SciFi Radfor SF
Radford, Irene
The dragon circle /

34028075642893
KT $6.99 ocm56029128
03/17/1

"YOUR CLAWS ARE RIPPING HOLES IN ITS HIDE."

The dragon called Irythros leaped free of the shuttle. Its talons screeched against the cerama/metal.

(*Forgive my trespass,*) Irythros said as he settled to the ground beside Konner.

The beast towered above him, as big as the shuttle. It spread its wings before furling them. The moonlight turned them into shimmering translucent veils. For a moment, Konner thought he could see star maps in the vein network.

Konner shook his head free of his fanciful thoughts. Dragons were planet bound. They might speak enigmatically with a great deal of wisdom, but they did not carry star charts etched into their wing membranes.

"Why did you seek me out?" Konner asked.

(*Hanassa speaks to the stars. We need to know why.*)

"But Hanassa is dead." Konner began to shiver with a new chill. Twice he and his brothers had thought they had killed the man. Twice he had recovered and come back to threaten their friends as well as themselves. The third time they had made certain he stayed dead.

(*The body of Hanassa died. Yet he still speaks to the stars. We need you to tell us why. . . .*)

THE
DRAGON
CIRCLE

THE STARGODS #2

IRENE RADFORD

DAW BOOKS, INC.

DONALD A. WOLLHEIM, FOUNDER

375 Hudson Street, New York, NY 10014

ELIZABETH R. WOLLHEIM
SHEILA E. GILBERT
PUBLISHERS

http://www.dawbooks.com

Copyright © 2004 by Phyllis Irene Radford.

All Rights Reserved.

Cover art by Luis Royo.

DAW Book Collectors No. 1301.

DAW Books are distributed by Penguin Group (USA) Inc.

All characters and events in this book are fictitious.
Any resemblance to persons living or dead is strictly coincidental.

If you purchase this book without a cover you should be aware that this book
may have been stolen property and reported as "unsold and destroyed" to
the publisher. In such case neither the author nor the publisher has received
any payment for this "stripped book."

The scanning, uploading and distribution of this book via the Internet or via
any other means without the permission of the publisher is illegal, and punishable by law. Please purchase only authorized electronic editions, and do not
participate in or encourage the electronic piracy of copyrighted materials.
Your support of the author's rights is appreciated.

Nearly all the designs and trades names in this book are registered trade-
marks. All that are still in commercial use are protected by United States
and international trademark law.

First Printing, August 2004
1 2 3 4 5 6 7 8 9

DAW TRADEMARK REGISTERED
U.S. PAT. OFF. AND FOREIGN COUNTRIES
—MARCA REGISTRADA
HECHO EN U.S.A.

PRINTED IN THE U.S.A.

This book is dedicated to all my
Circle of writer friends
Who have kept me going
Through thick and thin.
Thank you one and all.
Karen, Lea, Lace, Mike, & Bob

PROLOGUE

THE DRAGONS of the nimbus hear a new voice. Or is it an old voice become new. It speaks to the stars. We do not know this thing.

Stargod Konner, tell us who converses with the places beyond our ken. Tell us, so that we may be wary and know who listens to this voice and why.

CHAPTER 1

MARTIN KONNER O'HARA stared at the tiny device. Hardly as big as his palm and yet so dangerous. A red LED blinked at him in an ominously slow pattern.

He could almost hear it shout across the light-years "Here I am. Come get me."

It had to have been here for months, possibly a full year . . . since the last time he and his brothers had space-docked.

His ship *Sirius* was currently in silent orbit around an uncharted planet. While he made vital repairs, he had shut down all but the most essential systems, including spin. The star drive was quiescent, awaiting regrowth of a number of the directional crystals.

Konner and his brothers had just run out of time for repairs.

He pried the foreign device out from where it hid under the red directional crystal. It came away from the cerama/metal hull reluctantly. After a few curses, two broken fingernails, and a new set of bruises on his knuckles, he grasped the device in his palm, still blinking, still alerting authorities to his location.

How could she have done this to him?

Only his ex-wife Melinda could have taken one of

his patented locator beacons and perverted it so. Many had a motive to track the O'Hara brothers and their . . . independent cargo shipments. The Galactic Terran Empire called Konner and his brothers smugglers.

The people who received highly taxed and increasingly hard to get essential goods, like food, from the black market, called them saviors.

Melinda had more personal reasons. She had probably sold the frequency of this beacon to the highest bidder. Or bidders.

She could afford to spend a great deal of money to retrieve the damning evidence Konner had secreted aboard *Sirius* and a number of other key locations.

Konner wondered if Melinda would brag about her betrayal to their son Martin. Did she know how her need to banish Konner from Martin's life would destroy more than just her ex-husband?

When the Imperial Military Police found the beacon, they would also find a pristine world ready for exploitation. Konner shuddered at the thought of thundering tractors, a myriad of people, mechanical threshers, and machine after machine throwing out air and noise pollution. Chemical fertilizers would seep into the groundwater and run off into the rivers, making them unsafe to swim in, drink from, or fish out of.

Nine tenths of what the farmers produced would be shipped off planet to feed a hungry empire. The Coros would lose not only their way of life, but would have to learn to do with less than they had now.

The Galactic Terran Empire would not stop there. They would strip this place of every valuable resource, beginning with the timber and ending with the minerals, until there was nothing left. Then the inhabitants would dome their cities, breathe artificial air, eat tanked food, and sue for full citizenship.

And another bush planet would have to be found to feed the growing empire.

He had to destroy the beacon. Now. Before the IMPs found the right jump point to bring them here.

Konner bent his knees and pushed against the climbing rungs of the rabbit hole that afforded access to the outer array of crystals. As his body sprang back from his push through null g, he launched himself forward. Every ten meters he touched one of the climbing rungs on the inside of the conduit to adjust his angle of glide to match the curve of the saucer-shaped spaceship. At his back, the red directional crystals hummed a muted chatter only he could hear. As he sped along, the crystals became less harmonious.

One hundred forty-four directional crystals lined the outer rim of *Sirius*. They linked to twelve green driver crystals by kilometers of fiber optic cable. At the center of the ship, the drivers were linked to a single blue king stone. The two-meter-high monster kept the crystal drive harmonious and connected. In gravity, the king stone would weigh nearly one hundred fifteen kilos. But an active king stone never entered gravity. It had to grow in concert with its family of crystals in null g and lived at the center of the vessel where gravity from spin never reached.

He came abreast of the source of the strident note. A tiny crystal bud kept the port open while a new crystal grew at the center of *Sirius*. Five other reds had to be replaced as well. The disharmony among the array gave him a headache.

"Soon, friends. Soon you'll be whole again," he murmured soothingly. "And we can get out of here."

All the while his guts churned. Melinda had betrayed him to the Imperial Military Police.

If the IMPs showed up in this forgotten star system, they would take him and his brothers prisoner. Konner would never make it back to Aurora in time for his son's final custody hearing.

No wonder the IMPs had been able to follow Konner and his brothers across the galaxy. Their frantic flight from the law had kept Konner from meeting his son Martin at summer camp this year.

His fist clenched around the beacon. Would the boy be disappointed? Or would he even notice that his usual counselor had gone missing.

Five months ago, with the crystals damaged and the IMPs closing in, Konner and his two brothers had jumped blind into this uncharted star system three sectors off the maps. They had plunged into the adventure of a lifetime and found a place they could call home. A place where Konner could bring Martin to experience his true family away from Melinda's self-centered greed, amoral manipulations, and emotional abuse. As well as her lies.

And away from Mum.

Useless making plans now. As long as the beacon sent its signal, the IMPs could find the O'Hara brothers and terminate their dreams. All that had kept the law away from here till now was finding the weird jump point.

"We have to leave," he muttered.

He stared at the device again.

"We can't leave until the crystals regrow." Konner launched again along the narrow access shaft at the extremity of *Sirius'* rim. At the next hatch he grabbed a handle and changed direction. One deft somersault put him into the largest cargo hold.

Strangely, the load of black market pearls remained undamaged, despite the wild maneuvers through which Loki had put the ship in escaping IMP patrols. Konner had added to the hold the antique computers and lab equipment that had been left behind by the original colonists of the planet. A wealth of information about the first colony and the civil war that destroyed them lay encrypted on the hard drives.

From the hold, he dove into the crystal room. A vacuum-inducing force field encased each of the monopole drivers. Nitrogen flooded the field, causing the green crystals to spit out electrons along the fiber optics to the red directionals. Six new directional crystals stood in sealed baths shaped to the exact dimensions of the finished crystal. The original seeds stood at the peak of the bath cage and grew down and out. Limited by the cage and the precisely measured minerals in the baths, the red crystals would stop growing when they reached the shape and size needed. Each would need a little polishing and tuning to finish them, but they could be used the moment they completed growing.

Each bath was connected by fiber optics to the king stone and thus to every crystal on the ship. The ship's power, navigational, and communication systems had to grow as a family in order to synchronize and propel the ship across the vast distances between stars. More than that, the king stone had to be connected to a mother stone at its place of origin in order to find its way around the galaxy.

Konner had disconnected the crystal drive from its mother stone upon entering this star system. Just as Konner and his brothers were out of contact with Mum.

They weren't going anywhere until he reconnected that dangling orange fiber optic lying just outside the crystal circle. But if the ship could not find its way home with the connection severed, the IMPs could not find them through the connection.

Except for the damned locator beacon he still held in his palm.

"Another week to finish growing," Konner grumbled. "Another week for the IMPs to search for the jump point that should not exist but did."

Another twist and rebound took Konner up the gangway to the bridge. He slapped the comm port even before he anchored himself in his chair.

The lights blinked furiously red for an interminable ninety seconds. Then they dropped back to normal black.

"Damn!" Neither of his brothers had an active communicator close at hand.

"We haven't got time for this!"

A quick sensor sweep showed the inner planetary orbits free of man-made objects other than *Sirius*. He hadn't time to search the vast distances of the outer planets for a tiny moving vessel.

He pounded his fist against the edge of his interface. The locator beacon dug into his palm.

He had designed the thing to survive the fire and ice and massive radiation of space travel. He needed more weight than he had access to to crush the thing.

Only the sustained heat of molten lava at the heart of the planet would fry the femto-bots inside the beacon beyond their self-repair capabilities.

A half smile crept across Konner's face. He had access to that molten core. If he dared.

Could he face the ghost of Hanassa on his own?

*   *   *

"Captain Leonard, sir." Kat Talbot nearly squirmed with delight in her chair at the helm of Imperial Military Police Cruiser *Jupiter*.

Commander Amanda Leonard, captain of the *Jupiter*, glanced up from the screen full of reports she studied. She looked bored.

"Captain, I think I found it."

"Found what?" Commander Leonard lost the bland vacancy in her eyes. She touched the screen in front of her own chair so that it corresponded with Kat's.

"The jump point, Captain." Now Kat could not contain her excitement. "And the beacon."

"Show me," Leonard demanded. At the tone of her voice, the rest of the bridge crew keyed their own screens to share in Kat's discovery.

Lieutenant Josh Kohler, Chief Navigator and Kat's best friend aboard ship, flashed her a begrudging grin. They had a bet on this jump point. If she found it first, he would do her laundry for a week. If he beat her to the discovery, then she would sleep with him. Kat had no intention of allowing him to win the bet.

"Summon Lieutenant Commander M'Berra to the bridge, Englebert," Leonard said to the communications officer. Kat figured she would want the second-in-command in on this discovery.

Lucinda Baines, the diplomatic attaché who had hitched a ride aboard the IMP cruiser, hastened to Kat's side. She bent her petite body over Kat's shoulder, resting her hands on the back of the helmsman's chair. Her perfume suddenly overwhelmed all other scents. The usual citrus smell of the recirculated air took on rotten overtones, as if it had spent too much time in waste recycling and not enough in the scrubbers.

Kat shifted as far away from the woman as her station chair allowed. Then she highlighted the anomaly her sensors had discovered with her electronic pencil.

"I don't see it," Commander Leonard hesitated.

Kat brought up some new data. Commander Leonard's thick eyebrows raised as she digested a string of numbers and symbols that showed a femto's difference from normal space energy fluxes. In the past week of parking in deep space Kat, with M'Berra's help, had adjusted and fine-tuned the ship's sensors to detect smaller differences than any other IMP vessel could find.

And there was the beacon blaring through the tiny

hole in space. If you only knew where to look and what to look for.

Lieutenant Commander M'Berra ducked his curly black head as he stepped onto the bridge. He suppressed a yawn. Other than that single sign that he'd just gone off a twelve-hour shift, he looked as refreshed and crisply fresh as he had half a day ago. He immediately went to his station beside the captain. Leonard briefed him on the latest development in hushed tones.

"Are you certain that is a jump point and not just a reflection of the normal radiation currents?" Commander Leonard was known as a cautious leader. Bets aboard *Jupiter* favored that she'd easily make full captain, and get a bigger vessel at the next review board.

"Captain, sir, the outlaws jumped from these exact coordinates to somewhere. That anomaly is the only indication of something *different* about this area. And I am getting a hint of the beacon frequency that was highlighted on the memo from Command Base."

"Ms. Baines, do you have any objections to a further delay in delivering you to Annubis IV for your annual leave?" Commander Leonard asked.

"If the notorious O'Hara brothers disappeared from here, I have no objections to chasing them," the diplomatic attaché replied. Her eyes narrowed and the planes of her perfect face became sharper. "Commander Leonard, do you have to be reminded that capturing those three is highest priority for all Imperial Military Police."

Kat wanted to rear away from the menace in her tone.

Lucinda Baines, daughter of a planetary governor, granddaughter of an Imperial Senator, and greatniece of the previous emperor had a grudge against the O'Haras.

So did Kat.

"Inform Judge Balinakas that his services will soon be required," M'Berra ordered.

Ensign James Englebert busied himself at the comm board.

"Prepare for jump," Commander Leonard ordered.

"Aye, Aye, sir," Kat replied with enthusiasm.

CHAPTER 2

KIM O'HARA stared at the pristine piece of dried pulp in front of him. He'd spent hours peeling layers of stringy wood fibers, soaking them, and finally pounding them into an approximation of paper. Each day he made a few new pieces. Each day he scribbled notes recording the day's events.

Nearly five months had passed since Kim and his brothers had landed—almost on their butts—on a planet where dragons were real and magic worked. He had filled nearly three pages of his primitive paper with a description of Iianthe, the nearly invisible purple-tipped dragon. He'd given up trying to bind his scribblings. He now had five neat stacks of the papers, each confined within a separate box made of the same fibrous wood. One for each month of their time shared with the Coros—the name the local inhabitants gave themselves.

He could have cleared some space on a reader and used it as a daily log. He wanted more. He needed a journal he could leave behind, as well as an alphabet and basic grammar. Reading was a precious gift. He did not agree with his brothers that they should forbid the skill to the Coros. *His* people. He had to create something for them to read and learn from.

Enforced ignorance might keep the local tribes

from developing industrialization, but it would also stunt the growth of the civilization, stunt the minds and souls of people who deserved better.

Where to begin today? His mind spun with the facts of the harvest. Five acres of barley to cut tomorrow. Five acres of wheat threshed yesterday. Three acres of soybeans gathered and drying. The yield was bigger than he expected in all three fields.

Still, the harvest should stretch to feed them all if no more outcasts joined the village.

Two more refugees from outlying villages had made their way here today, swelling their numbers to seventy-five. Many of those who sought out the Stargods—Kim and his two brothers—had disabilities, missing limbs, or chronic ailments. Some of them had simple minds and damaged emotions. No one else wanted them.

How did he *know* to plant the extra acres to feed seventy-five rather than the thirty-two who began the village? How did he *know* events to come? How did he lay his hands upon an injury and make it right?

Time to think seriously about it. He gritted his teeth and grabbed a reader with a few gigs of free space. When he had a coherent text, he'd transfer his musings to his journal. Paper was too precious to waste.

Begin at the beginning, his mother's voice whispered in the back of his mind. Not quite Mum, though. The voice took on the sonorous overtones of Iianthe, the purple-tipped dragon.

Kim thought back to the beginning of the current adventure; to the day when he and his brothers had run so desperately from an IMP cruiser. The captain had seemed to anticipate every evasive maneuver, every jump through space, and every weapon blast the O'Hara brothers could imagine. It was almost as if the IMPs read his and his two brothers' minds.

Since then, Loki, the eldest brother, had developed and learned to control his telepathy. Quite possibly, in the stress of the escape from IMP patrols, he had broadcast his thoughts on a wide band.

Konner had begun to hone his ability to move objects with his mind. Mostly, he did it unconsciously in moments of stress.

Kim's precognitive talent kicked in when he least expected it. Aboard *Sirius* he'd had a vision of a safe haven inhabited by dragons. The vision had given him the symbolic coordinates of the jump point that had brought them here.

How to describe it?

He took a deep breath, felt refreshed, and filled his lungs once more. Ideas and flickers of memory crowded the edges of his vision. One more deep breath and . . .

He relived the numbness that shot through his body, the disembodied sensation of floating in a null g sensory deprivation chamber. Then the bright tangle of lights streaked across his vision. More than lights. Chains of light, each a different hue pulsing with life. Then blackness again.

He looked into the reader screen. Words scrolled rapidly across the screen as he dictated. The mini computer inside the reader prompted the word "void?" As good as any to describe the place in the mind between here and there.

His memory, triggered by the vivid description, pulled forth more images and sensations. Tumbling through darkness into atmosphere. The shuttle *Rover* tumbling toward a planetary surface and a . . . a dragon. A huge dragon with all the colors of the rainbow on its wing veins, horns, and claws, iridescent and awesome in its beauty, appeared out of nowhere. The wondrous creature shot forth a river of flame. Its dagger-length teeth and claws reached forward to rip . . .

Kim woke with a start and a whimper. He'd come out of the true vision with the same startling abruptness. Were the images more vivid in his memory than they had been originally? Or had the symbols become clearer with time and recall?

Only one way to tell. Deep breathing seemed to help the process. He'd read somewhere about mystic adepts who spent years learning how to breathe. Must have something to do with the infusion of oxygen into the red blood cells.

"I don't have years." He keyed a few notes about breathing into the reader.

Then he exhaled as much air as he could through his mouth, clearing his lungs of any leftover toxins and chemicals. When he felt as if his chest and backbone had nothing between them, he drew in a long healing breath through his nose.

Immediately, his vision intensified. Each basket and article of clothing strewn about the cabin he shared with his wife Hestiia came into sharper focus. This breath he exhaled as deeply as the previous one. A second conscious inhalation brought the now familiar dazzle around the edges of his vision. Rather than banish it, he nurtured it, giving the sparkles and half images a little time to develop. This time the aura remained as he got rid of that breath and took the third.

The void opened clearly before him. Pulsing chains of light and life invited him to explore. He reached for one that scintillated with every color and yet seemed to have no true color at all. . . .

The void snapped closed.

Kim landed on the packed-dirt floor with a thud. Rubbing his butt, he righted his stool and climbed back up on it.

His head ached and his stomach growled. He thought he heard a chuckle in the back of his mind. A chuckle with the deep bronze bell tones of Iianthe. Or did all of the dragons have the same bass voice?

Amazingly, all of his impressions and sensations revealed themselves in precise wording on the reader.

But what did it mean?

"Am I working magic?"

(*Magic is in the perceiving,*) the dragon voice said. It continued to chuckle.

* * *

Konner gulped. Before he could change his mind, he locked down communications and secured the hatch to the bridge. Then he jumped into a long dive for the launch bay where he'd parked *Rover*.

Before launching the shuttle, Konner tried to call his brothers again from the cockpit. The comm port remained silent. He set the device to repeat the call.

"Come on, Loki. Answer the damn phone." The light continued to blink red.

Konner vented the bay atmosphere as he opened the bay doors. He used the explosive release of the remaining air to push his shuttle out into the darkness of high orbit. He oriented to the planet beneath him. *Sirius* held position on the night side, over the horizon from the southern continent where he and his brothers had made homes among the Coros.

He passed his hand over the computer screen once more, in a pattern only he knew. *Sirius* disappeared from his sensors. His confusion field continued to work.

"What's so damn important you dragged me away from my work?" Kim O'Hara growled through the comm port.

Kim, the least likely to respond. The youngest brother had embraced the primitive life of the Coros. He'd taken a native wife. He'd announced his plans to remain dirtside when Konner and Loki returned to civilized space.

"Trouble coming. I need you and Loki to meet me at the landing site. Be there in one and twenty." Konner discomed before Kim could argue with him. Before Konner's own fears could choke him into immobility.

Ninety digital minutes later, they waited for him in the open meadow west of the village and tilled fields. The shuttle's landing draft blew their red hair and beards into their faces. Loki's blue eyes flashed with anger and he braced his long legs for confrontation. Kim leaned his lanky body against a boulder.

All three brothers had the same overt characteristics. But studious Kim was taller and more slender, audacious Loki broader, the shortest of the three with more brute strength. Konner was very much the middle brother in build and temperament, the placater, the one who tried to hold them together as a family when troubles threatened to split them.

"What?" Loki asked the moment the hatch irised open.

"Trouble. Get in." Konner pushed the shuttle toward a rolling launch before Kim had time to slap the portal controls closed. Both Kim and Loki stumbled as they fought for balance in the rapidly moving vehicle.

"What?" Loki asked again when they had all strapped in.

Konner tossed him the beacon.

Strained silence stretched. Konner realized he was holding his breath only when the pain in his chest became unbearable.

"Who?" Kim asked.

"Melinda. Who else."

"Aurora markings on the casing. Definitely manufactured in one of her factories," Loki mused turning the thing over and over. "But then she manufactures all of these things."

"Who else could modify it so that *I* would not find

it until I reset one particular crystal. None of my sensors noticed it. None of my routine inspections noticed it. The bit of recessed LED that shows was shadowed by an equally red directional crystal. The casing is painted the same gray-green as the rabbit hole. We got that color by mixing a bunch of left-overs from other ships. Only Melinda would have the audacity to try to match that paint or bribe the few people outside the family who had access to it."

Another long silence.

"So what do we do with it?" Loki asked.

"The lava core of the volcano."

All three brothers shuddered.

"I thought we decided never to go back there," Kim said.

"We have no choice."

"Are the IMPs within the star system yet?" Loki asked.

"Didn't take the time to do a full search."

"Mum will never forgive us if we get caught," Kim reminded them.

"Mum isn't going to like anything about this run." Konner checked the computer setting. Still on mute. None of them needed Mum's voice droning in their ears right now, even if it was just a mechanical device reporting the information of their interface displays.

"Can't we just dump this at the bottom of the deepest ocean?" Kim asked. His fingers ran over the sensor array with precision.

"Not deep enough," Konner replied. He kept his attention on the engineering rather than the mountain range looming ahead of them.

"What if we shot it into the sun?" Loki prompted. He piloted the craft with ease, posture relaxed, dominant left hand resting upon the joystick. He liked to interface with the ship directly rather than rely on computer readouts.

"Take too long to reach the sun's corona if we launch it from orbit. Besides, the window is wrong. *Rover* doesn't have enough power to get us away from the sun's gravitational pull once we get close enough, and we can't move *Sirius* until the crystals finish growing."

"How much longer on that?" Loki asked.

Kim frowned and turned his head away rather than face the issue of leaving the planet.

"A week at least. Maybe a day less," Konner replied. Even then he'd be cutting it close to make it back to Aurora in time for Martin's court date. He only had one chance to gain custody of the boy and he would not miss it.

They reached the yawning mouth of the mountain caldera all too soon.

They sat for a long time after Loki set *Rover* down inside the bowl of the volcano. The dust settled. The shuttle ceased to click as it cooled. Still they sat in silence. Waiting.

For what?

"We have to do this," Konner said finally.

"I'll stay and guard *Rover*," Loki said flatly.

"None of us should have to face this place alone. We all go, or we all stay." Kim swallowed deeply.

"We killed a man in there," Loki reminded them all.

"We killed a monster who tried to kill us and our villagers any number of times." Konner gathered a portable illuminator and a canteen. He tossed other survival gear to his brothers.

"We all go and face our personal demons together." Konner decided for them. "Come on. Let's get this over with before the IMPs have any more time to find us."

CHAPTER 3

LOKI STOPPED in the shadow of the ragged cave entrance. The sun beat down in a blinding glare upon the dry bowl of the caldera. High, steep walls of the blown-out mountain rose nearly one point five kilometers above him, trapping the heat and the dust, keeping out the wind. Nothing disturbed this lonely and hidden outpost in the Southern Mountains.

Even in the shade, sweat poured from his brow and back. He smelled himself and did not like the acrid taint of fear.

Deliberately, Loki scuffed the dust with his foot. Anything to delay entrance into the cave. He spotted traces of footprints, remnants of his retreat from this place a few weeks ago. He discerned the shape of his boots, Konner's lighter steps, Kim's bare feet, the tiny prints made by Hestiia, Kim's wife. In the middle, he barely made out the shuffling smudge made by Taneeo, the village priest. He'd been weak, ill, and sorely abused when they rescued him from violent Hanassa's clutches.

Then he saw something else. Someone with firm steps and a confident stride had been here. The most recent visitor had worn soft boots—unusual among the local population. Male by the length, breadth, and depth. Those prints were fresh.

"Wait!" Loki called to his brothers. They had already entered the relative coolness of the first chamber.

"What now?" Konner asked impatiently. He swept his illuminator along the walls, creating more shadows than it banished.

"Someone has been here. Recently," Loki said. He clamped his teeth shut to keep them from chattering.

"Rovers camp here when they travel the pass," Kim explained.

"Yeah. Rovers." Loki gulped. He took a swig from his canteen.

His family had given him the nickname of the Norse god known for his adventurous spirit and lack of caution. He was always the first one to wade into a brawl and usually the last man standing. Why did he fear this place so?

Because you took a life within these caverns, his conscience reminded him. That inner voice always sounded just like Mum. Anger began to replace his hesitance. Anger at Mum for her martyr complex and her manipulation of all three of her sons. Anger at himself for listening to her for so many years. Anger at Hanassa for being the bloodthirsty priest of the false god Simurgh. Anger at the dragons who had originally spawned Hanassa and then kicked him out of the nimbus for his lack of honor and his taste for human flesh.

He let the anger propel him forward. He caught up with his brothers and took the lead.

He could not help watching the ground closely for that alien footprint. It danced off to the side, then rejoined the direct route to the lower levels. A few paces farther on it disappeared again. Loki breathed a little easier.

The three brothers wound their way silently through the maze of caverns into the large room with a natural dais. At the entrance they all paused and held their breath.

Someone had placed a large, high-backed chair made of silver bloodwood in the exact center of the platform. Before it, a massive boulder had been carved and shaped into an altar. Outlines of a dragon dismembering naked humans, male and female, young and old, helpless and in their prime, appeared half finished on all four sides of the stone.

"The chair . . . it looks like a throne," Loki gulped. He could not stand to look at the grisly altar. He drank deeply from the canteen to keep his stomach under control.

His lover, Cyndi, would love that throne. She looked good in red with her blonde hair and fair skin.

"Who can tolerate sitting on that wood? The sap toxins would burn right through clothing." Konner squirmed uneasily.

"Hanassa would sit there. I don't think he'd notice a little thing like discomfort," Loki said quietly. Cyndi would also find a way to discount or avoid skin rashes and welts. Enhancing her looks was her primary occupation. That and defying her father.

"The dragons dumped Hanassa's body into the lava core," Kim reminded them. "He could not have survived. I know it, you know it. The dragons know it." He slapped his illuminator on his thigh with each statement.

"Maybe the Rovers?" Loki offered. Anything to banish the thought that Hanassa might still live to plague them.

Or his ghost might haunt them. Who else would *want* to erect and carve that altar? The rock looked untainted. At least it had not yet been consecrated with human blood.

"Maybe Rovers." Konner sounded as if he did not

really buy that explanation. The Coros blamed all misdeeds and bad luck upon the homeless tribes. "We need to get moving and destroy the beacon," he said. Now he took the lead and marched across the cavern toward the lava tube tunnel that would take them downward, into the bowels of the mountain.

"It's so beautiful." Kim drawled his words, his accent declining into the slow and drawn-out enunciation of the locals. He ran his hand above the intricate carving of the throne. He seemed to caress it without actually touching it. Horned dragon heads looked over the shoulder of anyone who sat there. Dragon wings formed the arms and sides. Dragon legs and large dragon feet with extended talons supported the piece. The openwork back looked like more dragon horns interlaced.

"They've left bits of the silver bark on the wings to represent the shimmering translucence of the membrane." Kim looked as if he was about to sit.

"Poison permeating the wood makes it red," Konner reminded the youngest brother. "Polish and time will reduce the toxins, but never eliminate them."

Kim sighed heavily as if breaking a trance. Then he rejoined his older siblings. "I wonder who carved it," he mused.

"I don't think I want to know," Loki said, careful to keep his speech crisp like any properly educated civil back home. "The artist's hands would be ruined forever from working with the raw wood."

"The artist who carved the altar would also have a ruined psyche after working those images," Kim said with a shudder.

They began the trek downward. The smooth lava tube tunnel offered an easy path. They made good time. The temperature rose dramatically with each half kilometer. By the time the path leveled off into another cavern, all three were drenched with sweat. They exhausted their canteens about halfway down.

"I'm so thirsty even that creek water will taste good," Loki admitted. He rushed to the streamside and splashed some of the sulfur-laden liquid on his face. He dipped his cupped hands once more for a drink.

"Hold on, Loki," Konner grabbed his shirt collar and pulled him away from the creek bed. "Let me test it first."

"What could change the content since the last time we were here? It's potable even if it does taste like morning breath with a hangover," Loki argued.

"This is an active volcano. The mineral content of this stream changes frequently." Konner knelt with one of his gadgets extended over the water. He dipped a sensor in and waited.

They all waited. Probably only a few femtos, but it seemed like an hour. The gadget beeped. Konner nodded.

Loki slurped up a double handful of water and spat it out. He screwed up his face at the foul taste. His brothers laughed.

"At least I wet the inside of my mouth," Loki excused himself. The sourness at the back of his throat overcame the strong aftertaste of sulfur. He sipped a few drops from his hands. It didn't taste quite so bad this time. A few more sips and he could tolerate enough to slake his thirst.

He noticed his brothers taking a few cautious sips as well. Eventually, they all drank their fill.

"The beacon," Konner reminded them.

As one, they rose to their feet and headed deeper into the maze of caverns. Half walls, boulders, stalactites, stalagmites, and columns forced them to take a twisted path that doubled back and wandered far from a straight line. Small dead-end rooms branched off the convoluted cavern. They paused at a metal door blocking a large room. They'd removed the computers and technical gadgets left there by the original colonists and stored them aboard *Sirius*. None of the locals could stumble upon the equipment and use it destructively without understanding it.

As Hanassa had.

Their steps took them past the site of their last confrontation with Hanassa, the place where Loki had pulled the trigger of a lethal needle rifle and killed the man. Each brother murmured a quick prayer and moved on.

Loki resisted the urge to make the sign of the cross. That was Mum's religion, not his. Still the old habit died hard.

Suddenly, the darkness and the weight of the mountain above pressed heavily against Loki. His breathing grew difficult.

He relived the moment he had last faced Hanassa. He raised his arms, as if still holding the needle rifle, took aim, and pulled the trigger. Cold sweat broke out on his face and hands. His knees trembled.

He saw again the hundreds of poisoned slivers of steel pierce Hanassa's back. Felt with him the agony as the deadly missiles passed through his body into the chest of Taneeo, his apprentice priest and hostage.

The world went white. Too bright.

As life escaped Hanassa, Loki knew several moments of deep agony of body and soul. And then nothing.

He shivered, remembering the cold numbness that had frozen his mind and his will to go on living.

He still dreamed that he died with Hanassa.

A hum began in the back of Loki's head. It sang in his back teeth and quivered along the fine hairs on his spine.

"Konner, is this what you hear when you work with the crystals?" Loki whispered.

"Similar. Nothing is as beautiful as the siren song of a crystal array in harmony," Konner replied.

"I have never heard a crystal array, Konner. This is irresistible." Kim smartened his steps and walked forward eagerly, the way he went to greet Hestiia.

A flicker of movement in Loki's peripheral vision diverted his attention from the allure of the hum. He turned quickly and swept his illuminator over the walls. The light glinted off dripping limestone. Ominous shadows played with his depth perception. Was that the shape of a man hiding behind a column? Or was it merely another stalagmite in the distance?

He shook himself free of the creepy imaginings.

Then he heard it. A low chuckle rummaging around his mind.

"Someone is here," he hissed to his brothers."

They halted in their tracks, not moving a muscle.

"Are you certain?" Kim asked. He stared around him, keeping the illuminator low.

"Yes," Loki breathed. "I can feel him."

"Him? Who?" Konner also searched the immediate environs.

"Not sure who. Only sure that a mind brushed against mine. It was . . . was totally alien."

Five months ago either of his brothers would have questioned Loki's statement. Since coming to this planet they had learned a new respect for psychic powers. Each possessed a different one. Loki was telepathic if he tried hard enough. Kim had visions of the future and the healer's talent. Konner could move things with his mind.

Each talent seemed to grow stronger the longer they stayed on this world of dragons and magic.

"We'll deal with the intruder after we dump the beacon." Konner moved forward.

Kim followed him, letting his illuminator wander from the direct path seeking anything that did not look right.

Loki took up the rear. He turned in frequent circles, checking behind him and off to the sides. Nothing showed in the feeble light. But the presence of "another" still weighed heavily on his mind.

They passed into the next cavern. The light was better here. Openings to the churning lava pool allowed the red glow from planetary fire to penetrate a few of the shadows.

The rusting hulk of an ancient steam generator, left over from the original colonists, loomed over them. The brothers had nicknamed the machine Big Bertha after a very cranky and very lazy aunt. Out of some superstition, Loki touched the boiler.

And jerked his hand away. He sucked on his palm, drawing out some of the burn.

"Why is this thing hot?" he asked around the fleshy part of his hand.

Panic lighted Konner's eyes. "It should be cool, unless . . . unless someone connected the pipes." He moved around the machine and shone his illuminator on the line of pipes that channeled creek water over the heat of the lava pool and into the boiler. Indeed, the broken and rusting pieces had been patched together with bands of bright bronze.

"Those welds won't hold." Konner shook his head.

"The question is who did it?" Loki persisted. He fought to control his own panic. "The only person on this planet with the technical knowledge to repair this thing, other than us, is dead." He gulped. "He *is* dead, isn't he?"

Silence.

"Isn't he!"

"He has to be. We watched Iianthe and Gentian dump his body into the lava pit," Kim insisted.

Loki replayed the scene from his memory, checking for errors. The two purple-tipped dragons had shrunk to the size of house cats. Eerily black and winged, they had grabbed the limp body of Hanassa in beak and claw, flown it through this side tunnel, and dropped it. Loki had not watched the corpse burn. He didn't need to in order to know it could not survive in any form.

"This beacon follows Hanassa into the pit before anything else diverts my attention." Konner ran into the nearest tunnel giving access to the open cauldron of churning lava.

At that moment the alluring hum increased to raucous song.

"The dragongate," Loki breathed.

The light changed from eerie red to a green-blue. The natural wormhole, born of the tremendous heat and pressure of the volcano, bridged the distance between the volcano and the depths of an ocean. And out of those watery depths loomed the biggest fish Loki had seen or read about on any of the worlds they had visited. The infamous behemoth. A voracious feeder, known to charge large boats and take bites out of the hulls.

"Shite, I need burning rock to destroy this thing, not water!" Konner shouted.

A mottled blue-and-gray hide made the behemoth nearly invisible until it was upon them. Its gaping maw showed row upon row of dagger-sharp teeth. Seven beady eyes probed the watery depths for prey.

Loki barely had time to breathe before the fish spotted Konner, turned, and lunged through the water into the mountain cavern. Konner reared back, stumbled, fell. The beacon rolled away from him.

A shadowy figure, clothed in concealing dark robes leaped out of the darkness, pounced upon the gadget, and raced off with it. He chortled and giggled as he pranced away.

"St. Bridget and the angels, he sounds just like Hanassa," Loki choked as he scrambled after the retreating shadow.

CHAPTER 4

M ARTIN FORTESQUE checked the corridor outside his suite. He'd already misdirected the normal surveillance equipment. This wing of the residence was empty of his many tutors, bodyguards, accountants, spiritual advisers, and athletic young sports companions, who were well paid by Melinda to see to Martin's well-being, and to keep him out of her hair. For once Melinda Fortesque had relaxed her vigilance over her son's safety—and his privacy.

Melinda carefully scheduled ten Earth Standard Minutes into her day to be a mother. The rest of her time was dedicated to making Aurora the wealthiest planet in the Galactic Terran Empire and the much larger Galactic Free Market.

"No one around to interfere," Martin chortled. He'd just spent two hours hacking into his mother's day-planner to make certain every one of his prison wardens believed that someone else occupied Martin's time.

He leaned back in his Lazy-former®. The inflatable cushions filled the contours of his posture and supported him while he concentrated on the blank white wall in front of him.

Where to begin?

"Scaramouch," he commanded his computer unit. "Bank balance upper right-hand corner."

A figure representing the total liquidity available to him appeared in both GTE credits and Adols, the Aurorian monetary unit. Not enough. For all of her wealth, Melinda kept her son on a strict and limited budget. Largesse came sporadically for reasons only Melinda understood.

"Scaramouch, holoimage of the HD™ 37000 jet pedcycle with optional foul weather bubble in lower left-hand corner. Full size." A three-dimensional two-wheeled vehicle with foot pedals for cycling, jet ports for minor elevation over obstacles, and collapsible wings for higher gliding materialized in the room. Only a slight distortion of sunlight coming in from a bank of tinted bioglass windows hinted that the coveted cycle was made only of colored light.

"Price of the HD 37000 above it, please." An astronomical figure appeared above the image in both credits and Adols. "Difference between bank balance and price of HD 37000 in the center."

The new figures represented an additional year of savings from his allowance.

"Well, Melinda told me to do my own birthday shopping. She's always saying I don't get enough exercise, so she can't object to the cycle in principle. Let's see what we can do. Scaramouch, show me Melinda Fortesque's day-planner for my birthday."

The computer already had the day memorized since Martin had accessed it several times in the last three AMs—Aurorian months. He skimmed the usual round of conferences, lists of judges and legislators to be bribed, and deadlines that littered his mother's life. Fifteen minutes allocated to an appearance before a judge. Not an unusual occurrence. Probably some paperwork designed to keep planetary laws within GTE guidelines while concentrating a maximum amount of power and money in Melinda's hands. After the court date, she'd budgeted an entire hour for his birthday celebration. The fact that it coincided with the evening meal surprised him. Mealtimes were prime opportunities to access business associates and rivals in supposedly casual settings. An Adol figure beside the mealtime must represent the amount of money Melinda was willing to part with for Martin's birthday present.

He raised his eyebrows, surprised at the amount. Quite a bit more than he expected.

"Wonder what she wants to bribe me for this time?" He mused. "Add this figure to my bank balance." He touched the day-planner image and dragged it up to the right-hand corner. The numbers ran upward.

Still not enough.

"Scaramouch, delete foul weather bubble from HD 37000."

The holoimage wavered and distorted, then reassembled itself without the protective force field that would keep rain, wind, and unpleasant temperatures from disturbing the rider. The price numbers flickered and changed. The difference between the price and the amount of money he might expect to tap decreased but remained far too high.

"Scaramouch, replace bubble. Since I've got to get creative, let's go for the whole thing." Martin memorized the number in the center of his field and blanked the screen. "Scaramouch, boot up BigMoney program."

Martin spent the next hour moving figures around the program. He bought some high risk stock with his available allowance and sold it almost immediately at a slight profit. He bought a confiscated cargo sitting in the police warehouse and sold it through the port authorities. That brought him closer to his goal.

Then something in the port records caught his eye. The entry was listed in bright red and displayed in letters three times the normal size.

"M. Konner O'Hara, ship *Sirius*. No entry under any circumstances on or before above date."

Martin looked closer. The "above date" was his birthday. Why had the port—and therefore his mother—banned Martin's summer camp counselor from the planet on his birthday?

Melinda sent Martin away for three AMs every year for "education and socialization opportunities." In other words, she wanted her son out of sight and out of mind. Konner O'Hara had been his counselor for four years. Except this year. Melinda had kept Martin home with no explanation other than a new tutor with loads of homework assignments.

Martin skipped back to his mother's day-planner. The judge to be bribed that day also included a court time handwritten in tiny letters rather than computer generated. An unusual entry. Electronic pencil markings could not be changed easily and Martin had yet to discover a program to hack them. The computer had difficulty reading the print and kept blanking it out.

Martin enhanced that portion of the schedule and set it on decode mode in case Melinda had gotten creative with her private entries. She did that every once in a while, as if she feared industrial espionage. She should.

"Final custody hearing. Make certain Martin has a new suit."

"I don't believe it. Melinda is actually going to go through the motions of obeying a law that is good for the masses but not necessarily good for her. She's going to let me choose my custodial parent. That myth she's been telling me, and everyone else, that she chose artificial insemination to gain an heir is a big fat lie! But why outlaw Konner. Maybe he knows my father. He could get my dad here in time for me to legally choose him instead of Melinda."

In order to maintain good standing with the GTE, Melinda Fortesque had to make a show of a republican government for the people who lived on Aurora—all of them her employees. Anything that she disliked or found inconvenient was taken care of with a bribe of money or influence. At some time in the past, she had allowed a law to pass that in cases of contested custody, the child had the right to choose his/her final custodial parent at the age of fourteen.

The fact that a hearing had been scheduled meant that Martin's father—whoever he might be—had challenged Melinda. He hadn't totally abandoned Martin.

"I wonder who my dad is?"

He zoomed back to the port authority and moved the order banning Konner O'Hara from Aurora to the previous year. No mention of banning him on or after the birthday and crucial court date. "Konner went out of his way to become a counselor at my summer camp. Maybe he's my dad."

Martin hoped so. The three Aurora months each summer that he spent with Konner represented more time than the accumulated amount Melinda allotted him on a daily basis.

"If he is my dad, then his name is on the custody suit." Martin hesitated. Did he dare hack into the official court records? The GTE maintained those records, not the local judicial system. If he got caught, even Melinda would have a hard time bailing him out.

He called up the message center of his computer. Sure enough, Bruce Geralds, his cabin mate at summer camp had left three messages. Martin opened them. All three were innocuous greetings and gossip about other friends.

Martin opened a mailbox and dashed off a hurried message for a conference. He needed the help of all of his friends to hack into the court records—especially Bruce whose father was a freelance bounty agent.

"Martin!" Melinda appeared in the center of his screen, life-sized and in three dimensions, as if she actually stood there. Her lustrous brown hair was sculpted into the latest fashion of the sleek professional woman. Her suit had cost the annual income of several small worlds. And anger blazed from her amber-brown eyes.

"What do you think you are doing with this money program?" she demanded.

"Just shopping for my birthday present, like you asked me to," he answered innocently. Hopefully she wouldn't find out until too late exactly what he planned to get for his birthday.

* * *

"Konner, grab the beacon with your mind," Kim called out to his brother even as he ran after the thief. They had to destroy the device before the IMPs found the jump point. Before Kim was forced to leave Coronnan and Hestiia.

Hestiia. A gaping hole opened in his gut at the thought of leaving her. Of never coming back.

Because once the GTE found this planet, nothing would be the same. The life they had built here would vanish as ashes from an evening campfire scattered, trampled, and drowned by invaders.

He and his brothers would not be allowed to return.

The black-clad figure darted through the maze of caverns. He stopped and looked at Kim from the depths of his hood.

"Show yourself, bastard!" Loki called from right behind Kim. "Are you afraid to show your face?"

The intruder giggled, high-pitched, hysterical. Insane. And took off again in a new direction. He danced and leaped and cavorted as if leading a festival celebration, all the while making certain Kim and Loki followed.

"He's toying with us," Kim panted. He put on a burst of speed.

"St. Bridget, and Mary, and all of God's little angels help me!" Loki cried as he took a flying leap.

Loki landed hard, fingers entwined in their quarry's cloak.

"Eeeeppp!" the man squealed. He flailed.

Loki tugged on the sturdy cloth. Not black. The ubiquitous rust color of the local shaggy cattle.

Kim grabbed the man's shoulders. Must be male by the breadth and musculature. He wore soft boots made of deer hide, the same as the footprint Loki had seen earlier.

And then the thief wiggled once and slid out of their grasp.

The intruder left Kim holding the cloak as he disappeared into the shadows.

Loki pounded the ground with his fist. He remained prone, shoulders slack in disappointment.

"I can't . . . get . . . it," Konner panted coming up behind them. "I can't find the beacon with my mind. And I don't have any Tambootie to augment my powers."

A hum began in the back of Kim's neck. His teeth itched and his feet did not want to remain still.

"The dragongate," he breathed. "It's opening."

"By St. Bridget, does this ghost know how to use the gate?" Loki looked up. Horror dawned in his eyes.

"If anyone but us knows . . ." Kim did not dare finish that thought. Instant transportation to almost anywhere on the planet offered near-limitless power. Another unscrupulous megalomaniac like Hanassa. . . .

"Hestiia knows," Konner reminded him.

"So does Taneeo," Loki added. "Hanassa sent him through the gate dozens of times while he was enslaved."

"We can trust them. Hestiia is my wife. Taneeo is a friend. He presided at my wedding. They understand why this must be kept secret," Kim insisted.

"Then who?" Loki asked. "Sure, we all want to trust everyone. But who else did Hanassa show this to?"

"There he is." Konner dashed after the flicker of movement at the edge of the light.

Kim and Loki stayed at his heels. They had to catch the man now. Before the IMPs locked onto the beacon and everything he held dear crashed around him. They ran full out. Kim's lungs began to strain in the heat. His thighs ached and his heart thundered in his ears.

The hum in the back of his neck set his teeth on edge. "He's headed for the dragongate!" he called out.

Big Bertha loomed ahead of them. The eerie red light from the lava grew brighter; took on tones of gray and pale green.

"Stop him before . . ."

Their quarry darted into the tunnel, little more than a silhouette. Did he have only two dimensions?

Kim blinked his eyes several times, trying to focus on the figure, find some point of familiarity, or substance in him.

"Good-bye, my friends. Even the dragons can't catch me." The stranger's voice deepened and rang through the tunnels. The soaring caverns took up the cry, twisted it, amplified the reverberating tones, and sent it back to them.

The hair on Kim's nape stood on end. Chill touched his heart.

Loki made the sign of the cross without breaking stride.

The light shifted again, going red and dark.

Konner came to a skidding halt at the lip of the volcanic crater.

A stream of lava flared upward coming within a thousand feet of the precipice where they stood. The heat threatened to scorch exposed skin.

"He's gone," Konner whispered.

"Where?" Kim asked. "Did you see where the dragongate took him."

"No place I recognized. Gray-green soil, rocks jutting through like broken bones in a compound fracture, scant plant life. Deep ravines revealing black rock beneath the soil."

"We have to find him."

"How?"

CHAPTER 5

KAT TALBOT yanked her safety harness across her shoulders and fastened it between her legs. All around her, the bridge crew copied her movements. All except Lucinda Baines, the diplomatic attaché. That august personage, not much older than herself, continued to brace herself behind Kat's chair, staring eagerly at the sensor readings.

"Are we truly on the trail of the infamous O'Hara brothers," Ms. Baines breathed.

"You won't be unless you find a place to strap in," Kat warned her. The woman's beauty and pedigree did not grant her special dispensation from the laws of physics. Scientists had yet to figure out how jump points worked. They only knew that they opened holes in space to distant places and that they were dangerous.

"Strap in, Ms. Baines, or get off my bridge," Commander Leonard ordered.

Ms. Baines flashed the ship's captain a resentful glare. Then she flounced over to a jump seat with a harness.

Kat slapped the jump alarm. A loud klaxon resounded throughout the ship three times, followed by the captain's prerecorded voice. "Prepare for jump. All personnel, prepare for jump." Thirty long

seconds later, each section of the ship reported in;
med bay, judiciary, anthropology, Marines, engineering, and all the other smaller departments that
kept the judiciary cruiser running. If anyone aboard
was out of position and injured in the coming minutes, they had only themselves to blame.

"I certainly hope this means we have finished this
wild-goose chase and can proceed toward civilization," Judge Balinakas intoned from the hatchway.
His stout body filled the portal, his black judicial
robes draped about him with majesty, reflecting the
glossy black of his hair. His swarthy skin had higher
color on cheekbones and nose than usual.

"Strap in, Judge," Leonard ordered. She gripped the
arms of her chair until her knuckles turned white. "I
am taking this ship in pursuit of criminals wherever I
must follow them. That is, of course, our mission."

"We are well overdue for our rendezvous, Commander Leonard. Not even the infamous O'Hara
brothers are worth yet another fruitless side trip."
The judge looked down his beakish nose at the captain of the ship.

"Take a seat, Judge, or suffer the consequences of
jump." She turned her head back to the screens,
clearly dismissing the man who represented a rival
authority aboard ship.

"I shall report you, Commander, for this devia-
tion." The judge did not seek the jump seat on the
opposite side of the hatch from Ms. Baines.

"Your conduct goes into my official report. Need
I remind you *again* that I am in command of this
vessel? You command only the judiciary process for
any criminals we apprehend." Leonard's voice
gained intensity and volume.

"Need I remind you that I have absolute authority
over this mission?" The judge remained calm.

"Bridge personnel secure, Lieutenant Talbot,"
Commander Leonard reported. "Take us into jump."

Kat slapped the final alarm.

Judge Balinakas remained standing.

Kat took a deep breath and began the sequence of commands transferring control to the central computer. No human could react fast enough during the sensory overloads of jump to navigate. Three hundred lives depended upon the computer's judgment.

"Someday, I'm going to prove that I can fly a jump by myself," Kat muttered to herself.

The klaxon sounded again. Three loud and annoying blasts that no one could ignore, including Judge Balinakas. He threw himself into the jump seat and secured his safety harness, every millimeter of his posture shouting resentment. He'd called the captain's bluff and lost the bet.

Lights flashed red and dimmed with each blast.

Kat's own jaw began to ache from clamping her teeth together to avoid biting her tongue.

The ship surged forward. Two gs, three gs. Acceleration pushed Kat hard against her chair. The high back kept her neck from whiplashing. Pressure built. She fought for every gulp of air.

Black stars crowded her vision. She forced her eyes open. She had to watch. Just once she had to see what jump was truly like.

Dry grit weighed heavily against her eyelids. She had to blink. Just once.

Before she could open her eyes again the pressure ceased. Gravity dissolved. Light vanished.

Kat lost contact with her body. She was only a soul drifting in a vast nothingness. Her mind tricked her into believing she witnessed bright coils of light pulsing with life. Each coil was a different color and brightness. They chained and twined together, braided and looped back upon themselves in an intricate mesh.

She could almost reach out and touch them. If the harness did not restrain her. If she had a body to be restrained.

Time passed. Aeons of memories flitted past her mind's eye. She tried to sort them, catch hold of one for longer than a single heartbeat. Each evaporated. Space ghosts without form or substance or purpose.

(*Why do you come?*) a deep sonorous voice that was many voices and minds combined echoed around her skull.

"Who are you?" She could not hear her words. A space ghost? Who else inhabited the empty places between the stars?

(*We are who we are. Who are you and why do you come?*)

"I come to find . . . myself."

(*Welcome.*)

The ship burst free of jump. Sensations slammed back into Kat's body, all at once, too quickly to absorb. She welcomed the headache as proof that she lived. The moment she had something to see, and eyes to see with, she scanned her instruments. Nothing looked familiar. The computer looped through incoming data from the ship's sensors. It found nothing familiar and repeated measuring the scan.

"That was definitely a jump point," Commander Leonard said. Her voice shook. The unflappable captain looked disoriented and uncertain.

"That was one hell of a jump," Chief Navigator Kohler said. He rubbed his eyes with trembling hands. His normally dusky skin looked gray.

"Longest jump I've ever endured." Ensign James Englebert, the communications officer on duty, said on a choking laugh, as if he had more than two or three jumps notched on his belt.

But he was right. The jump had lasted longer than usual. Although the ship's chronometer showed the passage of only a few seconds, Kat knew her body had passed through perhaps as much as an hour.

Jumps played hell with linear space and time.

"So where in Murphy's continuum are we?" Commander Leonard asked.

"I wish I knew, Captain," Kat whispered. "I think we are lost."

* * *

"I track the Stargods," Dalleena Farseer stated simply to the village headman. She had observed the protocols and sought him out first. But the tug on her senses drove her onward. Those she must find did not dwell here.

"Many seek the brothers from the sky. Why do you *track* our lords?" The middle-aged man with the heavy muscles of a warrior looked her up and down with care. The interest in his eyes had little to do with her femininity and a lot to do with her choice of words.

Not much of her body showed beneath her leather breeches, boots, vest, and linen shirt. Unlike most women of her acquaintance, she did not need to highlight the swell of her breast or the nip in her waist to earn her keep. She had other talents.

" 'Tis something I need to do," she replied.

"Why?"

"I need not explain anything to you without the courtesy of a name or hospitality." She stood firm, not wavering under his fierce gaze.

"Forgive my lack of manners, Tracker." The headman bowed his head slightly. But he never took his gaze from her eyes. "We have learned caution. Many seek the Stargods and their chosen people, the Coros. Some do not wish our saviors well."

"I have heard that the three brothers descended from the stars to save your people from a deadly plague. They also ended slavery among you." She scanned the array of houses behind the headman.

The town was nestled between the bay and the river, a half hour's walk above the flood line of either. Nearly one hundred sturdily built homes and a temple. No mistaking the huge building with the silver bloodwood columns topped by carvings of dragons. These people had worshiped the bloodthirsty Simurgh before the coming of the Stargods.

"My father still resents the loss of his slaves." A younger man with a hooked nose to match the headman's and a similar cast to the brown eyes, sauntered over from the largest of the homes, at the opposite end of the town from the temple. "I am Yaakke. My ill-mannered father is called Yaaccob the Usurper. You will not find the Stargods here."

"But they have been here. Recently."

"Your tracking senses are correct," Yaakke replied. "They came to bless the pregnancy of my wife. My sister is mate to the youngest of the Stargod brothers."

"Ah," Dalleena said. She turned in a slow circle, right arm extended, palm raised. West of this riverside town. Not far. Too far after a long journey afoot before sunset.

"I go to visit my sister," Yaakke said. "Would you care to join me in the boat journey? Company relieves the tedium of the travel."

"Boat? Yes, I will join you," Dalleena said with a sigh of relief. She could rest her aching feet. Gratefully, she followed the man to the riverbank.

After weeks on the road, he had offered the first evidence of actually having seen the Stargods. But everyone who lived south of the big river and north of the fiery mountains had heard of the three brothers who descended from the stars on a cloud of silver fire. Their great deeds done liberating the tribe of the Coros had become the subject of song and ritual.

Dalleena settled into the hollowed-out log of a

boat. "How did you smooth the inside so evenly?" She ran a hand along the inner sides, amazed that no splinters pierced her skin. Even the outside remained free of bark or ragged patches.

"A miracle of the Stargods." Yaakke grinned hugely. "There are advantages to allowing Stargod Kim to marry my sister." Then he handed Dalleena a paddle.

She looked at it skeptically. Tracking sometimes required her to travel long distances over a variety of terrain. The people who required a Tracker to find lost livestock, errant children, or missing lovers usually did all the work.

This time the quest was her own. Therefore she must work for herself. She dug the paddle into the water with strength equal to Yaakke's stroke.

Before long, her back and shoulders began to ache. Her palms blistered. The sight of the setting sun sparkling red upon the waters of the river numbed her mind and her talent. She knew nothing, felt nothing but the pressure upon her body each time she pushed the boat a little farther upstream.

"Nearly there," Yaakke told her. He pointed to a muddy embankment. Many feet and more than a few boats had slid up and down it. Two rafts and another log boat were tied to large stakes driven into the dirt on either side of the slippery access.

To Dalleena's surprise, Yaakke continued paddling beyond the point. Her shoulders ached even more. They had passed their objective and her guide expected more work from her. This was more tiring than if she'd walked!

"Ease up on the paddle," Yaakke called.

Finally. She obeyed him, resting the paddle across the boat sides. Her back slumped and her head felt a little too heavy. She should not be this tired. She worked hard every day on the family farm when she was not tracking. She could match muscle and stamina with any warrior.

Why?

Yaakke let the boat drift back toward the landing area, using his paddle to steer them closer and closer to the bank.

At last the boat grounded. Yaakke jumped out, calf-deep in the water. He grabbed the bow of the craft and waited.

"Are you getting out or not?" he asked testily.

"Oh," she replied dumbly. Heavily, she dragged herself out of the bottom of the little boat and into the water. The current tugged at her. She grabbed the boat for balance.

"Push," Yaakke ordered.

She did so. He hauled. Together they brought the craft up onto the bank. A crowd of people gathered above them, watching. When Yaakke had tied his craft to one of the stakes protruding out of the mud, a young woman jumped down and grabbed him in an embrace. She had the same set to her eyes as both Yaakke and his father, but a more delicate nose structure. Her thick brown hair cascaded down her back, covering most of her body. At first Dalleena thought she and the other women adhered to the old custom of not covering their breasts until a man had claimed them. Slave women were never allowed to cover themselves except out of doors in deep winter. A shift in Hestiia's posture, a ripple in her hair, revealed a halter woven of red cow wool above her leather sarong. All the women seemed to wear the same clothing with little variation.

Dalleena suddenly felt too tall, too awkward and out of place.

"My sister, Hestiia," Yaakke introduced them.

Dalleena gave her own name and talent, nodding her head.

"Welcome, Tracker." Hestiia marched over and stuck out her right hand to her.

Dalleena stared at the hand wondering if she was supposed to touch it.

Hestiia took the decision away from her, grabbing her by the elbow and shaking her arm. Dalleena returned the gesture as well as the woman's smile.

"Come, the hospitality of this village is open to you. We have hot food ready. My husband and his brothers should return any time now." The little woman led them up the bank and toward the cluster of cabins as if she held the honored place of headman.

Dalleena followed, curious about a village that allowed a woman to speak for them. At the top of the track, an ancient woman of impressive girth and swarthy coloring waited. She stood with hands on hips, legs spread sturdily, and a fierce scowl upon her face.

A Rover. What was she doing here? Rovers never settled in a village. Villagers never allowed them to linger near. Suspicion and distrust kept them always apart.

"I be Pryth," the Rover woman announced. "You be Tracker. Why do you feel needed here?"

"I do not know, only that something, someone needs tracking." Her senses awoke under the intense gaze of the old woman. Her hand burned and itched as it never had before. She raised her right arm and supported it with her left. Palm out she turned in a slow, methodical circle, pausing at every quarter of a quarter turn. Her head spun with the need to find the nameless thing before it destroyed itself. Or destroyed them.

But she could not find a direction to look.

CHAPTER 6

KONNER STARED into the campfire.
Villagers bustled around him. Women carried trenchers piled with roasted venison, chunks of wild yampion, a sweet tuber served raw or roasted or mashed with fresh milk, and globs of boiled greens dressed in fat and fruit vinegar.

The Tracker sat among the men across the fire from Konner. She did not participate in any of the usual female pursuits. Her eyes wandered restlessly around the village, across the sky, and toward the deep shadows beyond the fire.

Konner did not have the thoughts to spare this night to wonder why. All he could think about was the missing beacon and the audacious thief. Which led him back to Melinda and her betrayal of him.

Hestiia offered Konner a platter without meat. He waved it away.

She pursed her lips in disapproval and offered it instead to her husband, Kim.

He took it from her with a smile that lighted his face all the way to his eyes. Their gazes locked on each other, grew intense. His hand covered hers, lingered, and caressed before she relinquished the bark platter.

Konner turned his head away, embarrassed by

their intimacy, jealous and lonely in his own isolation.

Fifteen years ago he had believed he and Melinda could learn to love each other like that. She'd offered him one million Adols, the most stable currency in the galaxy, in exchange for a legal marriage ceremony. She wanted control of her inheritance, the corporation that owned the entire planet of Aurora. But her parents' will had specified she could not sit on the board of directors or have access to capital funds until she married or turned thirty years of age.

At twenty-two she decided to take control of her fate and made her proposal to Konner. He'd been only twenty and on his first solo reconnoiter for the family business. Aurora produced a number of high-tech items needed on bush worlds that could not afford to buy them legally. Mum had sent him to Aurora see if they could empty a warehouse without paying for the merchandise.

Then Konner met Melinda. They had spent a giddy week together on a newly opened bush colony world. No one had asked questions or required much in the way of paperwork before the wedding ceremony. Seven days of sex and wine and laughter and more sex had not been enough for Konner.

Within hours of returning to Aurora, Melinda had seized control of her corporation, had Konner arrested, and permanently exiled without a single fraction of a coin in payment of the prenuptial agreement.

Notice of annulment of the marriage appeared on the bush world within hours.

The humiliation and the loneliness burned so deep in Konner that he had not told his brothers about his marriage.

Loki planned and executed the theft from Melinda's warehouse based upon Konner's information.

Konner had participated in the plan without a single guilty thought to slow him down. Only Mum knew of his failed marriage, and she used the knowledge ruthlessly, to keep Konner in the family business when all he wanted was to go off exploring on his own. Mum promised him the time and money to fight Melinda for the prenuptial sums and custody of his son Martin when she completed a project of her own. The time never came when Mum had enough money to bribe the right officials to regain family citizenship. Without those essential papers, Konner had not a prayer of winning anything from Melinda in a legal court.

But he had kept a copy of the prenuptial agreement and stashed extra copies in key places.

Shame for his youthful misalliance still ate at him. His only consolation was a chance meeting with a mechanic who had worked a short time at the Aurora Space Docks and gave him the news that Melinda had a son.

As soon as Martin was old enough to go to summer camp, Konner made a point of working at that camp as a counselor. He'd forged citizenship papers to pass their security screen. He and his son had bonded over many an evening campfire.

Those flames had burned normal red and gold with a blue heart.

In front of him, on this early autumn evening on a forgotten planet beyond explored space, pale green flames around a deep yellow layer licked branches greedily. Copper sulfate, he told himself, made the fire burn green. Copper sulfate impregnated every living thing on this planet. He'd never get used to the colors. Wondered if his blood would turn green if he lived here long enough.

"I have to leave in five days," he said aloud. "I have to leave by then or miss my . . . appointment."

Loki nodded his acknowledgment. Kim frowned as he jerked his head down and up a single time.

Konner's brothers now knew of his court date on Martin's fourteenth birthday. He'd confessed everything to them after Loki had learned how to read minds with some regularity and consistency.

Pryth, the ancient matriarch of the village, stood up and began reciting a long saga of the first coming of the Stargods to rescue the slaves of Hanassa. She directed the story to the new woman, but included the entire village in her audience.

Konner winced. He'd heard this story every fourth or fifth evening sitting around the campfire during and after the communal meal. That he and his brothers were the heroes of the story embarrassed him.

One of the younger men picked up a skin drum and began beating the rhythm of the old woman's recitation. A middle-aged woman added deft tones on a reed flute to punctuate the story.

"You and Loki can't leave until we find the beacon," Kim insisted in hushed tones. "I won't have this planet at the mercy of the GTE, even if you two do leave."

"I told you that you should have dumped the beacon out *Rover*'s loo and let it burn up in reentry," Loki grumbled.

"No, you didn't. You weren't even there," Konner replied.

"Well, you should have thought of that solution."

"They are designed to withstand reentry and crash." Konner returned to his contemplation of the fire.

"So where did the thief go?" Loki leaned forward, shoulders and spine rigid.

"Raaskan," Kim hailed the village chieftain.

The man Konner and his brothers had rescued from a life of slavery and death as a sacrifice to Hanassa's god, ambled toward them. His soft leather knee breeches and vest molded to his muscular frame. The buttery color made a nice contrast to his permanently sun-bronzed skin. Konner guessed him to be in his early thirties, about his own age. But in this primitive society, just growing out of bronze and into iron technology, Raaskan commanded the same kind of respect as a senior CEO of a galactic corporation.

"Pryth always tells stories better than anyone else. She has an energy and sense of timing possessed by few," Raaskan said as he lowered himself to sit cross-legged beside Kim in one smooth motion.

Konner never had been comfortable out of doors before coming here. He preferred ships and big buildings filled with mechanicals. He could bond with machines more easily than people.

But something about these people and their simple values tugged at his heart with an emotion akin to his love for machines.

"Must be Pryth's Rover heritage. Her people are renowned for their ability to take ordinary events and make them into life-changing sagas," Konner replied.

"Pryth has been with us for more than three generations. We forget that she is not originally one of the Coros," Raaskan said.

"She has seen many places in Coronnan." Kim followed the casual conversational rules of this society. Pleasantries must continue for some time before coming to the meat of a subject.

Loki fidgeted beside Konner. The oldest brother did not like waiting. Any second now he would plunge in and demand information.

"Rovers wander far," Raaskan said. He nibbled a bite of venison from his trencher.

Kim turned his head away. Loki looked longingly

at the meat before yanking his gaze away to watch the women.

Hestiia and Raaskan's wife led a dozen villagers in a dance around the fire, acting out the story Pryth told. They recounted how Konner and his brothers had unleashed their magic—fully charged stunner guns—and blasted the sacrificial altar rock to pieces. No more would the stone taste human blood in homage to the winged god Simurgh.

"How far have you wandered?" Konner pressed Raaskan. "What have you seen beyond the meadows and rivers of Coronnan.

Raaskan clamped his jaw shut. He looked directly into Konner's eyes for long moments.

Konner did not look away. "You may speak of this among us."

"I flew with you, Stargod Konner, inside the belly of your white dragon that is no dragon."

"And when you traveled with my brother to the hills south of here," Kim said, "to the huge outcropping that juts out into the Great Bay so that you could bring a blacksmith to this village, did you see a land with tufts of grass more gray than green, with scrubby shrubs and long fissures cutting deeply to reveal black rocks, like the bones of the land scorched by the sun?" Kim easily fell into the convoluted formal language of the bard. He excelled in calling up language that spoke in metaphors as easily as fact.

The scientist in Konner rebelled at the imprecision these people loved. They liked many layers of meaning that they could peel away bit by bit to reveal truths of human nature that could not be quantified by science.

He ached to be gone from here, back on the space lanes where he knew the risks and the dangers and how to overcome them.

At the same time he knew he would miss the evenings spent in the community of friends sharing a meal, entertaining each other with stories and songs, and keeping the nightmares away with a cheering fire.

"I have never seen such a land," Raaskan admitted. "You must ask Pryth if her people know of it."

"Are there more Rovers we could ask? Clans who have traveled more recently than Pryth?" Loki asked. He twitched with the need to move.

"There are always Rovers. Finding them is not easy unless they wish to be found."

"Great!" Konner exploded, letting his words propel him upward. The momentum of anger fueled his muscles so that he did not need to brace or balance himself. "What good are these people? What good are any of you?" He stalked off into the night, tromping heavily through the underbrush.

He did not care how much noise he made. He did not care if he got lost. He just had to move; to do; to think.

His feet automatically steered toward the meadow west of the village where he had parked *Rover*. The cloaking field gave off a slight hum, more muted than the dragongate, a different frequency. This tone lulled the senses into believing it did not exist and neither did the object it hid.

Konner half smiled at his foresight in designing the system. After spending five months on this planet with its unique ability to augment psychic powers, he understood that the cloaking field worked with brain synapses to fool the mind.

A sliver of a moon showed just above the horizon. He slowed his pace.

He had to destroy the beacon. To do that, he had to find the thief. Should he go back to the volcano and wait for the dragongate to open to the same location as where the thief escaped?

That could take days, even weeks. The gate was unreliable and random in choosing its destinations. He did not have that kind of time to waste.

"I'll take *Rover* up at first light. I'll find that semi-arid land on my own."

(*Will you?*) a voice came to him out of the night.

"What? Who?" Konner turned in a full circle seeking the source.

Moonlight glinted off the nose of the shuttle. The cloaking field should mask even the reflection of light off the cerama/metal hull. He peered closer. His steps became more cautious.

(*Will you find the land that you seek on your own?*) the voice repeated.

The moon rose above the tree line at the edge of the meadow. To Konner's trained eye the outline of the shuttle became clearer, still insubstantial because of the cloak, but he knew where to look and what to look for.

Something marred the sleek silhouette of the vessel. A big lumpy something sat on the nose. A lumpy something with spikes. It looked a little like one of Mum's pincushions.

"Not again."

CHAPTER 7

KONNER SANK to the ground just outside the cloaking field. Evening dew moistened his knees. A chill breeze reminded him that summer had come to an end and he needed a shirt beneath his leather vest. Like the fine white one worn by the new woman, the one who dressed as a man and sat with the men rather than working with the women.

Still he sat there, staring at the nose of the shuttle.

"Iianthe?" he asked the living pincushion.

(*I have not the honor of purple tips to my wings.*)

Typical enigmatic dragon thoughts. If Konner did not know that Iianthe was another word for purple and that Iianthe's horns, wing veins, and wing tips were a shade of purple he would not have understood the statement.

"I am Martin Konner O'Hara," he said politely.

(*Irythros,*) the dragon replied.

"Irythros? Does that mean anything?"

(*I am Irythros. What should it mean?*)

"Does the word name a color in some other language?"

(*Ah,*) the dragon sighed in understanding. It remained silent so long Konner wondered if it would say anything more.

(*Some might believe my name means Red.*)

"Red. You have red horns and spines and your wing tips and veins are red."

(*Yes.*)

"Just like Simurgh."

(*Never!*) The dragon rose up on its hind legs, flapping its wings and roaring its displeasure. A single long flame shot forth from its open mouth.

"Touchy subject?" Konner asked. But then he knew it would be. "Dragons don't like to admit that one of their own became thirsty for human blood. You don't like to remember that you had to destroy one of your own."

The dragon's silence seemed to take on weight. Konner felt a heaviness in his mind that wanted to push his knowledge of Simurgh's true nature deep into the forgotten recesses of his lizard hind brain. A place that knew instinctive fear and had no sense or reason.

He fought the compulsion to forget.

"So, Red, are you waiting for me?" Konner crept a little closer.

(*Irythros,*) the dragon insisted.

"Whatever. Why are you here? Dragons don't show themselves to mere humans without reason." Konner dared rise to his feet. This brought his eyes level with the dragon's claws where they gripped the sleek nose of the shuttle. Each of those talons was as long as his forearm. He winced at the thought of punctures in the cerama/metal hull.

No mere dragon could pierce the hull of a shuttle designed to withstand the heat, radiation, and pressure of reentry, he reminded himself. Again and again.

"You are bigger than Iianthe," he commented, tentatively checking to see if any cerama/metal hull scales had broken off beneath the talons. He needed every one of those scales intact to protect the ship—from space travel as well as corrosion of the interior.

They all seemed intact. But he would not know for certain until the dragon moved.

"Would you mind coming down from there?" He looked up to where the dragon's eyes should be. Hard to tell in this light. Hard to tell in *any* light. His eyes wanted to slide around the dragon rather than look directly at it.

(*Is there a reason?*) Irythros asked. Suddenly, he snaked his head down to Konner's level.

Hot breath bathed his face. A spiraled two-meter-long horn of red and crystal teased his hair.

Konner resisted the temptation to jump back. He'd learned over the months of dealing with Iianthe, the purple-tip who was very fond of Kim and Hestiia, never to show fear. One had to earn a dragon's respect. They had no use for cowardice. They considered Simurgh a coward for hunting weak humans rather than more honorable prey, like the huge predatory fish in the Great Bay. Like the one that had startled Konner in the dragongate and caused him to lose the beacon.

Konner took three deep breaths to keep his feet from shuffling backward. The dragon exhaled.

Konner winced at the thought of the fire the dragon could produce. (They liked their meals cooked.) The wind that passed his ears was cool.

"I would like you to get off my ship because your claws are ripping holes in its hide," Konner said mildly.

(*Oh.*) The dragon leaped free of the shuttle. Its talons screeched against the cerama/metal.

The sound became needle darts in Konner's ears. Again he cringed but did not back away or cover the offended organs.

(*Forgive my trespass,*) Irythros said as he settled to the ground beside Konner.

The beast towered above him, as big as the shuttle. It spread its wings before furling them. The moonlight turned them into shimmering translucent veils. For a moment, Konner thought he could see star maps in the vein network. Or maybe transactional gravitons, the theoretical energy force that held the universe together and at the same time conspired to keep everything in place.

Overcoming the inertia of the gravitons posed the single largest obstacle to space travel. Or atmosphere flight, or rolling a cart.

Konner shook his head free of his fanciful thoughts. Dragons were planet bound. They might speak enigmatically with a great deal of wisdom, but they did not carry star charts etched into their wing membranes.

"Now why did you seek me out?" Konner asked again.

(*Hanassa speaks to the stars. We need to know why.*)

"But Hanassa is dead." Konner began to shiver with a new chill. Twice he and his brothers had thought they had killed the man. Twice he had recovered and come back to threaten their friends as well as themselves. The third time they had made certain he stayed dead. Two flywackets, purple-tip dragons shrunk to the size and shape of winged house cats, had dumped Hanassa's body into the lava pit. The same pit where Konner wanted to dump the beacon.

(*The body of Hanassa died. Yet still he speaks to the stars. We need you to tell us why.*)

"Speaks to the stars," Konner mused. "The beacon! You know where the locator beacon is. Can you take me to it so that we can destroy it?"

(*No.*)

Konner stared at the dragon, expecting the beast to fly away.

Instead Irythros parked his haunches on the ground and returned Konner's level gaze.

"You may be able to see in the dark, but I need more light to see you properly," Konner said at last.

(*Fetch it.*)

"You will wait?"

(*Yes.*)

For the first time in this bizarre conversation, Konner realized the difference between this dragon and Iianthe, the purple-tip who had helped him and his brothers through the last crisis. Iianthe spoke in bass tones very like a large bronze bell tolling across the landscape of his mind. Irythros was more of a tenor, sounded more like an Ubberlund doodlehorn chattering away with the crisp notes of a military march.

Konner wasted no more time. He touched the keypad in his pocket to banish the cloaking field and open the hatch. He'd stashed the portable illuminator just inside. A simple matter to grab it and exit without taking his eyes off the dragon for more than three heartbeats.

He blinked rapidly. Where had the beast gone? And why had Irythros contacted a human with such a very frightening and bone-chillingly cryptic remark?

* * *

Kim kissed Hestiia lightly on the cheek. "I have some work to do," he whispered.

She looked at him sharply. "Will you use the weed?"

"I don't know. Depends on what I find." He could not hold her gaze.

"You know it is dangerous."

"I know that Pryth thinks it is dangerous." He walked back toward their cabin, the one he and Hestiia had built for themselves the day they married. Well, actually, the village had built it for them as part of the wedding ceremony. They were still chinking the logs with moss and turf to insulate it against the winter cold. The moss they used was as ubiquitous as the red cow wool. It absorbed moisture in babies' diapers, became good tinder when dried, and insulated against cold and noise quite effectively.

Once inside the cabin, Kim pulled out his reader. It came to life precisely where he had finished his notes this morning. Before the hasty visit to the volcano, before the news of the beacon had upset the tidy life he had made for himself here.

He took a deep breath and concentrated upon the reader. He needed to record today's events.

The woman, Dalleena, and her supposed talent drew his thoughts away from the implications of the lost beacon. The locals respected her claim to track anyone. How did she do it?

For that matter, how did he achieve his own miracles of healing? Raaskan was alive because Kim, with the help of his brothers, had rebuilt the man's crushed rib cage and pelvis, using only the power of his mind. He had cauterized internal bleeding. And he had pushed a dislocated shoulder back into place. All without invasive surgery or the technology of modern medicine.

"Something born in me and my brothers lets us do this. So how do we access it on a regular basis?"

This morning, Kim had been on the verge of doing that with controlled breathing. But once he'd fallen out of the trance he'd been exhausted, ravenous, and nearly incoherent. "My body lacked the fuel to perform the magic."

His eyes sought the basket in the corner. Inside lay the wilting leaves of the Tambootie tree. Once before, he had ingested the essential oils that seeped out of the leaves. They had opened his mind and his talent, allowing him to perform one last miracle to rescue the

Coros from Hanassa's control. He had read Hanassa's mind from a distance of nearly ten kilometers.

"Just a little. I need just a little of the leaves to experiment." Without thinking about it, he had walked across the room and shoved his hand deep into the mass of leaves. His skin burned slightly from contact with the essential oils permeating the leaves. He withdrew his hand, grasping a particularly fat leaf dripping with oil. He licked it.

Colors burst upon his tongue. Outside, he heard every word whispered by his people. He shared Hestiia's concern for him as if experiencing his own emotion.

His vision sharpened on the periphery at the same time that he lost focus on things directly in front of him; as if he needed to look at life sideways, around the barrier of his own emotions and prejudices to get a clear view.

Halos enveloped every object in varying colors and brightness. He reached out slowly for the basket of Tambootie. His fingers had to stretch a long way into the corona, or aura, or whatever, before he touched the woven grasses of the basket. Further experiments showed the aura less deep on his bed and the stool in front of his working table. A quick peek out the door showed flashes of living fire surrounding the heads of all the people still gathered around the fire. He found Hestiia rapidly by the brown, rust, and orange flares growing out of her hair. Others he had to think about until he noticed distinctive colors and combinations for each person.

Darkness yawned before him. A bright tangle of colored chains similar in color and combination of colors to the auras beckoned him to grab hold and explore. . . .

(*Be careful when you delve into the realm of dragons.*)

Kim thudded to the packed dirt floor and promptly vomited.

CHAPTER 8

DALLEENA EXCUSED herself from the rapt company of the village men. Raaskan, the headman, and Yaakke from the other village, both had questioned her intently about her talent. Trackers were not born into every generation. Her family had produced one in each of three successive generations. Both men wanted her as an asset to the village.

Something bigger and more important drew her here. She had listened to reports of the Stargods for moons now. They offered a new view of life and spirituality. They offered freedom from the old ways.

And the Stargods had lost something important. She had to find it for them. Whatever it was, no matter what dangers lay in finding it. Her talent would not allow her to rest until the lost was found and the Stargods were safe once more.

Stargod Konner was not hard to follow. He had left a trail a child could see. She did not even have to engage her talent.

She followed him across two fields separated by a narrow creek. She jumped the creek without even thinking about it. Then over a small hill, with just enough elevation to obscure from the village what lay beyond.

Dim moonlight and a soft glow from the other side

of the hill lit her way. She used her eyes rather than her talent to pick her footsteps.

At the top of the rise she halted. Her throat froze. She forgot to breathe.

Shimmering in the moonlight a long white dragon rested easily on its haunches. That sight alone was worth a second glance. But the other dragon, the one that was hard to see, the one that demanded that she look anywhere but at it was even more beautiful. Illuminated by the Stargod's magical torch, she saw that dark red, the color of blood, outlined its horns, wing tips and veins.

She swallowed and stuffed her hands into her pockets. She must not cross her wrists, right over left, and flap them in ward against Simurgh, the winged god that had demanded blood sacrifice at every turn. Touching her head, heart, and each shoulder in turn, the ward of the Stargods, did not seem protection enough.

Beside the dragon stood a lone man. Stargod Konner. The dragon was a worthy companion of a god.

She swallowed her superstitious fears and walked down the hill toward the man and his dragon. A red-tip.

Simurgh had been a red-tip.

As she approached, the dragon took wing and disappeared into the night. Shielding her face from a blast of wind and dust raised by flapping dragon wings, Dalleena followed his flight path with her eyes. For half a moment she thought she saw a nearly transparent wing cross the moon. Then it was gone.

"Irythros!" Stargod Konner called. "Irythros, come back here. I'm not finished with you."

The dragon ignored him, of course.

"Dragons obey only themselves," she said as she came closer.

"Who are you?" Stargod Konner whirled to face her.

"Dalleena Farseer. I sensed that you had lost something."

"Sensed?"

She shrugged. "I am a Tracker. I find lost things."

"Why should I believe you?"

"You have my word."

He looked at her closely then. He focused on her eyes.

"I believe you. I shouldn't. But I believe you."

"What have you lost?" She could not break eye contact. The depth of his blue eyes promised her much. Promises she knew he would keep or die.

"Um . . ." he licked his lips.

She mimicked his action. Her throat still felt dry. She had to remember to breathe.

"We call it a beacon."

"A bee-kan."

"Close enough. About this big." He held up his hand and traced his palm. "It is made out of the same material as the shuttle." He gestured toward the huge white dragon beside them.

The beast emitted a low hum, but otherwise seemed strangely quiescent.

"I do not know this bee-kan." She placed her right hand flat upon the cool skin of the white dragon.

Her hand grew hot. Tingles shot up her arm to her brain. A numbness grew from a knot into a broad band at the base of her neck.

"Far away. I hear the bee-kan calling to its home. It calls to . . . a . . . king stone. It begs the king stone to come rescue it," she whispered.

She shook her head to free herself of the tracking trance. A little of the numbness eased. It would not leave her completely until she removed her hand from contact with the white dragon.

She lifted her hand. It felt too heavy. She braced her arm with the other hand and pulled back. Her hand was heavier still. Then she wrenched her arm.

Her hand remained glued to the shuttle.

* * *

Kim wrapped his arms around Hestiia, tucking her beneath his chin. She just fit there. Together they stood for long moments watching the last of the daylight fade beyond the western horizon.

"What troubles you, husband?" she asked.

His senses still reeled from the Tambootie. He dared not mention his reaction to the weed. He'd cleaned up after himself as best he could. But he had to lock his quaking knees and pretend nothing had happened.

"Kim?" Hestiia prompted him.

"Trouble comes," he replied.

"What form does this trouble take?"

Kim sighed. She'd not allow the subject to drop until he told her all. He did not like secrets. His family had too many. But some things were best kept private among his brothers.

"Tell me." She tried to step away from him.

He pulled her back against his body, savoring her warmth and her love.

"More people from my homeland approach. They will bring many miracles. But each miracle comes with a price. They will poison the air and water. Our ears will be assaulted with noise day and night until we can no longer hear birds sing or crickets chirp." How else could he explain the cost of industrialization?

Magic would do nothing to stop these people.

"Many, many more people will come to live here. At first the land will produce enough for all, but eventually the fields will grow tired and give forth smaller and smaller crops. My people will poison the soil to force it to grow more and more crops. And still more people will come, blind to the pollution, blind to the conflicts that arise when too many people fight for the same small piece of land. They will destroy everything we hold dear."

"Then we must stop them."

"Not so easy."

"But you and your brothers are the Stargods. Surely you and your white dragon *Rover* can defeat them, send them back where they came from."

"There are too many of them. They have bigger ships and more powerful weapons than we do."

"There must be a way . . ."

"We have one small chance. We have to find and destroy a small device before they find us."

"I saw the Tracker follow your brother Konner. She can help."

"I pray that she can." But Kim doubted it.

"Your silence tells me there is more trouble than a device that calls these Others."

"Are you sure you do not read my mind?" He kissed the top of her head.

"I know you well, husband. What else troubles you?"

"The beacon we seek was stolen."

"Who would dare!"

"Who, indeed?"

They both stared in silence at the silhouettes of trees against the last glow of light.

"Hanassa died. Your brother killed him. Gentian and Iianthe dropped his body into the fiery heart of the mountain," Hestiia said.

"Indeed. But Hanassa began life as a purple dragon, triplet to Gentian and Iianthe. But only one purple-tip may exist at any time. Gentian shrank to become a flywacket, Iianthe remained a dragon. Hanassa sent his spirit into a human body. Are we certain Hanassa's spirit died with his body?"

"Yes!"

"Then he must have had more disciples than Taneeo. We know how much our new priest hated Hanassa. We know we can trust Taneeo. Another must be haunting the caverns and making mischief for us."

"We must ask Taneeo. He would know if Hanassa trained any followers."

"I hate to bother him. He has not yet recovered from . . . from his ordeal." Ten drugged needles from Loki's rifle had run all the way through Hanassa's body into Taneeo's. One hundred or more of the needles had lodged in Hanassa's vital organs and muscles. The priest of Simurgh had died instantly. Taneeo had been knocked unconscious. Already weakened by months of privation while Hanassa's slave, the apprentice priest had taken a long time to recover from the wounds and the drugs. Even now, after more than a month, he failed to gain weight or rebuild muscle.

"We must still ask. Now better than later." Hestiia insisted. Decisively, she grabbed Kim's hand and led him back to the campfire.

A quick look at the assembly showed Konner and the new woman still missing. Taneeo had not made an appearance.

"I took food to his hut," Pryth, the old wisewoman said. "He often eats alone and sleeps early." She dismissed his behavior as normal.

But it was not normal. The Coros lived communally. The evening gathering was important to them. They sang, told stories, and shared their lives as no one on the civilized planets of the Galactic Terran Empire would. Survival on this primitive planet depended upon mutual cooperation and sharing of burdens.

"Perhaps I should examine Taneeo again. See if he needs healing," Kim mused as he and Hestiia trudged over to the circular hut set a little apart from the larger, square cabins of the rest of the village. With a bit more of the Tambootie, perhaps he could leech some residual poisons from Taneeo's body with his magic.

Hestiia politely rattled the strands of beads hanging outside the doorway. Kim counted one hundred heartbeats. Then he gave the beads a more vigorous shake.

No one answered.

"I'm coming in, Taneeo," Kim called as he ducked beneath the low doorway.

Inside, the single room was dark and deserted.

*　*　*

"St. Bridget!" Konner cursed. The Tracker woman had merged with *his* shuttle in a way he never could. If the ship wanted a human partner permanently attached, it should be him. Not . . . not this female from an alien culture. A *primitive* alien culture that knew nothing of machines or electronics or space travel or . . . or . . .

Damn.

"Um . . . has this ever happened to you before?" Konner stared at Dalleena's hand. He could not see where her flesh separated from the cerama/metal hull of *Rover*. He ran a blunt fingernail around the edges of the merge. One seamless bond.

Puzzled, he scratched his head.

"I . . . I do not usually have to touch the sheep and children who wander off to find them," she said. A tiny note of apprehension crept into her voice. Not panic. Not hysteria. Neither emotion would help and so she kept them at bay.

An eminently practical woman, to go with the

sturdy broad palm, nails cut nearly to the quick, and shortish fingers. A sturdy hand used to hard work.

"This certainly complicates life," Konner grunted as he walked around Dalleena to study the problem from another angle. He also studied her figure. Nice curves were outlined beneath her masculine clothing. She stood quite tall for a woman, as tall as many of the men on this planet. The top of her head reached the bridge of his nose. All of those curves would fit very nicely snugged against him. "Perhaps I should call my brothers."

"No!" Now she sounded closer to panic.

Konner cocked an eyebrow at her.

Immediately, she seemed to realize how her hasty reply had sounded. She squared her shoulders and returned his stare, measure for measure.

"Then what do you propose to do?"

She swallowed deeply and held out her other hand. He clasped it in his own. A tingle shot up his arm.

Who is this stranger, Konner? Mum's voice demanded in the back of his mind. Not Mum. The computer voice he had programmed to sound like Mum. He and his brothers had agreed that at times they needed her voice of authority to calm them when the IMPs were hard on their heels and all seemed lost. At other times they took immense satisfaction in telling the voice to "Shut up" and slapping the mute with enthusiastic vigor. Something they would never do in Mum's presence.

Dalleena's eyes opened wide and she bit her lower lip.

"You heard that?" he asked.

She nodded, eyes still wide.

He knew she was frightened, but she kept it under control. He liked that.

"Don't worry. Mum won't hurt you. At least not as long as you stay on this world," Konner chuckled.

"Your . . . your m–mother? This dragon is your mother?" Her knees knocked together and her face grew pale.

"Nothing quite so simple." Although to describe Mum as a dragon . . . Well, she did pretend to the wisdom of the ages and keep her own counsel. Margaret Kristine O'Hara could be as enigmatic as a dragon. She also defended her offspring with a ferocity reminiscent of a battle between a dragon and a behemoth.

Somehow Konner's fingers became entwined with Dalleena's.

Her other hand began to glow. And so did the hull beneath it.

Konner slapped his own hand atop hers, careful not to touch the cerama/metal scales. New warmth permeated his being from his points of contact with the strange woman.

"I expected the glow to be hot," he muttered. Just flesh. All he felt was soft, warm, feminine flesh beneath his hand.

He suddenly found Dalleena's lips very close to his own. She licked her lips. Their gazes met. The world seemed to stand still.

"Konner!" Loki called from the edge of the meadow. "Konner, we need you. Taneeo is missing."

"St. Bridget, his timing is perfect as usual." Konner broke free of the thrall of Dalleena's luscious mouth.

"Go," Dalleena whispered. She sounded more than a little breathless . . . and perhaps reluctant. "I will free myself. Somehow. They need you more than I do."

With the last statement she stood taller, straighter, and thrust out her chin in stubborn resistance to his charm.

"Fine." Inexplicable anger shot through him. Konner jerked both of his hands away from hers. The moment he was free of her, he regretted the distance between them.

Without thinking he clamped both hands around her right wrist, braced his feet, and pulled on her arm.

"If I can levitate a three-ton boulder, I can separate you from my ship and my life." He shuddered in memory of the disaster that had forced him to use the latent psychic talent in order to rescue Raaskan.

He should concentrate on separating Dalleena's flesh from the hull.

"Not so easy a task," Dalleena chuckled. She remained firmly attached to the shuttle.

Had she referred to the now famous levitation or to freeing her?

"Not easy, but possible." Konner shifted his weight and balance a little. With a firmer grim, he concentrated on the line of skin that met cerama/metal.

A ripping sound alerted him. He caught her as they tumbled away from the shuttle. She landed atop him on the ground. Again her mouth was a bare breath away from his.

"Free of the dragon, but not free from me," she said softly. Her gaze seemed concentrated on his own mouth.

Before he could reply, she brushed his lips with her own. Then she scrambled away from him.

He rose quickly, brushing grass and debris from his trousers and vest.

Now what? Clearly the woman wanted him. He could not deny the evidence that he found her very attractive. "St. Bridget and all the angels, I don't have time for a relationship," he muttered, hoping she would not hear him. "I have to get off this planet and claim my son. I have to find the beacon and keep the IMPs from finding us. I have to finish too many things before I get serious about a woman."

"I will meet you here at dawn. We will hunt your

lost bee-kan together," she announced and stalked back toward the village campfire. Not once did she look back over her shoulder.

Konner pounded his fist into the hull of the *Rover*. Pain immediately cooled his ardor . . . but not his frustration.

CHAPTER 9

"**I** AM WAITING for an answer, Lieutenant."
Commander Leonard drummed her fingers
against her screen.

"For the life of me, Captain, I can find no record,
ever, of this space configuration," First Lieutenant
Kohler said, shaking his head. His fingers never
stopped moving across his screen.

"Sir," Kat interrupted. Never good to jump into a
conversation with senior officers too quickly.

Commander Leonard nodded for Kat to proceed.

"Sir, there is a habitable planet. Fourth from the
sun. We are too far away to read signs of life. It looks
green. No man-made satellites. One moon. And I'm
getting a faint echo of the beacon."

"Communications, you picking up any traffic?"
Commander Leonard swung her chair around to face
Ensign James Englebert and his array of screens.

"Nothing coming from any of the planets, sir," he
replied. "Except that beacon. But *my* instruments cannot pinpoint a location. It seems like it's coming from
everywhere and nowhere."

"Any other habitable planets?" Commander Leonard asked.

"Not without artificial habitat," Kat replied.

"I would guess that if people lived on the inhospita-
ble planets, they'd have radio traffic," Englebert said.

"If our quarry did indeed come to this system through that wild jump point, then my guess is they would head for the one place they could breathe. Helm, take us in. Slowly, with due caution."

Kat smiled to herself. She set course for the little green planet. "Now we'll see what kind of audacity and courage the O'Hara brothers truly have. I'm sick of following legends and rumors. Time to bring them to justice."

*　　*　　*

"We'll find you, Taneeo," Loki said. "One skinny, young priest couldn't run too far away. There aren't that many places you could go."

He jammed a long branch into the green fire at the center of the village. The fat-soaked moss bound to the tip flared immediately. He pulled it free and held it up. The eerie light illuminated a small section of the compound beyond the evening gathering space.

Just on the edge of the light was the doorway to the large square cabin he shared with Konner. Kim and Hestiia had built their own home adjacent to this one.

Primitive. Logs crossed and stacked, chinked with moss and mud. Lots of the moss. For many months the thatched building had been home. A place to call their own. A home Mum had not invaded and stamped with her personality. He liked that. When he returned to civilization, he would insist upon a home of his own, a place where he could take Cyndi. A place where Mum had to knock on the front door to gain entrance.

Suddenly he wanted nothing more than to get away from the people of his village and their demands upon his time, his energy, and his integrity.

But first he had to find Taneeo. He was eldest. It was his responsibility. "It's not like Taneeo to be gone for more than an hour or so," he said.

"He's not well," Hestiia added. "Where would he go?"

Kim raised his own torch and illuminated another sector of the village.

"*St. Bridget,* I hope Taneeo hasn't been kidnapped by the ghost we encountered in the caves," Loki muttered. Surreptitiously, he made the sign of the cross. He found no comfort in his mother's ward against evil. What he truly wanted to do was cross his wrists and flap his hands in the gesture used by the locals to ward off the winged demon Simurgh.

"We could rescue him from kidnappers. Let's just hope he doesn't run into that big red bull who hangs out in the far meadow beyond the wetlands." Konner added his own torch to the pool of light.

"The priest is that way." The new woman, the Tracker, pointed in the direction of the wetlands and the bull. She started walking. Each stride was strong and confident, like a man's. She did not look back, as if she expected them to follow her without question.

"How can she be sure?" Loki asked. The hair on his spine bristled. Who was this woman to come into the village alone and start giving orders.

"She knows what she knows," Konner said. He followed the woman with the same long, determined stride.

"Konner?" Loki scrambled to follow, more worried about his middle brother than the little bit of dignity he forfeited with his hasty, ungraceful steps. "Konner never follows anyone. Not even me—or Mum."

"Looks like he found Mum's equal," Kim said with a chuckle. He and Hestiia paced alongside Loki, Hestiia taking two steps to every one of Kim's.

"I like Dalleena," Hestiia commented, a little breathlessly. "She will be a good addition to the village. To all of the Coros."

"Hmf," Loki grunted.

He caught up with Konner just as they all came

alongside the woman. She kept her right arm out-
stretched, palm facing forward. Kim and Hestiia
stayed a few steps behind, holding hands.

St. Bridget! They'd been married two months and
they still held hands, and smooched at any excuse.
Sooner or later Kim would come to his senses and
realize he had to leave the girl. Better sooner than
later. If they did not find the beacon soon, they'd
have to leave. Crystals or no crystals.

Loki did not want to be around to deal with the
copious tears that would fall upon the departure of
the Stargods.

Dalleena stopped short at the stone wall that divided the wheat field from the wetlands. The wheat
had been reduced to stubble over the last week. She
stepped forward, barked her shins upon the piled
rocks, then backed off one pace. Then she repeated
the process, seemingly blind to the obstacle.

"Doesn't she see the damn wall?" Loki growled.

"Apparently not. I guess that she has fallen into a
tracking trance," Konner mused.

"Trance?" Loki asked. "Like when Kim does his
healing magic?"

"Or like you when you eavesdrop, or like I do
when I 'commune' with the ship's crystals." Konner
sounded so calm, so trusting of this strange woman.

"This way," Konner said gently, taking Dalleena's
arm. He led her to a crude stile over the wall. She
followed docilely. But her right arm shifted to maintain her bead on whatever she sought.

Loki hung back. He did not want to leave the perceived safety of the cultivated fields. Primitive as
they were, these fields represented civilization. Beyond was wilderness, the unknown. Disaster.

He knew it. He knew it as clearly as he knew his
own name, and Cyndi's name, and how anxious he
was to return to her and claim her hand in marriage.

Once clear of the retaining wall, Dalleena moved

her arm back and forth, scanning, as if her hand were a sensor. Then she started off, faster than before. Her pace increased until she ran. She stumbled often, heedless of the rough ground and soggy patches. Konner was always there, steadying her, guiding her to an easier path.

Kim and Hestiia hastened after them.

Loki had no choice but to do the same. They had to find Taneeo. Had to protect their friend.

One thing Loki had learned over the past few months was that the Stargods did not let their people down. He'd be glad to get rid of that responsibility when he returned to civilization.

They circled the wettest of the wetlands. Not as soggy or dangerous now as when the brothers first landed on this remote little planet.

Konner's torch burned low. Loki's and Kim's didn't fare much better. The moss had its limits after all.

Dalleena kept moving. Could the woman see in the dark? Off to their left a series of barely perceived lumps shifted. One snorted and stood. The shaggy red bull warned them away from his harem.

Their path took them past the cattle and back around toward the cultivation.

"We could have gone straight through the barley to get here faster and safer," Loki complained.

"She follows the path that Taneeo took," Hestiia explained.

"Does she detect his scent?" Loki asked, intrigued despite his reservations.

Hestiia shrugged, as much as she could while keeping up the pace.

And then they were back in the middle of the barley. Loki dug in his heels. He nearly catapulted onto his face. The lump in the center of the field loomed menacingly. But this was no cow. This was a rock.

A rock that might be sentient. *The* rock that Konner had lifted with his mind to free Raaskan and save his life.

Taneeo sat at the base of the rock. He rested his back and head against the solid granite. His face was streaked with dirt, his trousers and vest ripped. His leg stuck out in front of him, twisted at an odd angle.

"We didn't kill him. We can't kill him," Taneeo whispered.

"Kill who?" Kim knelt before the village priest. He ran his hands over him assessing his injuries.

"Hanassa. Only the dragons can kill Hanassa."

The blood drained from Loki's face. The ghost of their greatest enemy was real.

*   *   *

Kim concentrated hard. His hands burned every time he came close to an injury on Taneeo's battered body. Two cracked ribs that would heal with time and tight bandaging. One eye swollen shut. The Bruise Leech® would take care of that. But that leg.

"We've set broken bones before, Kim," Konner reassured him with a firm clasp on his shoulder.

"Yeah. But I need the portable ultrasound unit. And some splints, and a stretcher and a bunch of stout men to carry him on the stretcher back home." A quick look around told him that Loki, as usual, was edging away from them—useless in a crisis. The oldest brother tended to charge into situations and then leave Kim and Konner to clean up the aftermath.

"Loki, he needs the US unit and the Leech. Can you get it for us?"

Loki bristled and clenched his fists.

"That is, unless you'd rather set some bones and . . ."

"Never mind. I'll get what you need," Loki grumbled. He turned sharply and set off across the acres of barley at a brisk trot.

"I'll go, too," Hestiia said quietly. "Pryth and Raaskan can help."

Kim's heart swelled. He knew she'd do her best to calm and soothe Loki. She was good at that. But would even Hestiia be able to ease Loki's mind tonight?

Firing the lethal needle rifle at Hanassa had cost Loki a great deal of emotional stability. Taking a life . . .

Kim shook his head to clear it of his own memories of the one time he had caused another man to die. Years later he still had nightmares about it.

Now to find out that perhaps Hanassa had not died must upset Loki's equilibrium.

Dalleena produced a skin of clean water. Kim accepted it gratefully. He took a long drink, offered some to Taneeo, and used the remainder to cleanse the priest's face.

"I tried to keep him out," Taneeo whispered. Suddenly he grabbed the fronts of Kim's vest with a strength that belied his injuries. "I fought him as hard as I could, Stargod Kim. I promise you I tried. But he is strong. Much stronger than I thought."

Taneeo swallowed with difficulty. Kim brought the guttering torch closer. What he had thought were streaks of dirt on the young man's face and throat turned out to be bruises. In the shape of fingerprints.

Kim's vision fractured and he suddenly saw ghostly hands clasping his friend's throat. He shook himself free of the frightening sight. He needed some Tambootie to make the vision clearer.

"Drink, Taneeo." Kim offered the skin of water once more.

"He punishes me. Even now he punishes me," Taneeo whispered. He clawed at his throat. Somehow his hands precisely fit the bruises.

Again Kim had to separate himself from the sight of a second hand atop Taneeo's guiding it, clenching it.

"Who? Who punishes you?" Kim pressed. He felt cold with the certainty he knew what was coming. If only he had some Tambootie, he could sort this out.

"Hanassa."

"We killed Hanassa. The flywackets dumped his body into the lava pit. No one, not even a dragon could survive the heart of the volcano," Kim insisted.

"Dragons are not limited to the life of the body," Taneeo squeaked.

"Dragons can't shapechange into humans," Konner insisted. "They can shrink to the shape of a flywacket, a flying house cat. If they choose human form, they have to—borrow a body. I wonder if they can later move from one body into another." He hunkered down beside Kim. The little lines around his eyes deepened and his shoulders arched toward his ears, sure signs of inner stress he did not allow to reach his voice.

"I have an awful feeling they can." Kim swallowed deeply, then turned back to Taneeo with resolution. "Whose body did Hanassa take?"

He had a sudden sinking feeling in his gut. How long could the ghost of Hanassa linger in the caverns before it forced its way into a human body? Which human?

Taneeo's eyes opened wide, staring into the distance. He gurgled and choked. "I fought him. I continue to fight. He will not have me!" Then his eyes rolled up and he slumped into unconsciousness.

A second aura appeared around his head, separated, and drifted free.

CHAPTER 10

DALLEENA STUDIED the white dragon. The rising sun cast interesting shadows upon the gleaming scales. Was that a slight indentation in the shape of a palm and fingers? She wanted to trace the outline with her finger, test the perceptions of her eyes with touch.

Resolutely, she crossed her arms under her breasts and buried her hands in her armpits. No sense tempting fate and permanently bonding with the dragon that was not truly a dragon.

An inner voice told her to leave. Leave the village. Leave the influence of the Stargods. Leave the all-too-handsome Stargod Konner. She had to forget his gentle touch, the way their bodies seemed to fit together when she landed atop him. No good would come from continuing.

But she had promised to track a lost one.

That nagging inner voice insisted that she had found the lost priest Taneeo. Did that fulfill her promise to Stargod Konner?

No, it did not. She still needed to find the bee-kan for Konner. Only she could do that. Her word of honor as a Tracker was at stake. She had to find the bee-kan. Then she would leave. As fast as she could. She would go as far away as she could and never, ever see Konner again.

No good could come from a relationship with a god. Even a temporary relationship. Hanassa, the priest of the god Simurgh, had spread his seed far and wide. No good had come to any of the women he seduced or raped. Unfortunately, or fortunately, most of the children of these liaisons had died young.

Dalleena had decided years ago that she would stay away from gods and their priests.

Resolved, she turned away from her scrutiny of her handprint on the white scales to watch the sunrise.

Konner stood right in front of her.

S'murghit, she had been so absorbed in thought she had not heard him approach. Unforgivable in a Tracker.

He stepped closer. Barely the width of her hand separated them. He bent his head just a little, bringing his mouth level with hers.

She moistened her lips.

"Are you planning on usurping control over my *Rover* again?" he snarled.

Dalleena reared away from contemplation of his delicious mouth. Her head banged against the solid surface of the dragon.

"Never. The thing is alien and dangerous. I do not know why you put up with the beast," she returned. Her head hurt. Her scalp tingled. And she'd caught another whisper of the strange feminine voice he'd called "Mum." What had it said?

Nothing complimentary, she was certain. Mothers never liked other women entering their sons' lives. Her own grandmother had complained constantly about Dalleena's mother for as long as she could remember. Right up until they both died in a slave raid led by Hanassa.

"Is the beacon still to the east?" Konner asked. He stepped aside and tapped the white scales in an interesting pattern right beside her handprint. Only after he dropped his hand did she notice a series of bumps and indentations.

The dragon hissed in response to the tattoo he'd beat on its side.

Dalleena jumped back.

The belly opened, like the pupil of a cornered animal's eye.

But no eye peered out at her from that opening. Just . . . just the inside of a cabin. A richly furnished cabin with soft cushions dyed a blue too vibrant to have come from any plant or mineral she knew, and strange storage chests made of a metal shinier than the new iron, and . . . all manner of things she could not identify.

Her head reeled trying to make sense of it all.

"Well, are you coming with me to find the beacon?" Konner asked. He marched up the two steps to stand in the doorway.

His angry tone shook Dalleena out of her befuddlement.

"The beacon is due east. At the other side of the sea beyond the Great Bay." She dug in her heels and braced herself, lest he force her into the dragon's belly.

"I need more information than that, Dalleena." He stood with hands on hips and a tense posture. "I have never explored the continent across the sea. You have to come with me."

"Not inside that dragon. I will not be its next meal."

"*Rover* doesn't eat people." Konner's entire countenance brightened. His eyes twinkled with mischief and his shoulders relaxed. The laughter in his voice sounded so inviting.

"Come along now. We can't waste any more time." Konner held out his hand.

She could not help putting her own hand in his

and letting him draw her up the two steps. Her hand lingered in his as she surveyed the inside of the dragon's belly. Most of what she saw still did not make sense. But she noticed that the too-blue cushions showed fading and wear patterns. The square edges looked frayed. Indentations marked the places where male bottoms had sat too often and too long.

A morsel of pride crept into her posture. She would never allow such wonderful possessions to be treated so carelessly.

"This way." He tugged on her hand, leading her to the right and the head of the dragon.

Dalleena promised herself she would explore the well-used cabin later. More curiosities awaited. Whatever magic this dragon possessed, it seemed designed to help Konner and his brothers, not devour them.

The Stargod held aside a shiny curtain. It had the same reflective surface as the storage chests. She had presumed it was just another wall. Curious. She fingered it, finding it slick, as if Konner had spread grease upon thin wood shavings. But her fingers came away clean.

What other marvels could Konner show her?

Eyes wide, absorbing as many details as she could, she entered what could only be a sacred temple. Soft flames from hidden candles glowed and blinked at her. Colored flames! Red and blue and yellow as well as the normal green. But not a normal green. Deeper and more intense than a saber fern just washed with spring dew.

Dalleena resisted the need to drop to her knees in adoration of whatever god Konner had dedicated this temple to.

But why would he worship another god? He was one of the three Stargods. He deserved adoration. He did not need to give it.

"Sit," he ordered her, pointing to a seat formed of metal and covered with the same worn blue cushions as the cabin.

Dalleena plunked herself down on the floor of the temple. She wrapped her arms around her knees and remained motionless. She just could not bring herself to sit where a Stargod had been enthroned within his own temple.

Stargod Konner frowned at her. "Don't be stubborn and ridiculous. I said sit and I mean there." He glared. His intensely blue eyes—the same color as the cushions before they had faded?—glinted with emotions Dalleena could not read.

She swallowed protestations of unworthiness. Somehow she sensed he would not respect groveling.

Hesitantly, she rolled upward without touching anything. Two short sidesteps took her to the throne. It swung beneath her, rotating in a full circle. She popped back onto her feet. "Is it alive?"

Konner chuckled briefly. Then he fiddled with something at the base of the chair. "Try it again. The chair won't bite." He gestured grandly for her to obey.

Dalleena bit her lip and lowered herself into the chair. She kept her weight balanced on her toes, ready to flee if anything moved.

The chair accepted her weight. Indeed, it welcomed her, snuggling to fit her frame.

"Now buckle up. I don't want you flying about the cockpit." Konner pulled long thongs about as wide as his palm over her shoulders and then fastened them to the chair between her legs. Then he sat and produced two more of the broad, flat thongs from the back of his own chair and "buckled up" himself.

He turned his attention to the altar of colored flames. As he touched first one and then another, the sounds within the dragon changed. It rumbled. It vibrated. The sunlight coming in through its eyes dimmed. If the thongs had not held her in place, she would have bolted. She could not. So she gripped the edges of her chair with her hands. Her knuckles turned white. Her fingers grew numb. And still she clung to the chair.

Then a tremendous weight pressed against her chest. She could not breathe. The meadow outside the dragon's eyes rushed past, faster than any person could run. Faster than a bird could fly. Faster than . . . than she could pray to whatever god might listen, even the hated and feared Simurgh.

"Easy, Dalleena. The worst will be over in a minute."

But it wasn't. On and on they sped. Faster and faster. The pressure increased. The landscape flitting past and . . . gulp . . . below them made her dizzy.

Desperate to maintain some sort of equilibrium she fastened her gaze on Konner. He remained solid, in place, and seemingly untouched by the terrible forces assailing them.

And then, with a jolting suddenness, they broke free of the pressure. And floated above the land.

"Is that the river?" Amazement overcame her fears. Birds flew. Dragons flew. Why not this bizarre dragon that was not a dragon. She had to trust that the beast would not spit her out to fall back to the land. She had to trust Stargod Konner to keep her safe.

"Yes, that is the river that gives the Coros life. And up ahead, that broad expanse of blue, that is the Great Bay." Konner pointed with his left hand, keeping his right on the array of winking lights.

"Will we see a behemoth?" She had only heard tales of the monster fish that had been known to take bites out of frail fishing boats, but when captured, could feed a large village for a week. And its thick hide could be tanned like leather to make warm winter clothing for most of a village as well.

"I doubt we'll see one, unless it comes to the surface." Konner frowned. His eyes clouded. "Can you point toward the beacon?"

Dalleena stretched out her hand, palm forward. She concentrated for a long moment on the small thing made of the same material as the hide of the white dragon. At first nothing. Then the tingling began in the center of her palm. Faint at first, then stronger.

"That way." She pointed straight across the endless blue of the bay that continued on into the distance until it met the sky. She shook her head with the enormity of their search. No one she had ever heard of had sailed beyond the reaches of the Great Bay.

Konner made a few adjustments to the lights beneath the flat surface in front of him. The nose of their dragon shifted slightly until it aimed precisely where her finger pointed.

"Will we fly to the edge and fall off?"

"No." Konner flashed her a grin. "The world is like a ball. There is no edge. A special energy called gravity keeps us anchored to the land so we do not fall off."

"But we are not on the land. We fly above it."

"I could fly up above the gravity." He pointed up through the top of the dragon. "I have a bigger ship up there that travels the stars. *Rover* isn't big enough or powerful enough to go beyond this planet."

"Oh." She did not know if she understood all that. The knowledge that Stargod Konner and his brothers could leave this place so easily only confirmed her hesitation to accept friendship or anything else from them. She must fulfill her duty. Nothing more.

She looked through the dragon eyes below them. The land gave way to the bay. She could see the muddy bottom beneath the surf. Must be high tide. Then she discerned the deeper channels through the mudflats. A miniature boat floated on the water, following one of those channels. Was that one of the waterdogs in the bow? The waterdogs had talents akin to Trackers. They directed the fishermen through deep water so that they did not run aground on the mud.

"They look so small. And growing smaller."

"Distance. A tree at the edge of the meadow looks no bigger than your hand. As you walk closer, it gets bigger and bigger. We are very far away."

"How far?"

"Higher than ten of the tallest trees you have ever seen."

She gulped. But her curiosity overcame her misgivings. A wispy cloud passed beneath them. More clouds appeared on the left, near the horizon. Dark clouds. "It will rain tomorrow."

"Probably," he grunted. "I hope Kim gets the last of the harvest in today."

They traveled on in silence for a long time. Dalleena had dozens of questions. He answered them politely. But she sensed he never gave her all of the information she needed to fully understand.

After a time she held up her arm again and scanned for the beacon. They came closer. But it was still very far away. She directed him to aim a little to the south. He did so.

Another space of time passed. They still traversed the ocean. She scanned again. Instead of the tingle in her palm, her entire body began to shake. Her muscles jerked. Forward and back, side to side. She swayed as far as the thongs allowed her.

"What?" Konner asked. He released his own restraints and jumped to hold her in place. "Dalleena! What's wrong."

Her teeth chattered. She clamped her mouth shut, lest she bite her tongue. Her throat swelled with the need to speak. To warn Konner of the strange apparition that pulled at her senses, demanding she find it.

"Up there," she finally managed. "In the sky. Beyond the sun. Something is lost. Something bigger than a behemoth. Much bigger than this dragon."

Then she forced her arm down and gripped the edges of the chair.

Konner looked up to the sky, then back to the flashing lights. Many more lights than before.

And then the strange voice of his mother spoke. "Warning. Open jump point detected. Unfriendly vessel approaches."

"You spotted the IMPs before my sensors did!"

CHAPTER 11

KONNER TOUCHED two interfaces and set the shuttle on autopilot. Then he returned his attention to Dalleena.

"How did you do that?" He ran his fingers over her damp brow and along the stress creases above her nose. Worry made him clench his jaw. He had to show a calm face. He had to keep her from going into hysterics.

"I do not know." She stared at her palm. The skin looked red, not quite raw, but definitely painful. "It burns," she whispered.

He should have known Dalleena would not panic.

"I have some salve for that." Konner released the first aid kit from its place beneath the console. His hands felt empty and cold when he released her, but the kit was awkward to haul into position with only one free.

A quick swipe of Electro-Steri® killed off any stray bacteria. St. Bridget only knew how much bizarre bacteria lurked on the planet. Then a squirt of cooling gel sealed the burn.

"What miracle is this?" She held up the hand. Already the redness faded as the medicines leeched the heat out of her skin before it could blister.

"Just keep your hand up, above your heart, for a

few seconds until the gel dries." He held her hand
in position. The softness of her skin despite the cal-
luses sent micro amps of electricity up his arm and
into his heart.

He jerked his gaze away from contact with her big
brown eyes before he lost himself entirely.

"Is this strange ship in the skies friend or foe?"
Dalleena asked. Ever practical. Ever logical. She returned to the cause of her hurt rather than dwelling
on the injury itself.

Melinda, Konner's ex, had taken to her bed for
three days when a splinter lodged in her finger on
their honeymoon.

"Most likely a foe." Konner let go of his memories
of Melinda gratefully. As soon as he retrieved his
son from her ungentle custody, he need never think
of her again.

He could concentrate on Dalleena.

No. His place was not on this benighted planet.
He belonged to the stars. He would not enter into a
relationship knowing he had to leave very soon.

"What must we do to evade this enemy? Or defeat
it?" Dalleena asked.

"Our first step is to find that beacon and destroy
it." Konner returned to his seat and put the shuttle
back on manual control. Without hesitation, he
boosted the speed. "The heck with fuel conserva-
tion." He pushed the speed up another notch. "If we
don't kill the beacon fast, we won't need the shuttle.
We'll need holes in the ground to hide in."

"I know of a number of caves on the headlands at
the south end of the bay. Children often get lost exploring them. 'Tis up to me to find them when they
go too deep," Dalleena offered.

"I'll keep that in mind."

The coastline came into view. Konner called up the
maps from Kim's initial survey of the planet. The
central continent dominated the scans. It spread

across nearly an entire hemisphere north and east of here. Only a few large islands and semicontinents, like the land of the Coros, dotted the ocean that covered the rest of the planet.

Konner and his brothers had dismissed the continent because the clusters of human habitation hugged the coasts with little or nothing in between. The climate of the interior appeared barely hospitable to human life.

He shed altitude. Somehow the initial survey had not picked up on the lively boat traffic that now came into view.

"Now where?" Konner asked. He might be close enough to pick up the beacon on one of his scanners. But he had to stay high enough not to disturb any locals.

"North. At the head of that bay." Dalleena pointed and he changed course.

The scanners spit images and a data stream into the interface. Then the beacon blipped. An obscure frequency well below normal scan ranges. If the IMPs did not know where to look, they would never find it. Another strike against Melinda. She had to have sold the frequency to his enemies.

Konner suppressed the boiling in his blood. Giving in to his anger with Melinda would not help him this minute. He needed to save his emotions and be in control for the court date.

And use his copy of the prenuptial agreement she had not honored.

He locked in the frequency and pinpointed it on the map the computer formed, layer by layer as he circled the port.

"Just wonderful." He nearly slammed his fist into the console. "An entire city full of people." Several thousand crammed into a tiny space. Any one of them could have the beacon.

Frantically, he sought a landing place beyond the

hordes of people, but close enough to walk into the city.

For some reason, the city seemed to be confined within a stout wall. It formed a large half circle around the harbor. Warrens of alleyways filled the enclosure. Buildings piled one atop another, threatening to tumble in a stiff breeze. The scanners picked up a large concentration of pollution in the water of the harbor. Mostly human and animal waste.

Konner wrinkled his nose at the thought of the stench of the city. Most civilized worlds were as crowded as this place. But air scrubbers built into the protective atmosphere domes replaced unpleasant odors with a citrus scent. Sewage disposal remained unseen and unsmelled, returning sanitized minerals and liquids to the environment and food tanks.

"Why do they not move beyond the wall?" Dalleena asked. She shifted her gaze from the growing map to the knot of dark brown below them.

Smart girl to have figured out the relationship between the map and the real view.

"I'm guessing the wall is protection. Marauders, dust storms, large predators. Something mean and dangerous lives in the steppes beyond that wall."

The land stretched out in near endless waves of undulating hills dotted with low shrubs, covered with tall grasses, golden in the autumnal sunshine, and creased by ravines. A few lakes glinted in the distance.

Konner decided to hide *Rover* behind a long hill that rose slightly higher than its fellows a few hundred meters beyond the city wall and away from the small flocks of sheep and goats that dotted the hillsides. Did the shepherds bring all of the livestock within the protection of the wall each night?

He circled around, banked, and cut the engines as he glided to his selected landing. He smiled as he rolled to a silent stop, completely hidden from the city. Loki could not have executed the maneuver any smoother or quieter.

Locking down the shuttle was an easy and familiar procedure. Collecting supplies required some thought.

"Water," Dalleena said. She looked around the cabin.

Konner touched the pressure panel on one of the cupboards. An array of native waterskins, cloaks, knives, and other survival gear tumbled out.

She sighed and rolled her eyes at Konner. Immediately she began to sort, stack, and organize the jumble.

"Water is in here." He stepped into the head and turned on the tap. Dalleena watched every move he made.

She quickly made sense of the sink and tap, filling the skins efficiently, with minimal waste. Then she inspected the shower with minute care. Very quickly she nodded in understanding. But the toilet seemed to mystify her.

"For waste," Konner informed her succinctly. A quick flush and the light of understanding dawned on her expressive face.

He felt inordinate pride in teaching her this simple thing. This one part of civilization that seemed so elemental.

"Hats," Dalleena said as she emerged from her inspection of the marvels of modern plumbing.

"Hats?" Konner looked up from his array of portable sensors and other gadgets. Almost as an afterthought he thrust six small diamonds into his pocket. The jewels were accepted as currency throughout the GTE when cash and credit limits did not cross borders into the Galactic Free Market—or black market.

"Hats?" he asked again as Dalleena peered into the corners of the supply closet.

"Desert sun. All of the locals will wear them as protection."

He nodded compliance. He added brimmed straw hats to the collection of gear.

And then there was no more reason to stall and every reason to find that bloody beacon and destroy it. He estimated they had approximately seven hours before the IMP vessel descended upon the planet.

After that, the history of the place, the very nature of society here would change irrevocably. For members of the Galactic Terran Empire could not leave a planet pristine. They always had to "improve." Improve, as in industrialize, exploit, overpopulate, pollute.

Destroy.

"Come on, we're running out of time." Konner flung the loosely woven cape of ubiquitous red cow's wool over his shoulders and began marching up the hill. He barely remembered to touch the remote to cloak the shuttle behind its light-bending force field.

Dalleena trotted behind him, uncomplaining, matching him long stride for long stride.

They crested the hill quickly. Looking downslope, the city lay before them, crammed into barely ten square kilometers. Every building was made of the same reddish mud bricks. At one time, the place had begun on a square grid with a well at every major intersection. But those spacious blocks had been divided and subdivided time and again. Alleys ran between buildings at odd angles. People crowded around the wells, now too few to accommodate them all. Dust covered everything, giving it a uniform reddish-brown pallor. No trees. No flowers. Nothing living except too many people and a few stray pigs and goats.

"Now where?" Konner asked.

"There." Dalleena held up her hand, palm out. She indicated an area near the port, north of center where a larger than usual congregation of people shoved and pushed their way through the narrow streets.

Konner took a bead on her direction with his portable scanner. Dead on. He could not have pinpointed the beacon any closer with electronics.

He hurried down the hill and through the open gate in the wall. Five gates. All open. No visible guards. Whatever the wall protected the locals from, must not come out during daylight, or this phase of the moon, or until it rained. Just not right now.

Unchallenged, they made their way into the heart of the city. Roughly clad people with swarthy complexions and blond hair bumped against them, shoving to get past, too eager to go about their own business to pay attention to two strangers.

But then maybe strangers were not all that unusual here. This was a port, after all.

The pervasive odors of rotting fish, salt water, and seaweed lay atop the more subtle scents of humanity pressed into too tight quarters, dust, and a hint of exotic spices.

"Where did all these people come from?" Dalleena asked in hushed tones. She clung to a bit of his cloak, as if she feared becoming separated from him. "Did they sail here from Coronnan?"

"Possibly. A long time ago." Konner did not want to give her a history lesson about the original human colonists who had fallen into civil war and genocide with a bioengineered plague. That plague still cropped up occasionally. He just hoped he'd managed to neutralize it last spring.

The babble of voices refused to settle into a recognizable pattern. The Coros spoke a dialect of Standard GTE, slowed to a creeping drawl and mutated over the last three hundred years. The denizens of this city spoke a rapid dialect that was similar. He almost caught a word here and there. And yet . . .

"Possibly they have been here as long as the Coros

have held their lands. My brother Kim will be very interested to study the history of these people." Perhaps the original colonists split, some coming here, others staying in Coronnan, before the devastating winter and crop failure drove Dalleena's ancestors to fight among themselves for generations until they fell back to bronze age technology and a tribal culture.

Perhaps there were many remnant cultures throughout this world. His feet itched to explore more. But he had to get the beacon. Now. Before the IMPs had a chance to pinpoint its location.

But once the IMPs landed, and they certainly would, now that they were in system, how could Konner and his brothers prevent them from informing the authorities back home about this pristine little planet ready for exploitation?

"The bee-kan is in there," Dalleena said. She nodded discreetly toward a jumble of people and makeshift structures.

Voices rose higher and higher as people shouted at each other, waving their arms in wild gesticulations. Konner was about to jump in and separate two men seemingly bent upon throttling each other. Then a few coins changed hands and one of the men scooped up the pile of goods between them.

"It's a *souk!*" Konner smiled with understanding.

"A 'sug?' " Dalleena asked, never taking her eyes off the arguments and exchanges.

"A market."

"Ah! We have these two times each year, at end of planting and end of harvest."

"That is a market fair. This bazaar is open every day. All year." They stepped beyond an invisible line that separated the normal crush of people going about their business from the frantic crush of people dealing with their business.

"Those metal disks they exchange. Are they markers against goods and services?"

"In a way. We call them coins where I come from. They are made of valuable metals."

"But what good are they?"

How to explain the concept of money to a woman who had only known the concrete evidence of barter?

Before he could think of a coherent sentence, she darted ahead of him. He had to hurry to keep track of her in the shouting and milling crowd. They wended their way around rickety stalls, fragrant cooking pits with roasting beasts, and cauldrons of aromatic stews. Everywhere people pushed and shoved and raised their voices, doing their best to separate Konner from the Tracker.

Then he caught a brief glimpse of her cloak. Good thing she stood nearly as tall as he, half a head taller than most of the shoppers and merchants. He elbowed aside an insistent purveyor of a frothy beverage that smelled strongly alcoholic, and stepped over a tumble of fabric rolls to keep her in view. Halfway around a cart piled with leather goods he saw where she had stopped.

Crystals and rough-cut gemstones dangled from the crossbeams of the stall. Agates and polished metal pendants were strewn about the counter. A beady-eyed merchant kept one hand on a dull green object the size of his palm while fixing his gaze upon Dalleena's face.

Konner's sensor went berserk, flashing lights and beeping in chords of tones.

A second dull green object nestled into a pile of gems in the back of the stall. Two of them? Where had the second beacon come from?

"How much?" Konner asked the merchant. His jaw trembled and his hands wanted to shake. He put Dalleena behind him, away from the lustful eyes of the thin man wearing a robe of garish-colored stripes and a matching turban. Unlike most of the people he had encountered in the *souk*, this man had pale eyes and sun-burned pale skin. He looked very much out of place in this land of dark-eyed and swarthy-skinned natives. Even his blond hair was too fair, almost artificial.

"The girl. I trade you the artifact for the girl." He grinned, revealing too-white, too-perfect teeth.

CHAPTER 12

Loki THRUST aside the leather curtain from the doorway of Taneeo's hut. He did not bother rattling the strands of wooden and clay beads hanging outside, nor did he ask permission to enter.

"Taneeo?" Loki called as he ducked beneath the low lintel of the circular reed hut. For some reason these people seemed to think that priests needed a dwelling without corners. Or amenities, by the look of the spartan interior. A reed mat on the floor. A single blanket of cowhide. A fired clay beaker of water on the dirt floor, and nothing else.

Nothing.

Not so much as a window to let in the glorious sunshine and fresh air.

The place smelled of sweat and vomit and sickness.

Loki did not believe Kim's tale of Taneeo possessing a second aura that separated from his body. Not one little bit. The boy had hit the Tambootie a little too hard in his magical experiments.

Taneeo hated Hanassa. He'd never allow his old master's spirit to possess his body. *Never!*

Loki refused to believe Taneeo capable of harboring the enemy in any form. If he did, then that would mean . . . that would mean that Taneeo had beaten himself in order to get rid of the offending spirit.

Impossible. No one could inflict that degree of injury to themselves.

Loki squinted and blinked, trying to force his eyes to adjust to the dimness. His mind knew Taneeo was here. He could "feel" the man's fearful shrinking against the wall.

Where else could the young man be but here where Kim had left him last night. He could not walk. Not with a broken leg and various other injuries.

"Taneeo," Loki said again, more gently.

A startled gasp came from the farthest curve of the hut.

"Didn't mean to scare you, Taneeo." Heat flushed Loki's ears. He squatted down, closer to eye level with the man.

Taneeo struggled to sit, dragging his splinted leg. He nearly collapsed twice as his arms and shoulders weakened with the effort. The pain in his cracked ribs must be excruciating.

Loki rubbed his side in memory of a vicious brawl on a bush planet notable only for its horse-piss beer and ugly women. He'd fought with a man twice his size, over the "honor" of a barmaid who did not want either man's attentions. Loki was lucky to walk away with only a cracked rib and a few bruises. The pain had taken his breath away and made his knees wobble until Konner got him to an ER. The medicos had bombarded his body with micro amps of electricity and ultrasound tuned to healing frequencies. Loki had whistled as he left the hospital mere hours after entering.

Taneeo did not have the luxury of modern medicine. Only Kim's limited magical talent that sped healing but did not cure. The portable ultrasound unit in *Sirius'* medi kit did not have enough power or life in its batteries to do more than indicate if Kim had set the bones properly.

Loki moved to help Taneeo to a sitting position.

The priest's instinctive jerk away from him kept him in place. "What do you want?" Taneeo's voice cracked with dryness. "To accuse me of treachery, as your brother did?" He glared at Loki with resentment.

Loki pushed the water beaker closer to him. The priest lifted it and drank long and deep. When he put the vessel down, he looked at a point above Loki's head and to the left.

"What do you want?" His voice was stronger, and clearer. "I am clean of the tainted spirit. I have fought him off and suffered the consequences."

"I need to know what happened to you," Loki said, careful to keep his voice even. "Who beat you?"

"I do not remember."

"You have to know something. Our enemy fought with you, broke your leg, cracked two of your ribs, and left you with a black eye that might permanently impair your vision. How could you forget that experience."

"I . . . I fainted. He came from behind."

A growl tried to climb from Loki's gut to his throat. He swallowed heavily to suppress it. "Did you see the man who attacked you?"

"Dark. Too dark." Taneeo turned his head away. He started to slip back down to his previous reclining position.

"Was the man dark?" Loki seized upon the adjective. "Dark hair, dark eyes, swarthy skin, like a Rover?"

Rovers, the local version of Terran Gypsies, used the blown-out volcano and the cave system as a way station in their endless wandering. They would have been the first humans to enter the scene of Loki's last battle with Hanassa. The spirit of Hanassa might have taken over one of their bodies.

Hanassa would then use that body to move closer

to his enemies. What better way to strike at the heart of the Stargods and their followers than to possess the body of their priest and friend?

Loki liked that explanation. It put a lot of his fears to rest and gave him a concrete enemy to hunt down and neutralize.

You mean murder, a little voice in the back of his head sneered at him. It sounded a lot like Mum.

No. He'd never take a life again. Even a miserable sadist like Hanassa had a sacred life force Loki must respect. His sanity would not withstand another episode like . . . like that time in the caves two months ago.

"Rover?" Taneeo's eyes brightened and cleared a little. He rested a little easier on his mat. "Yes! Yes, I do believe 'twas a Rover who attacked me. A very tall Rover. Nearly as tall as you and your brothers, Stargod Loki. But dark in every way. Dark of complexion and of spirit. His clothing . . . black tunic and trews. Black shirt. How do you suppose the Rovers mix a black dye for cloth and leather that does not fade?"

"They probably use the squid ink."

Just last week Kim had found a multilimbed blob of flesh on the beach that had produced a body fluid he could use for indelible ink in his endless scratchings and recordings of events and thoughts and who knew what else. He'd named the creature a squid after some long extinct denizen of Earth's oceans before pollution killed them all.

Loki frowned. He did not like the idea of Kim leaving behind so much information that could be deciphered by the locals. All three of the brothers had agreed that in order to keep this planet agrarian, prevent them from developing industry that would eventually cause pollution and drive them to quest for the stars, they had to forbid reading and the wheel from their culture. Otherwise, they'd become just another colony of the GTE.

Kim seemed bent upon violating the agreement. Loki made a mental note to gather up *all* of Kim's records and journals and take them with them when they left.

Otherwise, everything that was good and honest about this place would disappear. And so would the supply of fresh food Loki intended to sell on the black market back home. One cargo hold full of fresh vegetables would make his fortune for life. He'd finally have enough money to buy back his citizenship and marry Cyndi.

Loki could not allow this place to be despoiled. He had to stop Hanassa. All he had to do was find him.

"I will bring Pryth to you. She was born a Rover. She may be able to give us more information about your attacker." Loki rose from his crouch. He could not stand upright, even in the center of the conical hut.

"The old woman speaks not the truth. Born of Rovers, bred as Rovers. Truth eludes their kind as mist in sunshine. We . . . I will not speak to the woman!" With great effort, Taneeo turned his face to the wall.

"Pryth used to be your friend, Taneeo. She has helped us all with her wisdom and her knowledge."

"No more. She speaks for the tribe that shelters our enemy. She has *become* our enemy."

"How can you know that?"

"Even now she corrupts your brother. Together, they will bring change that destroys you."

"Kim," Loki whispered. "He's teaching some of you how to read." The truth washed over him like a cold dip in the river. He knew that Taneeo spoke true. He "felt" it in his mind as clearly as if he had read the priest's thoughts.

*   *   *

"Have you found anything interesting, Bruce?" Martin dictated a brief message to his friend.

Within femtos of sending his reply a message appeared in his mailbox.

"Couldn't wait to hear from you, Marty. My dad just accepted a contract with your mom. Usually he tells me where he's going and something about who or what he is supposed to find. This time he left abruptly without telling me anything. He didn't even come home between jobs. I thought maybe you could give me a head's up on what is so important that your mom hired a 'Sam Eyeam,'" Bruce's voice and image came through the computer screen.

"Now that is a good question," Martin muttered.

"This news comes right on top of finding a delete in the marriage records of Meditcue II. That delete has my dad's computer telltales all over it. I'm digging further. Too bad neither of us has a Klip. We could track Dad's activities a lot easier then. But, of course, they are illegal."

Martin gulped. A marriage record deleted by Melinda's private Sam Eyeam. Melinda was up to something. The timing was too coincidental. She didn't want key information to come up at the custody hearing.

If Melinda and Bruce's father had negotiated a sensitive contract, perhaps the man had come to Aurora for a private meeting. Data waves could be intercepted no matter how much security Melinda paid to put on them. Financial transactions tended to be more secure than private correspondence, but even then the data had to cross open space at many times the speed of light. Dedicated hackers could find even those messages.

He accessed his mother's appointment book for the previous month. Many meetings. Many contracts. Nothing resembling Bruce Geralds, Sr.

What about the AM before that?

Martin had to go through three more AMs and nearly a thousand entries to find what he was looking for. A cryptic remark, "Freelance. Midnight. Altered beacon," followed by an estimated expense account that allowed considerable travel was his only clue.

"Travel. He had to enter and leave Aurora space." Martin sent his snoopers over to the port authority. Sure enough, at 0600 hours the next morning, a private, one-man transport left the port. It carried Melinda's personal ID on the logbook.

"But Melinda was home that day. I remember because she introduced the new math tutor to me personally."

"Master Martin, I believe you are supposed to be working on wave differential equations at this moment, not playing with your friends." The image of the hated math tutor appeared in the upper right-hand corner of the screen. A twenty-something man with a sallow complexion and thin hair, who tried to look older by adopting a stern frown and an artificial touch of white at his temples, Adam Wun never approved of anything Martin accomplished.

"I finished the homework an hour ago," Martin replied. He pulled up his calculations and transmitted them to the tutor.

"If you completed all this so easily, either you were careless and made many mistakes, or you need more advanced work. I will have a new assignment for you as soon as I correct these equations."

"I'm due for physical training in ten minutes. You, Mr. Wun, will have to wait."

Fencing was one activity he enjoyed in the structured time Melinda arranged for him. Easy to imagine his opponents in the salle as his mother. He worked hard at aiming each lunge and thrust for her heart.

*   *   *

"Who are you and where did you come from?" Konner spat at the gaudy merchant with teeth so clean and firm they could blind a deer in the moonlight.

"I know not what you mean." The merchant backed up one step, holding his hands at chest level, palms outward. The gesture spoke of innocence.

Then his right hand snaked behind him to capture the second beacon.

He had used the same crisp dialect of Terran Standard that Konner used, not the languid prose of the Coros or the mutated dialect spoken elsewhere in the souk.

Konner raised one eyebrow in question and waited.

"I am but a seller of pretty trinkets," the merchant continued. Speaking too rapidly, as if to convince himself as well as Konner of the truth of his words.

"Then sell me the artifacts for a fair price. Both of them," Dalleena jumped into the conversation. "You paid nothing for them. They serve you no purpose."

"Ah, but they must serve you a purpose," the merchant crowed and smoothed his mustache and beard with one finger. "Else you would not be so anxious to purchase these pretty toys."

"The 'toys' serve only a captain of an IMP vessel," Konner said quietly. "I would make certain this . . . ah . . . sailor never finds them or the man who possesses them."

The merchant's eyes opened wide.

"Take the cursed thing, now. Before it is too late." The merchant pushed the beacon on the counter at Konner. The second one had disappeared into his clothing. Then he jerked his hand away from it as if burned. And soiled.

"Not until you tell me who you are and why you are on *my* planet." Konner folded his arms across his chest. He leaned slightly away from the proffered device, all the while seeking a telltale irregularity in the man's clothing for the second beacon. Where had it come from? More importantly, why did this black market denizen have it?

"I'm just trying to make an Adol." The merchant began folding his trinkets into brightly colored cloths. Still no sign of the second beacon.

"Here? This planet has little of value to the outside world. Few precious metals or raw resources."

Dalleena peered curiously first at Konner, then the merchant, seeking answers to the puzzling words they spoke.

Konner hated to do this to her. But they had to keep the conversation cryptic lest the locals hear and jump to wrong conclusions, and possibly drastic action to rid themselves of things they did not understand.

Konner and his brothers had survived one attack by locals only by cunning and a hasty retreat inside their shuttle. The shuttle was a long way away from this souk.

"If you cannot see the bounty of this place, then leave it to me and take this cursed beacon with you." The merchant strapped all of his wares, except the first beacon, into a crude satchel with straps that tied rather than buckled. He left the beacon on the counter.

"What I see is a man in a place he does not belong. Now who are you?" Konner reached across the plank counter and grabbed the merchant's robes at the throat.

"Sam," the merchant choked out, eyes wide and frightened.

"Sam Who?"

"Sam Eyeam."

Konner snorted at the old joke stolen from a children's text. Freelance agents, black market merchants, and bounty hunters all used the ubiquitous pseudonym. "You'll have to do better than that, Sam. What's your real name?"

"Yours first."

"Fair's fair. Konner."

"Not Konner O'Hara. Please tell me you aren't Konner O'Hara, the smuggler with two brothers." The Sam Eyeam closed his eyes as if in prayer.

"And if I am Konner O'Hara?" Konner did not release the man's robes. Off to the side, Dalleena began looking around hastily, as if she sensed danger coming closer.

Damn.

"If you are Konner O'Hara, then I will run away from this place as fast as I can, by as stealthy a route I can find, and never mention to anyone being here, or seeing you."

"You fear me that much?" Konner eased his grip a little. "Then give me the second beacon as well."

"I know nothing of a second beacon. Only this one given to me by . . . one I did not know. I will return the bribe that came with it."

Dalleena tugged on Konner's arm. "Men with clubs and whips approach. A large number of angry men follow them."

"Ah, the hue and cry has been raised. The locals do not like brawls of any kind in the souk." Sam ducked out of Konner's grasp, grabbed his satchel and . . .

And Konner stepped in front of him before he bolted out of the back of the stall. "Tell me why you fear the name Konner O'Hara so much. And where you came by the beacons."

Sam's gaze darted to the shouts rising from the dock side of the souk.

"Tell me, or I turn you over to them as a thief."

"I don't fear you. I fear the GTE. Anyone important enough to have a reward of 100,000 Adols has to be the most dangerous man in the galaxy."

"Melinda fears me that much?"

"Melinda Fortesque, the owner of Aurora?"

"My ex-wife."

"The father of her son!" Understanding seemed to dawn in his eyes. "Heaven help us all." Sam darted away.

"The second beacon . . ."

Dalleena grabbed Konner's hand and dragged him deep into the market at a breathless pace. She clutched one beacon against her chest.

"Wait! I have to know why he didn't detect my ship when he landed. Why I never saw his."

"Later. I will find him later. He is a Tracker. He will be easy for me to find. My talent will find his."

She was right. They had to take this beacon to the volcano and destroy it before the IMPs landed. Five and one half hours from now. Max.

"Let's go."

CHAPTER 13

THE AIR AT the head of *Rover* shimmered. Dalleena gulped. She dug in her heels. The caked dirt of the hillside crumbled under her feet. She continued her downward slide toward the dragons—the white one she could see and the red-tipped one that was almost visible in the harsh noontime glare.

"Now what?" Konner grunted and moved forward at a faster pace. He barely left a footprint in the ground at the speed of his passing.

"The Stargod does not fear the dragons. They are his messengers and allies," she whispered to herself. "If he has no fear, then neither should I." The thought did not reassure her. If the dragon wished, it could blast her with fire and eat her in one gulp.

Last night it had ignored her. Today it might be hungry.

The beast bent its head toward Konner. Steam or smoke rose in small puffs from its nostrils. Dalleena guessed it spoke to Stargod Konner in some mysterious way.

She struggled to remain upright, wrapping the shreds of her courage around her.

If she had nothing else, she had her dignity. If she died in the next moment, she would not quail before the Stargod. She was Tracker and had fulfilled her duty.

"I know," Konner said to the dragon. "Dalleena spotted them before I did."

So they discussed the invaders. Dalleena took her next step with a little more firmness than the last. *She* had served the god better than his dragon messenger did.

Then the beast turned one of its multicolored eyes upon her. Red glinted on the eyelid, echoing the color outlining its horns and wing veins.

Her stomach tied itself into a knot.

The red spiraled inward, drawing her attention, her consciousness, her soul. . . .

"Irythros, release her!" Stargod Konner shouted and slapped the muzzle of the creature.

The sound of his voice seemed to sever a physical tie between Dalleena and the dragon. She shook her head to clear it.

(*Apologies. I do not wish to offend.*) The dragon's eyes dimmed and it ducked its muzzle.

Dalleena shook her head again. "Did I truly hear him speak?" For half a heartbeat she shared a sense of deep shame with the beast. How could that be?

"Probably," Konner replied. He rubbed the knuckles of his left hand with his right palm.

"Apology accepted." She resisted a near compulsion to move closer and touch the place where Konner's fist had connected with its muzzle, just below the right eye. Hard to tell if the skin beneath the crystal fur bruised or not.

"Dalleena is under my protection, Irythros," Konner said. "Keep your hypnotic powers to yourself."

Dalleena tasted the strange new word. Hypnotic. It meant nothing to her.

(*Dragon dreams reveal a true nature,*) the dragon replied in a defensive tone.

"Unnecessary." Konner continued to stare at the huge creature with authority. "If you want to delve into the secrets of a human, go find the merchant who calls himself Sam Eyeam. He carries a second beacon that must be destroyed."

A niggle of pride ran down Dalleena's spine. This handsome man, this *god*, defended her before the most awesome being in her world.

"The news of the intruders is momentous, Irythros. I appreciate you bringing the news yourself. I have need of a favor, if you are willing." Finally Konner stroked the place on the dragon's muzzle that had begun to darken. The dragon leaned into the touch as it would a healer's caress.

(*Name your favor,*) the dragon nearly cooed.

Dalleena had to stifle a grin. This monster behaved as any steed, or dog, or cat, given adoring attention by its master.

"I have to drop this beacon into the volcano to destroy it. I would like to leave the shuttle hidden in the crater. The magnetic forces of the mountain will mask its presence from the intruders. Will you carry Dalleena and me back to the village from there?"

(*We cannot. The transition place of Hanassa is sacred. We may not go there.*)

The mighty wings of the dragon unfurled. He raised and dropped them once. Dust swirled into Dalleena's face. She threw up her arm to protect her eyes. With her other hand she groped for Konner. His hand entwined with hers.

The dust increased. The roar of the wind from pulsing dragon wings drowned out all other sound. All other thought.

Wind buffeted her, forcing her back and back again. She clung to Konner. She bumped against the solid hide of the white dragon *Rover*. And still the wind pressed against her, stole the breath from her, tried to crush her chest.

And then Konner was between her and the wind,

sheltering her with his body. She risked looking up at him. His eyes darkened. Barely a breath separated their lips. A strange stillness washed through her, replacing the terrible pressure of the wind.

Then the wind died. The agitated dirt settled on her clothing, in her hair, and on her face.

"He left," she said.

"In a huff," Konner replied, averting his gaze from her mouth. He heaved himself back, away from the shuttle and close proximity to her.

"Now what do we do?"

"We destroy the beacon."

"How? Do we return to the village of the Stargods?"

"I will leave you there before I go to the volcano."

"How will you return?"

"I must walk for many days, or trust my luck to the dragongate."

Dalleena crossed herself, swallowed her fears, and looked him straight in the eye. "So be it. I go with you."

* * *

"Captain?" Ensign Englebert sounded hesitant.

Kat stole a moment of attention from the helm to watch the communications officer's face. He looked puzzled.

"Watch it!" Kohler warned her quietly.

Kat jerked her attention back to her own screens and interfaces. She barely veered to port fast enough to avoid scraping *Jupiter* on a mid-sized boulder in a crowded asteroid belt.

At least Ms. Baines had retreated to the comfort of her cabin. Kat didn't have to worry about the woman watching and criticizing every move she made. Nor did she have to smell the cloying perfume.

"This space junk looks tricky," Kohler continued. "Computer can't find a pattern to the movement. We're going to have to wing it."

"Captain, can we get weapons on some of these rocks?" Kat asked.

Commander Leonard gestured to a pair of SBs to handle the chore. In three quick blasts, Kat had a clear path before her.

"Captain?" Englebert said again.

"Yes, Ensign." Commander Leonard did not look up from her screens as she answered.

"Sir, I'm getting an echo from the beacon. It's moving away from the primary."

"What?" Kat and Commander Leonard exclaimed at the same time. Kat dared not swing her chair around. A rock the size of a moonlet loomed before her. It tumbled fast enough to generate a gravity field.

"It's almost as if there are two beacons, sir," Englebert said.

"Impossible. Fortesque Industries swore they only built one at that frequency," Commander Leonard protested.

"I read the memo, sir. You can look for yourself. Something strange is going on down on that planet."

"If I may, Captain," Kat said, never taking her eyes or her hands off her screens. "The second beacon could be why we could not lock onto the signal earlier. We were getting echoes of both off the atmosphere."

"True, Lieutenant. Investigate further, Ensign Englebert. I want to know more about this.

"Uh, Captain . . ."

Leonard shot Englebert an impatient glance.

"Captain, sensors detecting a fireball on the big continent. It's burning hot enough to fry cerama/metal."

Kat gulped. What were the O'Haras up to?

"Status of the beacons, Ensign?" the ship's captain demanded.

"Both still beeping."

"Estimated time to orbit, Lieutenant?"

Kohler answered for Kat. "Five hours, twenty-seven minutes, sir."

"Providing someone doesn't start throwing these rocks directly at us," Kat muttered. Another blast from the pulse cannons sent a big one lurking behind the moonlet spinning out of their path. Chips from it splattered a sensor on the rim directly in front of Kat. She cursed.

A tech scrambled to get her a clear view again.

Kat veered sharply to starboard. Everyone on the bridge reached for safety harnesses. "If only I had a joystick," Kat breathed, "I could jockey around this planetary debris with no problems at all."

"Joysticks are not standard military equipment," Commander Leonard reminded her. "This is a Military Police Cruiser, not a cybernetic fighter."

"I know, Captain. Just wishing out loud."

"Are you sure you can get us through this safely, Lieutenant?" Leonard asked.

"Yes, sir. I'm rated ace on everything in the fleet. Just keep those cannons working on the little stuff and I'll get us around the big ones."

Kat let her eyes lose focus a moment while she listened to the crystal drive. She "felt" nearly every electron pulse shooting from the drivers to the directionals. Three arrays, all working off one king stone. She isolated the forward array in her consciousness. Suddenly the scene outside jumped into her awareness clearer than any computer display. She saw in her mind the position of every asteroid, moonlet, and chip. She understood the gravitational pulls from sun and planets upon each. She became a part of the web of transactional gravitons.

Her fingers flew over the computer interfaces on

her screen guiding the ship through the obstacle course.

"You're smiling?" Josh Kohler broke into her trance.

"Just meditating on what I'll do with my part of the reward from capturing the O'Hara brothers."

"Just keep your mind on steering this boat," Josh grunted.

Kat's smile grew broader. "I am, Josh. I am."

"The O'Haras may be the most wanted men in the Empire, but they aren't worth the lives of three hundred people and the loss of my ship, Lieutenant," Commander Leonard said. "Slow and easy. If you don't feel we can get through here safely . . ."

"I've waited too long for this moment to give up now, sir." Kat firmed her chin and narrowed her eyes. Nothing would keep her from finally confronting the O'Haras and bringing them to justice. Nothing.

*   *   *

I watch as Sam Eyeam meets another; one I should trust, but he smells wrong. They fight. The device that Stargod Konner seeks drops to the ground. It speaks to the stars in a voice we believed to come from Hanassa. Now we know that the man Hanassa has become wishes to misuse it.

The fight between Sam Eyeam and the one I cannot trust grows desperate. One man rises, grabs the device, and disappears into the dragongate. Who is left? I cannot tell from my watching distance. Dust obscures color. Injury disguises posture.

Ah, I see now that Sam Eyeam rushes to take refuge in a creature similar to Stargod Konner's Rover. This creature is bigger than Rover. I loose a little flame to encourage Sam Eyeam to emerge and speak to me.

He remains secreted. A little more flame. Too much? The creature catches fire.

The man jumps free and flees.

The heat from the fire singes my wing tip. I retreat to the clouds. Sam Eyeam and his device disappear from my senses.

*   *   *

Kim checked the village center. Two older women he knew only a little stoked the fire and hefted the stewpot onto the iron crane Konner had forged. Both women looked too frail for the heavy work. One had lost an eye, the other the use of her left arm. Both were past childbearing. No other village wanted them.

"Stargod Kim," the one-eyed beldame hailed him.

He smiled at them and took a moment from his mission to lift the heavy bronze cauldron onto the hook and swing it over the low fire. Enough distance separated the bottom of the pot from the flames to keep the metal from melting. An iron cauldron was near the top of the list of improvements for the village, as soon as Konner and his team of blacksmiths found time to forge one.

The old women returned his smiles with profuse thanks and bows and vows of eternal gratitude.

He scuttled into his cabin before they could enlist his help with something else. Everyone else who could work even a little was in the fields finishing off the harvest. A third grandmother watched the bevy of children too young to help. Five year olds helped gather the sheaves into stooks.

The perfect time for him to work in privacy without Hestiia hovering over him or Pryth clucking at him.

He did not wait for his eyes to adjust to the dim

light inside. He found the basket of Tambootie by
smell. As his pupils opened and he detected outlines
and shapes within the shadows, he thought that particular basket glowed with an unusual aura. A corona
of green mottled with pink, just like the new leaves,
shone around the entire basket. He picked out two
leaves, both mature, having lost all traces of pink.
Oil still gleamed slickly on the fat foliage, though
he'd picked these leaves nearly a week ago.

Checking once more that no one observed him,
Kim licked the oils. The now-familiar taste sparkled
inside his mouth. He felt lighter, freer, stronger, and
more alert. The dimness of the cabin receded. Every
object stood out in clear detail, as if he stood in bright
sunshine. Now he could truly work magic on
Taneeo's injuries, maybe speed the bone healing and
swelling. Perhaps even restore the man's full
eyesight.

And delve into his mind deeply enough to see if
Hanassa was still there or had left booby traps for
the Stargods.

He stuffed the leaves into his pocket and ducked
out of the cabin. The old ladies smiled and waved at
him once more. He ignored their invitation to talk to
them and perhaps get snared into helping with more
heavy chores. He had to act before the Tambootie
wore off.

At the entrance to Taneeo's hut, Kim barely took
time to rattle the strings of beads before entering. He
heard the rustle of someone moving quickly. To his
Tambootie-enhanced ears it sounded like a wind rac-
ing across the tops of the trees.

"S'murghit!" Taneeo cursed.

At least Kim thought it was Taneeo who invoked
the deposed winged demon. Who else would inhabit
this crude circular hut?

But the voice was deeper, raspier, harsher than the
young priest's.

Then Kim's eyes registered the shape of Taneeo's sparse belongings and the man himself by the light of the auras.

Taneeo seemed to be two men, one lying atop the other, each with his own separate aura, touching but not blending.

Kim blinked. The outermost halo of red and black faded to Taneeo's more usual green and blue spiked with orange pain.

What had he seen?

For a moment Hanassa's coarse features had masked Taneeo's.

Kim reached for the Tambootie in his pocket. Taneeo reached a hand to stay his movement. "Nay, friend. You need no more of the weed. I have rejected my former master once and for all."

"I wished to try more healing on your leg," Kim said. His mouth went dry. A dozen questions choked him.

"Do not bother, my friend and Stargod. Your magic cannot touch my wounds."

"How do you know that?" Kim knelt beside the pallet. The hut smelled of sweat and fear and fever. He held his breath.

Taneeo's aura spiked again with red and black, then calmed to its normal colors.

"Because Pryth has filled your head with false tales of your powers. You can do nothing for me. You only think you can because you listen to the ancient harridan. Go. Leave me in peace to meditate. I will heal in my own good time." Laboriously, he rolled to his side with his back to Kim. As clear a dismissal as possible.

Kim rose to his feet, swayed a moment. The Tambootie seemed to burn its way through his pocket, begging him to chew just a little. Already his vision dimmed back to normal limits and his ears felt blocked with the lessening of sounds reaching him.

"I have to try, Taneeo."

"No."

"We will never know if my magic is valid or not until I try. *I* have to know."

Had he seen Hanassa trying to invade Taneeo's body again? Or had it been a hallucination born of the Tambootie?

"Kim?" Loki's voice summoned him from outside. "Konner just commed. We've got trouble."

Kim closed his eyes and regrouped his senses. Already he longed for the clarity Tambootie gave his mind.

Clarity or hallucinations? He swallowed deeply and kept his hands out of the pocket that held the Tambootie.

Without another word he ducked out of the hut to join his brother.

Taneeo's grunt of satisfaction bothered him more than all of his other questions.

CHAPTER 14

"WHERE ARE the IMPs now?" Konner asked, closing down his comm unit.

"The Others come closer," Dalleena whispered. A glaze covered her eyes and she kept one hand extended toward the windscreen, palm questing outward.

"How much closer?" Konner spared her an extra few moments from his instruments.

The shuttle flew clear of the continent. The sea sparkled in the autumnal sunshine. He picked out the frolicking forms of dolphinlike creatures. The locals called them "mandelphs" and considered them warriors of old who had angered the gods. Their souls had been condemned to wander the seas for eternity. Their hunger for their lost humanity made them follow ships and rescue drowning sailors.

"Less than one third of daylight."

"Then they will have to orbit to pick their parking spot and deploy a lander. Six hours until they home in on the beacon's last location." He prayed to his mother's god and St. Bridget and whomever else might be listening that he destroyed the thing in time to confuse the enemy.

"Is it enough time?" she asked. At last she turned and looked at him full on. Other than wide eyes, she showed no trace of fear.

"Since I do not have to return you to the village first, we have enough time. Thank you."

She cracked half a smile.

"You realize that once we destroy the beacon, we will have a long and hard trip back to the village. Many days, with minimal provisions."

She nodded.

"Good girl." He patted her hand.

"I must see the task through to completion. 'Tis part of the code." She did not withdraw her hand from his touch.

This could get interesting.

"Whose code?" he asked, leaving his hand atop hers. "I wasn't aware there were any laws at all except for the ones Hanassa made up in the name of Simurgh to suit his own desires."

"The code of my father and his father and grandfather before him. 'Tis part of being a Tracker, seeing the lost thing returned to where it needs to be. Your bee-kan needs to be destroyed in the fiery mouth of the volcano. I will see it through." She looked off to their left, staring at the empty sea.

"I do not think that Sam Eyeam has the same Tracker code that I do."

"Why do you believe that?" Konner wished he understood why she considered the freelance agent a Tracker. Now if the man was a bounty hunter, a Tracking talent might come in handy.

"He did not acknowledge the secret sign I gave him."

"I did not see you . . ."

"I told you it is secret, passed from one Tracker to the other. Only we may know it. He does not know it. He does not follow the code."

"In other words, don't trust him."

They flew on in silence. Dalleena raised her free hand occasionally to sense the approach of the IMPs.

As much as possible, Konner slipped his fingers around hers. Sometimes she seemed hesitant to continue touching him, then she'd sigh heavily and relax into the gentle bonding.

"My villagers welcomed you without question. They honored you. I do not understand," he said after a while.

"Trackers are rare. We provide a service no other can. We earn our keep." Sam Eyeam could make more than his keep if he had a true tracking talent. A lot more.

"But my people did not question your word that you are a Tracker."

"I showed them this." Dalleena swept her mass of dark hair off to her back, then slipped vest and shirt free of her left shoulder.

Konner's gaze rested upon a small blue tattoo of a right hand, palm out. Meticulously drawn, he could almost pick out her fingerprints on it.

He dared look no further than the emblem. Her breasts swelled nicely above their confining band. He traced the tattoo with a delicate finger, wishing he dared drop his hand lower.

"Only Trackers are honored with this symbol. I had to successfully find three lost ones and return them home alive before I could call myself a Tracker."

She replaced her shirt and vest and raised her hand in questing pose once more. "They come. More quickly," she said quietly. Her grip on his hand tightened.

The shoreline of the Great Bay smudged the horizon.

A quick glance at his instruments confirmed the presence of a ship near parking orbit. Had they found and boarded *Sirius*? Had they left his ship intact? Or did they simply follow the beacon?

"They didn't stop to take in the sights, that's for certain," Konner quipped. But then, they'd had the beacon to follow and didn't need to do full surveys before making decisions about landing. How did they make it through the blasted asteroid belt so quickly? "We'll beat them to the volcano. Just." He boosted speed, heedless of the sonic boom he created and the vast amount of fuel he consumed.

Within a few moments, *Rover*'s instruments lost track of the IMP cruiser. "Damn. No satellites to bounce signals!" He slammed his fist into the console. He couldn't even tap into the more extensive sensors aboard *Sirius*. He'd parked her over the horizon to keep the locals from noticing a new "star" in the firmament.

The IMPs would not be so careful. They had no vested interest in keeping the locals ignorant of the outside and tied to a self-sufficient agrarian economy.

"Where are they?"

"They have not yet launched a . . . 'lander?' " Dalleena made the last word a question.

He jerked an abrupt nod that she had remembered the word correctly. Then he eased his speed up a notch. Inwardly he cringed at the thought of the noise his passage must create for the inhabitants below.

The Southern Mountains loomed ahead. Konner shed altitude and speed. The butterflies in his stomach grew to the size of bats.

Dalleena's knuckles turned white where she gripped her seat. Her sensing hand came up once more. She'd checked on the IMPs a lot since they had left the sea behind. And removed her hand from his, leaving him isolated and alone. "The . . . ship splits. Two pieces. One very large. One smaller. Moving fast. The lander?"

Konner gulped. Moving fast could mean any speed

to Dalleena who had grown up expecting paces no faster than the hybrid horses domesticated by the tribes.

"Faster than us?" he asked, not expecting an answer.

"Much faster. Spiraling through the air. Aiming for us."

"Damn." After a few seconds' thought he half smiled. "I'm not the pilot Loki is, but I still have a few tricks up my sleeve."

Dalleena cocked her head in question but said nothing. If she did not understand the phrase, she'd figure it out soon enough.

He liked that.

Abruptly he changed course and dropped altitude. Mountain peaks now rose above him. His magnetic readings began to spin. He let his mind go blank a moment before looking out the window. Spidery blue lines flickered in and out of sight. Lines of unexplained energy akin to transactional gravitons. Pryth and the dragons called them ley lines. They dribbled away to nothing in the foothills of the blown-out volcano. The eruption must have exploded with massive power to disrupt magnetic forces and the ley lines.

Konner could use the disruption to lead the IMPs a merry chase.

He popped up above the mountain peaks and the electronic magnetic fluctuations or EMF disruption long enough to give the IMP sensors a glimpse of him, way west of his target. Then he dropped down again and wove a serpentine course back north. When he judged himself far enough away from the volcano, he rose up again, briefly. Only long enough for the sensors to blip before he dove back down again.

If this IMP captain was even a degree less perceptive than the last one who had chased the O'Hara brothers, he should plot a trajectory based upon the last two sightings and look for the shuttle along the line of mountains running north and south to divide the continent nearly into two equal parts.

Konner circled around and took the fastest course toward the volcano, as high as he could, giving himself sufficient distance from the ground, but not to be out of the mask of EMF.

Dalleena bared her teeth at him in a half grimace half smile. "Is this what living in your world is like?"

"Pretty much." Konner suppressed a laugh of exhilaration as the broken mouth of the volcano crater came into view. He did not bother with finesse. He did not bother with comfort. He needed to set the shuttle down within the confines of the crater as quickly as possible.

Rocked and jolted by rapid changes from the VTOL jets he barely secured the vehicle before grabbing the beacon out of Dalleena's lap and diving out the hatch. She came right on his heels, not even wrinkling her nose at the hot dry air stench.

"What about the lander?" she gasped, trying to keep up with him.

"We'll worry about that later."

They maintained silence on the trek down into the heart of the mountain. Konner could tell that Dalleena was fairly bursting with questions. Still, she saved them. She even took his lead in sipping from the sulfurous stream, rolling the precious moisture around in her mouth before swallowing. The grimace on her face gave him a brief chuckle.

"You like this stuff no better than I," she retorted, then took a second, longer drink. This time she raised her eyebrows in puzzlement. A third mouthful and she quirked her mouth up on one side. A delightful dimple made the expression into a silent exclamation point. "I could get used to this."

"You may have to. The lava pit is over here." With careful, almost reverential steps he wound his way around the obstacles in the big cavern, through several smaller ones, each housing a generator or transformer, into the room where Big Bertha, the monster steam generator, dwelled.

Thankfully the dragongate remained silent, between cycles. He did not know if he would be able to think straight with the hum in the back of his head.

Dalleena stopped short at sight of the machine that filled nearly an acre of cavern. Her questing hand came up. She shook her head and thrust the hand forward with determination.

"Big Bertha is not lost," Konner chuckled.

"Perhaps not. But I think I may be." Tentatively, she used her questing hand to touch the metal surface of the generator. The first contact led to a more thorough tactile exploration.

"Come, we still have a chore to perform." Konner stepped into a side tunnel well away from the dragongate. No sense in taking a chance on the wormhole opening and taking the beacon to yet another destination. Though, if he could send it to the south pole, it might divert the IMPs long enough to finish repairs on the *Sirius* so that the O'Hara brothers could get the hell out of Dodge.

But that would not protect Dalleena and her people from the ravages of civilization that must follow on the heels of the IMP invasion.

He balanced on the edge of the lava pit.

The beacon weighed heavily in his hands. A stream of molten rock shot upward. Heat blasted him. Sweat broke out on his brow and back.

He had to destroy it. He and his brothers would deal with the IMPs somehow. He could not take a chance on another ship following the beacon here.

Without further thought, he hurled the beacon far out over the pit. A pitiful distance compared to the wide stretch of the opening. He watched it arc gracefully, a diminishing speck that dropped and dropped, a thousand feet or more into the roiling mass of the pit.

"Good-bye, Melinda. So much for your treachery," he sighed. He prayed that Sam Eyeam had taken the second beacon out of the system.

But it was already too late. The IMPs had found the O'Hara brothers and a pristine planet ready for exploitation.

The dragongate hummed loudly. Dalleena jerked her attention away from the tiny burst of flame that was the beacon. She cocked her head, listening acutely. Her right hand came up. Konner steadied her balance.

The gate silenced abruptly. Too quickly. Normally, it took a full minute to open completely and then another to close. This opening had lasted only a few heartbeats. Or had he been distracted with thoughts of the beacon and not heard the beginning of the cycle?

Too soon the thing began to hum again. He headed back to Big Bertha's cavern. Before he could gain a sighting on the dragongate tunnel, the thing reached a climactic pitch and grew silent.

"What the . . . ?" Konner nearly ran to the edge of the portal, Dalleena close upon his heels.

All he saw was the roiling mass of molten lava shooting flaming rock high enough to force him back from the lip as he flung his arm over his eyes to protect them.

* * *

The enemy is come. They cannot be allowed to destroy us or our home. We are responsible for the safety of this world. We will guard it at whatever cost. Even the death of the Stargods.

What is this? Sam Eyeam returns to my senses. He is stranded. He has no device that is the voice of Hanassa and speaks to the stars. He has no shelter, no food, no transportation. I must return him to the land of the Coros. But not too close. A band of Rovers will protect him as they wander westward. They will also keep Sam Eyeam from returning to the land of the Coros until his time is proper. Stargod Konner will find him later.

CHAPTER 15

KONNER STOOD in the dragongate tunnel for many long moments. He wished for a wrist chrono to time the portal. He'd left his on *Sirius*. What need of digital time in a society that measured its passage in seasons and generations.

He sighed heavily. What two places had it opened to in rapid succession before he watched it so diligently?

As best he could guess, the portal had not opened in half an hour. He could not wait any longer hoping that in the next few heartbeats he would see the green clearing across the river from his village.

In the last battle with Hanassa, he had destroyed the only remote that controlled the gate. The dragongate reverted to its own unmappable schedule.

"Dalleena, we'll have to take our chances with the desert."

"Shall we fill the waterskins at this creek?" She looked reluctantly at Big Bertha. He could not read her thoughts or emotions.

"There is a plateau nearby where the water is sweeter. We can harvest a few fresh greens there to supplement our rations." Time was he'd have been perfectly happy with reconstituted vegetable protein. Now he knew the true joy of flavor and texture, spices that burst upon the tongue, crisp vegetables, and juicy fruits. He had learned to appreciate sharing his meals. True food nurtured the palate and the soul as well as the body. After five months of eating food cooked over an open fire, he'd never settle for ship's rations in their Insta-hot® packets again. No wonder fresh food was the most valuable commodity in the Galactic Terran Empire.

On the trek back to the surface, Konner paused in the throne room. He scanned with his senses as well as his portable instruments for signs of recent habitation. The throne carved of silver bloodwood remained where he'd last seen it. The dust around the throne and the half finished altar remained free of new scuff marks since he and his brothers had been here . . . was it only yesterday?

The remnants of an old fire in one of the outer caverns looked cold and undisturbed. Whatever body Hanassa might inhabit, he had not come back since stealing the beacon and selling it to Sam Eyeam.

"Konner, wait," Dalleena whispered. She clutched at his sleeve.

Instantly, he froze in place. "What?" he mouthed.

She cocked her head toward the narrow opening with harsh sunlight streaming through it.

Then he heard what she had sensed. Voices. Footsteps. The hatch of a shuttle opening. The IMPs had penetrated *Rover*.

"Hide!" Konner shoved her behind him. Together they crouched behind an outcropping. He wrapped his arms around her, making them one object. With luck, and if God and all the saints looked upon them with favor, the desert heat concentrated into the bowl of the crater and the screwed magnetics would scramble their sensors.

"Lieutenant, I'm picking up a reading," an anonymous female voice announced in excited tones. No doubt she already had designs on the reward for the capture of any O'Hara. Doubled by Melinda if Konner were the one captured.

What could he do?

"We have to run back to the pit," Konner whispered to Dalleena. "The heat will confuse their instruments, and maybe the dragongate will open for us."

She nodded mutely.

With one ear tuned to the proceedings outside, he whispered, "Ready, set, go."

They pelted back the way they had come as fast as they could.

"Two of 'em. Running," the same female voice cried.

Dozens of feet pounded the baked dirt. Then came the distinctive thud and "Oof," of someone measuring their length against the ground, or one of the columns.

"Lights! Someone get some lights," an authoritative male voice called.

Konner ducked into the throne room. He risked his own light to orient his sense of direction to the exit. Together, he and Dalleena skidded around the corner and into the long tunnel that led downward. Ever downward.

Sweat dripped into his eyes and drenched his shirt. His mouth dried and his heart pounded too fast. The full length of his thighs ached and the soles of his feet burned.

At the creek, both he and Dalleena paused long enough to scoop up a few mouthfuls of water. If they were hurting from the mad dash through rough terrain with the intense heat, the IMPs must be in a sorry state. They had a few moments to breathe. And think.

"How do we get out of this?" he asked the air, not expecting an answer.

The dragongate hummed in the back of his mind.

Footsteps pounded on the long downgrade of the tunnel.

"Come." He grabbed Dalleena's hand and dragged her back through the maze of caverns.

Shouts sounded behind them as the IMPs emerged into the large room near the creek.

"Ewww! It smells like something died and rotted," a nasal tenor voice protested. It had the singsong pattern of one of the Hindu cultures.

"Sensor's scrambled," a female voice reported. Cool and precise. "Magnetics disrupted. This chamber is hotter than body heat. Can't get a definitive read."

More mumbles and grunts.

"Footprints, this way," yet a third voice cried excitedly.

The dragongate hummed louder.

"St. Bridget and all the angels, please let it be the portal I need," Konner prayed as he entered the short tunnel. He kept a wary eye on any signs of activity behind him.

Close. They came ever closer.

He couldn't let them find out about the wormhole.

The harsh yellow-and-orange glow from the lava below cooled to a soothing green. Bright sunshine on a circular clearing, ringed by Tambootie trees.

Konner grabbed Dalleena's face with both hands. Without thinking, he kissed her hard. He didn't want to let her go.

"That place is across the river from the village. Go!" Konner pushed her. "I'll find you. No matter what, I'll find you."

Dalleena stumbled over the ledge of the pit and into . . . the greens and browns swirled and shifted back to the normal colors of a volcano thinking about exploding. The insistent hum in the back of his mind died.

He dove back out the tunnel, running fast. He

shoved uniformed men and women aside, heedless of where they landed. All he wanted was up and out of this cave system; away from the dragongate.

"I must advise you that resisting arrest will not endear you to the judge." That had to be one of the lawyers. A judicial cruiser had followed them—a ship full of judges, lawyers, investigators, and police enforcement. That meant a minimum ship's personnel of three hundred.

Shite. They'd carry word of this planet back to civilization. The stories of its fertility would exaggerate into legend. Civilization would ruin and pollute the land as it had every planet the GTE had settled.

"Are we certain this man is our quarry?" asked the singsong voice. "Are we certain he understands our language?"

"I'll lead you all a merry chase right back to the beginning," Konner muttered to himself as he scooped up one more handful of water and braced himself for the uphill trek.

This time he set a moderate pace, needing the IMPs to follow him. Anything to keep them away from the dragongate. Halfway to the throne room he had to slow even more, dragging in deep gulps of air. His hands shook when he dashed sweat out of his eyes. The back of his throat tasted sour and gritty. He couldn't keep going.

He had no choice.

From the sounds behind him, the IMPs fared no better. Konner at least had spent the past five months working hard outdoors, plowing, planting, building a smithy and forging parts for *Sirius* as well as tools for the locals. Single-handedly he had dragged the Coros up from dependence upon bronze to a full embrace of iron. And in the course of that achievement, he had built muscle and stamina. The IMPs had been in space for months with no physical activ-

ity outside a gym in the heaviest gravity portion of
their ship.

If he stayed this far ahead of the main party, he
just might be able to gain access to *Rover* and take off.

They'd leave a few guards at his shuttle.

They'd shoot first and ask questions later.

He had to come up with a better plan.

Hard to think in this heat; working this hard. If
only he had a drink of cool water. A swallow would
help. He trudged on.

Visions of the cold waters of the Great Bay wavered before his eyes. A mirage. Surely a hallucination born of heat and dehydration.

Or a plan.

All he needed was a distraction.

"St. Bridget, send me an idea."

He burst into bright daylight, blinking and cursing.
Two uniformed men lounged at the hatch of *Rover*.
They'd slung their stun rifles loosely on their backs.
A third figure showed in the cockpit window. She
worked furiously and with frustrated gestures trying
to start the shuttle. She would not succeed. Ignition,
communication, and navigation were keyed to
O'Hara DNA.

Where the hell had they parked their lander?
Surely not in the crater.

Clearly the IMPS had not expected their quarry to
come running out of the caves alone.

Konner dove behind the nearest boulder. It was as
big as a hut and shielded him admirably. Finally he
had the time to breathe and think.

Not for long. IMPs had their limitations on bush
planets. But they were not stupid. He heard two sets
of footsteps approaching from two directions. Where
was the third?

He darted to the next outcropping, a nest of
smaller rocks.

Two weapons burped stunning bolts of energy. Both missed.

Konner ducked and rolled into his new position. The IMPs kept coming.

A quick glance between the rocks of his new shelter showed him three of his pursuers. They came at him cautiously, with silent but firm steps. Slowly. Each was balanced and held a stun rifle easily, comfortable with the weight.

If he crawled, he might make the next obstacle before they spotted him. Another quick look canceled that idea.

Then he heard the bulk of the party emerging from the caves. A full squad of Marines plus the lawyer, an anthropologist, and assorted forensic technicians.

"*S'murghit,*" he cursed. Three he might have handled. Twenty steepened the odds far above his budget of options.

He looked up at the sheer walls of the caldera. Aeons ago, the volcano had blown out its interior. The walls had been left so thin they collapsed back into the heart to form the crater. How stable were they?

He had one chance and one only. "Let's just hope this works." He'd worked a couple of miracles with his mind when he did not know what he was doing. Could he perform similar feats consciously?

He took a deep breath.

"I surrender!" Slowly he rose to his feet with both hands above his head.

The three IMPs closest to him looked skeptical. They swung back and forth, making certain the muzzles of their weapons covered a wide area.

"Where're your brothers?" the lieutenant called from the mouth of the cave.

A tech corporal beside him looked anxiously from Konner to her instruments. "I read only one civilian," she said. No emotion colored her voice.

"Where are your brothers, O'Hara?" The lieutenant approached with a confident swagger. Midthirties, unremarkable brown hair and eyes, politically correct stature. The top of his head might reach Konner's chin. And he had the muscle bulk of an efficient metabolism.

Kind of old to still be only a lieutenant.

"I'm alone," Konner called.

"Not likely. You three never go anywhere without at least one sibling. Where are they?"

Konner shrugged, keeping his hands up and nonthreatening. But he fixed his gaze high, about the middle of the slope above one of the smaller cave entrances. While the IMPs muttered among themselves, he concentrated on a rock teetering precariously on nothing but packed dirt. In his mind he pictured the rock rolling, gaining speed, collecting more rocks and debris in its path. Over and over, he willed the rock loose from its perch.

He breathed deeply. The picture of the rockfall became clearer in his mind.

And then he heard it happen.

Twenty IMPs looked up. Fifteen weapons swung up in the same direction.

Konner wasted no time. He dove for the next outcropping. Three meters closer to the exit. All the while he kept picturing the rock rolling down the steep cliff.

He heard the soft *chunk* of one stone bouncing off another. Then a sharper sound as the first hunk of rock slammed into a larger one. He spared a glance at the slope. Sure enough, a minor landslide had begun. The first rock had a long way to go and a lot of hillside to collect from before it reached ground. It gained momentum as it tumbled and gathered more of its kind in its wake. If the IMPs did not move soon, they'd be caught in a major cliff slippage.

All twenty of the GTE's finest law enforcement personnel stared at the cliff, dumbstruck.

"How did O'Hara know it was going to fall," one noncom whispered. Her words sounded loud in the hush that had fallen among them.

"Take cover!" The lieutenant recovered from astonishment first.

Konner launched himself toward the exit tunnel before anyone had a chance to think about him.

A mighty roar punctuated the sound of a rockfall. Konner risked a glance at the source of the sound. The vague form of a dragon outlined in red swooped into the crater belching flame.

"Thank you, Irythros."

(*They would hurt you,*) the dragon replied indignantly.

Then the dragon flew upward, the squirming, screaming body of the lieutenant clutched in one set of talons.

"They only wished to capture me and my brothers, not kill me! Put him down, Irythros."

(*Would capture not hurt you?*) The word "capture" appeared in Konner's head as himself imprisoned in a small room behind a glowing force field. Electronic force bracelets confining both hands and feet.

"Very much so."

(*Is that why you created the landslide?*)

"Yes, but you must not hurt the lieutenant. Isn't that part of dragon honor? You value life in the same way I and my people do. Put him down. Gently."

(*Very well,*) the dragon sighed. He almost sounded disappointed.

At the top edge of the crater walls, the dragon hovered and set his quarry down.

The lieutenant yelped. "Razor wire! What the frig . . ."

The dragon flew off.

Konner chuckled. Irythros had set the IMP lieutenant atop the rusting fence line erected by the original colonists.

Nineteen IMPs scrambled to find a path up the steep slope.

"That should keep them occupied while I get out of here." Konner took off again, forgotten by the law enforcement officials.

(*You may ride on my back.*) Irythros flew past the outside of the exit tunnel.

"I thought you could not come to this place."

(*You needed my help. Sometimes aiding brethren is more important than rules.*)

"Thank you." Konner allowed a moment of silence to emphasize his appreciation. "I do not wish you to get into more trouble with the nimbus. I have a better idea for getting out of here."

(*Be careful.*)

"Aren't I always?"

(*No.*)

CHAPTER 16

DALLEENA TUMBLED into nothing. Thoughts of a horrible death in the heat of the lava struck her dumb. She could not even scream.

Cool air drifted past her face. Cool?

She opened her eyes. Time and space twisted and distorted around her. She had no sense of up or down, right or left. Her head spun and her joints ached. Her stomach threatened to turn inside out.

A groan erupted from her throat. But she could not hear it. She decided to keep her mouth and her eyes clamped closed.

Contained within herself once more, her senses found orientation. She shifted to face up.

One heartbeat later, a firm surface pressed against her butt. With her fingers she explored the surface. Grass. Bracken. Stone.

Her eyes flew open. A near perfect ring of trees surrounded a grassy glade. She caught a whiff of the pungent Tambootie tree. Off to her right she heard the rippling of the river. Farther in the distance she picked out rhythmic voices chanting a harvest song.

Dalleena rolled quickly to her knees and then to her feet. She sought the protective shadows of the trees, all the while holding out her questing hand.

"Konner?" she whispered. The memory of his kiss lingered on her mouth.

The breeze in the treetops seemed to pick up her words and whisper them into the far distance.

Dalleena circled with her hand out. She had no sense of Konner, near or far. "Konner!" she called louder.

Her hand remained empty of directional tingles.

"That place is across the river from the village." She remembered his words. Did he mean here? "I'll find you. No matter what, I'll find you."

"I'm supposed to do the finding, Stargod Konner. So where are you?" Until she figured that out, she needed to find the village. He'd come looking for her there first.

She set her mind to picturing the village. Her questing hand came up and pointed directly in front of her. She followed her hand and the sound of the river. One pace for each of her heartbeats. Very shortly the expanse of the river came into view, shallow and narrow this late in the year. Once the winter rains began, it would swell. For now, she could probably swim to the other side with ease.

Before she plunged down the bank and into the water, she shaded her eyes and scanned the opposite bank. Two adolescent boys approached with fishing poles. She recognized the youths from the village.

"Wonder what tale they spun to avoid helping with the harvest," she muttered to herself.

One of the boys looked up at her words, as if he had heard her. He shouted and waved in greeting.

Konner was correct. She was just across the river from the village.

She pulled off her boots and tested the water with her toes. Cool. Refreshing after the intense heat of the volcano crater and caves. With a lace from the front of her shirt, she bound her soft leather boots together and slung them around her neck. Six steps brought the water up to mid-calf. Another five steps and it was deep enough to strike out with long strokes. Barely a dozen body lengths and the gravelly riverbed scraped against her toes.

One of the boys scrambled down the embankment. He offered her a hand out of the water. She accepted it, though she did not need assistance.

"You the Tracker?" he asked.

Dalleena nodded, wringing water out of her hair and shirttail.

"Stargod Loki has been looking for you and Stargod Konner." He looked beyond her shoulder as if expecting the errant brother to appear. Something in the urgency behind his words sent a frisson of warning up Dalleena's spine.

"He's not there," she said, trying to keep the worry out of her voice.

"Dalleena, where is *he!*" Stargod Loki called from the top of the embankment. His usually neat hair looked as if he'd combed it with repeated hand gestures, and bits of chaff clung to his beard.

"I do not know," she replied, more irritated than she intended. A knot of worry grew in her belly. She looked at the boys, all eyes and eager grins. And ears atuned to the slightest nuance of her voice.

She climbed the bank rather than voice her concerns in front of them.

Loki extended his hand to help her up the last steep incline.

She took it gratefully, hoping his strength would calm the shaking she could feel beginning in her hand and extending up her arm and shoulder and into her jaw. If she weren't careful, her teeth would chatter in a moment.

She should not care this deeply about someone she needed to find; only about the finding.

"Where did you last see my brother?" Loki pressed her in a quieter voice.

She drew him away from the edge of the bank and the listening adolescents. "We destroyed a bee-kan in the volcano," she said quietly.

"You found it! Where was it? Were you in time?" He grabbed both of her shoulders in a tight grip.

"We found it in a . . . sug." She fought for the word Konner had used.

"Souk. A marketplace," Loki confirmed. "Where?"

The top of a tousled head appeared at the edge of the embankment. Dalleena disengaged herself from Loki's hands and walked another ten paces closer to the village before speaking again.

"Far across the sea. A place where many boats gather and many numbers of people live in a very small space."

"A city on a harbor. Fine. Did you destroy it in time?"

Dalleena shrugged. "Intruders came."

Loki paled. He looked as if his knees would collapse. "No," he mouthed. "No," he said louder. "Not after all we've worked for. They can't come now!"

"They have come. About twenty men in a . . . a lander." She remembered the word Konner had taught her. "They chased us. Stargod Konner pushed me into an opening into the lava pit, but I landed there." She pointed across the river to the clearing.

"What about my brother? Didn't he follow you?" Loki's hands shook. He stared at them for a long moment, then stuffed them into his pockets. The face he turned to her was calm, but his eyes blazed with anger and fear and a number of other emotions she could not read.

"I do not know. He said he would find me."

"If he's still there, then the IMPs have him. He might be dead by now. We have to go into hiding. We have to . . ."

"We have to wait for Konner to return. He promised he would return. I believe him." This time she grabbed his shoulders and shook him.

He gulped and seemed to gather himself. "If you

could track the beacon across an ocean, why can't you track my brother in the volcano?"

"I do not know. I have never failed to find someone before. But he does not answer to my call." She held up her hand again and slowly turned in a circle.

Nothing.

"I must also tell you that a second bee-kan exists." She dropped her hand in defeat. That artifact did not tingle on her palm either. Her heart and belly began to feel as empty as her palm.

*   *   *

Loki's blood ran cold. Another beacon to find and destroy. Another trip into the volcanic craters. And IMPs beginning to crawl all over the planet.

He watched Dalleena's face and shoulders sag. She must know how dire their situation was. Moisture gathered in her eyes. He draped an arm about her shoulders ready to comfort her. He spent a lot of time comforting women on this planet. They seemed to enjoy the process of their weakness drawing his affections.

Dalleena surprised him. At his first touch she mastered the defeat in her posture and stepped out from under his embrace.

He raised his eyebrows. Not his kind of woman at all. His Cyndi could exhibit a spine of titanium when crossed, but she at least put on a show of needing a strong man to help her. She was the daughter of a planetary governor and knew when a woman should be soft and when she had to be strong.

The Tracker didn't know how to be soft. The men of the village had welcomed her as an equal. No questions about her masculine garb, her father, brother, or husband. She was a Tracker and that was all that was important.

Well, he could be strong and insistent as well.

"Try again, Tracker," he ordered. "I have to find my brother before the IMPs take him back to their ship."

She held up her right hand, palm out, and once again made a full circle. She paused briefly as she faced south by east, shook her head, and moved on.

"Nothing."

"What about where you paused?" Loki turned to face in that direction. All he could see were undulating hills of forest and meadow. Great swaths of pristine land waiting to be to put to the plow.

If the IMPs were already here, then the process of destruction was about to begin.

Unless . . .

"We can't let any one of those twenty IMPs from the lander, or the rest of the ship's complement leave the planet. We have to find and destroy the second beacon before another ship comes."

"We must kill the Others for what they have done to Stargod Konner," Dalleena said. Her voice sounded neutral, but her clenched teeth and fists told another story.

Loki's face grew cold and his stomach knotted. He'd taken one life. Even in self-defense, the death throes of Hanassa, the agony Loki's soul had shared with the man, haunted him still.

"I will not countenance their deaths. I must find a better way."

*   *   *

"Stand down, Lieutenant Talbot," Commander Leonard ordered.

Kat pursed her lips, biting back the angry words on the tip of her tongue. She wanted to pace the tiny office of the ship's captain. Protocol demanded that she remain at parade rest. She felt hunched and confined beneath the low ceiling. Her bushie height and long legs made all standard military living quarters claustrophobic.

Rigid training kept her posture erect even if her cap did brush the ceiling.

"May I ask for an explanation, Captain, sir?"

"If I give you one, it is not because I cater to your bloated sense of superior knowledge in this issue." Commander Leonard sighed. She fiddled with her electronic pencil and the series of screens built into her desktop.

A long stretch of silence. Kat did not break the tension with further questions.

"I do not want you taking point on the pursuit of the O'Haras because I believe your emotions are overriding your judgment," Leonard said at last. She did not look at Kat. For some reason, her screens seemed more important than her helmsman.

"Accompanying the next contingent of Marines dirtside is hardly taking point, sir." Kat almost snapped a salute to emphasize her words. At the last moment she realized the reflexive gesture was not necessary.

"I know you, Kat. You would not allow any mere Marine to lead." In the ship's convoluted hierarchy, the Marines ranked well below those who actually ran the ship, and below the judiciary arm that directed criminal investigations and capture.

Kat almost smiled.

"I obey *your* orders, sir. I take them very seriously. Leading the Marines is not an option, though most of the time they need to be led."

Commander Leonard swallowed a smile.

"You are too close to the issue, Kat. I will not have you turning a normal police pursuit into a personal vendetta."

"Sir . . ."

"I know your history, Lieutenant Talbot."

Kat clamped her mouth shut on her protest. No one knew her full history. No one. She'd made certain all records of her first seven years of life had been destroyed.

"I know that Governor Talbot adopted you when you were quite young. I also know that the O'Hara clan originated on your home planet. The connection is there. For some reason I will leave unexplored, you have a connection to the men we chase. You will have your opportunity for confrontation after they are captured. Not before."

Kat opened her mouth to say something, anything to get herself on the next lander.

"You will not sneak aboard the landers even if I have to confine you to quarters under armed guard, Lieutenant. Dismissed."

"Yes, sir." Kat saluted crisply, did a precise about-face, and marched out of the captain's office.

She muttered seven oaths in six different languages, none of them Terran Standard. If she disobeyed orders and sneaked aboard a lander, then her career was over. Everything she'd worked for, all of the disadvantages she'd overcome, were for naught.

Was revenge against the O'Haras worth it?

CHAPTER 17

"GET YOUR NOSE out of the book, professor, and come help us."

Kim looked up from his journal, blinking at Loki's silhouette in the open doorway. Dalleena stood just behind him. "What?" he managed to stammer, his thoughts still on the sequence of events he was cataloging for preparing the body to engage psi powers—or magic. He needed help if he was to understand how and why Taneeo had become Hanassa's victim once more. Kim was also puzzled about Taneeo's sudden antipathy toward Pryth. A few days ago they had been great friends, heads together discussing the value of this herbal infusion over that salve to treat a rash among the children who played too close to the wetlands.

Did his sudden dislike for the old woman indicate a residual of Hanassa's hatred for Pryth. If so, could that kernel of distrust leave a pathway for Hanassa's malignant spirit to return to the village priest?

Something about Konner's earlier communication. A warning of some sort. The locals and the planet were in danger from . . . His mind refused to focus on anything but the text he input to his reader. He needed to finish before the Tambootie wore off.

"You know we really should name this planet," he

mused. "I think we should start calling it Kardia Hodos, the name you suggested." Consolidating his thoughts on developing their psi powers was much more important than Loki's panics. Perhaps a little more of the Tambootie would inspire him.

"Later, Kim. We have a problem." Loki yanked the reader out of Kim's hands and tossed it aside. It landed with a thud on the mattress.

Kim winced. Loki's violent treatment of a reader indicated more than just his usual simmering temper.

"What is so important that you have to interrupt . . ."

"The IMPs have Konner."

The world stilled for a moment. Kim heard his own heartbeat.

"They've landed? Already?"

"Already."

"We have to evacuate. Raaskan mentioned some caves to the southeast. The harvest is almost in and stored. We can take everything. Pack it onto the backs of the cattle and the steeds. The women and children need to go first. The men should stay behind to dismantle the village, obliterate all trace of us . . . Hestiia. Where is Hestiia?"

"We need to rescue Konner."

"We need to rescue Konner," Kim echoed. His brother's words sank in. "We still need to evacuate. Raaskan can handle that while you and I find Konner."

"If we make certain none of the IMPs ever leaves this planet, we don't have to evacuate."

That thought stopped Kim. Could they strand the entire crew on this planet? Tantamount to a prison sentence for life. For future generations. That would be treating the IMPs worse than they had treated Kim and his brothers.

"They are foreign invaders. We are defending the

planet and its people by doing this," Loki said with force. Obviously, he had read Kim's mind again. He grabbed the front of Kim's vest and stared directly into his eyes. "We have to do this."

"How?" Kim swallowed his misgivings. For Hestiia and her people, for the future of an entire planet, they had to do it. They had to defend themselves against foreign invaders, just as Earth had defended itself against the Kree.

Kim did not like that analogy. Humans had stolen tech from the winged aliens and used it to expand their own empire beyond their own solar system.

"I shall gather warriors from all of the villages. We shall ambush the Others and kill them all. There are only twenty of them," Dalleena said from behind Loki.

"Oh, there are a lot more than twenty of them," Loki replied almost on a sneer. "Twenty came down in the lander. That was just the first wave. There are probably three hundred more up on the cruiser."

"Three hundred?" Dalleena looked as if she needed to sit down. "An entire city of the Others."

Then she jerked her head up and over to her left. Her nose worked like a cat's did when scenting the air. Then she raised her right arm to shoulder level, palm forward. She waved it back and forth until she settled on a generally easterly direction. "Konner," she breathed. A great deal of relief flooded her face.

Kim felt the same emotion.

"Where?" Loki and Kim asked on the same heartbeat.

"There," she pointed due east, toward the river mouth.

"Near or far?" Kim asked. He'd seen the woman in action last night. This was another talent he needed to record. The basket of Tambootie and his reader called to him, in an almost audible siren song.

NO! he told himself. First they needed to rescue Konner.

"Not across the ocean, but far." She began walking out of the village and along the riverbank toward the bay.

"I did not hear the shuttle go overhead," Kim said.

"You wouldn't with your nose in a book," Loki replied.

Dalleena just kept walking.

"Is he safe?" Kim asked her.

"Cannot tell." She stepped over a moss-covered log.

Last night she'd been oblivious to obstacles. Did distance from her target weaken her trance?

"We may need help," Loki said practically. "Raaskan, Yaakke, a few of the men with warrior experience. Weapons."

"Hestiia. I can't leave without telling her." Kim turned back. His wife would be in the fields with all the others, bringing in the last of the harvest. The wheat he had helped plant. The people he had helped rescue from a bloodthirsty priest. The village he had helped build. "I have to stay and defend this place." If he left now, he might never return.

Dalleena just kept walking.

"What about Konner?" Loki stopped long enough to stare at Kim. "What about rescuing our brother?"

"I don't know. I can't just . . . I . . ." For the first time in his life Kim knew the terrible indecision of choosing between protecting the people he loved as family and his brothers who had shared most of his life's adventures.

Dalleena just kept walking.

"I'll catch up. I'll bring men and weapons." Light dazzled around the edges of his vision. His gut churned with premonition. "I have to hold Hestiia in my arms one more time."

                    *   *   *

Kat prowled *Jupiter*. Each long stride only fueled
her frustration. The ship's passageways were too
small for her. The half-mile circumference and the
one-mile length of the torpedo-shaped vessel were
too short. There was not enough space to burn off
the energy that pulsed through her system. She
headed for the outer areas of heavier gravity. The
constant hum of the king stone at the exact center of
the ship quieted just a little. She breathed easier.

Good thing *Jupiter* possessed only one king stone.
If each of the three arrays of twelve drivers and one
hundred forty-four directionals—equally spaced
along the length of the ship—fed into a separate king
stone, she'd probably go crazy.

Or was that crazier?

Despite Commander Leonard's orders, she still
sought a way to get aboard the next lander to the
surface. She needed to confront the O'Hara brothers
face-to-face. *She* needed to be the one to bring them
to justice.

Her path led past the Marine ready room. Twenty
men and women strapped on spider silk armor,
cleaned and charged weapons, checked EVA suits,
and excitedly traded insults. Kat itched to share in
the precombat camaraderie. She'd done her share of
combat training. But since going into space, all of
her preparations had been with ship's weapons and
shielding, space tactics, and flight plans. Her dirtside
skills must be getting as stale as unscrubbed air.

Could she use that as an excuse to get a Marine
officer to request her presence in the landing crew?

"Balinakis is going soft. He's afraid of a tough
criminal recovery," a female corporal muttered. Her
short, squarish figure suggested civil lineage. But her

speech patterns and diction had a lisping whistle that came from a bush planet on the outskirts of GTE space.

Kat paused outside the ready room's open hatch to listen.

"I heard that the judge actually ordered Capt'n Leonard not to follow the marking beacon attached to *Sirius*," a tall, blond sergeant, decisively bushie in his size and speech, replied. "Clear violation of judicial protocol, if you ask me."

Kat knew that gossip and rumor flew through the ship at faster-than-light speed. Eavesdropping on enlisted personnel often provided her with more accurate information than official notifications. She pressed herself against the bulkhead, willing herself to remain unnoticed by the Marines.

"I'd like to see us strand the judge on a Bush planet and let Captain Leonard take his place. She's fairer and just as knowledgeable about the law," Sergeant Kent Brewster grumbled. That tall, dark-haired noncom had beaten her three times in poker, the only person aboard who could.

"We're Marines, not SBs," a young private protested. "We owe our loyalty to the judiciary, not the ship's crew."

"We owe our loyalty to justice," the female corporal sneered. "Fat lot of justice anywhere in the GTE." Her last statement was so quiet Kat had to strain to hear it.

A rumble of agreement rippled around the ready room followed by silence.

If she were leading this squad, she'd be hesitant to have so many bushies in the group. They sounded angry enough to find excuses to strand themselves dirtside. If this lot of combat veterans sided with the natives and mounted a defense against the rest of the crew, they'd have a full-blown mutiny aboard.

It had happened before. Three times in the last decade. Bushie crews had deserted ship en masse and sided with Free Market merchants. One crew surrendered to the Kree rather than serve under a particularly harsh civil captain.

Kat hastened back toward Captain Leonard's office. Now she had a reason to join the landing crew. Someone had to keep the Marines in line and fighting for the right side.

She ran right into Lieutenant Commander M'Berra.

"Excuse me, sir. I wasn't looking where I was going."

"Stand down, Lieutenant," M'Berra smiled. His large white teeth bit at his lip.

"I have serious breaches of loyalty to report, sir. I need to get to Captain Leonard." Kat tried edging around the big black man.

"I heard the talk as well, Kat." He looked back toward the Marine ready room. Still he did not budge from the narrow passageway.

"Then you know, sir, that I must report . . ."

"Consider your report given, Lieutenant." He stared at her with a stern expression Kat could not read. She was too far away from a crystal array for her senses to open and look beyond the surface of the man.

"Sir, in *Jupiter*'s best interest I believe I should accompany the next landing mission." Kat squared her shoulders and stared the man in the eye. They were nearly of a height. She could match him stubborn for stubborn.

"In *Jupiter*'s best interest, I am leading the next landing mission. You stay here and keep an eye on the rest of the Marines."

"But . . . sir."

"Stand down, Lieutenant. You have your orders. And not a word of this to anyone else."

"Yes, sir." Her words lacked her usual enthusiasm.

* * *

Konner ran his hands lovingly over the control interface of the IMP lander that had carried him far away from his enemies. Such an efficient machine, well maintained, responsive, and fast. It leaped to obey his slightest touch on the control screens. He didn't even need an electronic pencil to trigger the ignition.

But it had no personality. The ship's voice had no expression, no quirks, just the bland computer-generated tones, neither male nor female. Obedient and unthinking.

"Sorry to do this to you," he said to the colorless voice embedded in the computer.

No response. He hadn't asked for one. That blind obedience of a machine made his task so much easier. He'd never be able to consign *Rover* to the same fate. *Rover*, like *Sirius*, was nearly a member of the family.

"Autopilot on," Konner said firmly.

"Autopilot on," the computer confirmed. The sound irritated Konner with its artificiality.

He punched in the coordinates he wanted.

At the last moment he remembered to program in a thirty-second delay. Then he dove for the exit hatch, quite convenient to the pilot's seat rather than halfway back in the vessel as on *Rover*. The hatch closed automatically as soon as he cleared it.

With a roar that set Konner's teeth on edge and sent a flock of birds into squawking flight, the lander lifted straight up. Beach sand, small rocks, and bits of shell blasted his face. He had to turn and cover his eyes until the debris settled. He risked a look at the vessel as it reached an elevation of thirty meters. At that moment it shot forward. A nice arcing flight up to thirty-five hundred meters, then a straight plunge down into the watery depths at about the center of the ocean.

He watched it fall. "It's just a machine," he reminded himself. "The thing needed a bath anyway, to get rid of that green plant stuff in the outer atmosphere that eats metal." He needed to wash *Rover*. His mission to destroy the beacon had consumed his thoughts for the last full day to the point where he'd forgotten that little idiosyncrasy of this planet. If he left that chore another full day, the plant would begin to compromise the outer hull of his shuttle.

From orbit this world looked green because of a layer of diatomaceous plant life in the upper atmosphere. Passage through the layer left a coating of the metal-eating substance on the vessel. A quick dunk in the bay seemed to take care of it.

"I've got to go back to the volcano," he muttered. Exhaustion suddenly weighed him down. He had to sit a moment. The thought of a return journey to the crater, with twenty IMPs waiting for him with charged weapons did not entice him in the least.

Letting his mind go blank, Konner wrapped his arms around his knees and contemplated the waves lapping at the shore. Low tide. He guessed the sun was well past the zenith by now. He'd been moving every minute since he arose before dawn from a restless night. He'd been running nearly all of his life. Running from the law, running from Melinda, from Mum.

Running from himself.

Who was *he* when not running? A man more comfortable with machines than with people. And he'd just destroyed a magnificent machine.

The hairs on his right arm and at his nape tingled with another presence. He looked, expecting Dalleena. He'd only met the woman yesterday. But after today's adventures, he had grown used to having her at his side.

Disappointment sat heavily in his belly.

"Hello, Irythros."

The dragon sighed as it settled its haunches into the sand beside him. No words. He just sat beside Konner in companionable silence.

Konner felt like he should say something more, but the words lumped in his throat, along with his fatigue and his questions about himself and his life and what he needed to do next.

After many long moments, when the lander was out of sight and its distant roar but a memory, Irythros spoke. (*Your sense of duty is strong. Almost as strong as among dragons.*)

"Is that a compliment?"

(*If you wish.*)

"Right now duty and responsibility are not very attractive to me."

(*They seldom are.*)

Another long silence.

"I'm just so tired, Irythros. I want to stop running. I want . . . I don't know what I want."

The dragon let him think in silence.

(*I do not understand. You are an honorable man. Yet you flee the enforcers of the law. How can you violate law and remain honorable?*)

"Not all law is honorable."

(*Law is law.*)

"Not among humans. You saw how Hanassa perverted law when he was priest to the Coros. He created laws at his own whim and called it religion."

(*Hanassa did not create law. He dictated rules for his own convenience.*)

"Among my people that happens as well. They call it law. They have lawyers, people who do nothing but debate the law and make it more contradictory." Konner let that thought stand between them for a while.

The sun crawled toward the west, changing the angle of light. Shadows grew.

"When I was about ten years old, my father flew away on business. He promised to come back. We never saw him again. The planetary governor, a man appointed by our previous emperor, decided Mum made too much money from a small shipping business. He wanted that money. So he made up a lie and called it law. He sent armed men to arrest Mum. But a friend warned her. She managed to gather her children and flee. The governor's men arrived sooner than we expected. They set fire to the house. In the confusion, my sister Katie got separated and lost.

"Because we fled rather than allow ourselves be arrested, the governor convicted Mum of imaginary crimes *in absentia*. We lost citizenship. We lost our home. We lost our family. We lost everything."

(*And what of your lost sister?*)

"Mum is obsessed with finding her. Without citizenship, we don't have access to resources that will pinpoint her. Without citizenship, we can do nothing legally. So we operate outside the law, always in the hope of one day regaining what was stolen from us."

(*Your lawmakers act much as Hanassa acted.*)

"And so honorable men like me and my brothers must run from the law. And now the law has found us. I am tired of running."

(*Then you must stay.*)

"I have duties and obligations." To his son. To his mother. To the Coros. "And a finite amount of time before I must leave."

(*Then you must allow your enemies to find what you hold dear and make it dear to them.*)

"What is that supposed to mean?"

Irythros did not answer. He rocked to his feet and spread his wings. A few heavy steps with wings flapping and he took flight.

Konner watched him work his way to a respectable altitude before diving into the bay. He entered the water with wings tucked tightly to his sides, horns folded back. A small amount of splash accompanied him. Three heartbeats later, the dragon shot back to the surface with a huge fish wriggling in his maw. Irythros' wings snapped out and he took flight once more.

"I'll never understand how he maneuvers so much bulk so gracefully."

(*You must learn to make air and sea a part of your soul,*) the dragon chuckled as he flew away.

Before Konner could think of a retort, a shout from the embankment behind him drew his attention.

"Dalleena!" he cried as she trudged through the sand toward him.

His body and mind felt lighter. She was safe. He did not fully trust the dragongate he'd thrust her into because he did not understand it. He had not built it, did not know its specifications and vagaries.

He should have known she would be safe. This woman could survive many tribulations and learn from them.

"Dalleena," he said again and gathered her close to his chest. Where she belonged. He kissed her hungrily, as if he had the right. As if her familiar response to him had been a part of their lives forever.

Suddenly he knew what he had to do.

"Let's go surrender to the Imperial Military Police," he said.

CHAPTER 18

THE AIR LIGHTENED within the shadowed arch of a branch of a Tambootie tree in the clearing across the river from the village. Konner took a deep breath of lava-heated air through the opening wormhole. He waited on a count of one hundred. The greens and browns of the forest shifted, brightened, took on reddish tones. Luck smiled upon him. The dragongate opened.

"This won't be easy, but it's our only choice," he reminded his brothers.

"Let's go." Loki bent his knees, ready to launch into the dragongate the femto it fully opened.

"I still don't like this idea," Kim said sotto voce. "Someone could get hurt. Even killed. I don't like leaving Hestiia alone."

Konner grabbed his arm and dragged him through the swirling colors of the portal. He would not think about taking a life. Any life. All life was sacred. Even the IMPs believed that.

Kim grabbed at a low-hanging branch to keep from stumbling. Konner pulled harder to get him through the portal.

He lost contact with all of his senses. He thrust out his arms for balance. But his body was not there to respond. *I will not panic, he told himself.* He tried breathing deeply and regularly. Even though he could not feel his body responding, his mind calmed. The pattern and rotation of the wormhole began to make sense. If he followed this particular eddy of red . . .

He fell out of the portal into the narrow tunnel next to the lava pit.

Sweat streamed down his face and chest. His stomach turned sour in the heat. The smells of hot dust and sulfur could not mask the scent of his own fear. Fuzziness surrounded his vision. His knees wanted to give way. But this was his plan; he had to appear strong and determined for his brothers.

Kim still held the broken branch of Tambootie. A rash began to form where the essential oils in the bark and leaves had penetrated his hand. That should not have happened so quickly. Unless the dragongate intensified the reaction. Or Kim's system was saturated with Tambootie and only needed a little bit more to turn toxic.

Konner took the branch away from Kim. He considered dropping it back into the pit. But the leaves tugged at his senses. He concentrated on breathing, deeply, regularly. His mind cleared. Objects near at hand jumped into focus so clearly and precisely, they appeared to be almost enhanced digital images. He lost the limitation of periphery.

"Let me scout ahead," Loki whispered at the head of the tunnel. He peered out of the opening, took one step, and then two toward the rusting hulk of the generator.

Konner dropped Kim's arm. His left hand began to burn and itch where he held the Tambootie. He transferred the branch to his right hand. Instinctively, he sucked on the worst of the developing rash. Was this the irritant that had caused a similar breakout among the children? If so they had not been playing by the wetlands as they claimed, but had crossed the river and played in the forest against orders from every adult in the village.

Tambootie oils burst upon his tongue. His ears popped and cleared, his eyes honed in on the details of the cave. The solidified lava that encircled him paled and lost density. He peered right through the barrier to the larger cave system. Shadows of men and women wandered past. He saw insignia on collar and sleeve of each uniform, knew the ranks, specialty and . . . and name of each of the techs who prowled the lower caves for hints at the origins of the machinery left by the original colonists.

"Five down below. Confused and uncomfortable. Resentful of that discomfort," Konner said quietly. "They're worried about the water in the creek. The lieutenant issued orders not to drink it."

"How did you know that?" Loki whirled to face him. "Reading minds is my talent." He sounded almost accusatory. Jealous.

Konner thrust the Tambootie branch at him. Kim intercepted it. He looked at the bright green leaves, thick with oil. They'd lost the pink mottling of new leaves.

"We tried this once before, just before Hanassa tried to burn Kim as a sacrifice," Konner reminded them. "It enhances psi talents."

"The drug helped me listen to Hanassa's thoughts and comprehend his motives and his plot," Kim said. He looked back at the silent dragongate. "I knew then how to counter his megalomania. Perhaps, if I listen hard enough, I can find his ghost and the second beacon."

"Later. We need to concentrate on the IMPs. Give me a leaf. We need all the help we can get for this lumbird-brained plan." Loki grabbed the branch and began chewing on a leaf without bothering to strip it from the stem.

"Let's get on with this. I promised Hestiia we'd be home in time for supper. A promise I intend to keep," Kim said.

"And I promised Dalleena," Konner whispered, almost hoping his brothers did not hear him. At the same time he wanted them to know of his growing attachment to the Tracker.

"I vote we surrender to the most junior and gullible of the forensic techs. They have no authority." Loki marched forward.

"Inflate his ego with our surrender and he'll protect us with his own life," Kim chuckled.

Loki walked right up to a smooth-faced recruit—young enough to be on his first assignment—with a receding chin and dark blond hair plastered to his skull with sweat. More sweat stained his uniform shirt.

Loki tapped the boy on the shoulder.

The tech jumped and nearly dropped the instrument he pointed at a column made from cave drip.

"Easy there, son." Konner caught the instrument. He stared at the screen, saw a decimal point out of place and adjusted it. "It will read easier now." He handed the palm-sized gadget back to the boy.

They all stared at each other, shuffling their feet. The tech's mouth hung open in surprise.

"We surrender," Konner said. The corner of his mouth twitched.

"Su . . . surrender?" the boy gulped.

Konner did not need to read his name tag. "Yes, Mr. Saunders. Surrender. We are tired of hiding out in these caves and decided to let the Imperial Military Police feed us. Mighty hot down here." He wiped sweat from his brow.

The boy mimicked him.

"Mind if we get a drink?" Loki asked, taking his cue from Konner.

"I . . . I . . . my canteen is empty," Saunders apologized. He swallowed heavily, as if he had little spit to lubricate his throat.

"That's okay, we'll just get a sip from the creek." Konner began moving toward the stream. They had a lot of cave to traverse before they reached it. But the tunnel upward was right beside it. The Tambootie made him feel as if he could float there, or maybe fly.

"What does the kid want most?" Kim asked Loki on a whisper.

"What all nineteen-year-old men want." Loki shrugged. He looked at the boy long and hard. "Only he's twenty-one. Just inexperienced and socially immature. But good at what he does with forensics."

Saunders stumbled behind the three brothers. He touched his left hip as if expecting a weapon to be holstered there. He was a tech, armed only with instruments. He jerked his hand back and blushed.

"Inefficient of the lieutenant not to issue weapons to all personnel on a dirtside mission," Loki muttered. "Or at least provide more Marines to protect these kids."

"You never know when three desperate outlaws will surrender to you." Konner grinned back at his older brother.

At last they approached the creek. Beside it stood the muscle of the patrol. A squarely built woman surveyed the lower caves. She had a corporal's two chevrons on her sleeve and a stun rifle in her hands. Her dark hair was pulled back into a tight, no-nonsense bun. As Konner and his brothers approached, with Saunders in tow, she watched them warily, bringing her weapon to bear and pointing it squarely at Loki's chest.

He raised his hands in mute surrender. Kim and Konner mimicked him.

"Corporal Sanchez, mind if we get a drink?" Konner asked. The woman's name had jumped into his head at first sight of her. Strange that she thought of herself in terms of her surname rather her given name. He had to search a moment to come up with Paola.

The Tambootie still sang in his blood.

But what did she want most in life?

"Promotion," Kim whispered to him. "She wants control over those who don't measure up to her standards."

"Queen bee with a whole bunch of drones at her beck and call," Loki finished. He scowled. Konner knew Loki had never liked strong women with opinions of their own.

You don't know what you are missing, Konner sighed to himself with thoughts of Dalleena leading the others over the dunes with her hand extended until she spotted the one she tracked. Konner. She had not given up on him when he pushed her through the dragongate. He loved that she took action when she saw the need and never looked back with regret.

Kim looked at the cave ceiling and rocked back on his heels. A light whistle escaped his lips. His wife Hestiia also knew when and how to make decisions, take action, and defy the world when it needed changing.

From what Konner had heard of Loki's lost love, Cyndi, the planetary governor's daughter, she never decided anything—even the selection of a day's wardrobe—without long and deliberate consideration of all the options and the ramifications of each. Then she'd ask for a dozen opinions before selecting and changing her mind three times.

Loki stooped to take a drink, Sanchez followed his movements closely, keeping the rifle pointed directly at his back.

"Report," she barked.

"Th . . . they surrendered," Saunders stammered.

"Surrendered? Unlikely," Sanchez growled.

"True. We surrender," Konner said. He took one step closer to the creek. As foul as the water tasted, he really could use a drink. The heat from the lava core made him long for the hot days of summer in the desert as a relief. He noted the sweat stains on Sanchez's uniform, smelled the rawness of her discomfort as well as her frustration at being stuck down here when the action was supposed to be taking place above this cave.

"We need water. We're tired of hiding out and spending our lives on the run." Konner said. Both true statements.

"This water isn't safe," Sanchez spat.

"Sure it is. We've been living off it for weeks," Loki said. "We cured a plague with this water."

"If you've been here so long, then you must know where this machinery came from." Sanchez gestured with her rifle toward the various generators and transformers.

"Left behind by the original colonists," Konner said. He, too, stooped beside the creek. He took several long slurping drinks, then splashed more water over his face and hair, letting it drip down onto his vest and naked chest. The slight cooling helped banish his doubts about this plan.

Sanchez and Saunders licked their lips and swallowed. Konner deliberately took another long and noisy slurp of water from his hand.

"The remnants of the first colony are scattered all over the planet in small tribal groups," Konner continued. He splashed some more, making sure that some of the drops reached Saunders' pant leg. They evaporated quickly, but not before the kid felt a tiny dot of relief at those spots.

The young tech succumbed to the temptation of

the water. He pocketed his sensor and crouched between Loki and Kim. He spat out the first mouthful and screwed up his face in disgust. But then thirst and dehydration overcame the taste of sulfur.

"Very few of the tribal groups are united. The people seem *thirsty* for leadership," Kim said, looking pointedly toward Sanchez.

"Saunders, hold this," Sanchez ordered. She handed the tech her rifle. Dutifully, the boy stood and aimed the weapon in the general direction of the three brothers while the corporal drank. She was made of sterner stuff and swallowed her first taste of the nasty brew. She looked as if she might gag on it, but she kept the liquid down and took more. She, too, doused her face and head, then sighed in momentary relief.

Loki leaned back and looked directly at Saunders. "You know, I'm mighty grateful for the relief you are going to get me. Nothing like a nice long space voyage back to civilization to recover from this planet."

"Re . . . recover from what?" Saunders gulped.

"Being treated like a god by superstitious natives. I don't know about you, but after the first two dozen virgins, the routine gets a little boring. I'm ready for a woman of *experience*. But the locals don't think such a woman is worthy of one of the Stargods." He almost could not keep his chuckles under control.

Certainly Loki had shared his bed with more than a few women in the last five months. Konner, too, had sampled several. Kim had been satisfied only with Hestiia. But none of the village women had to be forced and few had been virgin. Vastly underpopulated before Hanassa's sacrifices depleted their numbers, the Coros had learned to value the birth of children and expanding the gene pool more than worrying about the identity of the father. In a com-

munal village, no child was ever orphaned or dispar-
aged for not knowing his father.

Then, too, the men of this planet took parental re-
sponsibilities seriously. Few children were born out
of wedlock, but the first one often came three or four
moons early.

"Now that tale is just a mite too tall to believe,"
Sanchez snorted. "Who would think you three
thieves are gods?"

"The locals don't know our history," Kim said. He
heaved himself to his feet.

"Time to report to the lieutenant. Saunders, bring
in the others," Sanchez said. "I imagine Pettigrew
will relish locking the infamous O'Hara brothers into
the deepest hole, in a heavy gravity hold aboard *Jupiter* and throwing away the key. We'll have you tried,
convicted, and into psychological rehab before the
next landfall." She grabbed her rifle away from Saunders and gestured with it for them all to stand and
march up the tunnel. "Which one of you stole our
lander?"

All three brothers stared at her blankly. Konner
willed his mind away from all thoughts of a transport vehicle. Any vehicle. He thought of Dalleena's
big brown eyes and long dark hair. He thought of
her quick intelligence and her courage in the face of
the unknown.

"Without the lander, how are you going to get
back to the *Jupiter*?" Konner asked mildly.

"We'll find a way to hot-wire your shuttle, if they
don't send down a second boat to retrieve us," Saunders said confidently.

"Don't be so sure of that," Konner muttered. He
glared at the kid from beneath lowered eyelids.

On the trek back to the upper levels Loki kept up
a friendly banter with the kid Saunders, lauding the
charms of the local women. The three additional

techs who joined them kept rapt attention on Loki's tales.

When they arrived at the hatch of the shuttle, a frantic quality permeated the men and women who bustled about, taking readings with sensors, jumping in and out of *Rover* and reporting back to the lieutenant who lay on a stretcher in the shade of one of the house-sized boulders. Long shadows nearly filled the bowl now that the sun came close to setting behind the western ridge.

Lieutenant Pettigrew struggled to sit up as Sanchez spat her report to him.

Instead of uniform trousers, his legs were now encased in a series of bandages. Konner looked up to the ridge where the dragon had deposited the man this morning. Sure enough the setting sun glinted off the rusting razor wire the original colonists had strung during the civil war that nearly destroyed the entire population.

He hoped the man's tetanus boosters were up to date. They were a long way from a new supply of any but the most basic of natural medicines.

"Which one of you stole my lander?" the lieutenant screamed at the three O'Hara brothers.

Konner and his brothers strove to return his glare with blankness.

"Don't answer that," the lawyer, Sasha Demochitsky called from a knot of IMPs on Pettigrew's other side. In a flash of images, Konner knew everything about her, including her passion for defending the downtrodden, convinced that the GTE accused bushies of invented crimes just to persecute them.

"You mean you didn't parachute down from your cruiser?" Loki asked. His eyes were wide and he sucked on his cheeks to avoid outright laughter. The way his eyes twinkled, he must be having a gay old time.

"You know damn well we didn't," the lieutenant began to froth at the mouth. He spat out the precious moisture.

Sanchez looked as if she wanted to spit, too, but conserved her bodily fluids for more important things.

The techs just found the sky fascinating.

"What do you know of the local cultures?" the anthropologist with the singsong voice rushed up to the brothers and shoved a recorder into their faces. "Are they ready to join the GTE or will they need persuasion?"

Arthur Singh, Ph.D. The title was as much a part of the man's identity as his name. Konner did not need to read this man's mind to know his prejudices against all bushies.

"Had any luck starting up *Rover*?" Konner looked over his shoulder at his shuttle, ignoring the anthropologist.

He saw three figures in the cockpit shaking their heads. "Didn't think so. *We* can fly all of you out of here. Our village women are preparing a hot dinner with lots of fresh water and ale. The river valley offers a much more pleasant climate, too. You and your men can refresh yourselves while you wait for someone to come get you."

A number of the people now milling about licked their lips.

These twenty IMPs had no true shelter and no conditioning to endure the extremes of the desert climate. In about twenty minutes the air would begin to chill as the sun set.

"What's our guarantee that you three won't attempt to escape again?" a sergeant asked. He stepped between Konner and the still spluttering lieutenant.

Konner had no trouble reading his name tag, Duggan. The Tambootie must be wearing off if he couldn't pluck the name from his mind.

"I must advise you . . ." Both men cut off the lawyer with a glare.

Corporal Sanchez relaxed a little. She clearly felt comfortable with Duggan's leadership. But not Pettigrew's.

Konner wondered which family had purchased Pettigrew's commission in the Imperial Military Police. How many promotions would their largesse buy? Mid-thirties and still a lieutenant. He'd not go much farther without a lot more money. And how could Konner and his brothers use that information to implement their plot?

"I'll see you all in hell before I, or my men, fly anywhere with you, O'Hara, unless you are in chains in the brig!" Pettigrew snarled. He lunged to his knees, grabbing at Konner's wrist. His fingers clamped tight, like force bracelet restraints.

His touch sent sharp pains through Konner's arm to his brain. The horizon tipped and twisted. Colors reversed. Pettigrew's head blanched to a grimacing skull.

Konner's head buzzed. His stomach roiled. And his heart felt crushed within his chest.

In that moment, with a trace of the Tambootie still augmenting his senses, he knew without a shadow of a doubt that Pettigrew would die and Konner would be responsible.

CHAPTER 19

KIM FOUGHT the urge to kneel beside the lieutenant and draw some of the poison out of his wounds from the razor wire. No sense in broadcasting his healing talent to skeptical IMPs.

"Lieutenant Pettigrew has become feverish from his wounds," Sergeant Duggan announced. Then he faced all three brothers equally. "Mr. O'Hara . . . um . . . et al . . . I will gladly delay your arrest for smuggling dangerous and outlawed substances, for resisting arrest, for unauthorized exploration of a lost colony, and for . . . whatever else is on the books against you and your brothers if you will fly us to a more hospitable place where we can get help for Lieutenant Pettigrew."

"And get communications working," a tech advised him. "This place is just plain weird. I can't get a signal in or out."

Kim found it interesting that the man had not asked them to use the shuttle to take them all immediately back to the cruiser in orbit. Why?

"We have enough fuel and lift to get us all back to our village," Loki said. "I'm the pilot in the family." He immediately marched toward *Rover* and entered the shuttle. Half a dozen troops followed him, holstering their weapons.

"We will, of course, need to use your communications equipment to signal *Jupiter* once we are clear of the magnetic disturbances here in the crater," Duggan continued.

"We expected as much," Kim replied. But they'd not get much use out of the system. Kim would make certain of that.

"Ah, Mr. O'Hara," Sanchez insinuated herself between Konner and the sergeant. "What was that creature that nearly killed Lieutenant Pettigrew, and how did you control the beast?" She cleared her throat. "An interesting potential weapon."

Konner smiled. "Irythros is very protective of me. He acts on his own initiative. Dragons don't take kindly to control."

"Just be glad Iianthe was not here," Kim added. "The purple-tip dragon dislikes strangers even more. Especially strangers who brandish weapons indiscriminately."

Lieutenant Pettigrew screamed something incoherent.

Sergeant Duggan gestured to another IMP with a medical caduceus on her collar. The blonde woman sprayed something directly into the lieutenant's face. He fell back against his makeshift litter with a thud and a grin on his face. The medic looked around as if daring anyone to question her cavalier application of strong sedatives.

"Drag . . . dragon!" Saunders and three other recruits within earshot crossed themselves. Paused. Repeated the gesture and began murmuring prayers.

Kim smiled.

This plan might work after all.

The sun was well down below the rim of the crater before all twenty of the IMPs were crammed into the shuttle. Sergeant Duggan and Corporal Sanchez elected to stand behind Loki and Kim, peering over their shoulders and marking every touch they made on the interfaces. Saunders took up a post in the cramped corner of the cockpit. He maintained a proprietary air about the O'Haras, as if they were his personal prisoners.

The engines fired to life at Loki's first command. The sensors and communications responded easily to Kim's touch.

"How'd you get a commercial shuttle to give readouts like that?" Sanchez gasped. "You've got every one of *Jupiter's* comm satellites on line and we aren't even out of the bowl yet?"

"Who says we have to leave original equipment intact?" Kim smiled at her.

"But the manual . . . ?"

"Got lost on the first shakedown run," Kim muttered.

"Bet Commander Leonard would give her eyeteeth for an array this accurate aboard *Jupiter*," Saunders said.

"Engineer Jorges would go flapdoodle and faint at the violations to the manual," Duggan chuckled.

The flight back to the village seemed to take forever. With the heavy load and limited fuel, Loki kept the speed and altitude low. The grumbles and mutters of discomfort from the main cabin grew louder with each kilometer. Then a few of the IMPs standing near portholes gasped. They were flying over the Great Bay. Phosphorescent life-forms crested the waves. In the diminishing daylight, the ocean sparkled and danced. A behemoth breached and splashed back into the depths right below them.

"Quite a place," Duggan said, his voice tinged with awe.

"We've kept the local culture primitive," Kim said. He wanted to say "unpoisoned" but bit his tongue.

"Makes them more malleable," Loki chimed in.

"They think these clowns are gods," Saunders added, as if he knew everything about the situation—or at least more than the sergeant.

"So we are landing half a klick away from the village and cloaking the shuttle," Kim explained. "And we would appreciate all of your people keeping their instruments and weapons holstered when in contact with *our* people. Your anthropologist should back us up on that."

"From what I hear, there's another instrument we don't have to keep holstered," Saunders said on a deep blush.

"Keep it to yourself," Sanchez barked before Kim could.

Suddenly, this part of the plan did not seem so good. Kim knew what they had to do, but to expose Hestiia and the rest of the Coros to these crude . . . barbarians . . . Marines!

Loki killed the internal and external lights.

"Brace yourselves. This isn't going to be pretty or comfortable," Loki called out. The shuttle bumped the ground, bounced, tilted, and thudded into place. All of the IMPs teetered and crashed into each other. The three O'Hara brothers shared a mischievous glance. They were strapped in and weathered the rough landing with ease.

"We're gonna crash!" A voice screamed in the back.

Surreptitiously, Loki moved his hand to another control while Duggan and Sanchez were righting themselves.

"Hey! The hatch won't open," a voice called from the cabin.

"Get us out of here. Life support is going down."

"I can't breathe."

"Lights! I can't see."

Duggan shoved aside the metallic cloth curtain that

separated the cockpit from the cabin. "Quiet down!" he ordered the troops. "We'll get you out in due order." Then he turned a malevolent visage upon all three brothers. "Open the damn hatch before I forget that all life is sacred and throttle the three of you with my bare hands."

"Certainly, Sergeant," Loki replied as if nothing were wrong at all. He touched a different control. All of the lights came on in a blinding glare.

Kim edged his hand toward the red triangle in the corner of his interface. Once the men were outside, he could render them all unconscious with a quick blast of the sonics.

Konner shook his head at him. "Not yet, little brother. Don't reveal your cards until the last chip is played."

"You've been quiet since we took off," Kim said.

Duggan bellowed orders for the orderly dispersal of his troops. Kim did not think anyone heard his own comment over the noise.

Suddenly the cockpit emptied of excess people and noise. Even Loki had disembarked. The silence seemed alien.

"How did you live with yourself when you killed that man?" Konner asked suddenly.

Kim searched his brother's face for signs of distress that triggered his question. The incident had happened years ago, but he'd never told his brothers until after Loki had been forced to kill Hanassa. Like Kim, Loki had shared the moment of death with his victim, nearly willing himself to die in the process.

"I had to go through the motions of living. For Mum. For you and Loki. I had to keep putting one foot in front of the other, day after day. Why? Did you kill someone on your adventures today?"

"No. I have not killed a man yet. But I had a precognitive experience. Must have been induced by the

Tambootie. I haven't done the deed and I already feel as if my guts have been ripped out." Konner slumped.

Kim had never seen him so upset. So . . . reduced.

"Then maybe you don't have to kill anyone. The one thing I have learned from experimenting with psi powers and Tambootie: the future is fluid. The few glimpses we get are warnings of one possibility. Each choice we make opens dozens of new possibilities. Maybe you were granted the premonition so you *won't* kill another human being."

"I certainly hope you are right." Konner looked a little brighter, a little less fatigued.

"Come on, big brother. Let's go get some supper." Kim slapped Konner on the back and urged him out of the shuttle.

Outside, they found the IMPs grumbling about the hike across open country to their destination. Duggan commandeered Kim and his brothers to handle the lieutenant's litter along with the medic. They led the way toward home.

Home. Kim savored the word. This forgotten planet three sectors off charted space had become home. The villagers and Hestiia were his family now. He never wanted to leave, even to see Mum one more time and explain to her why he had to stay.

Mum would get over his absence. He didn't want Hestiia to try to get over it if he left.

The savory smell of roasting meat and vegetables reached the troop before they sighted the cooking fires. All around Kim, men and women started licking their lips and hastening their steps.

"I thought you told the girls no meat," Konner whispered to Kim across the litter from him, and heedless of the medic in front of Kim.

"I did."

"Meat won't stop this greedy bunch of hypocrites," the medic snorted. "Every bush planet we encounter, that's the first thing they head for. I can't convince them they don't need meat to satisfy their nutritional needs. I can't tell them anything. They are too busy bickering among themselves to listen to anyone. You think the class system at the Emperor's court is strict? Try getting workshirts to sit down at the same table in the officers' mess with cleanshirts. Try getting the defense team to talk to the prosecution. Try getting forensics to talk to the Marines. Or one anthropologist to agree with the other on the time of day or day of the week. Then there's Captain Leonard and Judge Balinakas." She looked as if she wanted to pound her fist into someone's jaw—anyone who got in her way.

"In that case, half the plan is already implemented." Konner quirked up half his mouth.

But his smile did not convince Kim. "Must have been one nasty precog episode," Kim muttered.

"It was."

"Getting a headache yet?" he asked. His own head had begun to throb. Withdrawal from the Tambootie. He'd only ingested a small amount of the oils. His mouth salivated at the thought of tasting the oils again, of feeling the flavors burst upon his tongue and open his senses. His hands began to shake.

Just how addictive was the drug?

"Sometimes it takes a month to get the stink of meat out of the ship," the medic continued her litany of grief. "Even with the best air scrubbers available."

Kim looked closer at her uniform. In the gloom he thought he saw a name tag that said "Lotski." Did she have any gamma blockers in her kit to break addictions? Maybe all he needed were a few judiciously placed micro amps to the affected brain synapses. Then he could use the Tambootie with impunity.

The troop crested the last low hill before the village. The glow from the central fire lit the ridgeline.

"Duggan," Loki called the sergeant. "Best my brothers and I lead the group. Don't want you punctured by a spear or brained by a club. The blacksmith totes a really mean hammer."

The IMPs halted their plunge down the hill to wait for Kim and his brothers. The weight of the litter had slowed them down considerably. Or was it reluctance to let these invaders into their home?

Several figures stood between the troop and the fire. Backlit, Kim could not distinguish features. But he picked out Hestiia at the front of the welcoming committee. He'd know her anywhere. His heart speeded up in anticipation of holding her close once more.

He hastened his steps, forcing the other three with the litter to match his pace.

The rest of the waiting figures became clearer. All women. They moved forward bearing armloads of flowers, greens, and gourds. Just as they began bestowing their fragrant gifts upon the IMPs, Kim realized each and every one of them was naked to the waist.

Including his wife.

CHAPTER 20

DALLEENA SWALLOWED her embarrassment at having twelve strange men stare at her naked breasts. In her home village, and all the villages that had employed her as Tracker, she had been separate from womenfolk and their customs. She was Tracker, different, independent. She had worn men's clothing as a sign of her equality with them. Women had worn a simple sarong in spring and summer and little else until a man claimed them. Then and only then could they expect to cover their breasts in any but the coldest seasons.

Now Dalleena and all the other women exposed themselves to trap the invaders in their own lust. She swallowed her self-consciousness for the sake of the plan.

Then she caught sight of Konner staring at her. A deep frown creased his face. She straightened her shoulders with pride and met the next foreigner with a proffered blossom and a smile. Konner's scowl deepened.

Her assurance firmed.

The few women in the group of foreigners mimicked Konner's expression.

Then Raaskan, headman for the village, and three other men, wearing only their short buckskin trews and vests moved up and bestowed flowers upon the females. Bright smiles spread all around.

"Remember what happened to the *HMS Bounty* when they received a similar greeting from primitives," a man shouted even as he accepted two flowers from Poolie, Raaskan's wife.

"The mutineers from the *Bounty* succumbed to the allure of the native women and embraced a primitive way of life," Konner whispered in Dalleena's ear. "They went bush."

Dalleena just twitched her hips and moved on. She had one more flower to give. She stared at it a moment. Then she stepped daintily back to Konner and gave it to him. He dropped his corner of the litter abruptly. The injured man moaned and thrashed. The others set down the rest of the litter with a little more care. Not much though.

Kim rushed to Hestiia's side and draped his arm possessively about her shoulders.

Loki ambled toward the center of the group. He accepted a cup of ale and began a jolly round of swapping tall tales with the visitors.

Konner grabbed Dalleena about the waist with both hands. He looked at her long and hard from beneath heavy eyelids. Then he kissed her. Hot. Possessive. Insistent.

"You know what you have to do?" he whispered into her ear.

"But what do you *want* me to do?" Languor made her limbs heavy and her mind slow. The heat throbbing from his hands where he grasped her tightly sapped her strength and her will. She could no more separate from him now than she could cease to obey the tracking instinct.

"Later." Konner kissed her quickly and thrust her aside.

She almost stumbled. Strange, rough hands steadied her from behind. Those same strange hands began wandering all over her chest.

Dalleena gritted her teeth and turned to her would-be rescuer with a smile.

"You giving her up for the night?" a voice as rough as the hands asked Konner. The man had slowed his speech to a recognizable dialect. Probably the effect of hastily quaffed ale.

"Her choice," Konner replied. He turned his attention back to the now thrashing figure on the litter. "Always the woman's choice here. Not the man's." His voice grew heavy with warning.

Did she detect reluctance to leave her in his posture?

Pryth waddled over with her pouches of herbs and salves. She, too, had left her breasts uncovered. The pendulous sacs swung as she moved.

She and the blonde woman who had helped with the litter entered into a detailed discussion of infection that led to locking jaws.

Dalleena detected a sneer on the face of the man who tried to hold her. Then he turned his disproving gaze back to her and smiled.

"I don't like a lot of fat on my women," he muttered.

Dalleena decided not to take offense at his comment. Today. Tomorrow might be different. Deftly, she inserted her arm in his and led him to the cask of ale. His hand grabbed her bottom as she walked. She let her own hand drift about his hips until she found the square outlines of a comm unit in his pocket. She slid it free and tucked it into the waist of her sarong.

All around her the Coros, male and female, relieved their guests of every trace of contact with the mother ship. As they passed a one-eyed old woman, seated just outside the circle of light from the fire, they dropped the instruments into her lap. She then secreted them about her person with a near toothless grin.

Taneeo sat in the place of honor beside the fire with his splinted leg stretched out before him. He scowled into his cup of ale, never meeting the gaze of any who greeted him.

A shiver ran down Dalleena's spine that had nothing to do with the evening breeze on her bare skin.

* * *

Loki grabbed a handful of fresh vegetables from the heaping bowls scattered around the village common. The sweet yampion root crunched under his teeth. He let the tastes and textures linger in his mouth a moment before launching into his next recounting of his adventures. He carefully avoided mentioning that he had pulled the trigger on the needle rifle that finally felled his nemesis. This bunch of IMPs might be a bloodthirsty lot in comparison to most civils—those raised on civilized planets as opposed to those raised in the bush. Still, IMPs had taken oaths to uphold the sanctity of all life, even the lives of outlaws such as himself.

"So this guy actually slit the throats of his victims?" Sergeant Ross Duggan grimaced. Then he quaffed a cup of ale.

"And he enjoyed it," Loki said. "Three times we thought him dead. Twice he came back to life." And maybe a third time.

Loki looked around hastily. The hairs on his nape prickled as if someone watched him. Pryth, the ancient wisewoman and local healer seemed to follow his every move with her eyes. Had she been corrupted by the spirit of Hanassa as Taneeo suggested?

Pryth was strong of will as well as body. She had

never succumbed to Hanassa during his lifetime. Yet Loki could not trust her. She never accepted help if she had any other option. And she made her own decisions.

She was too much like Mum.

Loki could not trust her.

"We had no choice but to take him out the only way we could," he finished the story. He repeated to himself that he had had no other choice. He had to pull the trigger of the needle rifle and end Hanassa's tyranny over all of the Coros. He had to end the wholesale slavery. He had to destroy the bloody worship of the false god Simurgh.

No one else could have done it. No one else would have done it.

"Yeah, this place would never grow with a meat eater like that keeping the population down and instilling superstition and actually fostering slavery." Sanchez munched on a handful of crisp wild onions. She moaned in ecstasy as she savored each bite. "This place is some kind of Utopia. Can't see why you guys want to leave."

Loki grinned and handed the corporal a bowl of stewed sweet yampion. She had the compact stature of a civil, but something about her accent and the fierceness in her eyes suggested a different ancestry.

Duggan reached over her shoulder and snitched a chunk of roasted lily. He nodded his head in eager agreement with Loki's words.

A drum and flute began a lively tune.

"Who said we intend to leave?" Loki raised his eyebrows.

"But . . . but you surrendered?"

"Did we? Or did we kidnap you into the local version of Nirvana?"

A busty brunette, dressed only in a short sarong, grabbed Duggan's hand and dragged him toward the festival pylon standing tall at the center of the village. Long streamers of red-leafed vines trailed from the top. Flowers, grains, and tiny squash decorated the pylon as well as the vines. The brunette skipped and hopped in the opening steps of a celebratory dance. Grinning, Duggan copied her movements.

Loki allowed himself to be dragged into the dance with Sanchez.

Other couples joined them. Newcomers, men and women alike, had streamers thrust into their hands. The locals pushed and maneuvered them around and around the pylon until they were all quite dizzy.

All the while, the drum and flute kept up a throbbing and sensual rhythm.

More ale flowed.

Locals changed partners and places. Corporal Sanchez's sturdy hand caressed Loki's as she passed him. A thrill of excitement coursed through his body. Or was it revulsion. She was another strong woman who made her own decisions.

But, unlike Mum, her expressions remained open and honest.

Couples wandered off into the darkness, limbs entwined, mouths locked together.

Loki accepted the invitation in Paola Sanchez's eyes.

The drum pounded in time with the hot blood pulsing in his veins.

CHAPTER 21

MARTIN STARED blankly at the holoimage of the HD™ 37000 in the center of his screen. He'd left the image there to distract Melinda when she hacked into his system. No matter how many fire walls he erected, she always had better software. So he left decoys to send her off in wrong directions.

"Marty!" Bruce's image jumped to the top layer of programs running on Martin's screen.

"What? Did you find something?" Martin sent a series of algorithms and wave differential equations to sleep, boosting Bruce's image.

"I think I hit the jackpot," Bruce almost whispered. He looked over his shoulder as if he suspected adult eavesdroppers. "I found a minority report on the accident that killed your grandparents."

"A minority report?" Martin had never heard of such a thing connected to anything but judicial opinions.

"Yeah, an IMP detective wasn't convinced it was an accident. He filed a report differing from official record. The guy must have had enough rank and prestige the courts couldn't ignore it, but they didn't agree with his assessment. So they buried the report, pretended it didn't exist without actually destroying it."

"Does Melinda, my mother, know about this report?"

"Probably not. She didn't have my dad destroy it." Bruce grinned.

"What does it say?" Martin suddenly felt cold to the core of his being.

"Major Van der Hooten said, and I quote, 'Weapons residue on the hull surface indicates the vessel exploded from an external blast rather than an internal malfunction. Such residue is consistent with weaponry carried by independent merchants for defense against pirates.''

"An independent merchant? Anything else?"

"Nothing useful. I've got Jane Q backtracking flight plans for the dates one month either side of the accident. That would be a lot easier with a Klip, though."

"Good work, Bruce. And forget the Klip. We don't want to get caught tapping private data and draining power from bigger systems." Martin began to shiver. He did not like the implications of the minority report. His mother's corporation owned most of the vessels piloted by "independent merchants" who flew in and out of Aurora. Her parents had been barely out of the Aurora system on their way to the first jump point when the "accident" occurred. A small independent vessel attacking them would have to come from Aurora.

"Any luck on finding your birth certificate?" Bruce asked.

"No. No adoption papers either in any of Aurora's courts. Of course, Melinda could have gone offworld for my birth. Still, you'd think she'd want to stay here with her own doctor and nurses in a private clinic."

"That's what I think, too. Kurt has a new program for tracking deleted files. He's working on that marriage license. I'll have him download a copy of the software to you so you can check more deeply."

"Thanks, Bruce. I did find out that Melinda had Konner O'Hara arrested and exiled about a month after the date of the deleted record. Eight Terran months before I was born."

"Just long enough for her to confirm her pregnancy and be pretty sure she wouldn't miscarry." Bruce whistled through clenched teeth.

"Evidence is mounting that Mom married Konner, got pregnant, and then got rid of him," Martin muttered. "But why would she arrange her parents' death and not Konner's?"

"Look at the money trail, Marty. It's always about money."

"Something about the inheritance, I bet. I should be able to flush out a copy of my grandparents' will."

"If you can't get it locally, I might be able to find something at Earth Central. An inheritance as big as an entire planet would have to be registered there."

"Keep in touch, Bruce. This is getting interesting."

"Sure 'nough. Konner's a good guy. Best counselor at camp. We missed him this summer. Missed you, too." He signed off.

"Konner—Dad?" Martin tried out the sound of the word on his tongue. It sounded fine, slipped out of his mouth much easier than "Mom" or "Mother" when he thought about Melinda.

"Scaramouch, call up Super Snooper™," he ordered his computer.

The icon of two fencers clashing blades progressed back and forth across the screen indicating the machine needed time to process the request. Martin watched the chronometer tick off the seconds while he waited. When the fencers stabbed each other and their blood burst forth in a kaleidoscope of unrelated dots and lines, Martin donned his VR gear.

The dots and lines resolved into the three-dimensional image of a slender man with sharp features wearing a tweed Inverness cape and deerstalker cap who strode purposefully into the screen area. He carried a large meerschaum pipe and an old-fashioned magnifying glass.

"The game is afoot, Master Martin," he said in clipped tones. An edge of excitement tinged his voice.

"I need to know if anyone over at the port has noticed that I moved the 'no access' order for Martin Konner O'Hara, ship *Sirius*," Martin said.

"A disguise is in order, Master Martin." The detective shed his cape and cap to reveal the rough coveralls of a dock worker. He shifted his posture to suggest broader shoulders. His aquiline features spread and flattened.

These changes merely symbolized the signature masking taking place deep within the computer. Every computer on Aurora—except possibly Melinda's—had a registered signature that could be traced by the authorities back to the user. Alteration of that signature carried heavy monetary and criminal penalties. If he got caught.

Martin had no intention of getting caught. All he needed was one quick look at the harbormaster's calendar.

"You will need more memory available to complete this task, Master Martin," the detective said in a monotone—a clear indication that the huge Super Snooper™ program struggled to work within the constraints of Martin's computer. Melinda's would have been able to handle both the program and the holoimage.

"Scaramouch, cancel HD™ 37000." He waved his hand across the holo screen. In the wake of his gesture, a telltale afterimage of green fire followed his hand movement. Someone monitored his activity.

Guess who? Melinda. She was the only one in the

entire corporate headquarters/mansion who had the
hardware and software to beat him at his own game.

"Super Snooper, remove observer."

"Are you certain, Master Martin, that you wish to
alert the observer by forcing them out of the program?" The detective had resumed his costume of
Inverness cape and deerstalker cap.

"Alternatives?" Martin asked.

"Diversion." The detective smiled. Mischief glinted
in his holoimage eyes.

"Do it!" Martin agreed. The detective pulled a
leathersynth strap about one meter in length from
the capacious pocket of his cape. A canine—the likes
of which had never been seen on Aurora except in
holoimage—sprang from the white background and
loped over to the detective. It sat on the man's foot
and looked up at him imploringly.

Martin wanted to reach out and pet the creature.
He'd always wanted a pet, but Melinda had frowned
on the practice of domesticating alien species. Besides, she did not want to live with the dirt she supposed such creatures carried around in their fur. The
air filters in the mansion design could easily compensate for any foreign particles, but Melinda still refused Martin permission. She probably did not want
to deal with any being she could not control through
money or coercion. The emotions of love and loyalty
were too foreign to her.

On the holo screen, the detective snapped the end
of the strap onto the dog's collar, then he pointed at
the remnants of the telltale around the still intact
pedcycle. The dog sniffed around the image and then
took off howling in a new direction.

The detective let the long strap slide through his
fingers and turned back to Martin. "Toby will lead
the observer into the marketplace where you presum-
ably are shopping for your birthday present," he said

as he resumed his dock worker disguise. "Now, Master Martin, we shall proceed on our current mission.

The white screen dissolved to be replaced with the cubicle in the port authority offices where the harbormaster presided. The office was small but just as pretentious in furnishing as Melinda's. A large woodsynth desk filled nearly every square centimeter of open space. One blank wall was dedicated to holo equipment. Another wall looked out on the spaceport through a bioglass panel nearly as large and expensive as the one in Martin's suite. The other two walls were covered in holos of antique vessels designed for atmosphere flight only. Nothing lay upon the shiny surface of the desk; no notes, writing implements, day-planners, calendars, or maps. Since the demise of paper as a communication medium—even before faster-than-light travel—desks had become obsolete. Melinda Fortesque had one in her office that she used as a symbolic barrier between herself and whoever dared approach her. The harbormaster must have adopted the tactic in imitation of his boss.

The harbormaster himself leaned back in his Lazy-former® while he shifted icons around on his holo screen. Vessels and cargoes moved from box to box, indicating times and docks at the orbiting space station above Aurora. Shuttles indicated the ferrying of goods and personnel between the station and the big FTL vessels in orbit and the surface. Dock crews and equipment moved from the shuttles to assigned warehouses. Customs officials scuttled behind the operations every step of the way.

Martin's detective wiggled his way around the desk and stared at the screen from behind the harbormaster's shoulder, examining every aspect of the operation. Martin watched from the viewpoint of the doorway—without ever leaving his Lazy-forme® in his own suite.

A communication icon popped into the habormaster's screen. The port official froze his manipulations to touch the icon with a single fingertip.

Before the caller could appear on the screen, the detective used the interruption to step into the screen behind a warehouse.

Martin sensed his man working his way from one place of concealment to the next while the harbormaster yelled at one of his underlings for having lost a box of freeze-dried artichoke hearts intended for Melinda Fortesque. The Terran delicacy would not grow on Aurora. Melinda loved them and imported them regularly. Only she, on all of Aurora could afford the exotic food.

The calendar in the corner of the harbormaster's screen blinked twice and faded. A replica appeared in the center of Martin's screen, the harbormaster's office disappeared. The entry barring Konner O'Hara and his ship *Sirius* from landing on Aurora or docking at the space station for anything other than emergency repairs and medical service was still circled in red and remained on today's date. No one had moved it back to two weeks from Tuesday.

Martin breathed a sigh of relief. Deftly, he moved the item again to *three* weeks ago and recalled his detective.

He expected the man to walk out of the screen. Instead, a glowing green blob of light appeared at the bottom of the screen. It grew rapidly, expanding with many flashes of red, yellow, and purple flames bursting from its edges. Three seconds later, Melinda Fortesque exploded onto the screen. A lock of her sleek brown hair strayed from her coif and drooped over her brow. Her green suit jacket rode her shoulders slightly askew and a scuff marred her green shoes.

Whatever she had been doing had demanded all of her attention and energy.

"Yes, Melinda?" Martin ripped off his VR gear and faced his mother, trying desperately to school his face into impassivity.

"Martin, you have no business snooping around the docks." She didn't say he had no business using the Super Snooper™ software.

"But, Melinda, I wanted to know if my birthday present has arrived yet." Not a total lie.

"Konner O'Hara will not be bringing you anything. That man will never pollute our planet again." She nearly hissed in her anger. With a snap of her fingers, her red-circled entry moved to today's date with a permanent ban icon beside it.

"But, Melinda, he's my friend. Last summer he promised to come to my birthday party!"

"Last summer?"

"He's a counselor at my camp."

"Not anymore! He will be fired and blackballed as of today. And you are grounded. No more networking. I'm putting a lock on your screen. The only work you are authorized to do from now on is schoolwork. And don't try to get past me with your snooper software. It's outdated. I have the only copy of the upgrade. That's how I traced your activity. Now get back to your assignments. I believe you have wave differential homework. I shall also replace your tutor for allowing you too much free time for this—this disgusting activity."

Melinda dissolved from the screen, leaving Martin with a pile of graphs and equations. All traces of the pedcycle and his detective vanished along with Martin's hopes for escaping Aurora and his mother.

*   *   *

The one I should trust but cannot because he smells wrong seeks to deceive Stargod Konner. He plots in secret with the Invaders. What can I do? I dare not kill this man. *Dragons have made a pact not to kill these lesser beings. The rogue dragon, Simurgh, hunted them for many decades with malice rather than hunger. We will not follow his behavior. What to do? What to do?*

*   *   *

Loki woke with a smile on his face. Until Sanchez spoke.

"I hope you realize that last night does not mean I want any kind of commitment from you," she said.

Loki looked up through heavy eyelids. She stood over him, literally, feet braced on either side of his knees, hands on hips, and her lustrous dark hair cascading down her back.

She had donned her uniform shirt and underwear, scanty undergarments at that, but left off the trousers and boots. A magnificent Amazon.

Part of Loki thrilled at her stark beauty. The rest of him recoiled from her strength and decisiveness. In a brawl or wrestling match she might come out on top. He'd never lost either.

Sanchez reminded him of Pryth. He could not trust Pryth. Taneeo had warned him against the woman.

"Who said anything about a commitment?" Loki shrugged. "We were just celebrating the harvest. These people make any excuse they can to celebrate."

"If this place is as underpopulated as initial scans indicate, the influx of twenty newcomers to swell the gene pool is also cause for major celebration."

Loki stared at her without comment, wondering what leap of logic she would take next. Would she land on his side of the struggle for control of the planet? Or would she be like Pryth and betray him?

He'd trust Mum before he trusted Pryth or Sanchez.

"Though I did notice at the end of the evening all

of the couples were strictly local," Sanchez continued. "Most of my people are passed out around the remnants of the bonfire. I seem to be the only one who got lucky. Strange behavior for people more interested in genes than parenthood."

Loki nearly choked. "You noticed."

"Yeah, I noticed a lot of things. Like your people stole all of our comm units. I figure Captain Leonard will send down a rescue boat as soon as dawn reaches that volcano, our last known location. When they don't find twenty IMPs and three prisoners, and a lander, they'll come looking for the rest of us and spot your shuttle. What level of tech are you planning to bring these people up to? I presume you'll find a way to stall it just short of industrialization."

"What?" Loki sat up, scooting backward and drawing up his knees so that she no longer trapped him. "The . . . uh shuttle is cloaked. They'll never find it."

Sanchez shrugged, dismissing his comment. "You and your brothers aren't as dumb as Lieutenant Horatio Pettigrew. But your plan to entice the entire crew dirtside and then keep them here so your precious little Utopia remains a secret is obvious."

"Only if you say so." Loki stood up, ready to bolt around her and out the door. He should be whispering enticements to this woman to induce her to stay. Instead she laid out *her* plans as if organizing a battle.

"Why would you want to stay here, if, that is, I was planning such a thing?" he asked. He really did want to know, besides distracting her.

"Because back home my family is poor, and bushie. I enlisted ten years ago. Graduated first in my class at Basic and every bit of training since. If I'm lucky, I might make sergeant in another ten years. Meanwhile, dome-breathing rich boys like Horatio Pettigrew buy into a commission and get

promoted every time the family comes up with more
money. I figure I can sign on with some petty king
here and command an entire army." She shrugged
as if her explanation were obvious.

The movement drew Loki's attention to her well
proportioned attractions. He had a sudden image of
her striding into battle, wearing only a sarong and
carrying a sword and ax, yelling obscenities at her
enemies. His body grew tight with longing.

"How many IMPs will follow you?" Loki stepped
closer, ready to kiss Sanchez with all the passion he'd
reserved for Cyndi if she gave the right response.

"I can count on fifteen. Five already dirtside, ten
more on board. Duggan is the one we have to convince. Give him a job he can sink his teeth into and
he'll bring at least one hundred troops to our side.
Marines, communications, and forensic. Our other
anthropologist will go bush at the least provocation.
Don't count on Singh for anything."

"And I have just the job for Duggan," Konner said.
He poked his head around the curtain that divided
the cabin. Dalleena's head appeared just below his.
Neither of them had on much in the way of clothing.

Instead of surprise, Loki registered satisfaction at
the evidence of a growing relationship between the
two. Konner needed human companionship. He
spent too much time talking to his crystals and
machines.

"What job?" Loki and Sanchez asked in unison.

"Something big and dangerous that is keeping the
biggest port city on this planet from growing outside
some very stout walls." Konner stepped into Loki's
half of the cabin, pulling on his trousers as he talked.
"And your rescue boat will not find the shuttle. I've
got it cloaked."

"Like your mother ship. Best sensors in the galaxy
and we couldn't locate it. Not even by looking where

there appeared to be nothing." Sanchez grunted with something akin to admiration.

"Did you find another ship in orbit, possibly a small one-man merchant vessel?" Dalleena asked.

Where had she come up with the vocabulary?

"No, but I did hear reports of a fireball hot enough to burn cerama/metal. Hate to think what could trigger a fire that hot on this primitive place."

"Sam Eyeam," Konner breathed. "Did he and the second beacon survive?"

"Second beacon still beeping, last I heard," Sanchez replied.

"What?" Loki took a step closer to his brother.

"Tell you later." Konner grabbed his shirt and finished dressing.

"Could Irythros set fire to Sam Eyeam's ship?" Dalleena asked. She moved closer to Konner as if seeking shelter.

"Unknown."

"Irythros, the dragon?" Sanchez looked as if she needed to grab a weapon.

"Yeah, a dragon," Loki replied. He began to make connections. Sam Eyeam, the name most black-market merchants took to hide their true identity. A dirtside ship on fire. A dragon in the vicinity.

And a second beacon.

He shuddered and resisted crossing his wrists and flapping his hands. He did not want to think about the possibility of a human being caught in that blaze.

"If we open up that port to more than a small portion of the coast," Konner continued, "we'll have the beginnings of a major trade network. We need trade to grow to a high medieval level of society and technology."

"You'll also need sailing ships and some primitive navigation," Loki mused. Better to concentrate on future plans than dwell on yesterday's horrors.

"I've got just the people you need for that." Excitement glowed in Sanchez's eyes. "You two just signed on your first ally." Suddenly she looked quite beautiful.

Loki wanted to trust her. He really did.

CHAPTER 22

"THERE'S A ROGUE dragon preying on trading caravans," Konner told Sergeant Duggan. He made up a reason for the port city to remain huddled behind stout walls.

He sat beside the blond sergeant on matching rocks near the communal fire. Konner absently stirred his morning porridge with a wooden spoon. The grain mixture was sweetened with berries and fresh milk. Normally, he gulped his breakfast, too concerned with what he had to do that day to think about the fuel he put into his stomach.

Now he contemplated how well the cereal "stuck to his ribs." He often went five or six hours after breakfast without even thinking about food.

If he thought about what he needed to do today, he'd feel guilty about the lies and deceptions he spread among the IMPs.

"What concern of mine is a rogue dragon?" Duggan asked. He, too, stared at his bowl. "This is really good. I could make a fortune packaging and selling this back home."

"The GTE won't let anyone make a fortune on food." That at least was the truth. He had to give each and every member of the *Jupiter*'s crew a vested interest in preserving this planet. "The powers that be will move in their corporate employees to run the farms. All surplus goes into Imperial warehouses for distribution."

"Smugglers could make a great deal of money . . ." Konner turned a blazing smile on the man.

"But we'd have to keep this planet's existence a secret from the rest of the galaxy," Duggan finished for him.

"How big a cut do you want?" This was the hard part. Talking money when all Konner wanted was to grab Dalleena and run for Aurora. Martin's fourteenth birthday approached. Two weeks from today. Would the crystals aboard *Sirius* be ready?

Rover ran low on fuel. He needed to steal the next lander from *Jupiter* and drain its fuel cells.

"Not certain you can give me what I truly want," Duggan said quietly.

"This planet is under populated. You could claim a big hunk of it and crown yourself king."

"Can you get my parents and my wife and kids out of debt indenture?"

"Shit! Which planet?" Only fringe worlds of the Galactic Free Market (translate that as pirates) still practiced debt indenture. Konner and his brothers had taken refuge on most of them at one time or another.

"Mehican V."

"Shit." The worst pirate world in the known galaxy. No laws. No rulers. Just bullies lording it over weaker folk. Weaker translated as poorer, less cruel, or less self-serving. Debt indentures might as well be slaves working mines and factories in bleak conditions.

"Yeah. Shit. Only reason I signed on with the IMPs was to earn some cash to pay off the debt. Trouble is the interest grows faster than my annual salary."

"You help us and the first profit goes to paying off those debts."

"What about your own profit? Heard you three are trying to bribe your way back to citizenship. You need to clear your names. Going to take a heap of A dols to do that."

"Auroran currency is the most stable in the Empire. Melinda Fortesque owns all of Aurora and therefore all of the A dols. She has a big grudge against me. Getting my hands on any of her money is next to impossible." Going to be hard enough to liberate his son from the woman's greedy claws, even if he won legal custody.

"Do we need to take care of this rogue dragon in order to open up more farmland?"

Konner took a deep breath before spitting out his next lie.

He couldn't do it. Duggan was being honest and helpful.

"Truth is, I don't know what is preying on the largest port city we've found. I do know that we need those trade caravans to bring produce to a central market."

"Let's go scout the territory." Duggan stretched up and stood. He looked at his bowl quizzically. "We supposed to wash these or something?"

"Big cauldron beside the fire. Filled with warm water and a root that makes good suds. Also a fine antibacterial." Konner stood and added his own empty bowl and spoon to the mix. "Uh, rinse your spoon and keep it. Along with your utility knife. We all carry our own utensils. That way we don't deprive someone else of theirs if we happen to be away from home."

"We've got mess kits aboard the lander . . ."

"Ditched it."

"In the ocean?" Duggan looked pained. "We could have cannibalized it for tools, bedding, canteens, rations . . . survival."

"I know. Hurt like hell to kill a machine, but it

had to be done. I couldn't let *Jupiter* find us too quickly by locking sensors onto the lander. But now I can't even steal fuel from it."

"Shit! Now what do we do?"

"Set a trap for the next lander?" Konner grinned at his new friend.

"Guess we better find something to do away from camp before Pettigrew starts bellowing orders." Duggan rotated his shoulders and surveyed the perimeter of the tidy village.

"And Arthur Singh, Ph.D, tries to convert us to the joys of rejoining civilization."

They both grinned at the man who stretched groggily on the other side of the fire. His turban tilted over one eye and his uniform looked as if a dragon had stepped upon it. He held his head in his hands and moaned.

"Hangover," Duggan said and pointed the anthropologist toward the bright-eyed medic who was dispensing analgesic sprays to all comers. "His first, I think. Guess he didn't recognize your local brew as alcoholic since it didn't come with a label. He's big on putting labels on everything, including people."

"Pryth has taken Lieutenant Pettigrew to . . . ah . . . her bosom so to speak. We won't worry about him for a while."

"Pryth?"

"Local wisewoman and healer."

"Big—?" Duggan held his hands in front of his chest, cupped.

"That's our Pryth. Earth Mother personified. She won't take any nonsense from him and she'll probably keep him restrained to let his wounds heal."

"Can't exactly call her an 'Earth Mother' since we aren't on Earth."

"We've been thinking about that. Haven't agreed on a good name for this planet yet. We certainly need something better than MKO-IV."

"Something close to the heart." Duggan grew silent for a moment while he stared at the flames beneath the cereal cauldron. "*Jupiter* is very close to Captain Leonard's heart. As long as there is a ship in orbit and a chance to fly it home, Amanda Leonard will not leave *Jupiter*."

Was he envisioning his ship going down in flames?

"All we have to do is get the orbit to decay. Once it passes through the outer layer of atmosphere, the green diatomaceous plants will eat the hull beyond repair. We have to bathe *Rover* every time we return from visiting *Sirius*."

"Not enough." Duggan shook his head. "She's smart. She knows that ship inside and out. You don't have enough firepower to take it away from her. You have to destroy the king stone before Leonard communicates with civilization. As long as the king stone is intact, this enterprise is in danger."

"I have to destroy a king stone," Konner muttered. The giant blue crystals that communicated along transactional gravitons to mother stones and kept the rest of the crystal array working as a unit lived. All life was sacred. He'd already had a premonition about killing a human being. Killing a king stone . . . "I'd rather rip out my own heart."

*   *   *

"Maybe we should uncloak again," Loki suggested, nervously tapping his fingers against his thigh. The three brothers and Dalleena lay prone beneath *Rover*, waiting, watching the sky.

"Patience," Kim counseled him. He, too, felt the urge to move. He settled for running his hands through his unruly red hair. He tugged at the leather thong that tied the mane at his nape.

"How long has it been?" Loki asked.

"Less than ten minutes," Kim replied. He looked

up at the sun's position and checked it against the
length of the shadows. The Tambootie in his system
told him more precisely the time, their location, the
nearest magnetic pole, and that he needed another
dose to keep those senses enhanced. But he could
not determine the location of the lander *Jupiter* had
launched just after dawn local time.

"If we uncloak again, they'll know the blip on their
sensors isn't a fluke," Loki said.

"It takes more than ten minutes for a lander to fly
from the volcano to here," Konner spoke up at last.

He'd seemed very moody this morning for a man
who had found his soul mate. At least Kim presumed
Konner and Dalleena had found each other last night.
The way their shimmering auras merged when they
leaned their heads together told him more than the
whispered confidences they shared. Dalleena had no
business on this adventure. But Konner had insisted.

Kim should have brought Hestiia with him. His
wife had more right to accompany them than the
Tracker.

Right had nothing to do with it. Skill and talent
decided the duty roster, he reminded himself. He
winced at how his vocabulary returned to the jargon
of space farers and how his speech seemed more
clipped and rapid after only a few hours in the company of the newcomers. The lazy dialect of the locals
lingered on his tongue and he savored the poetry of
the idea behind the words. Efficiency lost importance
among people who measured time in moons, seasons, and generations rather than digital femtos and
metric minutes.

"They come," Dalleena said. She held her right
hand up, palm outward, facing south."

"How far?" Konner asked.

Dalleena raised her left shoulder in a half shrug.
"Far. They come closer."

"They must have emerged from the shadow of the volcano," Kim mused. Communications, sensors, magic went haywire within the confines of the crater. The meadow outside, where the water was sweeter than in the cave offered marginally better electronic performance. "So what do we do when they get here?"

"You, Kim, surrender to them. Offer to lead them to where the others are hiding. Loki and I will take the lander back to *Jupiter*." Konner did not look happy about that.

"The rest of the crew will have to evacuate once we break the king stone." Loki looked positively gleeful. "Once we do that, the crystal circles will lose connections and stop working, their orbit will decay, and the ship will crash. The crew will have ample time to evacuate with adequate supplies."

"You should take Ross Duggan and Paola Sanchez with you. We should cannibalize as much as possible from the ship. Like fuel for *Rover*," Kim suggested

"No." Konner put on his stubborn face, jaw thrust out, eyes narrowed, and shoulders reaching toward his earlobes. "If something goes wrong, they'll be tried for mutiny. Maybe treason. I won't let them take that risk."

"Not your choice," Sergeant Duggan said. He walked boldly up to their hiding place beneath the cloaked shuttle. Corporal Sanchez stood right behind his left shoulder where she was in a good position to protect his back.

"You can't see us," Loki choked.

"I can if I know what to look for and where. Besides, you three are making so much noise even Pettigrew could find you."

"The Others wander," Dalleena said. She held her hand out, more to the north.

"They are probably following the signature of the

lander. Salt water will confuse the signal. What part of the ocean did you ditch it in?" Ross Duggan asked.

"Deepest trench I could find," Konner grunted.

He and Kim got to their feet at the same time. Both reached to open the hatch.

"Time to uncloak again," Kim said.

"I can do this, little brother," Konner muttered.

"But you don't want to. Let me help, Konner." Kim tried to place two fingers from his dominant left hand upon his brother's temple. Experimenting with Hestiia had helped him find this the best way to enter a person's mind and soothe disturbing dreams and thoughts.

Konner ducked away from his touch.

"I know what I have to do, Kim. You can't ease that burden."

"It should not be a burden."

"But . . . a king stone?" Konner shivered.

"Maybe Loki or I should dismantle the king stone. Neither of us is atuned to the crystals as you are."

"That is just it. One cannot remove a crystal from the array unless one is atuned to them. Especially the king stone. It has its own defenses."

Kim gulped. "You should not do this alone. I'm coming with you and Loki." And he'd take a stash of Tambootie with him, in case he had to intervene with more than his wits and his strength. He fingered the dry leaves in his pockets. Was it enough.

A roar approached from south by southeast.

No more time to think. The IMPs had found them without uncloaking again.

"We have to do this. To preserve our home. To save Hestiia and all the rest," Kim muttered to himself.

"Amen," echoed his brothers and their two new allies.

"Something is wrong." Dalleena looked at her tracking hand. "There are two landers." She shifted her palm to face due east as well as south.

"We need two distractions now." Kim pounded his fist into his other palm.

The first vessel approached slowly from the south. It circled three times and hovered before settling to the ground thirty meters from the cloaked shuttle. The long tubular vessel, painted black with white IMP insignia looked alien and menacing in the waving grassland. Five heavily armed Marines poured out of two hatches. They surveyed the area with weapons at the ready. Three techs holding sensors emerged more slowly. They sported holstered pistols, and rifles slung across their backs.

"That's Lieutenant Commander M'Berra. Executive officer of the *Jupiter*." Sanchez pointed to the ebony-skinned man with tight black curls clinging to his scalp who jumped down and surged forward, pistol cocked and trigger finger itchy. He had the tall stature of a man raised on a bush planet. Unusual for a bushie to rise so high in the ranks. His family must be very important back home.

Another ten Marines followed him out of the lander. Immediately, the vessel lifted and hovered.

The second lander touched down, deployed another twenty Marines, and took off. The two craft circled the area, one clockwise, close in. The other circled higher, in the opposite direction two kilometers out. Both ships opened ports for pulse cannons.

"Now what?" Kim slumped down and stared at the grass. "They are smarter than we expected."

CHAPTER 23

*I*RYTHROS, *I need your help*, Konner called with his mind. If only he had a bit of the Tambootie that Kim touted so highly.

"Loki, your telepathy is better than mine. Call a dragon," he whispered.

One of the techs jerked his head and his instrument in their direction.

Konner held his breath. No one moved. The tech shook his head and moved his instrument around. Lieutenant Commander M'Berra waved his troop forward in the direction of the shuttle. They, too, remained silent.

Only a matter of a few steps before they ran into *Rover*, even if they could not see it. Upon contact, their instruments would penetrate the cloak, understand it, and never again be fooled by it. With that information, *Jupiter*'s crew would be able to find *Sirius*.

He needed to act. Fast.

"Just be ready to disappear." Sanchez scooted out from under the shuttle. Before Konner, or anyone else could stop her, she ran around the vehicle and approached the IMP squad from an angle at a fast trot.

"Hurry," she said, breathless. More breathless than

she should be after such a short sprint. "They're after me. They . . . they have a dragon!" She pointed to the east and north, across the river.

Instantly, all the techs shifted their instruments away from the shuttle to the direction in which the corporal pointed.

"Calm down, Sanchez," Lieutenant Commander M'Berra said. He placed a comforting hand on Sanchez's shoulder. "You must be hysterical, Corporal. There are no such things as dragons. Now report. Slowly. Calmly. And rationally."

"Yes, sir. Thank you, sir." Sanchez took two long slow breaths. The techs and their protective phalanx of Marines edged a little to the north and away from Konner and the others.

"The locals welcomed us with open arms and a feast last night," Sanchez said. She shifted her weight and shuffled. Her movement forced M'Berra to make nearly a quarter turn.

"When we woke this morning, all our comms and equipment had been stolen, the locals had disappeared, and this immense creature was perched on a boulder the size of a house staring at us. Lieutenant Pettigrew tried to shoot it. It attacked. Then the noise of the landers frightened it off. It . . . it flew, sir. On wings a full five meters wide." She gulped. "I believe Lieutenant Pettigrew is injured, sir. Legs a mess of abrasions. Medic Lotski has nothing but water to wash the wounds. Everything else was stolen, sir."

"Why in Allah's name did Lieutenant Pettigrew trust the natives. And where is the lander?"

"I do not know, sir."

"Where are the rest of your squad, Corporal?" M'Berra sighed heavily and shook his head.

"Back this way, sir." Sanchez pointed upriver, well beyond the village and the shuttle.

Duggan ground his teeth.

Konner touched the sergeant's shoulder, much as M'Berra had calmed Sanchez.

"Sensors indicate a population center of about one hundred bodies due east of here," a tech pointed his instruments directly at the village, half a klick away.

Konner swallowed his frustration.

"Corporal Sanchez?" M'Berra raised an eyebrow in question.

"Could be, sir. I got twisted around running to catch you. Lots of landmarks look alike. The natives took all my equipment. I ran too fast to observe my position as carefully as I should." She wiped sweat off her brow and looked very pale. The medic grabbed her elbow to steady her as she swayed in her tracks.

"One fine actress," Loki mouthed without a sound.

M'Berra activated his comm. "Find a landing place with good cover and wait for us," he barked.

"What about the smugglers?" a sergeant reminded his commander.

"They aren't going anywhere. Our first responsibility is to our own." M'Berra stalked in the wake of the tech toward the village. The entire squad followed without question.

When the last of them disappeared over the rise and the roar of the landers had receded south, Konner crept out from beneath the shuttle and its electronic cloak.

"Now what? Sanchez saved our skins, but we didn't get a lander. Nor did we get fuel for the shuttle." Disappointment rode heavily on his shoulder.

He breathed easier, though. Relief. He would not have to kill a king stone today.

*   *   *

"Magnificent woman," Loki let his gaze linger in the direction Paola Sanchez had disappeared with the landing squad. "Too bad she isn't my type."

His brothers looked at him strangely.

"Open your eyes, Loki. She is precisely your type," Kim chuckled.

"She's too much like Mum," Loki protested.

"Not in the least." Konner smiled and looked lovingly at Dalleena.

Loki's back itched with something more than physical irritation. Could they be right?

He decided to change the subject rather than examine his emotions too closely. "How far away do you suppose the landers went?"

"Couple of klicks from here," Duggan said with a shrug. "The pilots don't want to be too far off, in case the villagers, or the dragon, gives them any trouble. But I wish Paola hadn't gone down a crystal conduit without a sensor like that. She'll be up on charges before the day is over once M'Berra discovers she lied." He rubbed his knuckles against his teeth in a worrisome gesture.

"Don't worry. We'll find a way out of this. Now let's see if we can find the landers." Loki slapped his new friend on the back hard enough to shake him out of his doldrums.

"Minimum flight crews aboard. But every member of *Jupiter*'s crew is fully trained and most are combat veterans. Even the judge and lawyers," Duggan said.

"I'll fire up *Rover*'s sensors and find the landers," Kim said. He keyed open the hatch. "We've got some stunners and probably the element of surprise."

"We'll have to uncloak to get a reading," Konner warned him, hard on his heels.

"You aren't the only one who manipulates systems beyond factory specs." Kim smiled widely.

"The landers are there." Dalleena held up her hand palm out and faced due west. "A short walk, hardly a full sun mark."

Duggan looked to Loki for an explanation. "Primitive timekeeping. One sun mark or one candle mark is roughly one hour."

"About three klicks." Konner beamed with pride as he pulled Dalleena against his side. "She's almost as good as your sensors, Kim, and untraceable."

"Get the stunners, Kim. We're walking," Loki called to his youngest brother.

"A body could get mighty tired of walking," Duggan grumbled.

"Get used to it. Once we take care of this little problem, walking is about the only form of transport," Loki replied. "Unless you want to round up some wild horse hybrids. Locals call them steeds. That's a good name for them; can't really call them horses anymore."

"Um, Loki," Kim stammered as he handed out stunners, even to Dalleena. "I think I should go back and check on Hestiia, the village . . ."

Loki snorted. Kim wasn't complete anymore without his wife. A total waste of a good man.

But he had to admit that when Hestiia stood at Kim's side, his logic was clear, he acted more decisively, and he led the natives with superb instincts.

"Pryth and Hestiia have taken them all to the next village. Hestiia will be safe with her brother and father," Konner said. "M'Berra will find only his own people trussed up like wild lumbirds ready for the spit."

"You could have told us that!" Loki protested.

"Didn't want to spoil the surprise." Konner and Dalleena grinned at each other like moonstruck Acadian Jolilbirds. They mated for life, and if one lost a partner, never found another mate, and often died of loneliness and a broken heart.

Loki shivered at the thought of tying himself so completely to any woman. Even Cyndi. Certainly he planned to marry the love of his life, but he'd never imagined either of them being completely faithful. Life was too full of adventure for that.

Paola Sanchez would demand monogamy from her mate. And St. Bridget help the man who strayed from her side. Good thing she'd announced that she expected no commitment from Loki. She had a larger agenda than finding a spouse.

"What about Taneeo?" Kim asked. "Is he still free."

"Hardly, with splints on his leg and his other injuries." Konner shrugged. "Even if he does harbor Hanassa's spirit, he can't move around enough to betray us."

"I don't like that Captain Leonard sent M'Berra down with the second wave," Duggan said, rubbing his knuckles across his teeth. "She usually saves her big guns for more desperate situations."

"She's lost track of twenty of her crew and an expensive lander. I'd be part of the second wave if I were her," Loki replied.

"Not our captain. She stays with the ship unless she has no other options. That's accepted military protocol. And believe me, you don't want to get her into a corner with no options. She's one fierce lady with a mind as sharp as a laser cutter."

"Was, um, er, the *Jupiter* chasing *Sirius* about five months ago?" Loki's stomach felt like it wanted to sink to his toes.

"Yeah, we were. Thought the captain would split a few skulls when Command called her off the chase. She wanted to capture you guys like her life depended on it."

"If *Jupiter* was called off the chase five months ago, why are you all here now?"

"Captain Leonard got hold of the report of how *Sirius* disappeared through an uncharted jump point. She detoured from delivering a diplomatic attaché to chase you down."

"Tenacious, isn't she?"

"Obsessed."

"Just like Mum?" Kim piped in. His voice sounded mischievous. His face looked grim.

"Just like Mum. This mission could be a real pain in the ass," Loki muttered. He shook his head.

An idea slammed into his brain with the force of a pulse cannon.

"Your Captain Leonard wouldn't be tall and red-haired, would she?"

"No. That would be Lieutenant JG Kat Talbot, our helmsman. Captain Leonard has black hair and blue eyes. Pale skin and a figure to make a man look twice. Maybe four times. But she's all business aboard ship. Doesn't tolerate flirting among the crew, especially not with her."

"This Kat Talbot . . ." Loki prompted. "Tall with red hair. Green eyes?"

"Green eyes that spit fire. Another woman you do not want to cross."

Just like Mum. *It can't be. I'd know if it was her. Wouldn't I?* Loki could not dismiss the nagging questions.

(*Would you?*) The voice in his head flitted by so quickly he almost did not hear it.

"Yeah, I'd know," he replied, as much to himself as that obscure mental intruder. "I'd feel her in my thoughts and dreams. *I'd know.* It's my responsibility to know." He kept walking toward the two landers and whatever encounter lay ahead, wishing he'd never discovered this godforsaken planet MKO-IV.

*   *   *

Commander Leonard drummed her fingers on the arm of her chair on the bridge. "What is going on down there?" she asked the air.

Beside Kat, Josh Kohler hunched in on himself as if trying to make himself invisible. He did not want to capture the captain's attention when she was tense, concerned, and thinking out loud. He could end up cleaning bilges for breathing wrong.

Any of the bridge personnel could.

"I told you this detour was unnecessary and dangerous," Judge Balinakas said calmly. He punched notes into his handheld, recording every misdemeanor.

Kat presumed on Leonard's superior rank by answering her question without having been specifically addressed. "If you ask me, sir, the O'Haras have begun a guerrilla warfare campaign." She sat up straight and caught the captain's gaze with her own. She had too much at stake to let a superior officer's bad mood get in the way.

And she did not trust M'Berra or any of the Marines dirtside to complete their mission successfully.

"I did not ask you, Lieutenant. But go ahead, explain your thoughts." The captain leaned forward. She kept her face and expression neutral. Her right fist continued to clench and release her electronic pencil.

"Classic opening sortie, sir. Ambush and retreat. Force the enemy to commit more troops. Those, too, will be sabotaged. Cut communications and supplies. Lure more troops dirtside. My guess is that they will try to eliminate, incarcerate, or seduce most of ship's personnel to the planet, then sneak aboard and steal *Jupiter*."

Leonard's electronic pencil snapped loudly in the silence that followed Kat's words.

Kohler flinched as if his neck had been the intended victim instead of an inanimate tool.

Leonard turned and glared at Balinakas, daring him to add his now familiar diatribe.

"Alert. All ship's personnel. Secure all launch bays. I want armed troops stationed in or near each hatch with full counter-grav gear," Leonard nearly shouted into ship's comms. Without equipment to neutralize the heavy gravity of the outer sections of the ship, troops would have to be rotated every hour to avoid undue fatigue and physical stress. "No ship comes aboard without command codes and passwords. Sight recognition is not enough."

Somewhere deep in the ship an alarm blared in response to the captain's orders. Faint echoes filtered through to the bridge. Leonard did not relax.

Kat grinned to herself. She'd taken steps to prevent a mutiny without violating her orders not to speak of the complaints she'd overheard.

"Captain, if I may suggest . . ." Kat prompted.

Leonard pursed her lips in disapproval, then nodded for Kat to continue.

"I would like to set a trap for my . . . for the outlaws. Let them come aboard. Lull them into believing we are unaware of their presence. Then set an ambush for them in the heavy grav section, where their maneuverability is limited and we have the advantage of counter-grav units."

"I don't know . . ." Leonard looked long and hard into the eyes of every person on the bridge. No one offered her any alternatives.

"Dangerous," Balinakas said. "But I like it. Easy to set up and execute and we get out of here all the faster."

"What makes you think they will come aboard, Lieutenant Talbot?" Leonard ignored the judge.

Kat noted a few drops of blood on the captain's fingers where the broken electronic pencil had cut her. She proffered the first aid kit from beneath her console. Leonard nodded brief acknowledgment of needing it. She sprayed an antibiotic cleansing compound onto her fingers, followed by a touch of sealant. The blood evaporated and only a little telltale swelling lingered from the injury.

"I have studied these men, Captain," Kat said. "None of their operations have been on this scale before. But they've never had an entire bush planet at stake before. They will fall back to patterns that have worked in the past. Just bigger and a little more complex."

"An entire bush planet at stake," Leonard repeated.

"Aye, Captain. What else would make them linger here long enough to risk capture?"

"Do it, Kat. Do what you have to. I want those bastards captured, tried, locked up, and mind-wiped by shift change in the morning."

Kat jumped to her feet, saluted, and jogtrotted to the exit hatch. Her heart nearly skipped a beat with excitement. After twenty years, she'd have vengeance.

CHAPTER 24

"WHO'S ABOARD the lander?" Konner asked. He and his party lay flat in the tall grasses one hundred meters from the first parked lander. The second lander lay two klicks west and out of sight. Dalleena had led them to this spot without hesitation and without error.

"Pilot and copilot, both armed, and a sentry, probably a corporal armed to the teeth and capable of killing you with one hand tied behind his back and both feet in shackles," Duggan replied.

"I thought IMPs weren't allowed to kill anyone," Kim muttered.

"Marines are trained to the extreme. Have to know how to kill in order to disable. At least that's the theory. A lot of bushies go into the Marines. Their viewpoint is slightly askew of standard GTE." Duggan grinned sideways.

The sentry emerged from behind the lander, making a circuit of the craft, rifle at the ready, two pistols holstered at his hips, a knife in his belt and another in his boot. He scanned every sector warily.

Konner kept his head down, hardly daring to breathe. The sentry returned his gaze and his rifle aim to their direction several times before moving on to the front of the lander.

They'd not approach him undetected.

"I haven't done anything like this before unless I was desperate with the adrenaline pumping like mad," Konner whispered to himself. He hefted a palm-sized rock he found conveniently by his hand.

"A simple thrown rock won't divert him for long," Duggan warned.

"I'll just graze his temple a bit. Enough to knock him out without hurting him," Konner replied, weighing the rock and judging its mass.

"At a hundred-meter distance?" Duggan raised his eyebrows skeptically.

"Try some of this. It might improve your aim." Kim handed Konner a Tambootie leaf with a grin. His eyes looked a little bloodshot and unfocused. How much of the weed had Kim taken?

The leaves looked a little dry and wilted. Kim had probably been toting them in his pocket since yesterday. No oils to lick off. Konner nibbled a bit of the leaf tip.

Kim nodded approval.

Loki took a second leaf from Kim and devoured the entire thing in three mouthfuls. He smiled dreamily.

"I am champagne and my body is the bottle that barely contains me," he said wistfully.

Konner took a bigger bite of the leaf. He felt too light to remain lying prone on the ground. He wanted to fly!

Kim offered Tambootie to Dalleena. She shook her head and kept her hands tightly clasped.

Duggan's eyes grew wide, but he did not take any.

Konner hefted the rock in his hand one more time. Then he peered at the sentry. His vision focused in on the precise spot on the man's temple he wanted the rock to hit. High enough to render him unconscious, low enough to avoid permanent injury.

As he narrowed his focus, fuzzy blue lines snaked across the land beneath his feet. The same web of energy he likened to the transactional gravitons that held the universe together. He shifted his balance a little. His left foot touched one of the lines. Energy pulsed up his leg to his arms and his eyes.

The Tambootie hit a high note in his blood, threatening to shatter glass, or the stone in his hand.

And then he tossed the rock. He followed it with sight and mind. The gravity-defying flight made him laugh.

The sound must have alerted the sentry. He turned to face him. The rock thudded against his forehead, right between the eyes. He sagged. His knees collapsed. He fell forward.

"St. Bridget and all the angels, have I killed him?" Konner immediately sobered. His heart beat too fast. Black spots burst before his eyes followed by a too white light.

"Easy," Kim whispered. He clamped a hand on Konner's shoulder. "Not dead. Just unconscious. I felt it, too. He's not dead."

Konner clung to those words as he gasped for breath. If he shared this much with a man he merely injured, what would it feel like when he had to kill someone?

He crossed himself, muttering prayers.

Loki jumped up and ran toward the lander, Duggan right on his heels.

Dalleena helped Konner to his feet. He fought for balance, leaning too heavily on her.

"Go," she said to Kim. "Help your brother Loki. I have Konner. I will protect him."

Kim nodded and followed Loki. He caught up with him and Duggan at the open hatch.

"Do you know how dangerous that Tambootie is?" Dalleena said. Anger deepened her frown.

"Yeah, I am getting that idea." His vision flashed and once more he felt the splitting ache in his head. His knees threatened to give out, just as the sentry's had.

"The more you use, the more you need to use. And more often. The need for the leaf never leaves you."

Konner's view of the dangers were decidedly different from hers. Addiction was moot with gamma blockers, available in any advanced med kit. But this awful sharing of emotions could kill him eventually. Especially if he managed to end someone's life while in a Tambootie thrall.

"My father used the Tambootie to increase his tracking skills. The stuff killed him in the end," Dalleena continued.

"We have to help my brothers," Konner muttered. He took one hesitant step. His knees held. He took another and almost fell. Dalleena kept him upright though he could see the strain in her arms and face.

"I can walk," he insisted. He visualized himself darting the one hundred meters to the lander. Then he was doing it, faster than he should have. His breathing came easy and his heartbeat did not rise.

Dalleena had a hard time keeping up with him.

One of the pilots glanced out the cockpit windscreen at that moment and spotted Konner. A hasty conversation ensued between the two. Konner read their lips and knew they quickly organized their own defense. They drew their weapons.

"Why can't these things ever go easy like we planned?" Konner asked the sky.

(*Because life is never easy.*)

"You got that one right."

Still feeling as if he could fly, Konner launched himself into the open hatch. His head connected with the midriff of one of the pilots. They went down in a tangled heap. While the IMP fought to catch his breath, Konner knocked the stun pistol from the pilot's grip and restrained both wrists in one of his hands.

"Get up very slowly and raise your hands," the other pilot said. His voice was low and menacing.

Konner looked up to find a stun pistol aimed at his eyes.

Very slowly he disengaged from his victim. The man still breathed heavily, but he no longer gasped from the stunning blow to his diaphragm.

"Now who are you and why did you attack this vessel?" the IMP asked. The pips on his collar made him a first lieutenant. The sprawled man was a junior grade. He'd be the copilot. The senior officer held him captive with that stun gun. Was it larger and more powerful than most?

"Martin Konner O'Hara, at your service." Konner made a slight bow, still keeping his hands up.

Where were his brothers?

In his mind, he saw Loki beckoning him to ease backward.

Konner shuffled his feet and nearly tripped over the copilot. He flailed his arms seeking a balance he did not need. The Tambootie in his blood kept him light and placing his feet without error.

The pilot stepped forward instinctively to keep Konner from falling.

Loki's hand shot out from the cover of the hatchway and grabbed the pilot's ankle. He yanked. The pilot fell. His gun spun away.

Konner caught the weapon neatly and trained it on both men.

"Tie them up and leave them outside," Konner ordered. "Kim, use the comm system to jam all dirtside frequencies. Loki, fire up the engines. Dalleena, you and Ross go back to the village. Keep track of the others."

"Konner . . ."

"I'll be back. I promise."

"Be careful."

"Aren't I always?" He cocked her a wide grin.

"No." She sounded remarkably like the dragon with that comment.

Their tasks accomplished, Loki slammed the hatch shut. "Let's go kill a king stone," he said with glee.

"Kill a king stone. I have to kill a king stone."

In that moment Konner knew he couldn't do it. He had to find another way.

(*There is always another way.*) Was that the dragon or Mum who spoke?

*   *   *

Konner, you travel too far and too fast. Betrayal awaits you where you go and when you return. Look before you leap into the void. Reach for us when you do leap. No one else can catch you. We will aid you the only way we can. The invaders will not survive.

*   *   *

"This is too easy," Kim said quietly.

Loki edged the nose of the bulky lander into its docking clamps. "Just like we planned," he chortled. "They asked for codes. We gave them codes. They opened the bay door and we docked."

"They will wonder why twenty-plus Marines and three prisoners do not pour out of the hatch at touchdown," Kim reminded him.

"Requesting decontamination and temporary quarantine." Konner spoke into the comm.

"State your problem, Lieutenant," a brisk feminine voice filled the cockpit.

Shivers of familiarity ran up and down Kim's spine. Where had he heard that voice before?

"We encountered some bushies, ma'am. The prisoners have been living among them for quite some time. They may be carrying a local plague. We have all been exposed."

Loki grinned from ear to ear. "We did encounter a local plague and were exposed to it."

That was months ago. Kim remembered his own bout with the debilitating fever, locking jaw, and dehydration. He'd almost lost Hestiia to the bioengineered disease left over from the original colonists and their civil war. Hestiia had lost their child before she knew for certain she carried it.

Kim still ached for the loss of the babe. They needed to wait another moon or two for Hestiia to fully recover before they tried again. A secret smile crept across his face.

"Docking bay three cleared of all personnel. Decontamination in progress," the feminine voice came over the comm.

The shiver of familiarity became a frisson of disquiet. Kim knew that voice. Knew that woman from somewhere.

"Now we get out of here, before they realize this ship is empty," Konner whispered."

"The hatches are sealed until the decontamination is finished," Kim replied in an equally hushed tone. He had a feeling that familiar female was listening.

"There is always an emergency exit. Into the rabbit hole with the crystals if nothing else," Konner said. Any ship that used a crystal drive had to have access to the outer circle of red directional crystals. In the torpedo-shaped cruiser, three separate circles, evenly spaced the length of the craft, kept it on course and spinning for gravity.

All three brothers scanned the bay for signs of an access hatch.

"There." They pointed to the imperfection in the hull plating. Just the barest sign of a crack and latch.

With the uniform gray-green paint on bulkheads and hatch, only those looking for it would notice it.

They made for the exit. Konner led them along the rabbit hole. They climbed. Gravity pulled at their muscles. In moments Kim was sweating, breathing heavily. He felt as if he crawled two hand-widths above the floor. Every meter presented a new, sharply-pointed red crystal ready to spear him if he lost his grip.

Konner had suffered a similar injury aboard *Sirius*. Kim had healed him with magic, without knowing how or what he did. He had no confidence that his brothers could tend him as well.

He needed more Tambootie to strengthen his body and his will.

Sirius didn't produce this much gravity while spinning. But this was a much bigger ship. It had to spin faster to generate gravity in the interior portions, making the outer rim proportionally heavier.

At last Konner paused. Seemingly, they had traversed half the diameter of the cruiser. But they had passed only one other hatch. If he remembered correctly, they had come only one eighth of the way around.

"Loki, can you sense another mind beyond this door?" Konner whispered.

Loki held his hand flat against the bulkhead beside the hatch. After a moment he shook his head and shrugged.

"There's a long tunnel to the main corridor about as long as the docking bay is wide. It's empty. Can't tell what is beyond."

Without another word, all three pulled stunners and aimed at the hatch. Konner flipped the latch and waited. The hatch opened a crack. No voices. No unseen hand eased the portal farther open. Loki nodded and swung through, pushing the hatch with his feet. Another uphill crawl. Because of the spin, "down" seemed to be the rabbit hole. At the end of the tunnel he shifted his angle of approach. A cautious look around the exterior and he pushed up through a hatch in the deck of the corridor. He rolled onto the deck and came up in a crouch, weapon at the ready.

Kim counted to ten and followed his brother. Eventually he, too, rolled to his feet, alert and ready to fire his weapon, or jump back into the tunnel. The corridor was empty. He scooted to the side to make room for Konner.

Konner heaved himself upward onto the deck. He stayed on his knees, breathing heavily, pale and sweating.

"Maintenance," Loki mouthed. "Mid shift. Bet they are all in the mess hall."

Kim nodded his acknowledgment of the assessment. But something wasn't right. With nearly three hundred people on board, in uncharted territory, with men and a lander missing, surely someone should patrol every corridor at all times.

"Well, if it isn't the infamous O'Hara brothers dumped right into my lap," the familiar female voice from the comm system sneered.

Kim looked in the direction of the voice. A tall woman, as tall as Loki, with a cap of red curls, long legs, and green eyes that spat fire, stood in the shadow of a cross corridor to their left. Her khaki uniform with emerald trim was crisp and clean and shouted authority. She leveled a needle rifle at his heart.

Counter-grav units strapped to the soles of her boots and just above her elbows gave her the advantage of maneuverability.

All three brothers froze.

"Lieutenant JG Kat Talbot?" Kim asked.

"I bet she was christened Mari Kathleen O'Hara." Loki grinned from ear to ear.

"And if I was, why shouldn't I nail all three of you to the wall?"

"Because IMPs don't kill."

"I've cleared this corridor. Captain won't ask questions if I dump your dead bodies out an air lock. No one with a conscience will come looking to save you."

"Then you will not shoot because the blood in your veins speaks to the blood in mine," Kim said calmly. He felt the draw of kinship. Her physical resemblance to himself and his brothers said more than words.

"If blood speaks so strongly, why didn't you come back for me twenty years ago?" She let loose with a single blast from the stun pistol in her right hand. The bolt of energy landed at Loki's feet. The counter-grav equipment made her body jerk with the recoil.

All three brothers jumped away.

Kat lifted the muzzle of the needle rifle. It rested easily in her left hand—a miniature counter-grav unit clamped to the butt negated the weapon's weight for her. Her trigger finger twitched nervously.

"We did not go back for you because we could not go back." Loki took one cautious step forward, hands raised. His stunner dangled uselessly from a wrist cord. "Not then. Not with Imperial troops authorized to kill Mum."

"Imperial troops do not kill. All life is sacred," she snarled and let loose another blast from her pistol. This one sent Konner scrambling to his right, farther away from her. Closer to the next cross corridor.

Kim coughed heavily as he scrambled left. Kat sent him a scathing look. Had she seen how far away Konner had gotten?

"Tell that to Governor Mitchell," Loki growled

back. "Dead men—or dead women—tell no tales and carry no lawsuits back to Imperial Justice on Earth. We've been on the run for twenty years because of that man."

"Mitchell is dead," Katie said, quite calm. Her eyes looked dead. She'd lost the fire. "I watched him die."

She did not add that she had shared the moment of death. She did not have to. Her eyes said it all. That fact alone made her one with her brothers. They all had borne the curse of nearly following victims beyond the mortal realm.

"Mitchell's decrees of outlawry remain," Loki said. Bitterness colored his words and his posture.

"Mitchell's falsified evidence against Mum remains." Kim took up the recital. He forced a loving tone into his words. He tried to reach out to her with every scrap of healing empathy he could. If only he had more Tambootie! "We've been running away from a dead man for twenty years, Katie. But not for one moment did we forget that we left a family member behind. We've been trying to find you for twenty years."

"You didn't try hard enough," she spat. "And my name is Kat. Kat Talbot, I took the name of the man who adopted me. The man who loved me as a daughter. The man who was there for me when my *family* deserted me." She aimed the stun pistol and blasted again.

Kim knew she would do it. Knew precisely where she would aim and that she had as good accuracy with her right hand as with the needle rifle in her left. He did not move out of the way.

He had to give Konner a chance to disappear.

Pain lanced through his bare left foot. Flame shot up his leg followed by numbness. His knee was on fire.

And then he fell. He tried to catch himself against the bulkhead. He couldn't find it with dead hands.

"She shot me!" he mumbled through leaden lips. "My own sister shot me."

Konner took off into the blind cross corridor without a backward look, as fast as the heavy gravity would allow him.

CHAPTER 25

K ONNER KNEW what he had to do. He had to abandon his brothers, much as they had all abandoned Katie twenty years ago. He hated himself for leaving Kim wounded.

Kim must know that he had to leave. They had planned for this. At all costs Konner had to dismantle the king stone.

None of the IMPs could be allowed to leave this planet. Ever. All communication with civilization must be severed. The king stone was the key.

(*Do not forget the other beacon,*) a disembodied voice warned him. (*One you should not trust has the beacon.*)

"Later. First things first." He ran. A blast from Katie's stunner nipped at his heels. He ran faster.

She had the advantage of counter-grav. But her quarry had split. Which would she keep under guard?

He heard footsteps behind him.

His heart thudded. The heavy gravity dragged at his muscles. He kept going.

Right ten paces, left two. He grabbed the rungs of an emergency ladder and pushed himself up to the next deck and slightly lighter gravity.

The footsteps behind him fell away. He thought. He couldn't be certain. His heart pounded in his ears so loudly he heard nothing else. Too fast. Gravity was too heavy. He had to slow down and think.

This corridor ended in a blast door. Kat had said that she'd cleared the area before confronting her brothers.

Konner spun the lock. It slid open.

He heard voices off to his left. A cross corridor ahead. People. IMPs.

He ducked into a storage locker. Cables and grapples and magnetic couplers filled every available inch. He pried a space for himself between two neatly stacked coils of cable. One long breath in and out. Then another and a third. His pulse calmed to a more reasonable level. He listened. A coupler pressed painfully into his back. One hundred heartbeats later the voices moved on.

Not bothering to fully close the locker, he crept out. Now where? He had to work his way into the heart of the ship to the king stone.

Konner drew his stunner, a toy compared to the pistol and the needle rifle his sister packed. He checked the charge and the setting. Mid range. A solid hit to the chest would render most adults of civil height and mass semiconscious. No sustainable injuries. But this crew seemed to have as many bushies as civils. Their greater height and weight might take a stronger charge.

The vision of Lieutenant Pettigrew's death's head grinning at him wiggled into his mind once more. He left the setting in the middle. He'd take his chances.

One corridor at a time he worked his way inward, toward ever decreasing gravity. The area grew more and more populous. Everyone carried a sidearm. Many packed larger weapons. He detected no more needle firearms. They were illegal after all. So why did Kat have one?

Knots of people gathered around viewscreens

peering at the planet below them. Two fistfights broke out when someone refused to give way.

Konner gulped and pressed himself deeper into the shadows. The fight broke up. Three men drifted away directly past him. They searched the area warily, but their gazes slid right over him without a flicker of acknowledgment.

Maybe the Tambootie continued in his system, allowing him to misdirect their attention.

He passed crew quarters and a mess hall. The scent of textured protein and tanked greens did not entice him at all. Voices raised in disagreement sent him scuttling past the open hatchway.

Just beyond the mess hall, he found a lift, an open affair, merely a series of platforms rising on a continuous belt. Beside that was a closed stairwell. He took that up one level. The corridor there seemed to go only north and south. He couldn't see any cross ramps going east-west or up and away from the concentration of gravity.

Up two more flights. He found it! A ramped passage going east-west. He stepped into it. On the bulkhead a terminal blinked at him. He pressed two buttons and found a map. But he did not truly need it. He could hear the crystals whispering to each other up ahead.

Gravity eased. He moved more quickly. Each step bounced and threatened to send him in oblique directions. He could not afford the time recovering from rebounding off the bulkheads.

Concentrate, he admonished himself. *One step in front of the other. Straight lines. Straight ahead.*

The crystals came alive in his mind. One king stone and twelve drivers. Always a symmetry of twelve. But this ship had three circles of drivers, twelve each, at bow, aft, and midship. Each ring of drivers had one hundred forty-four directionals spread around the circumference of the torpedo-shaped vessel. *Sirius* had a more efficient design—to Konner's mind—with a single ring of drivers around the king stone and a directional circle around a saucer.

He heard/felt the magnetic monopole drivers sharing the nitrogen that bathed them. They spat energy along fiber optics to the twelve directionals assigned to each driver. Each crystal was connected to the others. They needed no opposing pole to complete them. They had a circle of like crystals. An entire family of green drivers, red directionals and a single blue king stone that interpreted computer commands for direction and speed. Every crystal in the three arrays was grown together. The king stone maintained an invisible tether to a mother stone at the place of their birth. As long as the king stone was in communication with its mother stone, it could always find its way home. It could also communicate with every other king stone tethered to the mother faster than the speed of light.

Crystal scientists theorized that the stones used the invisible transactional gravitons to communicate almost instantaneously anywhere in the galaxy.

Konner had seen the local equivalent of transactional gravitons crisscrossing the planet below. He'd used the energy in those blue lines when he needed to move heavy objects with his mind. Could he use them to throw his thoughts across great distances as well?

He sped onward toward the sealed door and the crystal he had to kill. Without the king stone, the crew would have to manually input each tiny correction into each driver and directional. The strain of the constant work allowed shifts of only two hours with the next four hours in heavy, drugged sleep.

Konner had seen men go mad after only two days of maintaining a crystal array. They became so atuned to the crystal matrix that they could no longer communicate with humans.

* * *

"St. Bridget and all the angels!" Loki exploded. He dove for Kat Talbot's knees. The heavy gravity made him sluggish. She sidestepped easily, buoyed by her counter-grav units.

Loki snagged her ankle with one fist. His palm covered the power unit of the counter-grav. He switched it off and yanked her foot out from under her. She fell atop him, unbalanced in the heavy gravity. The needle rifle skidded across the deck. She still had the stun pistol. Grasping it, she slammed both fists into his kidneys.

Loki rolled and gasped. Fire raced up his back. *Jaysus*! She was strong.

But the counter-grav units had reduced the force of her blow. He'd be bruised but would recover.

He twisted, pinning her beneath him. She writhed like a Denobian muscle-cat, spitting and hissing curses in at least three languages.

He had the advantage of weight and reach and a hundred barroom brawls where fair had nothing to do with winning. He made certain he switched off both of her arm counter-grav units. Her muscles grew slack beneath him.

Kim groaned. They both stilled. Loki watched as Kim's eyes rolled up and he passed out.

"Jaysus, Mary, and Joseph, what did you do to my baby brother?" Loki stared into Kat's eyes.

"Baby brother? That's Kim?" she breathed.

"And you have no grudge against him. He was but a toddler when we lost you. You were barely two years older. Hate me, and Konner, we were teens and should have gone back for you. Hate Mum for failing to find you later. No way you can blame Kim."

"You all look so much alike . . ." she said quietly. Beneath him, her stomach muscles contracted.

Either she prepared to deliver a massive blow to his head or she was going to vomit. He hoped the later, as he crawled over to where Kim lay.

Kat rolled to her knees and retched. Dry heaves. They had to hurt under these g forces.

Loki busied himself with checking Kim's pulse. Slow and steady. His eyes dilated when Loki rolled back the eyelid. He'd live.

Konner had taken responsibility for the king stone. Loki had to make sure they all escaped. That meant keeping Kat occupied and the corridor clear.

"The docking bay was empty. Should have been three more landers there," he said casually. And another five in a bay on the opposite side of the ship. Plus a number of smaller shuttles and fighters.

"On the surface. Deployed in a broad search," Kat replied. She seemed to have regained control of her stomach, but stayed on her knees, holding her head in both hands. She probably lied about the ships. All O'Haras inherited the ability to spin yarns at will. "I swear I only stunned him. He's not dead, is he?"

"You'd know if he was. You'd share the passing with him, maybe even let yourself pass beyond the barrier with him." Loki grabbed a pair of force bracelets out of Kat's uniform pocket. Before she could recover, he slapped them around her wrists. Two thin strands of plastic, linked by an electrode. Every movement of the wrists and hands sent jolts of electricity through the special conductivity of the bracelets. Loki had endured incarceration with bracelets before. They were no fun.

Kat would have to have more endurance and will-power than he had to do more than sit quietly and answer his questions.

"How long will your captain keep this corridor free?" Loki grabbed her stun pistol and slid it through his belt. It rested neatly, as if it belonged there. The rifle he kicked farther down the corridor, never wanting to touch such a weapon again.

Kat stared mutely at the force bracelets.

"I asked you a question." He grabbed the bracelets by the electrode.

Kat gasped and paled. Her lips remained sealed.

"You're tougher than I thought. But then you are an O'Hara." Loki stepped back and thought a moment.

"Help me get Kim back to the lander."

"No."

"What do you mean, 'no?' "

"I am a prisoner of war. I do not have to aid and abet the enemy."

"We aren't your enemies. We're family."

Again she remained silent. But this time her venomous green eyes were riveted on him.

Loki squirmed. She looked very like Mum in that moment. He'd never been able to withstand Mum's stare. He always succumbed and told her everything when she fixed her gaze upon him like that.

"Very shortly, all hell is going to break loose and you will want to be in the docking bay." Loki looked around for an easy way to get them back into the rabbit hole without impaling Kim on a directional crystal. Or better yet, convince Kat to escort them through the corridors.

The heavy gravity of this deck was wearing on his thought processes. Or maybe the Tambootie he had ingested earlier had worn off.

"What can you three do to bring down an IMP cruiser alone?" she scoffed.

"Never underestimate the ingenuity of your brothers," Loki returned. He knelt and checked Kim again. His eyes opened and closed fitfully as he fought back to consciousness. Having him awake would help, but the numbness in his legs would take too long to wear off for him to handle the rabbit hole by himself let alone be of much use out here.

"Where is Konner?" Kat sat up straighter and looked around. "He disappeared halfway down that corridor." She jerked her head in the direction she had chased the middle brother.

Loki smiled and held her gaze. He could be enigmatic, too, when he wanted to.

"If I remember correctly, and I remember everything in precise detail, Konner is the engineer in the family. He was always dismantling things and rebuilding them better," Kat mused.

She sat in silent thought for a moment. "Oh, my God!" She struggled to stand. She winced several times as the force bracelets shot jolt after jolt of electricity through her.

Loki did not offer to help her.

"He's going to destroy the king stone. Why?"

"If you'd paid attention to the surveys of the planet below, you'd know," Loki replied.

"Every crewman and officer not assigned otherwise has their noses glued to portholes and surveys. This is an uncharted system with a habitable planet. They are all excited."

"And getting greedy. Big bonuses for discovering habitable planets. Bigger bonuses for discovering lost colonies," Loki said.

Kim stirred and moaned. But his eyes opened and stayed that way. He moved his head cautiously, checking his surroundings. Then he opened his eyes wide and moaned.

"She shot me. My own sister shot me."

"Yep. And she'll do it again if we give her half a chance." Loki handed the stun pistol to Kim. "Use it if she tries to escape."

Kat snorted.

Loki helped Kim to sit up, bracing his back against the bulkhead. His long legs straddled the hatch to the rabbit hole.

"You getting any feeling back?" Loki ran his hands down Kim's legs, looking sharply for any muscle reaction at all.

"Flashes and tingles," Kim replied.

Loki could not read his reaction as his youngest brother eyed their sister.

Come to think of it, she was mighty quiet, concentrating on the electrode of the force bracelets.

"Try to move your legs, Kim. You've got to be up and running by the time Konner finishes."

Kim's knee twitched under slight pressure.

"Breathe deep and even. Concentrate."

Kim flashed him a grin as if he knew more than Loki about the subject of breathing.

"He recovers fast," Kat said. She finally looked up from her study of the bracelets.

"We all do. A matter of survival."

"And possibly something else?" She twisted her wrists. The bracelets flashed. She winced.

The bracelets weren't supposed to flash. The current threading through the conductive plastic was designed to be silent and invisible.

Loki shifted his attention to Kat and the bracelets. Did they rest a little looser on her wrists than they had a few moments ago?

"You can't open the bracelets without a key," Loki said, somewhat puzzled. "I'm an expert with those things and I know the locks inside and out. You can't open them." He walked over to her, bent on examining the lock to make certain.

While he crouched beside her, Loki relieved her of the counter-grav units and strapped them to his own arms and feet. All the while he studied his sister and how she held her wrists.

"Wanna make a bet I can't open my own bracelets?" She smiled sweetly even as she lunged to her feet. She kept her hands together as she shoved them into Loki's jaw.

She no longer had the counter-grav holding back her blows.

Black-and-yellow stars burst before his eyes. His balance tilted. He shifted his weight forward. Veteran of too many brawls, he knew how to compensate and stay upright under a sucker punch. Without thinking, he swept one leg behind Kat's feet.

She fell backward. The bracelets dangled from one hand only. Her left swung back, preparing a new blow. If she was like the rest of the family, her dominant left hand was free.

Bad news.

Kat twisted as she went down and caught herself. She drew her feet back under her and jumped upright, only slightly hindered by the heavy gravity.

But she jumped back, toward the cross corridor.

Loki cursed himself. He should have manacled her feet as well. She had two more sets of force bracelets in her uniform hip pocket.

He dove after her, still fighting for clear vision and balance.

He caught up with her easily, propelled by the purloined equipment. She did not go far before he grabbed her right shoulder.

Too late.

Her left hand slapped a comm unit set into the bulkhead just below a ship's diagram.

"Captain Leonard. They're going after the king stone!" Kat yelled.

CHAPTER 26

KONNER FLEW into the crystal room at the exact center of the ship. The king stone and the first twelve drivers lived here.

He could not think. He just had to do.

An engineer turned at the sound of the portal irising open. Konner let loose with a blast from his stunner. It caught the man square in the chest before he had time to sound a protest. His body plunged backward, toward the bulkhead. In null g he bounced off the exposed pipes and conduits and spun in a new direction.

The recoil from the gun sent Konner into a roll. He compensated, firing in the opposite direction.

But the crystals' chatter rose to an unharmonic seventh chord.

Konner braced himself low against a driver crystal to prevent recoil from his weapon that would send him flying about the room.

A second and a third man went down as easily as the first. They, too, were propelled from wall to wall.

The crystals shrieked at the disruption of their routine maintenance.

Konner closed his ears and his mind to them. Deftly he caught each of the engineers and tethered them to the leashes attached to the bulkheads. If the ship had to dive into evasive maneuvers, the momentum could severely damage vulnerable humans. They had to have the leashes handy at all times.

Crystals, however seemed to glory in the challenge of rapid changes of direction and speed. As long as they were connected to the king stone. Without it, they grew confused and spurted energy in odd, and often dangerous, directions.

At the consoles around the room he checked each display. One of the drivers was out of alignment. It needed to be rotated a micrometer or two. It happened sometimes after a magnetic storm or when the ship achieved too low an orbit too quickly. The unusual planetary magnetics of MKO-IV could be playing havoc with the crystals.

Every instinct in Konner demanded he perform the adjustment.

Blindly, he slapped every console into sleep mode. Each crystal had to come off-line in order. No time for the long safety protocols. He had to get the king stone disconnected quickly.

First he cut the flow of nitrogen to the stones. The gaseous fuel flooding the crystals caused the monopoles to spit energy along the miles of fiber optics to the directional crystals. He could shut off the fuel source, but the stones still had massive amounts of energy contained within their force field.

Konner braced himself against the console labeled due north of the king stone. He found the fiber-optic cable in the first position. "Let's hope these guys use standard left to right." He closed his eyes, said a brief prayer to whatever God might listen, and pulled.

The cable did not want to let loose its connection. "S'murghin' stubborn dragon!" he yelled and yanked with all his might.

The cable broke loose.

The crystals shrieked loud enough to wake the techs.

Konner flew to the opposite bulkhead. He grabbed a leash with one hand to keep from bouncing around the room. "Hush now. This is for the good of my people," he whispered to the crystals.

Sparking energy spat from the end of the clear tubing. He capped it with a special clamp from the workbench beneath the console.

The south console was now directly beneath his butt. He loosed the first cable and began working on the number one here. It, too, resisted his attempt to disconnect it. But, eventually, it yielded to his pressure.

Too much time. He had to get on with this. On to the west and east consoles. Each disconnect came a little easier than the last. He was down to the last twelve when the clamps ran out.

Curses streamed from his mouth. He had to improvise. How?

Praying the next crystal did not decide to blast him he tied an overhand knot in the cable just before its connection to the console. Then he gritted his teeth and prepared to endure pain.

The cable came free. A dribble of sparks leaked out, not much in comparison to a fully live fiber optic, but enough to light a small city for a day. He kept his hands above the knot, hoping he remained safe. Now to keep the leaking energy from making the cable dance about. He wedged the knot between two exposed pipes along the bulkhead. So far so good.

At last he had all one hundred forty-four red directionals free of the king stone.

The king stone whined and strained loud and long as it sought to compensate for the loss of the center array by tapping into the other two circles of directionals at the bow and aft.

"I'm sorry." Konner felt as if his heart might break. With a few commands to the computer, he isolated the other two circles of directionals.

Now he had to tackle the twelve green drivers.

The king stone wailed a mighty protest. The big blue stone was dangerous when isolated. At any moment it could unleash forces no man had encountered and lived.

Konner could not listen. He could not think. He had to keep going now before he lost his nerve.

The green drivers were bigger than the reds and channeled proportionally larger amounts of energy. The cables did not want to knot. The leakage was more volatile. His hands grew raw from contact with the raw power.

The crystal techs began to stir in their tethers.

Konner looked over his shoulder for any indication that the blue king stone would protect itself and its family of crystals from disconnection and death.

"I have to do this," Konner apologized to the stone.

A headache slashed Konner like a laser wrench to the base of his skull. Too-white lightning flashed before his eyes, nearly blinding him.

"I'm sorry. But I have to do this. There is no other way."

(*There is always a better way.*)

Was that the stone speaking to him?

No, it could not be. The stones might be alive, but they were not sentient.

Were they?

The voice became a chuckle. The headache eased. But it did not go away.

Konner took a deep breath and cut the connections to the other two circles of drivers.

The force field went down.

The king stone was now alone.

He thought he heard a sob.

The ship lurched slightly. He grabbed hold of the console edge to keep the null g from throwing him into the bulkheads along with the semiconscious engineers. Without the crystal arrays, the vessel no longer compensated for collisions with space fragments. Most were too small to notice. Anything larger than his fist could throw the vessel off alignment.

Surely someone would notice that the arrays were off line and come to investigate. He had to hurry.

He took a deep breath to steady himself. Then another. The crystal chatter became less strident. Almost took on meaning. He inhaled again. Held it. Let it go until he felt as if his belly button met his backbone.

His focus grew more acute in the center. Fuzzy layers of bright yellow and blue surrounded the crystals. He peered more closely and saw deep into the core of the king stone. Light and energy blossomed outward, enveloping him.

He had to touch the blue stone.

Slowly he approached the stone and placed his hands on it, near the base.

Awareness of his body drifted from his mind. He knew only the channels to each crystal. A tiny beacon called to him from far, far away.

The mother stone.

If he just reached a little, he could touch her, become a part of the massive family of crystals communicating throughout the known galaxy. Every ship became a part of him. He understood each of their idiosyncrasies. They teased him. Flitting in and out of his perceptions, needing him to adjust this, fix that, align a pathway through the universe to connect them all.

He sighed. A sense of family welcomed him. Stronger, keener than the domineering embrace of his mother, the grudging respect of his brothers. More massive than the love that he shared with Dalleena, but not better.

Dalleena.

He knew what he had to do.

Still dazed from the oneness he shared with the stone, he withdrew his mind.

And then he twisted the king stone free of its base.

The king stone screamed. The sound battered his ears and his mind.

He jerked his hands away from the stone's agony.

"I can end your pain," he whispered. He grasped the stone with both hands. The cool facets blazed hot and angry.

He ignored the pain and yanked the king stone free.

Tears ran down his face. He cradled the stone in both arms, ready to hurl it against the bulkhead. But he couldn't. He was the stone. The stone was he.

He'd rather kill a man.

(*There are always alternatives.*)

Sobbing openly, still holding the king stone as if it were an injured child, he stepped out of the crystal circle.

"Put it back," an angry female demanded. "Put it back or I shoot you with a full load from this needle rifle."

CHAPTER 27

KONNER STILLED. His emotions evaporated. "If you shoot me, you damage the king stone."

He shrugged, shifting his grip on the king stone. In null g it weighed nothing. But the two-meter length of the thing made it awkward. By the time he reached the docking bay on the outer rim, the crystal would weigh more than he did.

Before that, he had to get past Commander Amanda Leonard, captain of the *Jupiter*. She blocked the only exit to the crystal room.

The engineers thrashed against their tethers. The simple straps would not restrain them long.

If only he had some way of getting Commander Leonard out of the way, for just a few seconds.

Nothing loose floated about the crystal array. Everything was strapped down and out of reach. As was his stunner.

Leonard raised her rifle and took careful aim. "In null g the stone will not drop. I'm a crack shot. I can kill you with a single needle in the eye." The newest upgrade had the option of firing a single needle. The weapon Loki had used to kill Hanassa could only fire a wide spray.

Konner couldn't take the chance she was bluffing with the capabilities of her weapon or her ability.

Well, the magic had been working for him so far. He concentrated on his stunner, holstered on his belt on the right side, for easy draw with his left hand. He shifted the king stone again, bringing the left end up in front of his face.

"Care to take a chance on hitting the stone?" he asked. The words spilled forth, but his mind was on the stunner, willing it into his right hand where he cradled the base of the crystal. "Those things don't shoot on a straight line. They spray the needles across a target area. You'd also hit one or more of your own crew behind me." He pretended ignorance of the new design.

The stunner remained in place, impervious to the prod from his mind.

How comfortable was Amanda Leonard in null g? She seemed to have braced herself against the door-jamb to keep herself in place and prevent recoil.

Konner was in the middle of the room with only some fading directional crystals, barely a meter high, as a brace. Just a little spring upward would propel him as high as he wanted to go. The right amount of pressure against the balls of his feet would keep his movement slow, give him more control over his trajectory.

Without thinking further, he sent himself up. Maybe he could kick the ship's senior officer in the temple and knock her out.

Commander Leonard followed his passage with the muzzle of her needle rifle.

Then the stunner nudged his right fingers. He was so startled at the delayed reaction to his mental command, he almost brushed the weapon aside. Before it floated away, he snagged it with one finger. A little shift of his hand and he had it braced against the crystal and his index finger on the trigger.

No way to aim. No time to regret.

"Sorry about this, Commander." Konner pressed the firing button on the black box of the stunner. A bolt of red energy hit Leonard on the side of her face.

She slapped the place as if she had been bit by an insect. Her fingers caught the tail end of the stunning blast. Her hand fell to her side twitching as her knees collapsed and her eyes rolled up.

"Hey," one of the engineers shouted.

Konner twisted and shot all three of the tethered men. They rocked like pendulums at the end of their leashes. The recoil sent Konner against the bulkhead near the ceiling joint. He banged his head against the cerama/metal plates. Black stars bloomed before his eyes.

And so did the web of blue energy connecting the transactional gravitons and the planet. The crystal in his arms seemed to expand as it drew the energy inside itself, inside Konner.

How could the king stone still be connected to the rest of the universe? Did it communicate with the mother stone even now?

He swallowed, trying to understand.

The crystal array came closer. Konner fought to restrain his drift across the room. He checked the air circulation ducts. He should be moving toward them as unseen compressors moved the air about and scrubbed it of CO_2.

No, he was moving toward the center of the crystal array. The king stone wanted to go home. He could not allow that. He had to get back to the docking bay. Fast. Before either Commander Leonard or the engineers awoke and sounded an alarm.

Cautious about recoil, Konner twisted around. Then he pushed against one of the driver crystals. He aimed for the hatchway and the exit. Years of practice in free fall made his aim true. But he had to shift the king stone to keep from banging it against the doorjamb. A damaged stone would solve many problems. It might also kill him. At least break his heart.

An image of Dalleena rose before his mind's eye. He smiled. If anything could heal him after a catastrophe with the crystal, she could. He did not want to put that kind of burden upon her. He had to protect the stone.

At the next intersection Konner pushed against the first solid object he encountered. He sped down the long ramp to the next level. Near the end of it, gravity began to grab him. He anticipated and landed with both feet on the deck, knees bent. And another long spring until heavier gravity forced him back on the decking. With each pace toward the outer decks and each descent down a ladder, the stone grew heavier in his arms. By the time he reached normal Earth gravity, sweat poured down his face and back. His toes were bruised and his calves ached.

He spotted the passageway he needed into the heaviest gravity and hoped he'd land somewhere near his brothers. He needed help with the stone. His fingers were numb from grasping it so tightly. His shoulders felt as if the stone were wrenching both his arms free of the joints. Air burned all the way down his throat to his lungs.

His heart beat too quickly and irregularly.

And still he felt the giant crystal pushing him backward to its home. It screamed in his mind at the loss of its family.

"I promise, I'll reunite you to at least one array," Konner soothed the crystal.

It did not believe him.

"How about if I find a new task for you?" Though what that would be, he had no idea.

"Intruder Alert! Intruder Alert!" A male voice came over the comm system. He sounded so calm.

"All crystal techs report to manual stations. Repeat, all crystal techs to manual. This is an emergency. All decks, all shifts. Be on the lookout for the O'Hara brothers. They are aboard. Do not shoot. They have the king stone. Repeat. Do not shoot them. Approach and apprehend with caution.

St. Bridget! Konner was willing to bet that all the bay doors had been sealed. No one was leaving the ship with the king stone or without it.

*   *   *

What are we to do with the intruder in orbit? Stargod Konner tells us we cannot allow it to fly away. This requires much thought and subtle action.

We have powers we have not used in centuries. A little tug here, a push there. The intruder will not stay in orbit long now. Nor will they fly away.

*   *   *

Dalleena lay flat amid the tall grasses on the verge of the plowed fields. From here she could watch the village. Raaskan, the headman, and his wife Poolie lay just beyond her.

Inside the village, dozens of armed men and women from the landers ransacked the huts, pulling out baskets of food, tools, clothing, everything portable. They laughed and hooted over the fine spears and arrows men had labored over for many nights around the fire. They gobbled handfuls of raw grain and spat them out again. One woman tore off a hunk of dried meat with her teeth. She made an ugly face and spat. One of her teeth came out along with the soggy blob of jerky. She howled and rubbed her jaw. The others nearly doubled over in laughter.

"All our stores gone to waste," Raaskan muttered as he pounded the ground with his fist. "They'll squander every morsel of grain, every basket of jerked meat. And we will starve this winter. I have had enough of starving." He began to rise, eyes glinting dangerously.

"No!" Dalleena and Poolie both said through gritted teeth. They hauled him back into the protection of the grasses.

"We saved most of the stores. Stargod Konner told us to leave behind just a little as bait," Dalleena reminded him.

"We did not save enough to feed our village all winter," Raaskan replied, still scowling.

One of the intruders looked their way, narrowing his eyes.

Dalleena held her breath, willing the man to forget he'd detected movement out of his peripheral vision. Apparently, she did not have Stargod Loki's talent for influencing minds. The man turned and fully faced her and the others. He raised his weapon and shouted something at his comrades. She had to concentrate a long time to understand the rapid stream of clipped syllables.

"Jimmie, did you see anything?" The guard took a step forward. "I'm going to investigate. This place is spooky. Cover my back."

A second guard stepped into his place, weapon at the ready, eyes scanning the fields, back and forth. Back and forth. He'd spot anything that moved. "Watch your step, Brewster," he said.

The first guard, Brewster, came closer. His weapon moved with his gaze across the stubble in the fields. For half a heartbeat, his gaze lingered right above where Dalleena crouched. Then he moved on, stepping cautiously, alert to his surroundings.

Silently, Dalleena cursed whatever gods had cursed the people of the Stargods. Then she cursed the intruders from another world.

The guard looked sharply above Dalleena's head,

toward the marshlands that separated the fields from the pasture of wild cattle. He raised his weapon and aimed.

"What?" Dalleena mouthed to Raaskan.

He shook his head.

One finger length at a time, Dalleena turned her head in the direction where the guard looked so intently. Raaskan and Poolie edged backward, deeper into the high grass.

"S'murghit!" Another curse escaped her lips, this one not so silently.

"Halt!" Brewster called. He shifted his attention and his aim up, away from Dalleena, toward the tree line.

Dalleena froze. The ground beneath her vibrated slightly. She placed her tracking hand flat upon the dirt. Many feet. Human feet. tramped toward her.

She risked turning her head a little farther.

A wild red bull, his long fur ruffling in the breeze, sprang to his feet. No longer warily chewing his cud, he pawed the ground and lowered his head at the line of men approaching.

Taneeo, the priest with the broken leg, led two dozen men. He had discarded his splints. He walked with only a slight limp.

How? After only two days! Stargod Kim must have worked a wondrous miracle for such a cure.

Then she noticed that each man in the line carried one or more of the weapons and communications devices the villagers had liberated from the intruders last night. They carried them across open arms and open palms.

And Taneeo carried a bit of white cloth dangling from a stick.

She recognized the fine weave of the "handkerchief" Konner had used last night to cleanse his face before retiring.

CHAPTER 28

"**A**T LEAST WE can tell Mum that you are alive," Kim said to his sister. He studied her intently for familial resemblance.

Her sparkling green eyes were truer in color than Mum's paler hazel. All three of the boys had midnight blue eyes. Kat Talbot had the same length of leg, red hair, and fair skin as the rest of the family. Mum was shorter but not by much. Their father must have been quite tall.

Kim had no memories of his father other than a long shadow offering comfort when he awoke with a nightmare.

Hard to tell if Kat had a figure at all beneath the now rumpled uniform. But she gave the impression of lean fitness.

She possessed a dangerous, feral quality, ready to lunge at any moment without warning; even with force bracelets restraining her wrists and ankles above her soft ship boots.

Kim edged a little away from her.

They sat along the interior bulkhead, resting as much as possible in the heavy gravity.

"You expect to get out of this escapade alive? Your Mum will be lucky to ever see you again," Kat said. She'd lost the sarcasm in the last half hour. "Do you have any feeling yet?" She touched his right leg tentatively with both hands. Hard to separate them with the force bracelets.

Kim fought to keep from twitching under her touch. Survival might depend upon the element of surprise. For the first time in months he wished his boots had not worn out. Boots would hide his feet when he flexed them, trying to restore circulation and feeling.

"Barely." Kim sighed deeply. "When you go dirtside, will you tell my wife that I died honorably, from battle wounds?" He tried to make his expression imploring. "I just hope our son will understand why he does not have a father."

Both Loki and Kat raised their eyebrows at him. Kat looked a little wistful. And sad. No one had ever found their father.

"I have a nephew?" she whispered.

"You didn't tell me that Hes is pregnant again," Loki said accusingly.

"Not enough time," Kim shrugged off the half-truth. Last night as he lay beside Hestiia he'd placed his hand upon her belly with affection. She'd been asleep when he finally crawled into bed after hours of experiments with the Tambootie. With the drug still coursing through his veins, he had sensed an extra presence beneath his fingertips. A heartbeat. A stirring of personality. "I only found out last night myself."

"And you can tell so soon that it's a boy? I thought the natives were primitive." Kat sat up a little straighter. Alert curiosity banished her soft expression "Even the most sophisticated medical equipment cannot determine fetal gender until the end of the first trimester."

"We don't need medical equipment. We just need Kim on this planet." Loki looked very smug.

"Explain."

"Psi powers augmented by local conditions." Kim jumped to explain before Loki went off into some wild tale.

Kat's face went blank. She was hiding something.

Kim caught Loki's gaze. He nudged his brother with his mind to read their sister's thoughts.

Loki's eyes crossed. He concentrated for a long moment then shook his head. "She has erected barriers." He sounded exhausted. The Tambootie must be wearing off.

"Psi powers have never been documented," Kat said. She sounded as tired as Loki.

"Just because they have not been documented, does not mean they do not exist. We discounted them, too. Until we went dirtside here." Loki picked up the train of thought.

"This planet is magical. But it won't be for long once your esteemed GTE gets hold of it," Kim continued the persuasion. "The first thing the GTE surveyors will do is kill all of the dragons."

Kat shifted her attention from one brother to the other. "Dragons?" she gulped. "Dragons do not exist."

"They do here," both brothers jumped in.

"I've ridden on the back of one," Loki said. "More magnificent than piloting any craft built by humans."

"You've had psychic experiences, haven't you, Kat," Kim pressed her. "Probably just flashes. Hardly enough to document. But enough to make you wonder."

"What happens to you, Kat?" Loki asked. "Do you sense what others are thinking? Do you know what will happen before it happens? Or do you move things with your mind? Like the force bracelet you opened earlier."

"Perhaps you have touched someone who has received a mortal wound and watched them heal beneath your hands," Kim added. To emphasize his point he raised his right knee, the one that should still be paralyzed, until she touched him.

She gulped and opened her mouth as if to speak.

"Intruder Alert! Intruder Alert!" came over the comm system. The lights turned red and began to flash.

"Captain Leonard must have found Konner." Kat struggled to her feet. The force bracelets must be burning into her flesh. She reached with both restrained hands for the stunner that should have been holstered right at her hip.

Loki held up the weapon with one finger. He grinned sardonically. "Looking for this?"

"You have to get back to your ship immediately. Before she seals all the doors." Kat looked frantically up and down the corridor.

"You come with us, Kat," Loki said with the authority of the senior member of the family.

"You need to find out what your mind is capable of, Kat," Kim added. "We can help you do it. But only if we have some time, free of pressures from your crew."

"Where the hell is Konner?" she asked rather than answering.

"Here," Konner said from the end of the cross corridor. "Loki, I need help." His voice came in gasps and grunts.

Both Loki and Kat took off down the corridor, as fast as they could in the heavy gravity. *St. Bridget,* how much pain could she endure before she collapsed? Kim followed more slowly. Every joint and muscle from his waist down ached from the stunner blast. The gravity did not help much.

Kat seemed to be made of sterner stuff than he.

He found Loki and Kat supporting the magnificent blue king stone. Konner slumped against the bulkhead, half upright. Sweat glistened on his skin and soaked his shirt.

Loki and Kat tugged in opposite directions, neither willing to give up possession of the crystal.

"Can't you three get it through your thick heads? If you won't run far and fast right now, your only hope is to turn yourselves in, without violence. I'll see that you get a fair trial," Kat yelled.

"There is another way," Kim said more calmly than he felt. Alarms blared all around him. He sensed panic heading toward them.

Then he heard a fierce pounding upon the sealed doors on either end of the corridor.

"There is only one way in the GTE. Obedience to the law," Kat argued. "You three may be my long lost family, but my loyalty is to the GTE, this ship, and my captain."

"Our loyalty is to the family and the people dirt-side who depend upon us for safety. Neither the family nor our people can have that within the GTE," Loki spat. "You are invading private space."

"You are coming with us, Kat," Kim said. He closed his eyes and prayed for forgiveness. With luck his mental plea would reach her.

Then he slammed his fist into her jaw.

He just barely caught her end of the king stone before she collapsed against the bulkhead.

"Grab her, Konner. We are getting out of here. All of us." Without looking back, Kim led his brothers to the nearest rabbit hole hatch. His back and leg muscles screamed in protest and threatened to buckle with every step.

* * *

Loki checked both of his brothers where they slumped in the cockpit of the lander. The king stone rested snugly in crash webbing. Why had Konner insisted on bringing the monster? Escape would be so much easier without the crystal.

Kat fought her force bracelets from the jump seat where Konner had deposited her. Her wrists had already turned raw. At this rate they'd soon bleed.

"Will you please give me the codes to override the captain's seal on the bay doors?" Loki asked Kat with a veneer of politeness.

"Go feed yourself to your dragon," she spat and tried to kick him.

He dodged her blow and caught her knees with one hand. Slowly he lifted, throwing her balance back against the bulkhead.

"This is the last time I ask politely, baby sister. Mum always taught us to be polite. Will you please give me the codes?"

She glared venom at him.

"Okay, we do this the hard way." He dropped her knees abruptly. Her feet landed with a thud. She winced from the pain of the force bracelets.

"I have a little Tambootie left in my pocket," Kim said. His voice sounded strangled. All three of them were exhausted and hurting from too strenuous activity in too heavy gravity.

"What is this Tambootie?" Kat asked.

"Give it to me. We need those codes." Loki put out his hands.

Kim deposited one partial leaf and several fragments into his palm. He kept the largest piece for himself, chewing on it hungrily.

Loki's skin begin to tingle upon contact. One layer of fatigue washed away from him. He popped all of the pieces into his mouth. He sucked on them a moment, moistening the dried leaves and drawing out any lingering oils.

A now familiar rush of sensation sharpened his

focus. A layer of energy emerged from atop every object. Mostly he saw a white after shadow. But when he looked at Kat, flares of bright red shot forth from her brow and the top of her head. With her red hair, she looked like a sun's corona.

Or the lava pit boiling beneath the blown-out volcano.

Loki banished thoughts of that place. Too many bad memories crowded out what he had to do.

"What are you hiding, baby sister?" he asked quietly. Immediately her corona of colored light shrank and blanched to a mere glare.

Loki clenched his eyes closed a moment and shook his head.

"Breathe deeply," Kim coaxed him. "Inhale long and hard. Exhale long. Get rid of all the air inside you. Good. Now inhale. Exhale. Again."

Loki obeyed the soothing voice. More layers of fatigue and worry slid off of him. He opened his eyes again.

Kat sat before him. If he looked closely, he could see through her skin to subcutaneous fat, muscle tissue, and bone. Her jaw muscles tightened. She ground her teeth.

Fascinating.

"Deeper," he whispered to himself. "Deeper."

Her skull seemed to dissolve before his gaze. He thought he saw tiny bolts of lightning firing across the surface of her brain.

"Past the brain, into the mind." Deeper he went, following chains of synapses into the center. The chains became tunnels. They took on colors. Yellow for muscle reactions, blue for autonomic functions. Green for memory. Red for knowledge.

And a black wall standing between him and the piece of knowledge he desperately needed.

"Open," he commanded. A few bricks seemed to fall away from the wall.

She threw up new ones as fast as he tore down the old.

"She's blocking me," Loki said. At least he hoped he said it.

"Relax a moment. Gather your resources," Kim instructed. His voice remained quiet, calm, soothing.

Loki withdrew to the outer surface of her mind. Then Kim began talking. He spoke of fathers and sons. He whispered about the sweetness of holding his baby son when the child arrived. He spoke of Konner's loneliness, missing his son, and needing to get back to Aurora in time for the custody hearing. He talked of Mum's obsession with finding her missing daughter.

The black bricks began to crumble and thin. Kat had held firm against frontal assault. She dissolved under the subtle pressure of her own need for family.

How did Kim know what to say to her? He'd taken the Tambootie. It must have opened his telepathy.

Loki turned his attention back to his mission. The moment he sensed Kat relaxing, he dove through the barrier in her mind.

A beautiful black rose opened before him. The lush velvet petals spread. Each one contained a string of numbers. Some made no sense to him. But deep within the rose he found what he needed. Three words followed by six numbers.

"Got it." He pulled out. Dizziness and disorientation. The cockpit looked strange, harsh, unreal. Nothing fit. He put out his hand expecting to brace himself upon the back of the pilot's chair. He missed by three centimeters. The rest of the cabin tilted to the right by the same distance.

Konner slid an arm beneath Loki's shoulder. Kim just sat and grinned.

"Breathe, Loki. You have to breathe. It takes a moment to clear your mind after an intense session," Kim said quietly.

"You've been practicing," Loki said. His words sounded slurred.

"You should, too. And so should Konner. We have to be able to control these powers."

"Let's worry about that after we get out of here."

Loki opened an interface with *Jupiter*'s computer. He scanned the menu presented on the screen.

"Is it voice activated?" he asked, keeping his back to Kat.

Kim watched her. He was better at reading faces. He'd alert them all to minute changes in her expression.

No answer from either of them.

"Konner, hack into the system. I need to override voice and go to manual."

Konner swung around and began working the co-pilot's screens. Some of the worry lines had eased around the middle brother's eyes. "Good to go. You have a manual connection to the central computer."

Loki typed in the three words and the string of numbers.

Access Denied. The words flashed before him. *Access Denied. Begin countdown to automatic defense system.*

Loki gulped. He swung around to face his sister.

She smiled blandly at him. "I'll die before I give you the correct codes. We'll all die in thirty seconds."

CHAPTER 29

"WE HAVE TO HIDE!" Dalleena said as she slithered backward on her belly. She'd moved only a few feet when her bare feet touched mud. She shuddered. She hated swamps. The murky water and unknown depths hid bloodsucking creatures, flesh-eating reptiles, and plants with leaves as sharply edged as one of the new iron knives.

Or so she believed.

Taneeo and his followers continued to march toward the intruders, weapons and communications devices still proffered as peace offerings. The men's eyes did not focus. They stared blindly ahead, walking as if bewitched.

Taneeo grinned widely. He almost sauntered in triumph. The limp evaporated with each step.

"I must stop the idiot," Raaskan said. "How did he escape Pryth's vigilance?" He tried to stand. Once more, Poolie held him in place. Nearly as tall as Dalleena, she was strong from long hours of working the fields and spindle.

Raaskan glared at his wife.

She returned his gaze levelly and with meaning.

"Taneeo has to learn that not all problems can be solved with peace and compromise," he hissed.

"Especially when it means he's betraying us," Dalleena muttered. She didn't care if the others heard her or not. She was leaving. One of them had to remain free and safe to tell Konner and his brothers about Taneeo's betrayal and the defection of half the men from the village.

Gritting her teeth, she dared the swamp. At least the mushy edges of it.

When her knees felt soggy, she risked rising to a crouch. From that position Taneeo and his men were clearly visible. The intruders still gathered twenty paces away. They carried their weapons warily and balanced on the balls of their feet, ready to run forward in attack, or flee as events evolved.

Neither group seemed to notice the rustling grasses where Raaskan and Poolie crept toward Dalleena. Beside a rotting tree snag they peered around, seeking the best path. Dalleena motioned retreat.

"Big Red," Raaskan whispered. He jerked his head toward the shaggy wild bull that had risen to its feet.

It plodded toward the marshy verge of the pasture. Morning sunshine showed the sharp tips and smooth curve of his horns. From tip to tip, those horns spread as wide as a man could spread his arms. Big Red's cows shifted their grazing closer to the tree line, away from the village and the armed intruders. Their red fur seemed to fade to gray and shadow as they merged with the protective cover. Movement alone would betray their presence to predators.

Big Red, on the other hand, drew attention away from his cows. He pawed at the ground and bellowed his annoyance at the proximity of so many people.

The bull stood between Dalleena and safety. He made enough noise to attract the attention of the intruders, across three fields and a swamp. Laughter from the intruders at the bull's antics. They did not fear it. They should.

"Stillness," Raaskan said under his breath. "The hunted stands so still he blends into his cover. The hunter cannot see him until he moves."

Dalleena took a deep breath and willed herself to obey. Every instinct in her body told her to flee.

If only Konner were here to protect her.

But he, too, needed to stay free of the invaders.

If only she could hear the words passed between the Others and Taneeo.

The priest made a gesture and each of his followers moved forward in turn and deposited the weapon or communicator he held at the feet of the foremost guard. Other intruders crept out of the village. The ones with the most decorations on their clothing grabbed guns and comms from the growing pile first.

When all of the stolen gear had been returned, the intruders, as one, turned their weapons upon Taneeo and the others.

They crumpled to the ground, startled looks frozen on their faces.

Fine thanks for their act of goodwill.

Dalleena swallowed back the bile that threatened to choke her.

Poolie rested a hand upon her shoulder in mute comfort. "We saw much the same actions from Hanassa before the Stargods liberated us from him. But Hanassa drew blood and gloried in death. The invaders have only stunned the traitors. These weaklings fear death and do not kill lightly. We must use this against them."

"Yes, we must," Dalleena agreed. "I will watch. You two go and gather the others. You are more used to hunting stealthily than I. Go in secret. After sundown, before moonrise, we will liberate our neighbors. Also in secret."

But Konner and his brothers would return before then. She had to warn them. She would not allow them to stumble into a trap as wicked as a patch of devil's vine.

How could she watch the village and wait for Konner at the place he told her he would return?

*   *   *

The betrayal becomes obvious. We must stop this. But we cannot. With our magic and awesome defenses, too many innocents would be caught in the storm. Even a dragon dream will not affect the traitor. For he is one of us.

We will concentrate on the Others. We can accomplish something positive there. We pull upon the ship in orbit with our united minds. We will it to crash and never fly again.

*   *   *

"Read the codes back to me from right to left," Konner demanded. His voice sounded harsh, bruised to his own ears. He didn't have time to worry about it.

Twenty-four, twenty-three. The computer counted down the seconds.

"Um, 763997 Alpha, um," Loki stammered.

Konner watched his brother's eyes swivel right to left, left to right, and back again.

Nineteen, eighteen, seventeen.

"Standard protocol is left to right," Loki protested.

Konner felt like shaking his older brother. "Kat is left-handed. Like the rest of us. Her brain wants to read right to left even though she's been forced to learn to read left to right. Give me the codes backward."

Kat opened her eyes wide. Her nostrils pinched and she clenched her teeth. He had guessed correctly.

Ten, nine, eight, seven.

"Alpha 7997367, beta, omega, pi." Loki looked deflated.

Konner punched in the code. His fingers moved rapidly over the interface. The countdown stalled at *three*. The bay doors creaked open, slowly. Oh, so very slowly.

He breathed in short gasps.

Kat slumped against her jump seat.

"Strap in, everyone. We're blasting out of here. Fast. Before Commander Leonard has a chance to scramble fighters." Before the doors finished opening.

Konner punched in the launch protocol. Engines fired beneath him. Cockpit lights dimmed.

He felt lighter. His lungs drew in air more easily. Gravity lessened its drag on his muscles.

That had to be his imagination. His body reacted to the surge of adrenaline and made him feel lighter. Momentum should keep *Jupiter* spinning and, therefore, the gravity at a normal rate far longer than this. Planetary gravity should only assert a minute influence on the ship at this time.

He prayed. All they needed now was for the ship's orbit to deteriorate too quickly, before Commander Leonard had time to evacuate all personnel and salvage much needed stores.

Would hearing the death screams of hundreds of trapped innocents be worse than his vision of Lieutenant Pettigrew dying?

He had to weigh the loss of innocent lives among the Coros if he failed in his mission to ground the IMPs for all time.

Konner's hands began to shake.

"This is going to need some finesse, Loki. Can you take command?"

"Finesse is my middle name," Loki said on a big grin.

"No, it isn't. You are Mathew Kameron O'Hara," Kat said.

"A lot you know," Loki said back. "Let me show you some real flying. Hang on."

Kat snorted. But she held on to the edge of her seat between her knees as best she could. The simple waist restraint on the jump seat offered only minor protection.

Konner's head snapped back as Loki slammed the lander forward. Gravity increased with acceleration as it compounded the spin on the primary vessel. Pressure built in his chest. He found it difficult to breathe.

He heard metal scrape against metal. His teeth ached and his spine cringed. The lander edged through the partially opened doors with no room to spare.

Then they burst free of the cruiser. Gravity fell back to an acceptable level. Loki flipped the lander around to circle *Jupiter* and aim for the planet.

A squadron of fighters scrambled into position to block them.

"We'll have to shoot our way through," Loki muttered.

"The weapons array lay at Konner's fingertips. Everything looked odd, out of reach, misplaced. Kim monitored sensors and engineering. The layout was backward from *Rover*. Konner should have engineering and communications. Kim should have sensors and weapons.

"If I know Captain Leonard, she's ordered her flyboys to take out the cockpit," Kat said. A smug smile crept across her face. "They'll leave the cargo area intact. She wants the king stone back. She won't let your death stand in her way."

"We've a few tricks up our sleeves," Loki muttered.

"Why didn't you just smash the crystal, Konner? Life would be easier," Kim asked.

In the back of Konner's head, he heard the king stone crying out to its family of driver and directional crystals. It had never been alone since before it was a tiny seed in an omniscium bath.

"Look out! Vultures at three o'clock," Kim shouted.

Konner slammed his palm flat on the interface, firing whatever responded. He closed his eyes and prayed that the fighters would veer away and no one would get killed. Least of all the king stone.

*   *   *

Loki closed his eyes and pushed the throttle forward. One nice long smooth motion. Acceleration pushed him back into his chair. He listened to the ship. Listened to the constant hum of active minds. Waiting. Waiting until it felt right.

He jerked the ship right and "down" relative to his internal horizon. Only when the ship began to shudder from the speed and angle of reentry did he ease up. Still without looking he thrust the controls to port, up, down, starboard, down.

To his right he heard Konner mutter a prayer every time he fired weapons. Kim shouted orders to both of them. Kat sneered at every word said, every action taken.

Loki tuned them out. Now he listened for the planet. The obscure, primitive, raw, and unforgiving place that had grabbed his heart and promised him everything he'd dreamed of. The place he had to protect at all costs.

Without the king stone, the IMPs could neither leave, nor communicate with civilization. If every crystal tech aboard took continual shifts of two hours on, four off, *Jupiter* might achieve something close to light speed. Not enough to make it to the jump point in less than a year. Without the king stone, they could not jump. He had to keep them from retrieving the stone. Even if it cost him and his siblings their lives.

Why hadn't Konner smashed the crystal when he had the chance? But he could not read his brother's mind and evade the fighters.

Up, down, port, and starboard, always angling closer to the planet. The green atmospheric layer glowed beneath him. He plunged into it. Leveled out. Shot to port.

His right side tingled where a bolt of energy seared the edge of the cockpit. A strange whistling came to his ears. More than tinnitus ringing against his eardrums from the rapid changes in direction and acceleration.

"Sensors clogged," Konner said on a sigh of relief. He'd not be shooting any weapons for a while.

"Femto point hull breach," Kim reported. As he said the words, he unstrapped and reached for the repair kit.

"What is that stuff?" Kat leaned forward to peer out the windshield.

"Diatomaceous plant life, lives in the uppermost reaches of the atmosphere," Kim replied. His hands were busy with a caulk gun filled with liquid cerama/metal. It would harden quickly and seal most small holes up to the diameter of a man's pinky finger.

"It eats the metal out of the hull alloy unless we bathe the shuttles every trip," Loki added.

"No wonder the planet looks green from space," Kat said. Curiosity seemed to have calmed her antagonism.

Loki felt like he had to say something. Anything.

He couldn't think what. The ship and his evasive course demanded all of his attention. If he thought about his maneuvers, he'd overthink and make a mistake.

He kept up a course that made the foothill approach to the volcano look flat and easy. Occasional shots zinged past them. A few came close.

"They are shooting blind," Konner said quietly. He looked pale and shaken. Shooting back at IMPs had never bothered him before. Why now?

Loki was a fine one to ask. He'd killed a man, Hanassa, and nearly followed him into death, linked to his mind by psychic talents.

Another shot pinged the tail of the lander in a glancing shot. Enough to send him careening into a spin.

"Have the fighters got new technology for listening to us?" he asked, not expecting an answer. "Tech we don't know about."

Kat said nothing. She looked pointedly at the ceiling rather than return his gaze.

"Not that I've heard," Konner said. He usually heard about every innovation, public and military. "But we've been gone for months. Between civilized worlds for months before that. I thought I was up to date when we jumped to this planet. Maybe I wasn't."

Kat bit her cheeks and kept her mouth closed.

"Okay, little sister," Loki whispered. "I'm trusting your silence to be a 'yes' answer. Not a word out of anyone. They may be listening to echoes of our voices." Loki abruptly changed course. He nosed upward. A sharp climb almost took him out of the green layer of microscopic plants that should have blinded the IMPs' ship as well as the lander's sensors. He'd never spent so long a time in the green and wondered how much damage the plants would do to the hull before they safely hit dirtside.

The shots continued, barely missing. They must be following engine emissions.

"Going back to surrender?" Kat asked hopefully.

Kim grabbed the ubiquitous duct tape and started strapping it over her mouth.

Loki put the lander into a dive and shook his head at Kim. No sense in maintaining silence.

"Not on your life. I wouldn't give Captain Leonard the satisfaction," Loki whispered.

"You may have severed communications, but we have a diplomatic attaché aboard. Her father will move galactic parliaments to get her back."

A funny feeling began jumping in Loki's sternum.

Kim moved to close Kat's mouth with duct tape anyway. Loki shook his head "no."

"You haven't been in orbit long enough for the GTE to triangulate your position," Konner said, also on a whisper. He didn't sound as happy as he should. "And I'm betting that when you found the jump point you did not have time to transmit the coordinates."

Kat just sat there smiling smugly.

Damn.

"The diplomatic attaché can't be too important if she allowed the captain to divert onto a wild lumbird chase," Kim said. He shrugged.

Loki breathed a little easier. The last time he'd communicated with Cyndi she had said she'd enter the diplomatic corps before she married the sniveling flunky her father had selected for her. But Cyndi would never allow a mere commander captaining an IMP cruiser to divert her for long.

Unless . . .

"Whose idea was it for *Jupiter* to sit long enough to search for the jump point?" he asked Kat, looking directly into her eyes, praying that he'd be able to detect a lie.

"Mine," she replied. "I knew you had disappeared at those coordinates. I've been searching for you guys for a long time. Easy to convince my captain that IMP priorities required us to investigate outlaws and smugglers before shuttling a dippo around the galaxy."

"And you just happened to mention to your blonde dippo why you could not deliver her to her destination on time," Loki said quietly. His gut wanted to sink to his feet.

"Of course." Kat did not contradict the dippo's hair color. "As soon as I mentioned the name O'Hara, she agreed wholeheartedly that we must pursue you. In fact, Lucinda Baines even took a turn at the sensors."

"Shit."

Loki forgot evasive maneuvers. He forgot the king stone. He did remember to polarize the hull as he put the lander into a steep dive into the atmosphere. Like he should have done in the first place. Instead he had needed to show off for his long-lost sister and impress her with his piloting skills.

Nothing would impress Kat. She was an O'Hara.

Dirtside, he and his brothers had allies. The O'Haras were gods on the planet below. A few fighters would not have a chance there.

But he left his heart and his enthusiasm aboard *Jupiter*.

"Cyndi," he muttered over and over. Lucinda Baines. "Cyndi" to friends and her lover. How could he justify stranding every last person aboard *Jupiter* dirtside when one of them was the love of his life. The reason he had endured Mum's manipulations and obsessions just to get enough money to bribe his way back to citizenship.

He'd never get that precious change in status on the official database.

And he'd never earn Cyndi's forgiveness for hijacking her transport and stranding her in the middle of nowhere.

CHAPTER 30

(W*ELCOME! Welcome, welcome,*) Irythros chortled in Konner's mind. The red-tipped dragon flew loops and twirls around the fighters and the lander.

"You're going to crash into that thing!" Kat choked.

Konner's respect for her courage rose a facet. She didn't scream, though clearly she wanted to. She clenched her eyes closed and began murmuring some personal prayer. He couldn't catch the words.

"Irythros is smarter than we are," Konner replied, almost chuckling at the sight of the red-tipped dragon. "He will avoid us."

(*Of course I will. Only a yearling silver dragon just out of the nest has so little control over his wings that he would make contact with* Rover,) the dragon crowed.

The others in the lander did not react as if they heard Irythros. He must be transmitting on a tight beam to Konner only.

Hello, my friend, Konner replied, also on a tight beam. This telepathy talent was growing stronger with practice. Or maybe proximity to the dragon helped him. *Any news?*

(*Trouble.*) The joy vanished from the dragon's voice.

What kind of trouble? Alarm built in Konner. Fear

of IMP troops capturing and molesting Dalleena crowded out coherent thought.

(*Your mate is safe,*) Irythros reassured him. (*Safer than you. I must protect you when, and however, I can.*)

Konner's head emptied of external thoughts. He felt a little light-headed and disoriented.

What in St. Bridget's name did the dragon mean?

(*We of the nimbus have exiled the one you call Sam Eyeam, though he gives himself another name. But the beacon still speaks to the stars. One you should not trust has betrayed you.*)

Who, Irythros? Who should I not trust? Konner asked. Worry began to gnaw at his stomach and the back of his neck.

(*We of the nimbus may not speak his name.*)

Hanassa.

Irythros squeaked a loud protest that stabbed at Konner's eardrum as well as his mind.

"What is that thing?" Kat asked. Her voice still sounded strained but she had opened her eyes.

"That, baby sister, is a dragon," Loki said. He beamed with pride.

"St. Bridget, those things really do exist," she breathed. Now she leaned forward for a better look at the creature through the windscreen. Sunlight sparkled along his crystalline fur, reflecting it back to them in a myriad of prisms.

"Is that blood showing through his horns and wing veins?"

"Doubtful," Kim replied. "Each adult male dragon sports a different color. I understand the females are iridescent, all colors blending into no color at all. This one still has hints of silver in his hide—signs of a juvenile. They are born a dark pewter color and get more silvery as they mature until they are as transparent as glass. By my guess and from what Iianthe has told me, I presume the purple-tip and this red-tip are from the same litter. They are less than three decades old." He too leaned forward.

"Litters? Not clutches?"

"Litters. Our dragons are mammalian, bearing live young, suckling them. They have fur instead of hide. Each hair is like an individual crystal that directs the eye around the dragon," Kim continued to lecture all he had learned about the elusive creatures.

"How long is a year on this planet?" Kat cut off his monologue. She sat back, gathering information now as well as satisfying her curiosity.

Konner needed more information, too. What kind of trouble did Irythros warn him of?

"Three hundred fifty-two point six local solar days," Konner replied, forcing his mind back into the conversation. He'd spent time observing the stars and moon, verifying what the computers had told him. He agreed with the calculations, but found satisfaction figuring it out for himself.

"And how long is a day around here?" Kat tried to look casual, but she kept leaning farther forward for a better view. The huge continent below them gave way to the ocean. Soon they would be over the Great Bay and home.

"Twenty-seven Earth standard hours," Konner replied. He suddenly realized he'd had no trouble adapting to the longer day or shorter moon cycles. As if his body knew what his mind only recently began to accept. This planet was home.

His lover lived here. This was home. But, oh, how he missed traveling the stars. There had to be a way he could do both.

Presuming they all survived the coming encounter with the IMPs.

Irythros continued to fly around them, more maneuverable than the man-made craft. He offered no more conversation, even when Konner prodded him mentally.

Loki slowed the vehicle as he descended. The atmosphere glowed around them from the heat of their reentry. Shields automatically slid across the windshield, deflecting light as well as heat. The interior lighting snapped on to compensate. Yellow-red light similar to Earth's sun.

And seemingly alien to Konner after five months of the redder but dimmer light of Star MKO in the local heavens.

"Any sign of pursuit?" Loki asked.

"Can't tell. Sensors still gummy from the green layer. We need a bath before we land." As Konner spoke, Irythros plunged into a steep dive. He entered the choppy waters below without a splash. Seconds later he swooped up. A fish, nearly as large as himself, was clutched in his talons.

"Can your dragon sense intruders?" Kim asked, eyes glued to the dragon.

Konner stilled himself, waiting for the clarity of mind to listen to the dragon. His vision dimmed. Colors lost intensity. Edges lost their definition. And then . . .

(*I caught it!*) Irythros chortled. (*I caught a behemouth. Tonight I feast.*) With his last words the dragon dropped his prey upon an open desert behind them.

Konner cringed, almost hearing the thud of its landing through his contact with Irythros. The fall killed the monstrous fish. Then the dragon landed gracefully beside his dinner and loosed a long spurt of green fire.

Irythros continued to ignore Konner's mental probes.

"Dragons are civilized. They cook their food before dining," Loki informed their sister.

"Nothing about this place is civilized. Yet. Including you three."

"You'd be surprised, little sister," Konner said. His mind remained open to the dragon. He listened to his siblings with half his attention. "Loki, let me take control. I want to try something the dragon taught me."

Maybe Irythros would release more information if he saw the lander and its passengers as kindred spirits.

Reluctantly, Loki shifted piloting interfaces to Konner.

"What are you going to do?" Kat asked skeptically.

"Drown some unwanted passengers." Konner grinned at her. If she was ever to be part of the family, she had to learn to accept their teasing.

She blanched at Konner's words, but held her tongue.

"No. You aren't going to do what I think you are going to do." Loki looked pale as well. His fingers curled and brushed his interface. He wanted control of the lander back.

"Why not?"

"Because this thing was built by the GTE, not to our specs." Loki's voice rose an octave as he braced himself for a steep dive.

"We'll see." Konner let go of his contact with Irythros. He'd learned enough from the dragon. Now he needed to listen to the ship. "Kim, does this thing have atmosphere wings?" he asked. His voice came out hoarse and barely above a whisper.

"Little ones," Kim replied. He moved his hand to a lever above his head. The manual override. If the craft lost power, the wings could catch the winds and glide to a softer landing than a straight plunge. Modern pilots rarely used them for anything but emergencies. There wasn't even a place on the pilot screen for activation.

"Little is all I need." Konner adjusted his angle of entry and slowed.

"One hundred meters to impact," Loki said. He called out the numbers as they descended.

Twenty meters above the water with the engines slowed to a near stall Konner called out, "Wings. Now."

The lander shuddered and creaked and abruptly slowed.

Two heartbeats later they impacted the water. Konner's head whipped back and slammed into the headrest of his chair. His teeth clanged together and he bit the inside of his cheek. He tasted blood.

His spine jolted. An ache spread outward.

Their world became blue. Bubbles streamed past them along with fish and seaweed. Light played games with shifting currents. He wanted to linger and observe. He couldn't.

Fighting gravity and pressure, he reached for the interface. The ship did not respond.

Water trickled in from around the seal of the tiny hole in the hull. Steady drops hit Konner's face. The trickle became a stream.

* * *

"Sluggish as a garbage scow!" Loki spat. He wrenched control away from Konner. "Kim, get the sealer out. Now!"

Kim reached for the tube of cerama/metal caulk. He moved gingerly, not jarring his body further.

The lander wallowed in the water and sank deeper.

"I'll have you know, this lander is the latest model. Engineers can't design anything better!" Kat spluttered.

"You could design something better in your sleep," Loki replied. "Not even a joystick to control this heap of junk."

"Imitating dragons diving into the depths of the ocean is not the kind of maneuver any sane pilot would put a ship through," Kat retorted. "If you'd just let me . . ."

"Forget it, Kat. You may be the best pilot the GTE can produce, but I taught you how to fly." Loki's fingers flew over the interface. Hard as he looked, he could not find anything resembling full manual control. The computers kept compensating for every correction he made.

"Our father taught me how to fly before he left. You just followed up on his lessons," Kat retorted.

"You know, if you hadn't put that red-tailed spiny lizard inside her pants when she was five, she might be more cooperative." Konner grinned at Loki.

"That was you!" Loki spluttered. "You put the lizard on her. I was there to protect her."

"But it was your idea," Konner protested.

Loki couldn't even remember what game had inspired the prank.

"Manual is in the kneehole. Far right corner," Kat said. She sounded as if she begrudged the information. At the same time a memory clicked behind her eyes. That look always led to mischief; mischief that got Loki and Konner into trouble with Mum. "I'd have had us out of here by now if you'd just let me . . ."

"Forget it. I'm in charge," Loki spat at her. "You can help Kim seal around the windshield. I'm surprised this barge has held together this long!"

"Manual is a last resort," Kat continued. "You shouldn't reach for it, unless you are desperate."

"We are desperate," Konner whispered.

Loki glanced at Konner. He was pale and sweating.

"I know I copied every last move Irythros made. Including the twist upon entry. It should have worked."

"But we don't have a tail as long as the body for a rudder and you didn't collapse the wings the moment we entered the water," Loki reminded him. He reached left instead of right. If manual control was a last-ditch effort, then it would be opposite the dominant hand of most pilots. But convenient for the left-handed O'Haras.

Kat swallowed hard and scrunched her eyes closed the moment Loki found the toggle. She obviously did not like that he could second-guess her even without using telepathy.

"Wings?" Konner looked a little brighter. "Are they down now?"

"Kim, do it!" Loki called

The ship shuddered slightly as Kim shoved the lever upward. The wings locked into place with a clank that reverberated around the cockpit and inside Loki's skull.

He clenched his jaw against the beginning of a headache as he manipulated for manual control while trying to keep one eye on the windscreen and the other on the interfaces. "Damned inconvenient release when you're desperate," he muttered. At last the computer released control. The interface went blank, a small joystick rose from the panel.

Loki breathed a sigh of relief. The ball fit loosely into his palm. Designed for someone with smaller hands; a smaller *right* hand. A quick rotation of the stubby control and he had the feel of it. The lander's nose edged upward. It nudged something pliable, but heavy.

A startled dolphinlike creature stared at him through the bioglass windscreen. It blinked, then nosed the craft. When it encountered the resistance of the screen, it bounced back, working its fins and tail to maintain position.

"That must be a mandelph!" Kim exclaimed. He brought his nose up to the screen and made faces at the creature. "The original colonists brought dolphin embryos from Earth. They had genetically engineered language into their intelligence, looking for partners in fishing and exploration. But the creatures disappeared. The colonists thought they died out when released in the wild. But they went feral. Maybe interbred with something native. Local fishermen gave them the name because they have been known to help drowning fishermen back to shore and are quite adept at stealing fish from the nets. No one has mentioned anything about them speaking to humans, even telepathically."

"Is he always so . . . ?" Kat asked.

"Kim is our family scholar. He reads everything and remembers every word. He's collecting local lore now," Loki said. A smidgen of pride swelled in him. He'd helped Mum teach Kim how to read and encouraged the boy to study everything that came to hand since he could never go to school while they were on the run. Kim had quickly outstripped the tutorial programs available through local educational systems. Now he qualified for three doctorates. Someday, when he was no longer on the run, he would collect them.

"But how did you find out about the original colonists?" Kat shifted her gaze from the curious sea creature to Kim.

"We found journals. A full record of . . ."

"If this is a lost Earth colony, then why are the locals so primitive? No communications to monitor, no industry, nothing but farms and those are few and far between."

"Their own technology killed them. We don't intend to ever let that happen again," Kim said. Anger made his voice husky.

"This planet remains free of GTE interference," Konner added with equal vehemence.

"That's why you stole the king stone."

"That's why we stole the king stone."

"Make me understand why you think primitive

life in the bush is more valuable than all the benefits of the GTE," she pleaded.

"We'll show you as soon as we get this garbage scow out of the water," Loki reassured her. "Observe closely, because if you do not understand, you will never leave this planet again. None of your people will be given a chance to hint to folks back home that this place exists."

Kat snorted as if she did not believe him.

Loki gritted his teeth. She was more stubborn than all three O'Hara brothers combined. Maybe as stubborn as Mum.

With that thought he shuddered.

All he needed was *another* strong-willed woman in his life.

So why did the image of Paola Sanchez rise before his mind's eye rather than Cyndi, the love of his life?

CHAPTER 31

DALLEENA WATCHED the Others in indecision. Her tracking talent sensed that Konner returned. She knew that water surrounded him, but he did not drown. Had he flown another vessel into the Great Bay? He did not need her at the moment. But she needed to tell him that Taneeo had disappeared in the move to the other village, then reappeared with two dozen men in thrall and returned all of the weapons and comms to the Others.

She also needed to warn Konner about the Others. They had broken a flag of truce. They honored nothing.

Even now the guards tramped about the fields and swamps, crushing delicate plants and heedlessly scattering wildlife in all directions. One of them took aim at the red bull with his long weapon.

The bull! The heart of the village livestock.

He could not be allowed to kill the beast. They would have to borrow a bull from a neighboring village—rarely a wise move for many reason—or wait for one of the calves to mature.

Saving the bull was more important than watching the intruders from her hiding place. Raiders. Nothing more than pirates.

She abandoned her hiding place and ran full tilt for the man taking aim at the bull.

The belligerent, red creature pawed the ground, head lowered, nostrils steaming, preparing to defend his territory and his harem.

Too far away. She increased her speed. Her lungs labored. Her heart pounded. Her legs strained. Her feet burned with power and speed.

She saw the IMP's finger tighten on the trigger.

"No!" she screamed.

The man barely shifted his attention to her, but his grip on the trigger eased.

Dalleena took a flying leap, knowing she must fall short.

Miraculously she collided with the man. They tumbled to the ground together. His gun flew away.

The bull charged. The ground thundered beneath Dalleena. She looked up. Enormous horns filled her vision. The tips gleamed sharply.

She thought nothing. Said nothing. Only stared in horror at approaching death.

All around her, she heard shouts and screams of panic and warning.

The shooter tried to scramble from beneath her.

And then those monstrous horns scooped her up and sent her flying over the top of the bull's head.

She landed hard. Something snapped. Something else crunched.

Black stars crowded her vision. She could not breathe. She could not move.

Pain filled her being. Fiery lances shot through her with each attempted breath. Death. Release.

If she died now, would Konner know that her last thought was of him?

* * *

"Something is wrong," Konner said as he jumped out of the lander's hatch.

Loki had parked the vessel three klicks from *Rover*, well away from IMP patrols.

"Of course something is wrong," Loki said as he joined Konner on the ground. "Our home is swarming with IMPs."

They watched the enemy prowl around the village. Few strayed more than a single kilometer from the cluster of their comrades.

"Dalleena is not here." Konner made a rapid circuit of the lander, searching with all of his senses for sight, sound, smell, or *feel* of Dalleena anywhere in the vicinity.

"She would be here if she could." Kim placed a soothing hand upon his shoulder.

"Konner, you only spent one night with the woman. Maybe she's had second thoughts." Loki shrugged his shoulders.

Konner pinned him with a glare.

"Okay, maybe she is special to you. But any one of a hundred things could occupy her right now, including spying on the IMPs. Maybe she's just late."

"No. I know she's in trouble. I know it here." Konner pounded his gut with a fist. "And I know it here," he said more softly, open palm atop his heart.

"Trust your instincts," Kim agreed. He paused in the hatchway long enough to assist Kat down. The force bracelets still limited her movements.

"Well, if we're going to help your lady, shouldn't you remove these?" Kat held up her hands.

"Your word of honor as an O'Hara that you will not try to escape." Loki planted fists on his hips.

"My word of honor as an officer of the Imperial Military Police that my duty is to escape and warn my superiors of your threat to the stability of the Empire." She assumed a posture as arrogant as Loki's even with the force bracelets inhibiting her arms.

"The bracelets stay." Loki insisted.

"I wish I had Dalleena's tracking talent. Then I could find her," Konner said. He set off toward the fields beside the village. She was supposed to have watched the IMP intruders from a safe distance.

(*Listen to your heart,*) Irythros said into his head.

Konner stopped short. He paid no attention to his siblings as they plowed into his back.

"Speak plainly, Irythros," he commanded.

(*Be still. Listen.*)

"Basic technique for working magic," Kim whispered into his ear.

"You heard him?" Konner did not think anyone could overhear a private conversation with a dragon. Unless the dragon wished.

"That was more than just one dragon talking. I still have a minor connection to Iianthe. Through him, I heard them all speak." Kim shrugged as if listening to dragons was an everyday occurrence. For Kim and his Tambootie, it might be.

Kat came up beside them and rolled her eyes. "More mumbo jumbo. Why not use the sensors to isolate groups of people. Surely the natives have had enough separation from humanity to have a slight DNA variance."

"Tech doesn't solve every problem," Konner nearly shouted at her. "The locals are as human as you and I. Three hundred years isn't enough for genetic drift."

"Don't be so bushie defensive," Kat snarled. "I didn't intend it to be an insult."

"We have to do something with the king stone, Konner." Loki placed a reassuring hand on his shoulder. "Soon. Probably before we can look for Dalleena. This is the first place the IMPs will look for it, as soon as they realize we've left the ship."

A moment of panic grabbed Konner. He had to

find Dalleena. But the entire future of this planet depended upon keeping the king stone out of IMP hands.

Why hadn't he just smashed it?

Because it was alive and he could no more kill the crystal than he could murder a human.

"You may have to choose between saving the king stone and saving Dalleena," Loki reminded him.

"I'll scout the village." Konner checked the position of the sun. Still plenty of daylight. "You three transfer the stone to *Rover* and recharge the fuel cells. I'll be back in an hour. Then we'll look for a place to secrete the stone."

"What kind of place. I'll review the maps . . ." Kim said.

"I'll know the place when I see it." Konner stalked off. A plan nudged his brain. But he couldn't do anything about it until he knew Dalleena was safe.

He began walking.

"Take me with you, Konner." Kat hurried to catch him.

"Why? So you can escape?"

She answered him with silence.

"You stay here where our brothers can keep you out of trouble."

"Define trouble."

"Mari Kathleen O'Hara Talbot." He turned his back on her and kept walking.

The distance to the village had never seemed longer. Before the circle of huts came into view, Konner angled south to keep small hills between him and the intruders. Then he crawled through tall grasses to the edge of the plowed fields.

The moment he dropped to all fours, he heard/sensed frantic movement off to his left. He risked a peek above the tasseled tips of the wild grass. Five uniformed IMPs carried something away from the bull's pasture. Medic Lotski forged ahead of them speaking rapidly into her comm unit.

Konner wished he were closer. At this distance he could not identify the injured person. Too many people crowded around the inert figure to determine clothing, size, or coloring.

A terrible feeling gripped his gut.

He crawled closer, using the distraction of a serious injury or illness among the IMPs to move faster than he would if armed patrols still swept the area.

He noted a number of natives bound with force bracelets and crude rope on the far side of the fire. Taneeo among them. Yaaccob, the village elder from the neighboring community hunched in the middle of the group, working silently at his rope bindings.

Konner watched the IMPs carry the limp figure into the largest cabin, the one he shared with Loki. The home he had invited Dalleena into last night. As the men carrying the burden maneuvered through the narrow doorway, Konner caught a glimpse of dark leather trousers, the legs stuffed into crude boots. Above the waist, he saw a white homespun shirt and leather vest.

His heart leaped to his throat.

Dalleena!

CHAPTER 32

MARTIN FORTESQUE faced his mother.
In person.

No hiding behind a computer-enhanced vid screen. He had to do this in person.

"Mother . . ."

"I told you to call me Melinda." She continued working at the stack of messages on her personal desktop. The entire surface was nothing more than a compressed vid screen that allowed her touch point corrections. A miniature electronic pencil dangled from her subdued earrings. She detached it from the molecular adhesive of the gold jewelry and highlighted something on her desk, then returned the tool to its resting place. "You are nearly grown now. Soon I will train you to help me run the corporation. In business circles we must appear as equals even though I will always hold a controlling share of stock and votes on the board of directors."

"Mother, will you look at me when I speak?" Martin couldn't keep the childish waver out of his voice.

Something in his tone must have startled her, for she looked up sharply, narrowing her eyes to look directly at him. And only at him.

Perhaps she had a scrap of motherly emotion in her after all.

Before she reverted to corporate coldness, Martin plunged forward with his planned speech.

"Mother, I need access to systems beyond my tutorials."

"Why? So you can interfere with my shipping manifests again?"

"No." That was strictly true. Martin had no intention of messing with shipping *manifests*. "It's for a school project. I need to do some research."

"Such as?" Melinda touched a corner of her screen. Martin had no doubt his full curriculum spread before her in minute detail.

He had to make this sound good.

"I . . . ah . . . I'm doing a report on the changes in shipping lanes since the advent of the armed conflict with the Kree." The only other sentient beings humanity had encountered since entering space had proved belligerent in territorial disputes. So far, those had been few and far between. However, the GTE had taken pains to stay out of sectors now claimed by the winged creatures.

Most of the population went about their lives as if the Kree did not exist and nothing barred the expansion of the almighty GTE. Those who lived near the border prepared for all-out war. Corporations that built their fortunes on interstellar trade had to be aware of the constantly changing boundaries and currencies.

"An admirable project, Martin. I shall review it when you are finished. Our business will benefit from such a study." Melinda made an adjustment to Martin's curriculum. "You are now free to use the system. But if I discover you tampering with anything, there will be repercussions."

Martin backed out of his mother's office as rapidly as he could and still remain upright. The moment the door whispered closed, he turned and ran back to his own suite.

Time had grown short. He had to remove port restrictions for *Martin* Konner O'Hara quickly. (And hadn't he and his friends had a time hacking his father's full name out of an obscure database on an even more obscure bush world.) Those port restrictions were the only things keeping Martin's father from coming to claim him. He was certain of it.

"Martin." Melinda's voice chimed through his personal chip embedded behind his ear.

"Yes, Mother?" He had no doubt she could hear him through hidden comm ports in the palace corridor.

"I have ordered you a new suit for your birthday. Be available for a fitting at seventeen hundred hours."

"Why do I need a new suit? I have six that still fit very well."

"We have an important appointment on your birthday. You must look your best."

"What appointment." Martin knew. But he had to play along as if his mother was as omnipotent as she pretended.

"An appointment that will ensure our future together. Never forget that you are my only child and heir." Melinda disconnected with a slight popping sound.

Martin was left with a vacancy between his ears from the absence of sound.

Come and get me, Dad. Please come and get me soon. We can't let her win this one.

*   *   *

(*South*.) A dragon voice spoke directly to Kim.

"Iianthe, greetings," he said. He peered at the cloud cover seeking the only purple-tipped dragon in the nimbus. No mistaking the deep, sonorous tones of his old friend.

(*What you seek is to the south.*)

"Loki, I think we are heading back toward the volcano," Kim told his brother. They stood beside *Rover*, waiting for Konner.

"More magic and hoodoo voodoo?" Kat asked sarcastically. She lounged against the shuttle as if she had no cares. But she worked at the force bracelets continuously. Her wrists looked like raw meat.

Kim spotted a flash of sunlight on a transparent wing. "Maybe we should let her ride the dragon who guides us." Kim looked at her levelly, with a half smile.

She blanched but returned his gaze with courage. Her chin lifted just a little in defiance.

For a moment Kim was proud of her. He just wished she recognized the family connection and cooperated more.

But if she capitulated too easily, would she be a true O'Hara?

"Loki! Kim! They have Dalleena. She's hurt. Bad." Konner pelted toward them, gasping for breath between words. "They've also captured Taneeo and about two dozen men from the other village."

A series of sharp feedback squeals brought him up short. He whirled around to face the direction he had come from.

Flashes of red pain filled Kim's vision. He felt the hot burst of energy against his skin and his thick skull. A need to bellow, paw the ground, and charge filled his being.

Then nothing. A great emptiness spread outward from Kim's navel.

"St. Bridget, they've killed the bull." Kim's mouth hung agape.

"Are you certain they shot the bull?" Konner started toward the pasture, then stopped short.

What could any of them do? Why would the IMPs intentionally kill a living animal? Supposedly they considered all life sacred. Civilized members of the GTE did not eat meat because they refused to take a life. Any life.

"How civilized are the Marines among your crew?" Kim turned slowly to face his sister.

Kat shrugged. "Many are bush born. Sergeants Duggan and Brewster are barely civilized."

Bushies ate meat in order to survive. The GTE demanded nearly all of their grain, fruits, and vegetables as payment for protection, medicines, and technology among the far-flung worlds. Bushies lived as exploited colonists. They could not enter the GTE as full members with voting rights or self-rule until they industrialized, gave up their uncivilized dietary habits, and domed their cities.

How could these IMPs appreciate the value of a single bull beyond a meal for the troops?

"They won't get away with this," Kim vowed.

"You can't stop them," Kat reminded them.

"I can make them pay."

"How? You have only a few weapons and fewer numbers," Kat continued.

"We have the king stone," Konner said. His voice was cold. For the first time that Kim could remember, his brother sounded mean.

Then Konner looked back toward the village. His face crumpled with despair. "I have to go to her."

"As much as we hate the IMPs," Loki said, placing a hand upon Konner's shoulder. "They have better medics, equipment, and medicines than we do. They won't let her die. Lotski is one of the good guys. She won't let a patient die."

"But what if it's the plague?" Konner balanced on the balls of his feet, ready to run toward Dalleena.

"We sowed the entire area quite liberally with selenium this summer," Kim reminded him. "The bioengineered virus is now inert. You found the cure, Konner. You know we eliminated the plague."

"What if . . ."

"No. Do not think about it. We have work to do. You have to tell us what to do with the king stone."

"He could give it back," Kat offered.

None of the brothers listened to her.

"Without the king stone, *Jupiter*'s orbit will decay and the ship will crash. Your people are stranded here, Kat. They invaded and lost. They have to learn to live among us on our terms. We can't let any of you leave. The GTE must never be allowed to pollute our home," Kim told her.

Konner stepped into *Rover*. "The dragons say we need to go south. Let's fly."

Kim placed his hands on Kat's shoulders and pushed her to follow Konner.

"Irythros spoke to you?" Kim asked Konner as they settled into their familiar places in the cockpit.

"The entire nimbus told me to find what I seek in the south."

"I got the same message. Do you think they mean for us to return to the volcano?"

"The strange magnetics would certainly help hide the crystals," Loki agreed. He gave Kat's force bracelets one more check before taking his place in the pilot's chair.

The cockpit only had three chairs. The brothers had never anticipated needing a fourth. So Loki placed their sister on the deck and restrained her with various cables crossed around her chest and hooked to the bulkhead of the cockpit. In a moment of compassion, Kim placed a cushion from the lounge behind her back and neck. She sighed in relief but said nothing.

"I have something better in mind than that haunted volcano." Konner looked smug.

"Do I dare ask what?" Kim asked as Loki sent the shuttle forward into takeoff.

"A place to hide us as well as the entire crystal array."

"Are you thinking what I think you are thinking?" Loki looked both pleased and pained. He shook his head and set course due south.

"The cloaking I developed for both *Rover* and *Sirius* is nothing more than a confusion field," Konner explained.

"Like those nearly invisible dragons?" Kat asked. "I should have guessed. They warp light rays defying the eye to look anywhere but at them, at the same time they challenge you to look nowhere else. Damn. Now I know where you hid your ship in orbit. I looked right at it and forgot I'd seen it." She hit her forehead with both palms.

She grimaced and eased her hands back into her lap.

Kat would be looking to steal the key to the bracelets at every turn. Being an O'Hara, she'd likely find it.

Kim reminded himself to keep a closer eye on her.

"If you are using the entire crystal array, then we need a roughly circular place," Loki mused, biting his lip in thought.

Kim took his eyes off Kat long enough to load maps and surveys onto his screens.

"If we were riding dragonback, we could fly lower, spot the place with our eyes," Konner said as he leaned over to check Kim's charts.

"There." Konner pointed to the top of one of the foothills to the Southern Mountains. A pass through the chain of peaks ran close by.

"Far enough east and north of the volcano that the volcano's EMF won't mask it from sensors," Loki objected.

"I don't need EMF to hide us. That's the right place. I can feel it." Konner sounded triumphant.

Kim felt a nod of agreement in the back of his mind from the dragons.

Loki shrugged and corrected course. The land beneath them began to rise as they neared the mountains, leaving the river plains behind.

"I'm willing to bet that when we get there, we find a confluence of ley lines," Kim said. He couldn't help but smile. With ley lines under his feet and Tambootie trees in the nearby woods, he could experiment with magic to his heart's content. Who knew what powers he would develop, pass on to his children. Perhaps even teach Hestiia to share in the powers.

"Ley lines?" Kat sat up straighter against the bulkhead. Her improvised crash harness strained against her shoulders.

"Think of theoretical transactional gravitons," Konner offered.

Kat's emerald-green eyes did not light with recognition.

"A web of energy that holds the universe together," Kim explained. "King stones use the lines of the web to maintain contact with the mother stone and facilitate faster-than-light communications. Ley lines are similar, but on a planetary basis. We don't know if they are connected to the gravitons or not. I suspect that we tap into them for energy to fuel our psi powers. The number and consistency of the lines here augment our talents more than anywhere else." Even more so with a good dose of Tambootie. Kim dug in his pocket seeking a scrap of a leaf, anything to help him think straight.

He came up empty. His hands began to shake and his head ached. He clenched his fists and bit the inside of his cheeks to cover his aching need for more of the drug.

Kat slumped against the bulkhead where she sat. "More magic. You three are really giving in to bush madness."

"We don't see it as madness, Kat," Kim said quietly. "We see it as salvation for ourselves, the family, maybe even for the entire GTE. The exploitation of people and resources has got to stop. We won't let it come here."

"The emperor is trying," Kat replied defensively. "He has introduced legislation to allow bush planets membership in the GTE without doming and industrializing."

"But he hasn't succeeded in reversing the mind-set of six hundred billion people," Konner added.

"Not even a majority of the six thousand members of Parliament," Loki finished.

"When I can see a transactional graviton, or ley line, or whatever and feel the energy coursing through my body, then I might begin to listen to you." She set her face, O'Hara stubbornness written all over it.

"A confluence of ley lines coming right up!" Kim laughed to cover his trembling voice. A neat clearing, almost perfectly circular came into view. He drank in the sight, knowing he had come home.

Tambootie trees filled the nearby woods.

CHAPTER 33

KONNER GUIDED the king stone into a hole a meter and a half deeper than he was tall. He and his brothers had used the laser pulse from *Rover* to define the hole. Then counter-grav equipment purloined from the IMP lander lifted the chunk of dirt in a solid heap. It lay to the side of the hole, ready for deposit around the king stone once Konner had the stone anchored in position.

Now Loki held the shuttle in a tight hover directly above the center of the hole. Kim kept the cables wrapped around the crystal from tangling. At least he tried. His movements seemed clumsier than usual. The blue crystal spun frequently and Loki had to raise the stone higher while Kim untangled it.

Kat sat at the edge of the clearing, worrying her force bracelets. A frown drew deep lines beside her mouth and between her brows.

"A little to the left, Konner," Kat called out.

"Quiet. I can see where it has to go," Konner spat back at her. But he edged the cable a little to the left.

The crystal ceased dropping. "Another meter, Kim."

"We're out of cable," he called back, over the roar of VTOL jets Loki used to keep the shuttle in place.

"Damn!" Konner jumped down into the hole. He

wrapped his arms around the stone. The weight of the thing shook his balance.

"I need your help, Kat."

"Not on your life, O'Hara."

"I'll take the bracelets off you."

"Promise?" She stood up and crossed the distance at a near run. Her face brightened.

"No, Konner. Keep her restrained. I'll come down." Kim looked as if he'd jump the eight meters from the shuttle to the ground.

"Kim, you'll break your neck. Where will she go if she tries to escape? She'd need a week or more to get back to the village on foot.

Just then, the stone jerked upward out of his arms. Kim waved frantically. The shuttle's nose jerked up and so did the king stone.

Konner stumbled. His nose crashed into the packed dirt on the side of the hole. Then the rest of his face followed.

"One of my last memories of you is with grime smudged all over your face from the fire at the household compound. You haven't grown up much in the last twenty years," Kat chuckled. She winced as she braced herself to jump into the hole beside him.

Once on his level she sobered. "You smiled at me and took my hand as we ran away from the noise and confusion. Your teeth showed bright against the dirt. I thought that everything would be all right just because you smiled for me, Konner. You don't smile enough."

"You pulled your hand out of mine, Katie. Why? I followed you, but lost you in the darkness. Why, Katie? We could have both gotten away if you'd just stayed with me."

She looked away a moment while she fished a handkerchief out of her front pocket. Her movements were awkward. The pain must have been incredible.

"I forgot Kim's teddy bear. I knew he wouldn't sleep without it." She swiped at the dirt on his face with the handkerchief. It came away filthy.

"Let me get those bracelets off you." He avoided the emotional moment by retrieving the electronic key from his inside vest pocket. He slapped both pockets. Both were flat and empty.

"Looking for this?" Kat held up the black remote.

"Yes." Konner grabbed it back. "How?" he asked as he pointed the gadget at the electrode between her wrists. A brief buzz from the bracelets and the wrist circles snapped open at the electrode.

"I picked your pocket between wiping your face and distracting you with poignant memories." Her half smile came back.

Konner returned it. Then he waved at Kim.

The shuttle lowered once more, and with it the king stone.

Konner wrapped his arms about the giant crystal. Kat did the same on the opposite size. Together they balanced it while Kim cut the cable from above. With feet braced, they both lowered the crystal until it rested firmly in the depression filled with fiber optics at the bottom of the hole.

The flat bottom nestled into the dirt as if coming home. For the first time in hours the strident wail of the crystal separated from its family shifted to a more harmonious note.

"It's happy here," Kat said. She looked surprised.

"It will be happier when I restore the array." Konner kicked some additional dirt against the base of the stone and stamped it down.

"Why do I think it won't move, even without bracing?" Kat did not assist in planting the crystal.

"Because your psychic talent is kicking in and you can hear it sing."

She shook her head and clambered out of the hole. Konner followed her. They watched as Loki lifted the pile of dirt with the counter-grav and dumped it back into the hole. It mounded slightly. Konner wondered if he should tamp it down, make the excavation less visible.

Kat moved to board *Rover* the moment Loki settled the shuttle on the far side of the clearing.

"Now where?" she asked.

"You stay here." Konner left the mound of dirt. Rain would settle it better than he could and a storm was building off to the east. He smelled the cold moisture.

Both Kat and Kim looked surprised.

"I have to go to Dalleena." Konner took a deep breath to control the anxiety that had not left him since seeing his lover carried into the hut by the IMPs. Limp. Unresponsive. Bleeding.

"Kim, you and Loki need to start removing the central array of driver and directional crystals from *Jupiter*. I'm going after Dalleena. Taking Kat with us is too risky. She'll have too many opportunities to reveal our plans to the IMPs. We can't take a chance on anyone finding this place before I finish the confusion field or all personnel are evacuated and the landers deactivated."

"I have a wife, too, Konner. I need to check that Hestiia is okay."

"You'd know if she wasn't." The two brothers stared at each other in a moment of understanding. "The last we heard she was whole and hale. Dalleena isn't."

"We'll need help with the crystals. Hestiia, Raaskan, and a few others, I think," Kim replied hastily. "We stop long enough to pick them up."

Konner nodded and boarded the shuttle, pushing Kat aside.

She tumbled onto her backside. "And what am I supposed to do while you are gone?" Kat asked. She hadn't gotten up from her ignominious position. "I'll be all alone! I might be attacked by wild animals. Or wilder natives. I'll get cold and hungry. I'll be alone!"

Konner flipped a serviceable iron knife so that the blade tip embedded in the ground half a meter from her hand. A blade he'd forged and polished himself. He'd even bound it with strips of sinew to a section of deer antler for a hilt. Kat would never understand what a precious gift he gave her.

"Learn to use this for defense. For cutting bracken for a bed. For digging roots to eat. I recommend the bulb of the yellow flowering plant beside the creek. Fire is optional, if you can figure out how to start one by striking sparks off the knife blade with a rock. Use the knife for cutting branches to build a lean-to. Vines make very good twine. The presence of the king stone will probably protect you from wild animals bigger than you are. I'd advise you not to leave the clearing until one of us returns for you, though. There are bandits in these hills, Gypsies, too—the locals call them Rovers. They don't have the same sense of honor as we do."

"You're abandoning me again. I should have known."

"Stranding for a few hours. Not abandoning," Kim clarified for her. "We'll be back. We keep our promises."

"You didn't twenty years ago."

"You'll never know how much trouble we went through to go back for you and find you gone. Presumed dead," Konner said bitterly.

"And what am I supposed to do while you go off adventuring?"

"Think about circles." Konner slapped the hatch control. It irised shut slowly. He did not turn away from her penetrating gaze until several layers of cerama/metal separated them. Still he felt the green fire sparking from her eyes, stripping him to his soul, and finding him wanting.

Guilt slammed him in his face. In his worry for Dalleena and the fate of the planet he had forgotten his primary goal: to gain custody of his son.

Time leaked away from everything he held dear.

* * *

Kim gathered Hestiia into his arms the moment he cleared the hatch of *Rover*. He clung to her a long time while Loki and Konner barked orders to the villagers. His wife fit tightly against him, her dark curls just reaching his chin.

"Beloved," Hestiia whispered. She tried to draw away from him. He tucked her closer. "Beloved, I have dire news."

"It does not matter. I have you in my arms. All is well," he replied, trying to believe his own words.

"Taneeo has betrayed us."

Kim stilled in diappointment. "I guessed he would, but I did not want to believe it. He is our friend. We saved him from Hanassa. I thought he was stronger," he said sadly. Lumbird bumps rose on his skin. A sour taste began in the back of his throat.

"Taneeo led two dozen men, some from our village, some from Yaaccob's village. They returned weapons and comm units to the Others," Raaskan added. Carefully he related what he had seen.

A chill ran up Kim's spine.

"Taneeo is not Taneeo," Pryth said as she surged through the crowd toward Kim and his brothers.

"I agree, he's not been himself since . . . But I thought he had overcome Hanassa's pressure. I thought his will was stronger."

"Another is now Taneeo." The old woman turned and parted a way through the crowd as a ship through water. Hardened warriors, children, and matriarchs shifted to allow her easy passage.

"At least we know who now hosts Hanassa," Konner said quietly.

As one, the villagers crossed their wrists, right over left, and flapped their hands.

Silence hung over them like a heavy cloud.

"We don't have time to deal with this," Loki said. He began pacing in front of *Rover*'s hatch. "We need to get the crystals from *Jupiter* and get back to Kat before she finds a way to escape."

"After dark I will take a group of females to rescue our people from the Others." Hestiia straightened away from Kim. "We will deal with their treachery." A hard glint came into her eyes.

Her fierceness almost frightened Kim.

"I sure would not like to be Taneeo at about sunset," Konner muttered.

His brothers nodded.

"Let Pryth lead the women. I want you with me," Kim insisted to his wife. "I do not want to take a chance that you might be captured," he said more quietly, for her ears alone.

"It is my place as the wife of a Stargod to lead . . ."

Kim stopped her protest with a finger across her lips. "I need you with me. I trust you to help. Not all of our people have the . . . ability to assist us." Many of the villagers would be so frightened of flying in *Rover* they would be useless in retrieving the crystals.

"Right," Loki said. "Raaskan, Poolie, you two come with us." He pointed to several others who had proved themselves more adaptable to change than others.

"I'm staying here. I'll see to Dalleena," Konner said firmly.

"Fine. Whatever." Loki jumped aboard *Rover*, ushering half a dozen villagers into the cabin.

"Loki, Konner, are we sure we want to do this?"

Kim hesitated to move to the lander. The sight of his wife, their friends, all they had to lose could not soothe his conscience. "We are going to strand three hundred people on this planet. Separate them from their friends and families, put an end to all of their hopes and dreams."

"It's not the same, Kim," Loki barked. His face flushed with anger. Or was it guilt?

"It is the same. We are going to imprison these people against their will."

"They would do the same to us," Konner reminded him.

"Does that make it right?" Kim began to shake.

"No." Konner said. "It does not make it right. But we have to weigh the welfare of our people against what would happen if we do not do this."

"They are invaders," Loki insisted. "Humans resisted the Kree when they invaded Earth. We have the same right here on our home."

"I go on the record as having serious reservations against this." Kim clenched his teeth to keep his chin from trembling.

"Fine. You record it later. Let's get this show on the road!" Loki dismissed the problem by marching forward to *Rover's* cockpit.

"We will find a way to make it right, Kim," Hestiia whispered. "After we ensure the safety of our people."

"I certainly hope so." Kim reluctantly climbed into the lander.

CHAPTER 34

CHAOS. LANDERS, shuttles, jolly boats, and fighters fled *Jupiter's* launch bay and scattered in all directions. Some headed for the ocean directly beneath the ship's decaying orbit. Others sought a more hospitable landing place.

At least some of the scout ships must be seeking the king stone. Loki did not believe they would find it.

He slid *Rover* into the loading bay just as the doors began their slow slide closed. Kim squeezed in behind him with the lander.

Waiting for bay doors to close, force fields to reestablish, and atmosphere to fill seemed to take forever.

In the meantime, lines of IMP personnel formed in the corridor beyond. Their strident voices leaked through the sealed hatch. Fists pounded upon the bulkhead demanding entrance. Tension crawled along Loki's spine like a thousand itching bugs.

"Why the panic exodus?" Kim asked over the comm. "The orbit should not be decaying yet."

"Did you notice some slowing in the spin?" Loki replied. "Something other than normal gravitational pull is already affecting this ship. At this rate, they'll be lucky to get everyone off, even using escape pods. The fact that we have one of the landers and Konner ditched another means more trips back and forth, using up more fuel, and twice the panic."

And military discipline had broken down. Severely. Why wasn't the infamous Commander Amanda Leonard commanding an orderly escape? Where was the captain of *Jupiter* anyway?

"While they run to and fro without thinking, we can move in with minimal interference." Kim sounded defeated already. His guilty conscience must really be bothering him.

Or was it the Tambootie he had stuffed in his pockets before liftoff? The kid definitely needed a long treatment with gamma blockers.

Loki did not have the luxury of a conscience or an addiction. As the eldest, he was responsible for the family's safety and their success.

"Let the droids refuel," Loki told Raaskan. "After that, no one but us gets aboard these two ships. And keep an eye on Kim. Don't let him do too much. Think about his orders before you do anything."

"I shall lead the foraging party for the red crystals," Raaskan said quietly. "I have memorized the plans. Stargod Kim should remain here to help guard the ships."

Loki nodded agreement. Under the influence of so much Tambootie, Kim might bond with the directional crystals and take off on some lumbird-brained excursion of his own.

"What about the people pounding on the doors?" Hestiia asked. She looked as if she wanted to throw the hatch open, or maybe grab a spear and run all of the IMPs through.

Part of Loki wanted to give in to the pleas of the people waiting outside the doors and give them a ride back to the planet. He did not dare. They had other means of escape. *Jupiter* should not crash for several weeks yet. Possibly months or even years. Plenty of time to strip the ship of everything usable.

Except the spin had already begun to slow. Momentum should have kept it going for weeks. Why weren't the techs making corrections manually?

Raaskan relayed the orders to his small band of warriors. Each was armed with iron knives, clubs, and/or iron tipped spears. They looked a fearsome bunch. More fearsome than fearful, he hoped. Bringing them along had been a calculated risk. They'd never encountered null g before. They'd never seen a spaceship.

But they were survivors one and all. And they obeyed the Stargods with unflinching loyalty.

Kim grabbed two antigrav cargo sleds from the racks along the bulkhead. Raaskan relieved him of the burden. Hestiia and Poolie each grabbed two more. Loki took the last two and parceled them out among the villagers. That left four men, including the two brawny blacksmith apprentices to guard the shuttle and the lander. And Kim. Enough.

Gravity remained here in the outer section of the ship, not as heavy as the last trip. Enough to make the antigrav sleds necessary.

Kim directed four men from his crew to begin loading the sleds with the small red directional crystals from the nearest rabbit hole. One hundred forty-four of the small red stones would take time to load, but should offer no great challenge.

"I'll stay here and supervise. Can you get the drivers?" Kim asked. His eyes looked bloodshot and he moved sluggishly.

"Twelve greens shouldn't present a problem. Getting from here to the crystal room and back again will be the problem. Konner insisted we need the drivers from the midship array. They are a fraction bigger than the aft and bow circles. How do we keep the evacuees from breaking in here and stopping us?"

"Give me two minutes at the sensor terminal."

Kim grinned, more sarcastic than humorous. He nibbled on a leaf of the Tambootie. Then he nearly skipped toward the computer terminal near the hatch into the corridor as if no more than normal g pressed upon him.

Loki shook his head at the immediate change in his brother. He vowed to himself that as soon as they returned dirtside, he'd get Kim those gamma blockers.

"Can you hack your way into bridge controls from here?" Loki asked Kim. Meant for recording quartermaster manifests, the terminal had limited access to the primary systems.

"Doubtful. But I can screw up a lot of signals. Anyone bothering to look at screens will see that the bay doors are damaged and the bay is empty and open to vacuum." Kim began working away at the touch screen.

Within a few moments, the line of desperate people fled the corridor, seeking another escape. Loki heard cries of dismay. They pushed and shoved each other ruthlessly. One small woman had trouble turning and moving with the flow. A heavy duffel bag on her shoulder already overbalanced her.

"Out of my way, SB," a squarely built man with a blind justice insignia on the collar and cuff of his black uniform snarled. He had a prow of a nose beneath black hair and beady eyes. "I'll have your stripes for blocking my way. I'm the judge. I ordered this evacuation. Now everyone out of my way. No one gets off this boat until I do." He shoved the woman viciously, slamming her into a bulkhead.

Her head smacked against the cerama/metal walls. The judge did not even look back at her. Blood trickled down the side of her face.

The crowd ignored her. They stepped around her. One slight man tromped on her sprawled legs trying to get out of the way of a bigger man.

Loki bit his lip. He gulped hard. She needed help. He should go to her. He didn't have time. *She* was not his responsibility.

Hestiia prodded his back. "We have to get going. She is the enemy. Not our concern," she said.

"I can't just leave her."

Loki's stomach sank. He had to obey his conscience after all.

* * *

Kat looked up at the thick cloud cover. A raindrop plopped onto her cheek. Then another struck her eye. She blinked rapidly to clear her vision.

"Nacring Nebulae!" she cursed. "First they abandon me. Then they kidnap me. Now they've stranded me in the middle of the bush in the middle of a rainstorm with only a primitive iron knife."

She turned slowly, trying to get her bearings. Which way led back to the village where her crewmates had landed?

Thick clouds obscured the sun's position. She'd never find north without help.

"I don't dare strike out on my own." She almost wept. "I don't even know which direction to go, even if I knew which direction to take."

She clenched her fist around the hilt of the weapon. The chunk of horn hacked from some poor animal warmed under her touch, seemed to mold to her grip. She stared at it a moment.

"Well, if you want to work, best we get started." She clamped her mouth shut on the last words. "What am I doing, talking to an inanimate object. A knife, by St. Bridget. A bloody *knife*."

The barbaric weapon did not answer her. Of course it wouldn't. She hadn't expected it to. She just needed to hear the sound of her own voice to convince herself she wasn't dreaming. That wasn't stepping over the line into insanity.

Was it?

Insanity? She'd invoked a saint she had not thought about since early childhood. Governor Talbot—Dad—had followed a different faith from her birth mother. She no longer believed in saints and miracles, or dragons and unicorns. She believed in her own hard work and intelligence.

Surely she could tame one wild clearing in the middle of nowhere long enough to give herself shelter and some food.

Her stomach growled. "Why didn't I bother with lunch before those barbarians invaded my ship?" she moaned.

(*Because you were too excited at the prospect of meeting your family to eat.*)

"Who said that?" Kat turned rapidly, scanning the clearing for intruders. She kept her knife at the ready. It balanced easily in her hand. She saw no one to use the weapon on. Not even a small rodent that might become dinner.

Then she shuddered at her primitive thoughts. No matter how desperate, she would not succumb to killing an animal, taking a life, merely to serve her noisy stomach. Maybe if she missed a meal or two a few of the extra inches on her hips would dissolve.

(*You must eat to keep your energy and your mind at peak functioning.*)

"Who is hiding in the bushes?" she demanded. She charged a large clump of greenery slashing with the knife. She bounced against flimsy branches. Her weapon embedded in the trunk. As she wrenched it free, she kept looking over her shoulder for the speaker.

A low chuckle came from behind her.

She whipped around, brandishing the knife. Nothing. No one. He had sounded so close.

Who?

Maybe she was going insane. People stranded on bush planets did that.

Maybe she was only hungry. Konner had said something about the bulb of a plant with yellow flowers, down by the creek.

Where in the frocking black hole was the creek?

(*Listen.*)

Sound advice. Her brain must be working properly and her imagination only put voice to it. A bright tenor voice. Too high to be one of her brothers. Too slow and drawling to be one of her shipmates.

She stood still and listened to the clearing. Birds chirping. Insects buzzing. Wind and rain. Grass growing. Trees reaching out with gratitude for the moisture . . .

"Stop that!"

Another low chuckle.

Then she heard it, beneath the other sounds, a soft ripple of water, faster than the dripping rain, gentler than the wind. She headed toward the sound.

Her nose worked in wonder. Gone was the citrus smell that permeated ships and domed cities. Green growth, falling leaves, sap from a softer wood, and the faint musk of an animal in rut flooded her senses. And over it all she inhaled the clean scent of vibrant life.

Her skin prickled from the cooler air. She rubbed her arms for warmth. The ground beneath her feet became spongy and descended at a gentle angle. Kat pushed aside drooping ferns. One of the fronds sliced her palm. She jumped back startled. Then she stared in fascinated horror at the drops of blood welling up from the wound.

A string of curses escaped her.

(*Suck it,*) the voice in the back of her mind suggested.

She knew she should. Enzymes in her own saliva

would begin the clotting and healing process. But the thought of tasting blood sent waves of revulsion through her. All of them knotted in her stomach.

If only she had a med kit she could spray the wound with a cooling gel that would clean and disinfect as well as seal it. Cool. She needed something cold to slow the bleeding. Then pressure and elevation.

(*The creek.*) This time the voice coaxed as if dealing with a small child.

In the bush she was an infant.

Not quite an infant. She'd taken shore leave on bush planets before. She'd aced three advanced survival courses. St. Bridget, she'd been born and raised in the bush. She knew what to do.

Always before, she'd had the option of an emergency beacon and extraction if she became overwhelmed, or hurt, or ill. Not here. Not now. She had to think and act in her own defense.

"The creek it is. I just hope I don't get infected with some exotic bacteria that causes my flesh to rot and slough off, leaving me a living skeleton."

(*Hardly.*)

She was getting used to the voice now.

Avoiding the ferns and placing her feet carefully, she descended a few more steps to find a wide pool fed by a small waterfall and draining by a narrow defile into another steeper fall. She plunged her hand into the pond. Cool water soothed the slight burn of the wound. After a few moments she lifted it free of the gently lapping water. Several moments passed and only a few beads of blood appeared. Satisfied, she looked for something to press against the wound.

All she could find was her trouser leg. Dared she risk getting her hand dirty again on her grubby uniform? Captain Leonard was finicky about uniforms. Kat followed her example and never allowed anything to mar the sharp crease on her trousers or the grime to show. Instantly, she felt grubby and itchy. The rain did nothing to cleanse her of the sensations. Surely kidnap and stranding in the bush offered an adequate excuse for a less than pristine uniform.

She pressed her palm against her thigh. What was one more stain? Still she wanted a bath and a clean uniform. NOW.

"I'm as bad as a dome breather," she admonished herself. "This isn't building a shelter or providing me with fuel."

She looked for yellow flowers. Three stalks of them to her left drooped under the weight of the rain. A few thrusts of the knife loosened the soil at their base. She tugged them free. Sure enough a fat bulb grew at the end of each plant.

She shook off loose dirt. Too much remained. Back to the pool. She had to kneel in the muck at the edge, further staining her uniform. After swishing the knife and vegetation in the water, some splotches of soil and rotting vegetation clung to both. Nothing for it but to use her hands to scrub.

A little pressure from her fingers cleared off any remaining debris. She let her hands linger in the soothing water. Not as cold as she expected. The feeder creek looked like it cascaded straight down the nearest mountain glacier. It should numb her skin by now.

"Hot springs?" she asked the air.

No answering voice, just a sensation of a nod of agreement.

She'd have to remember the hot spring when the rain chilled her to the bone.

"A fire. Konner said I could start a fire by sparking a rock off the knife blade.". If there was any wood dry enough to burn.

Cautiously, she broke a path back to the clearing,

being careful to avoid the fronds of the plant she
named saber ferns. Beneath some of the taller shrubs
she spotted small twigs and branches that had broken off in an earlier season. These she gathered. By
the time she made one full circuit of the clearing, she
had an armload of bigger branches.

"Now if only I can remember the formation for the
most efficient fire." She'd aced the classes on survival. As she'd aced all of her classes and graduated
a year early. So why had what she had learned about
fires slid out of her brain like hot grease poured
down a drain?

"What good was it to finish at the top of two
classes and be denied assignment for years?" she
muttered the old grief. Flying admin touch screens
for four years while training on every vessel in the
fleet and earning graduate degrees did not advance
her career. Space time alone granted promotions.
Well, she had some space time now and look where
it got her. Stranded on a bush planet by her own
flesh and blood.

"I'll get you for this, Brothers O'Hara. One way or
another I'll see all three of you mind-wiped or dead."
Resolutely, she set about stacking her wood. When
she ran out of fuel, she sat back on her heels and
admired her construct. Text book construction. But
would it work?

(May I light this for you?)

Kat looked up and stared straight into the swirling
eyes of a red-tipped dragon, steam trailing from its
nostrils, teeth longer than her knife blade dripping
with saliva.

She fainted.

CHAPTER 35

L OKI GRABBED the latch. He had to help the trampled crew woman. The rest of the mission had to wait. Hestiia followed him into the corridor, right on his heels. She stared about anxiously as Loki stooped to touch the stranger's neck.

Her pulse beat strong, if a little too fast. Her eyelids fluttered.

"Let me help you up," he said quietly, hoping for a soothing tone. He checked her insignia and name tag at the same time.

She opened her eyes and gasped. Her eyes threatened to roll up in another faint.

"I won't hurt you. My word of honor," Loki protested. He grasped her elbow and lifted her.

She scrambled to pull away from him.

"SB Lee, compose yourself," he ordered.

She nodded at his authoritative tone, blinking her almond-shaped eyes rapidly and chewing on her thick lower lip. Then her expression brightened.

A lone straggler hastened down the corridor, checking monitors every ten paces. He had a duffel matching SB Lee's slung over his shoulder.

Lee shrugged off Loki's helping hand and rushed to the newcomer's side. Jabbering explanations, they turned away from Loki and Hestiia. They seemed more interested in finding an escape vessel than reporting the presence of intruders.

Loki breathed a sigh of relief.

When the IMP couple disappeared around the curve, Loki led his troops toward the center of the ship.

They made good progress in the outer level. As they climbed, gravity lessened. At first the bushies smiled and bounded from corridor to corridor. They hopped and rebounded, delighted with the lessening gravity.

The next set of stairs upward gave them all fits until Loki got behind and pushed everyone and the sleds up. Then the fun began. All seven of Loki's charges began bouncing off bulkheads, ceilings, decks. They abandoned their sleds in order to experiment with the novelty of micro gravity.

Normally reserved and thoughtful, Hestiia turned a double somersault in midair. She quickly learned that she could increase her speed by grasping her knees and tucking her head.

Poolie walked delicately upside down. She took small, mincing steps and managed to maintain her orientation.

Niveean, a stout and seasoned warrior, lost his lunch in a cross corridor.

Loki stood back and watched for several minutes. As much as he wanted to rush to finish his job, he knew his helpers needed time to learn to move without the anchor of gravity and the orientation of a horizon. A few moments of play now might save them an hour of mishaps later when the sleds were laden with precious crystals.

Two dozen IMPs jogged toward them. At fifteen meters' distance, they stopped abruptly and brought their weapons to bear. Counter-grav equipment gave them stability in the .3g sector.

Loki gulped.

"State your business, bushie," the sergeant spat. His voice sounded a lot like one of his weapons would when he pulled the trigger.

"We're crew, in native disguise. Deep cover. We're salvaging for dirtside survival. Commander Leonard's orders," Loki returned. He refrained from saluting.

"Command code?"

Loki spat back the data stream he'd gleaned from Kat's mind. The one that opened the launch bay doors.

The sergeant nodded abruptly and signaled his men forward. They pushed past Loki and his natives, weapons shouldered.

At least some semblance of military discipline remained, even if it was lax. Leonard should have changed the command codes.

"You'll never be experts, but I think you can manage in null g now." Loki called his group together. "Follow me, move cautiously. Remember the bounce is strong. Keep your movements small and slow."

They had a few mishaps on the journey inward. The sleds did not want to move straight, especially up stairs. Niveean never did find a firm orientation and retched three more times before they reached the crystal room. He continued to plow forward, a small measure of the courage bred into him by centuries of warfare. A warrior endured pain and privation in order to protect his honor and those he held dear.

The chaos of the IMPs fleeing a sinking ship looked organized compared to the mess in the crystal room. Six techs flew, literally, from crystal to terminal to workbench and back again. They rebounded expertly into proper trajectories, grasping familiar handholds to brake or redirect their flight. Fiber optics, cables, and tools trailed in their wake, presenting hazards to the unwary. One woman worked frantically at a terminal trying to become the king stone for this array. The expression on her face showed the strain of thinking and entering commands at speeds beyond normal human capability.

Hestiia watched them with her mouth half open. Awe brightened her countenance.

Twelve beautifully clear, green crystals dominated the room, each a meter high, bigger around than a blacksmith's well-muscled upper arm, and sharply faceted. The bright glow of life had burned low in their cores. Unless their connection to a king stone was restored soon, they would die. Loki had to get them back to the clearing quickly and reconnect them as a family.

"If you are trying to stabilize *Jupiter*'s orbit, your job is futile," Loki announced to the techs.

"Fearsome Kahli!" one exclaimed. "It's him again."

"The O'Hara," stated another.

"Stinking bushie!"

At the last insult, anger burned Loki's cheeks. Every one of the men and women in their ugly khaki coveralls had the short, compact stature of civils, civilized citizens of the GTE. Sonic bathers. *Dome breathers.*

"I'll have you know that I bathe every day in real water with soap," he replied coldly. He could not give in to the temper that demanded he lash out with fists and feet. Too much depended upon getting the crystals safely back to the clearing.

Loki moved to the first driver crystal. Konner had disconnected them. The stones would not lash out with burning energy if disturbed. He twisted the first one and lifted it out of its socket. Tens of meters of fiber-optic cable attached to it tangled between the stone and its designated computer interface.

"Stop that. You're killing the ship!" A tech tried to pull the green crystal from Loki's grasp.

"That is the idea, odiferous civil. This ship will crash and you and your mates will be stranded dirtside forever," he snarled. He jerked to his left, pulling the stone away from the tech. The abrupt movement sent him spinning.

Niveean stopped Loki with a strong hand.

The tech hit the bulkhead. His head slammed against the unforgiving walls with a sickening thud.

"Techs, take care of your buddy. Time for you to join the rest of the rats fleeing this ship," Loki ordered.

If a person could scuttle in null g, the techs managed to give that appearance as they hastened to take one of their own to the nearest medical facility.

Loki gently placed the crystal on the sled. The fiber optics tangled and coiled around his feet.

"May I assist?" Hestiia asked. Even before he could answer, she began separating the fiber optics at the source.

In a remarkably short time, Hestiia had untangled the cables as if working with a very fragile yarn.

The woman at the terminal continued her futile task, never looking up. Every micron of her attention belonged to her task.

Would she even notice when her green crystals left the array and she had nothing left to command?

"This is for your own good, ma'am." Loki pressed two fingers hard against her jugular vein until her head lolled forward. Before she could recover consciousness, he lifted her from her chair and placed her outside the room, slumped against a bulkhead.

Then he exhaled sharply. Followed by a deep inhale. He felt better. His mind cleared of the red mist of anger.

"Hestiia, you and Poolie work on the cables . . . er . . . ropes." He had to remember to use vocabulary they understood, though they learned fast. Faster than some civils. "Men, you free the crystals, carefully wrap the ropes around each one and load it onto a sled."

They obeyed without question and treated the crystals with care and respect; more so than many civils would have.

"Well done, my friends. Now we have to get them back to the launch bay. Avoid contact with any of the . . ." How to describe the IMPs? "The Others. These stones are very valuable. They will help defend the Stargods and our people in the weeks to come."

They all nodded solemnly. Hestiia and Poolie both placed a hand flat against their bellies in an instinctive protective gesture. Time to get them back into gravity. Too much time in null g during gestation kept babies from developing correctly.

The corridors seemed more crowded on the return journey. Perhaps because Loki tried to avoid contact. He feared an overzealous Marine might try to retrieve the crystals. Niveean, the warrior, became their lookout. He directed them into shadowy hiding places Loki never would have considered viable.

They had just crept out from one such alcove beside the hatch they needed to take them back to the launch bay when a woman in a bright suit of fashionable cut stepped in front of them. Her blonde hair looked as if she'd combed it with her fists. Creases marred the sharp tailoring of her trousers. Scuffs showed on her dainty boots.

She pointed a needle pistol at Loki's eyes.

"Hello, Cyndi," Loki gulped.

"Bastard bushie. Why are you trying to kill me?"

CHAPTER 36

(*RYTHROS*.)

"Is that a name?" Kat mumbled. She kept her eyes closed, not wanting to acknowledge that she had fainted or why.

(*Yes*.)

A pregnant pause. The voice waited for a reply.

"Kat Talbot, Lieutenant JG assigned to IMP Cruiser *Jupiter*. Helmsman."

More silence.

"Not enough? Yeah. Mari Kathleen Talbot."

(*O'Hara*.)

"O'Hara by birth, not by choice." Kat opened one eye warily. She still saw the dragon. Immense. Shimmery in the fading light. Red outlined its horns and wing veins. It blinked a translucent membrane over the red-and-silver eyes. The swirling pupil opened wide, drawing her into unknown realms of thought and imagination.

She slammed her eyes shut against the invitation to trust her soul to this creature's scrutiny.

A sense of hurt and embarrassment spread outward from the back of her neck.

"Sorry, critter, but my thoughts are my own. You may not have them."

The dragon lowered its head. In acceptance? Or to skewer her with the spiraled horn on its forehead?

She scrambled backward rather than take a chance. She found the knife still clutched in her left fist.

Konner had said she could defend herself against animals bigger than herself with it. She snorted in derision. The knife would prove useless against this beast.

"What do you want from me?" She sat up straight. The dragon did not come any closer. Rolling to her knees and then her feet, she kept the knife ready. She figured the half-furled wings would be vulnerable. If she damaged one, the beast would not be able to take wing and follow her through the underbrush.

Provided she could get away before it flamed her. The smoke kept curling from its nostrils in mute reminder that it liked to eat its meals cooked.

"What do you want from me?" she repeated.

(*To help.*)

Puzzled, Kat stared at him, braving those hypnotic eyes. "Why?"

(*You are of the blood of the Stargods. You need help. I must aid you.*)

That made no sense at all.

"I am not even certain I believe you exist. Why should I ask for help?" Dismissing the beast as an obvious hallucination—prolonged exposure to the alien air must have made her feverish—Kat knelt before her pile of brush, picked up a nearby rock and struck it against her blade.

A feeble spark died before jumping onto the kindling.

(*Allow me to light the fire, please.*)

"Go away. You do not exist."

A sharp prod to her back brought her to her feet, swinging the blade.

The dragon had lowered the tip of its spiral horn level with her chest. (*I exist!*)

"Okay, okay, I believe you."

(*No, you do not.*)

"Well . . . I can barely see you, and then only in certain lights. All the science I know proves that dragons cannot exist in this dimension within the physical laws of the universe.

(*If you ride on my back and see the ley lines, will you believe?*)

"Now I know you are a product of my imagination."

(*You said this to Stargod Konner.*)

"But . . ."

(*Come. Mount. I will show you.*) The dragon crouched down and extended its foreleg.

Kat gulped. Then she squared her shoulders, anchored the knife inside her belt, grasped one spinal horn, and heaved herself aboard. The dragon did not wait for her to settle her butt before it bounded three steps across the clearing, flapped its giant wings, and leaped above the trees. Chill wind and rain rushed past them. The ground and trees fell away. A cloud enveloped them in thick mist.

She swallowed, trying to keep her stomach and its slight contents in place. She clung to the horn in front of her with both hands. Another horn braced her back. She clamped her knees tightly against the dragon's back. Through the insulated cloth of her uniform she felt the animal's muscles ripple as it worked the wide wings. She risked a look at the translucent marvels of flight.

Fascination overcame her fear. In her mind, she saw the air currents vector across the wings. The beast would not tumble from its flight path unless injured. She was as safe here as in any craft built by the Imperial Military.

Maybe safer.

Then she gloried in the sensation of freedom. How often had she dreamed of flying without a craft surrounding her?

"Which direction?" she shouted over the rush of air in her face.

(South and east.)

"Why there?"

(*Because it does not rain in the desert.*)

"No rain. No clouds. We can see the ground."

(*And the ley lines.*)

"What exactly are ley lines?"

(*Life.*)

"What is that supposed to mean?"

The dragon banked into a wide circle, moving farther east than south. If her sense of direction was correct. Up here, shrouded in mist, nothing seemed real. She'd lost her horizon and landmarks.

"Why are we changing direction?"

(*To avoid the place of Hanassa.*)

"I've heard that name somewhere."

(*Your brothers.*)

She could not remember in what context she had heard the name, only that she had. Painstakingly, she dredged up every word of her conversations with her brothers. Nope. No mention of Hanassa.

"Why do we have to avoid this place?"

(*Evil. Can you not feel it? Can you not hear it?*)

Then she sensed a vibration that might be a pinging in her ears. The sound of a distress beacon.

Adrenaline shot through her. "We have to help them."

(*Hanassa lies. Never believe anything that comes from Hanassa.*)

"Is Hanassa a man or a place?" A burning sensation on her right shoulder drew her attention. The distress beacon broadcast to all of her senses, demanding she come to it.

(*Both.*)

"But the beacon . . ."

(*Is false.*)

"The second beacon. Why are there two? I thought the bounty was for only one."

A mental shrug from Irythros. Good thing only his mind responded. If he'd rotated his massive shoulders, she might lose her grip.

They burst clear of the clouds. Bright sunshine pelted her eyes. She closed them tightly, then opened them slowly, getting used to the change in light by degrees.

Jagged mountain peaks tipped with snow stretched from left to right in a broken chain. They seemed close enough to touch, yet so far away as to be unreachable, even on dragon back. She tried to pick out a pass through them. Faint traces of trails showed possibilities, all too rugged for any but the most intrepid traveler.

Her uniform had not been designed for high-altitude open air flight. The cold settled into her bones and would not let go. Her fingers and toes grew numb. Her teeth began to chatter.

The cold squeezed her bladder.

Did Irythros increase his speed?

She hoped so. She did not know how much longer she could endure without losing her grip upon his horn.

Without a chrono, Kat had no way of determining the passage of time. Flight across the mountain range could have taken digital hours or mere femtos.

Then, quite suddenly, with no warning at all, the mountains fell behind and a vast desert opened before them. Irythros shed altitude. The air temperature warmed. As they dropped closer to the scrubby plateau, Kat forgot her physical discomfort. She forgot her need to relieve herself.

"Hundreds of square klicks of nothing but a few low shrubs, rocks, and dust."

(*Look more closely.*) Irythros skimmed the surface.

She caught a glimpse of movement. A lizard scurried beneath them, frantically seeking shelter from the huge predator. It finally crouched in the shadows cast by a cluster of rocks.

"So there is life in the desert. It isn't empty."

(*Look more closely.*) Irythros surged upward and stabilized about one hundred meters higher. He flew a lazy circle.

Kat peered down. "What am I supposed to see?"

No answer.

She checked the horizon. Mountains on three sides, in the distance she caught glimpses of a deep river valley emptying into the sea. A magnificent landscape. But then hundreds of bush planets had awe-inspiring vistas.

(*Look deeper.*)

"Beneath the soil? Are there subterranean streams?"

(*Deeper into your self. Look with your other sight.*)

The hot desert air penetrated the synthetic fabric of Kat's uniform. She began to perspire. Sweat dripped into her eyes. The salty moisture stung. She dared not lift a hand from her grip of the horn to dash it away. She blinked it away and wiped her cheeks on her shoulder as best she could.

When she looked again, her eyes detected an altered spectrum. Reds shifted toward blue, greens toward yellow, and the light slanted in from an angle at odds with the westering sun. She blinked again to clear her eyes of salt.

Colors became prisms. Individual drops of moisture became crystals.

And then she saw it. Them.

A giant web of blue energy. Random lines crossed, merged, veered off in new directions. No uniformity or symmetry. Just pulsating life.

"I believe," Kat breathed.

(*First you must touch a ley line and understand.*)

"It's getting late. Maybe another day."

(*Now.*) Irythros shed the last hundred meters of altitude with a stomach-jolting dive.

Kat clung to the spinal horn with all her might. Acceleration flung her against the horn at her back with the force of at least two gs. Not so bad a pressure in an enclosed craft. Dangerous in the open, with no buffer from the wind that tore at her hair and ground her face with grit.

Blessedly, the dive lasted only a few femtos. Kat alighted from the dragon with shaking knees. "May a Denobian muscle-cat develop a taste for your flesh," she cursed. Then added a few more in three languages.

Irythros glared at her, unappreciative of her creativity.

"And may the fleas of a thousand camels infest your lair," she added for good measure.

The dragon's skin rippled the length of his entire back, as if it itched.

(*Find your ley line and learn it,*) he snapped and turned his tail toward her. It thrashed the ground in agitation.

She skipped away from him. Only when she was out of reach of the lethally spiked tail did she look around and assess the landscape.

"As soon as I find one of those ley lines, we can leave?"

A sense of agreement, but no words formed in the back of her mind.

Kat heaved a sigh of resignation and walked a little farther away. Her soft ship boots scuffed the loose red dirt. The light breeze picked up the loose grains and swirled them away. Heat baked the chill of flight from her bones and flushed her skin.

She wouldn't last long out here without water, skin

protectors, and a hat. Best she get on with this. Stalling and denial would not get her out of the desert.

A deep breath inward and she allowed her eyes to unfocus. Nothing. Maybe if she let some sweat drip into her eyes again, she could let the fractured sight line reveal the energy beneath the ground.

Nothing. Another deep breath of the hot dry air. She almost coughed out the grit that permeated everything. Her exhalation went on and on. She couldn't get rid of enough tainted carbon dioxide. When she thought her lungs would collapse, her body shuddered and jerked and took in a huge gulp of fresh air. It still tasted of dirt but seemed to fill every crevice of her being with . . . clarity.

Blue lines jumped into view. Some fat, others skinny. Farther apart than she'd expected from her first glimpse from one hundred meters up.

Now what?

(*You must take the energy into yourself and understand it.*)

Kat took another deep breath, this time for courage. Was she about to be electrocuted? Torn apart by antimatter? Sucked into another dimension?

Well, if the lines killed her, she'd likely die more quickly and with less pain than from exposure in the desert.

She picked out a particularly fat line about one hundred meters to her left. As she approached it, she noticed that if she followed it back toward where the dragon crouched it met two more lines, forming a kind of pool or knot. Instinctively, she headed for the junction.

Irythros nodded as if in approval.

Keeping her eyes slightly unfocused and her breathing deep and even, she stretched forth her left foot, letting her toes brush the silvery blue that wanted to elude her, like mercury released in null g.

A tiny jolt crept up her leg as far as her knee. She jerked her foot away. Not exactly a jolt, more like a thrill. Enticing. Probably dangerous.

She checked out the dragon again. He had not budged.

"Again?"

No response from the dragon.

This time Kat placed her left foot fully inside the pool. Tingles slid up her limb, climbing higher with each breath. When it reached her heart, gravity seemed to disappear. If she lifted her arms just so, she might truly fly. Alongside the dragon rather than atop him.

Addicting. She brought her other foot into the circle of arcane power.

The world tilted, colors shifted.

Her senses opened. A cacophony of insects buzzing, wind sighing, burrowing animals digging, the dragon's innards boiling, ready to flame something. She heard it all, became a part of it all, shared the life of each entity. Suddenly she knew what it meant to be a dragon and breathe fire upon a fresh kill and savor the rich flavor of broiled meat. She understood a mouse's need to dig a deep burrow to hide from the elements and predators. She became the air with a deep urge to flow from here to there to balance air pressure. Massing moisture buoyed her.

She had purpose. Life had meaning if only she reached out and grasped it.

Her mind opened and she knew how to reach out telepathically, to equalize weight and mass and lift anything with her mind. If she thought about the future, she could catch glimpses of possibilities. . . .

Like a king stone reaching out to its mother stone, Kat extended her senses upward, outward. She brushed past *Jupiter*, acknowledged *Sirius*, and sped onward, seeking something familiar. A home. Mum?

She conjured an image from memory of a woman nearing forty Earth Standard Years, taller than mid-height but nowhere near as tall as her oldest teenage son. Her features took on care lines from worry. Kat gave the woman her own nose and chin but softer eyes that lighted with love whenever she looked upon her four children. She had to have red hair, like each of her offspring, but with gray hints at the temples.

With the image came the brush of a mind. Just a hint. Nothing more than knowing that the woman existed, alone, frightened, worried, and . . . obsessed.

Her obsession turned inward. Grew malignant. Shifted focus. The need to amass more money outweighed the purpose for that money. She would never have enough wealth to go in search of her daughter. That quest might end in failure. She'd failed at so much already. The need to make more and more money was something she never failed at.

Abruptly Kat dropped out of the trance. She swayed as her mind plummeted back into her body. For one hundred too-rapid heartbeats reality took on the pallor of the unreal.

When she thought about the enormity of her mental journey, Kat stumbled.

She caught her balance on Irythros' muzzle. Then she straightened, more sure of herself and what she had to do than she had been in many years.

She blinked, puzzled by the uncertain light. While she had been . . . elsewhere, day had turned to night. Stars shone brightly in the skies, alien constellations teased her mind with mythical creatures and heroic figures behind them.

"How long was I gone?"

(*Not long. Day turns to night quickly here.*)

"Thank you, Irythros." She caressed the soft fur of his muzzle gently. "Now I know what my brothers call magic and why it works. I do not agree with the life path they have chosen, but I understand it."

(*Then we can return.*)

"Will you take me to my people?"

(*Of course. Where else would we go?*)

CHAPTER 37

STRANGE FACES crowded around Dalleena. They drifted in and out of her field of vision. The sounds of their senseless jabbering left her bewildered, uncertain, frightened. So intense. So rapid in their dialogues.

Desperately, she tried to get a sense of place. The light was wrong. Yellowish. Harsh. Her eyes did not want to open to confront it.

She let go of her need to know for a moment. If she could just relax and let her senses take in the flood of information, she could sort it out later.

A vague recollection of flying soothed her. She had flown with Stargod Konner. He had shown her the wonders of her world from the inside of his magic dragon. Not magic, she reminded herself. A machine. A very complicated machine.

One day, perhaps, he would allow her to control it, to feel the rush of air beneath the wings and the speed of flying across the vast ocean in a few hours. Fishing boats needed many months to do the same and rarely undertook the perilous journey to the other side of the world.

She wanted to fly again. In the machine called *Rover* and in Konner's arms. The wonders of the last two days flooded her with warmth. She felt herself smile and sigh contentedly.

The barrage of voices quieted. Good. They confused her so that she could not think, could not sort through what her senses told her.

Another long space of time. She thought she slept. The light changed. Dimmed. No longer harsh, just . . . different. Finally, she opened her eyes.

Starlight glimmered beyond the window. She knew where she was now. The cabin of the Stargods. The bed she had shared with Konner last night. Where was he now?

Beyond the curtain that separated the two rooms of the cabin, she heard a murmur of voices. He must be there, talking with his brother Loki. Too many voices. One feminine. Kim and Hestiia must have joined Konner as well.

Why had he left her alone?

She tried sitting up. Pain lashed across her middle. Her breath caught and she cried out.

Memory returned. The bull. The intruder with the gun. The bull charging. The wide horns filling her vision. Flying through the air. Landing heavily, too heavily, hearing something snap. Something else crunched.

If she did not move, she could breathe through the pain. Every muscle stilled. A gnawing ache persisted.

Then true fear assailed her. The IMPs controlled the village. Konner and his brothers had gone to steal something very important from the intruder's ship, far up in the sky, near the blanket of the night sky.

She wanted to cry with loneliness and pain. She dared not. Until she knew the extent of her injuries and her status with the Others, she had to remain strong. And silent. Listening and watching.

Stillness was good. She could control the pain and her breathing if she remained motionless.

A shadow blotted out the stars for a moment. She held her breath. Then a familiar scent wafted across her face. Her heart warmed.

"Konner," she breathed.

"Dalleena, sweetheart." His lips whispered across hers.

"Are we safe?" She barely heard her own voice.

"Not completely. What happened? Are you ill?"

"Hurt. The bull." She gasped for air. Her chest did not want to expand far enough to let her bring enough in. "One of the *Others* was going to shoot him. I could not let him. Ruin village if lose bull. I tackled. Bull charged." Each phrase came out more broken than the last.

Stillness, she reminded herself. After several long moments she could breathe almost normally again.

Konner hushed her with a hand over her mouth. He made a brief but thorough examination of her body with gentle hands.

"Gored?" he asked.

"Broken ribs. Don't know what else."

She sensed his nod more than saw it. "Immobility cast across your belly. Head?" His fingers found the bindings on her brow.

She tried to shake her head no, but it hurt too much, all the way down her spine to the backs of her legs and up over the top of her skull into her eyes.

He must have felt her wince.

"Concussion. Painkillers. Can you be quiet if I help you out of here?"

No! Her mind and body protested the thought of moving. But she had to trust Konner. The Stargod must know what was best for her.

As long as he remained by her side, she could endure anything. She hoped.

"Yes." She breathed deeply, preparing herself for the sharp onslaught of pain.

He ripped something from her wrist. Just a tiny prick of discomfort compared to the thought of actually moving her body. A few drops of moisture trickled across her hand. Then he removed a patch from her temple. It came off with a sucking sound. She winced again as several hairs tore free with the patch.

A quiet chirp, like a baby bird, began. The soft voices on the other side of the curtain ceased.

Dalleena felt them listening.

Konner hurriedly replaced the patch. The bird ceased chirping.

"I'd better check on that," a female voice said.

Konner faded away from Dalleena. One of the yellowish lights glowed brighter, closer. It appeared around the edge of the silvery curtain that separated the two rooms of the cabin. The too-steady light reminded her of an overlarge fish eye glowing in the depths of the Great Bay at midnight on the dark of the moon.

Soft footfalls behind the light explained the slight bobbing motion the eye made. Still it did not flicker like a normal candle or oil lantern. Dalleena studied the area illuminated by the eye, memorizing the placement of the few articles of furniture and the baskets of clothes and tools. Konner was neater than his brother, but still not overly concerned with the clutter that blocked direct pathways. Some of the baskets showed signs of having been pushed hastily aside to clear a broader path.

Of the person behind the light, she could see nothing.

Dalleena lay still, barely daring to breathe as gentle hands probed the patch on her temple and then ran down her arm.

"What have you done, silly girl?" The woman

shook her head as she laid the light down on top of
the machine beside Dalleena. The new position of the
light allowed greater visibility. Words flew rapidly
from the woman's tongue. Dalleena had to listen
carefully and sort them through several times to
make sense of them.

"If you are awake enough to rip out your IV, I
guess you don't need it anymore." The woman
stared at the transparent snake in her hand. Instead
of a head, it had a long metal tongue at the end. A
tongue that was so sharply pointed it could easily
penetrate flesh. Moisture dripped from it onto the
floor.

"You'll feel the lack of pain meds, but I think we
can leave this out. You'll be able to eat and drink in
the morning. Then we'll get a real ultrasound unit
from *Jupiter* to hasten the healing." The woman set
aside the snake.

"How about another session with the US?" The
woman sat on a stool beside the bed. She retrieved
a small device from her pocket. With a quick flick of
the woman's hand, Dalleena's shirt fell open. She
placed the small device upon Dalleena's ribs, right at
the sorest point. Something thick and hard lay between the device and her skin.

The immobility cast?

After several long moments the woman sighed and
lifted the device. "Enough for now. That should
speed the healing and let you move a little easier.
But you have to leave the monitor alone for now."
She pressed the temple patch tighter against Dalleena's skin. "Now go to sleep. That is the best medicine
for broken bones and a bump on the head."

The woman left as quietly as she had come, taking
the light with her.

"She woke up and ripped out her IV. Must have
panicked. You know primitives. They fear anything

they haven't seen before," the woman explained to her unseen companions.

When their soft murmurs resumed, Konner eased back beside Dalleena. Where had he hidden? The light had been powerful enough to eliminate all but the darkest recesses of the room.

He fumbled with the machine attached to the patch by a stiff string. Then he removed the patch again. The bird remained asleep.

"Not a sound," he breathed.

She nodded her consent. Then he gently helped her to roll to her side and drop her feet to the dirt floor. Her body was on fire with pain. She kept moving, knowing if she flopped back upon the bed she would never get up again. The effort made her hold her breath against crying out.

Tears pricked her eyelids. She clamped them shut while she breathed heavily.

Konner sat beside her. She leaned into him, grateful for the support of his body. He draped one arm around her hips, placing her own arm around his.

"Together," he breathed and stood, carrying her with him.

She wasn't ready. Agony sent her head spinning. She had to close her eyes again to maintain her balance. But she was up. The worst was over.

She hoped.

One step at a time, halting for her to catch her breath with each one, they walked to the curtain. Konner breathed deeply, three times. Then he gently eased the silvery material aside.

Dalleena nearly stepped back into the darkness at the sight of a blonde woman and two men, all in the mud-colored uniforms of the Others, sitting on stools of curious construction around a small table. They held flat things in their hands, like leaves but sturdier, covered in bright colors and designs. Surely

they must look up from their intense study of the
leaves and see Konner and herself.

As if she had commanded it, the blonde woman
looked up and stared right at them.

Dalleena held her breath.

Konner kept his body between her and the intruders and kept walking, slowly, quietly.

The woman returned her gaze to her leaves. Her
eyes did not focus upon Konner and Dalleena.

Dalleena held her breath until they passed through
yet another of the silvery curtains. The night was
warm and the intruders had not closed the door that
Loki had installed just days before. He had been
proud of his accomplishment, showing the others
how the door would keep out the cold, wind, and
rain better than blankets woven of red cow fur.

Outside, Dalleena breathed short gasps of the
humid air. The intense pain of getting out of the bed
faded to sharp aches. She breathed again, shallowly.
The air was heavy with recent rain and more to
come. It smelled wet, clean, better than the closeness
of the cabin. Clouds obscured the stars. Rain would
fall again by dawn. She and Konner had to be far
away long before then.

How? Already her knees wanted to buckle from
the strain of walking through the pain and the dizziness from the lump on the back of her head. Konner
kept her upright and moving. Konner showed her
the way through the sleepy patrols around the perimeter of the village. Konner gave her the strength
and courage to keep moving when all she wanted
was to fall upon the ground and sleep until the ache
went away.

Finally they reached Petram, the huge boulder that
had refused to be moved from the middle of the
fields.

Gratefully, Dalleena leaned against the rock. The

cool surface soothed her sweating body. She hoped she wasn't feverish from her injuries.

Konner scanned the skies and restlessly paced around Dalleena and the rock. She was afraid the sentries would see his movement, a darker shadow in the night.

"Konner, you have to know. Taneeo betrayed you. He . . ."

"I know. Raaskan told us. Pryth led a band of women to rescue the men. We will question Taneeo later."

"Then your people are safe from the Others?"

"For now. But they are not safe from Pryth." He almost chuckled.

"Now what?" Dalleena whispered. She doubted she could walk much farther without more rest, and nourishment. And more rest.

"We wait." They still spoke in hushed tones mindful of how sound carried on the still night air.

Dalleena was more than willing to wait. Not move. Just exist. She shifted against the rock and started to slide to a sitting position.

"Don't." Konner was beside her before she could do more than bend her knees. "If you go down, we'll have a s'murghin' difficult time getting you back up. We won't have a lot of time once things start happening."

"Like what?" She had to keep talking, keep him talking in order to stay awake. Her entire body felt too heavy to remain upright. And her torso ached. The pain reached all the way up her spine to her head and then darted between her eyes.

A refreshing breeze wafted across her face. It became a wind.

"Our transport just arrived," Konner said.

She felt the smile in his voice.

Dalleena dared move her eyes beyond the dim outline of his face. A larger shadow directly behind him blotted out the rest of the darkness.

"Oh," she moaned. "I do not think I can climb atop a dragon."

"You have to, Dalleena. This is the only way I can get you to safety."

CHAPTER 38

"CYNDI, HONEY," Loki pleaded with the irate woman before him. "You know I would never deliberately hurt you."

"Do I?" she snarled at him. "Now answer my question. Why are you doing this?"

"It's a long story. One that will sound better around a campfire with a good dinner inside you." Five months ago, Loki had scorned the evening ritual. At this moment in time, he wanted nothing more than to be in the middle of one.

"Campfire? *Campfire!*" she shouted. "You expect *me* to contaminate myself with smoke, and meat, and . . . and *unscrubbed* air?" Lucinda Baines, daughter of a planetary governor, granddaughter of an Imperial Senator, and great-niece to a previous emperor, shuddered with genuine fear. Her attention wavered and her grip on the needle pistol loosened.

Niveean, the silent warrior, pushed off the bulkhead to his left and slammed into Cyndi. Startled, Cyndi did not begin to struggle until they slid toward the deck.

Loki grabbed the loose pistol and tossed it to Hestiia. "Don't use it unless you have to, to save the crystals. Get the crystals to Kim," he commanded. He lunged into the fray, heavily and clumsily.

Hestiia, Poolie, and the others grabbed the sleds and disappeared down the last hatch.

Cyndi kicked and tore at Niveean. She twisted herself on top of him. Each movement became slower in the heavier g. The big man kept his arms around her in a wrestler's hug.

Loki fell short of his target. With his head in the middle of Cyndi's back he locked his arms around her legs. She kicked back, connecting hard with his upper thigh. The heel of her fashionable shoes gouged his flesh. He gritted his teeth and hung on. When he knew his grip was firm, he flung his legs wide, encircling hers. They tumbled backward, Niveean on top of both.

She heaved against Loki. He pressed harder.

Niveean scrambled to his knees and then to his feet. He grabbed the jamb around the hatchway. His breath came in short sharp pants.

Then Loki pressed their limbs together in an odd parody of a lovers' embrace.

Loki rolled, keeping his arms around Cyndi. The open hatch downward toward the launch bay was at his elbow. "Duck," he screamed in her ear and swung his feet into the opening.

She barely obeyed him in time. The top of the hatchway scraped her flying hair close to her scalp. With a little yelp of surprise, or indignation, he couldn't tell which, she complied.

They fell heavily.

Still locked together, they slid down to the lowest level of the ship. The extreme gravity—less than when Loki had left the launch bay an hour ago—grabbed hold of them. They landed heavily on a pile of tarps and rolled.

To their right, Kim was helping his wife and Poolie steer the sleds into the launch bay. The corridor was otherwise empty.

"Loki, we don't have the time or resources to tend a hostage," Kim warned him.

"This one we have to take extra special care of," Loki grunted. Slowly, he disentangled himself from Cyndi.

"Who?" Kim asked. Then his eyes widened as he saw Cyndi's face.

"I believe you two have met," Loki said as he assisted Cyndi to her feet. He kept one hand firmly locked on her wrist. His grip must be painful to her, but she said nothing, only glared at him.

"A few years ago," Kim admitted. He turned his back on them and pushed Poolie and the second sled ahead of him into the bay.

"You owe that man your life," Loki reminded her. "Remember that and stay out of trouble."

"I owe you and your brothers nothing, Mathew Kameron O'Hara. You sabotaged this ship. You endanger my life now. Mine and everyone's aboard this ship." She hung back, bracing her feet wide.

"I always knew that life with you would never be easy," he grunted. Before she could reply, he slung her over his shoulder, clamped his arms around her legs, and lurched into the launch bay.

"Put me down, you barbarian."

"Quiet." He swatted her bottom. "There was a time when you liked being mauled by this barbarian."

"Never again!"

He did not care. He had better things to do with his life than cater to this spoiled dome breather.

* * *

(*Iianthe,*) the dragon announced his name.

A niggle of disappointment crawled up Konner's spine. He had come to think of Irythros as his personal dragon. Iianthe seemed more attached to Hestiia and Kim. Konner had to remind himself that no one "owned" a dragon. Wild creatures, they belonged only to themselves and to this planet. They assisted and advised humans as their whims and sense of honor dictated. Humans had little if anything to do with the decision.

"Konner." He bowed slightly to the purple-tipped dragon. "Give him your name, Dalleena. Dragon protocol."

She wheezed something that approximated her name. Konner did not like her labored breathing or how heavily she leaned against him.

"Sweetheart, we have to leave," he urged her forward. She shuffled her feet heavily. "It's for the best, Dalleena, no matter how much it hurts. I could not have gotten you away from the IMPs tomorrow."

She nodded her mute agreement and trudged the few remaining steps to the huge beast who waited for them.

Then the significance of the dragon name penetrated through Konner's worry about Dalleena.

"Iianthe?" Konner peered more closely at the purple-tipped dragon crouched in the middle of the field. "I expected Irythros." Where was the red-tip? They had planned for him to meet Konner and Dalleena.

(*Elsewhere*,) Iianthe responded to Konner's unspoken question.

"Welcome, Iianthe," Konner bowed again to the dragon. "May we ride upon your back to the place of safety?" He did not have time to debate with the dragon. He needed help getting Dalleena away *now*.

(*Yes*.) The deep bronze bell of Iianthe's voice reverberated on the back of Konner's tongue and at the base of his spine. (*Irythros sends greetings and a warning. You must beware of the one you trust. The one who does not smell correctly; the one who still speaks to the stars.*)

"And who might that be?" Typical cryptic dragon speech. Konner had no more time or patience for it. Why couldn't they just come out and say what was on their minds?

Iianthe did not reply.

Sighing heavily, Konner reverted to the purpose of this meeting. "If you speak of Taneeo, then we know of his betrayal. Pryth deals with him now. My lady is injured. Can you crouch lower to make climbing easier for her?"

(*You must carry her.*) With that pronouncement, Iianthe spread out, bringing his belly into contact with the ground and his left foreleg lower.

"I worry that our combined weight will damage you." Konner eyed the makeshift staircase of the dragon's limbs.

(*Do not.*) The dragon made himself flatter yet.

"Easy, love. This is going to hurt, but only for a little." He scooped Dalleena into his arms.

She groaned and her head fell against his shoulder. Before he could think twice about his actions, he hastened along Iianthe's foreleg to his shoulder. He had to shift Dalleena's weight to grasp a neck horn for balance as he heaved her upward between two spinal horns. She came awake again with a pain-filled gasp. She clutched her middle with crossed arms.

"Hey, you!" an IMP guard hailed them from the village compound. He brought his weapon to bear.

Konner scrambled up behind her. "Now, Iianthe." He slapped the dragon's side.

Iianthe took five steps, working his wings frantically.

A blast of energy shot from the IMP's weapon.

"Fool, you could kill her!" Lotski, the medic, cried. She clung to the guard's arm, tugging at his rifle.

Iianthe took three more long strides. His wing action seemed slower. He still did not have enough momentum or lift to fly.

Konner tried hunkering lower. Dalleena groaned as he pressed against her back. Her injuries would not allow her to bend.

Another bolt of energy slid past them. Voices rose in disagreement.

At last, after lumbering across three fields, Iianthe lifted in flight. Konner breathed a sigh of relief. Dalleena slumped against him.

And a low moan filtered into the back of Konner's mind.

"Iianthe? How fare you?"

(*Not well. I must land.*) With that pronouncement, he dropped rapidly below the tree line, onto a small knoll beside a tributary river. They had covered less than fifteen klicks' distance from the village

Konner dropped to the moss-covered rock. He let his hands roam over the dragon's hide, seeking the source of injury. He did not get far before he noticed the left wing drooping, only half folded. A little more investigation showed a deep burn where the lower wing bone met the spine.

"How can I help you?" he asked, careful to keep his hand off the injury.

(*Remove your lady from my back, Stargod Konner.*)

"Down is easier than up," Dalleena attempted a grin. She fell more than climbed down into Konner's arms. The jolt sent her groaning again.

Konner cradled her close to his heart. Tears smarted in his eyes. Disaster piled on complication. He bit back his own cries of frustration and disappointment.

Somehow they must make the best of this awful situation.

Before he could voice his thoughts, a soft silvery light emanated from the dragon's hide.

Konner blinked. The light grew to engulf him. It brightened until he had to close his eyes. Even through closed eyelids, the light nearly blinded him. He turned his back to the dragon's light, still protecting Dalleena in his arms.

With the light there came a hum. Unlike the song of the dragongate, this music tickled his mind with elusive harmonies and tunes.

Finally, the glare around them softened and receded. He opened his eyes and turned back to face the dragon. He nearly dropped Dalleena in surprise.

"Iianthe?" he asked of the black cat that crouched before him. No ordinary cat, this one had wings. One of them drooped.

(*Who else?*)

"You transformed into a flywacket. Never thought I'd live to see it happen." According to Hestiia, only a purple-tipped dragon could perform this miracle.

(*See and believe.*)

"Oh, I believe. Now what?"

(*We rest. Dalleena and I must huddle together for a time. You should build a fire, fish, bathe, refresh yourself.*)

"Never question a dragon." Konner shrugged and set Dalleena down beside the black cat. She draped an arm around the solid feline body. They leaned together, supporting each other.

The hum intensified and grew louder.

"Ultrasound," Konner murmured. "The original ultrasound for healing was a cat's purr."

No comment from either patient.

Konner set about his chores. Fire. Food. Bath. Sleep. Morning would determine if they could continue their journey. For now they were hidden from the IMPs.

CHAPTER 39

"WHERE IS EVERYBODY?" Loki asked as he stomped down the ramp from *Rover*. "We need to get started on building our defenses against the IMPs. We need plans and tools and Konner."

Kim had already disembarked from the stolen lander. He had an arm around Hestiia's waist and seemed oblivious to all else.

"What?" Kim asked, lifting his gaze from his wife.

"Konner. Kat. Where are they?" Loki knew a moment of panic. He suppressed it. If he showed weakness, they'd never get anything done. His people would doubt his wisdom.

All his troops looked about, puzzled by the emptiness of the clearing.

"Someone started to build a fire," Raaskan offered.

"Probably Kat. Konner knows how to build a better fire than that." Loki kicked at the pile of branches. It toppled easily. Lights from the two vessels illuminated the clearing but did not penetrate the tree line beyond.

"What do we do with the crystals?" Poolie asked. Like Kim and Hestiia, she and Raaskan clung to each other as if they had been parted for years instead of hours.

"Is this what you brought me to?" Cyndi whined from the hatchway. "There isn't even a building or a road, or other people or . . . or . . ." She bit her lip and turned her head away.

Loki caught a glint of moisture in her eyes.

"Sorry. Life is primitive out here in the bush. We survive by our wits and make what we need." Loki had no sympathy for her. Why had he ever believed himself in love with this spoiled dome breather?

"Primitive? Primitive implies rudimentary amenities. This is barbaric!" Cyndi's voice became shrill.

Loki blocked out the stream of invective that followed. "Stay aboard the shuttle, Cyndi. You'll only get dirty if you try to interfere." He might just deck her himself if she kept up her complaints.

Wisely, she retreated with a pout and an angry glint in her eye. The last time Loki had seen that expression on her face, he'd made love to her to soothe her mood. His aggression had excited her and her mood changed rapidly.

He'd not resort to that method of appeasing her again.

"What do we do with the crystals?" he asked Kim.

"Konner knows where he wants them placed," his brother replied.

"Can we not duplicate the distances on the mother ship?" Hestiia asked. Her ability to learn new vocabulary and make associations never ceased to amaze Loki.

"I know the specs for *Sirius*'s crystal array. But that's a star drive. St. Bridget only knows if Konner needs the same ratios for a confusion field." Loki shook his head and began pacing off distances.

"He's created a confusion field around *Sirius* with our crystal array," Kim reminded him.

"Then let's break out the laser sight on the needle rifle. That will give us distances to the picometer. Something to do while we wait. Save time once Konner gets here."

"I'll build a proper fire," Hestiia said. She disengaged from Kim's embrace with a quick kiss to his cheek. She and Poolie cleared away the ineptly piled wood and began anew with a wad of dried moss and ferns. By the time the first crystal rested beside a small cairn of rocks marking its eventual resting place, the women had a fire blazing and something cooking over it.

The rain showers held off.

"How are we going to bury these things?" Loki looked up from his measuring of the last driver.

"We'll think of something." Kim shrugged.

"We can dig," Raaskan said.

"With what? All our tools are in the village, half a continent away."

Everyone sobered a few moments.

"We fly," Hestiia replied blithely. "We can bring our villagers here at the same time."

"We'll need three trips with both vessels for that." Loki marked the place for the next crystal with three small rocks. Niveean carried a green over to him. "We're running low on fuel cells again and no way to recharge them."

"We have sunlight," Kim suggested.

"That will take weeks, if we ever see the sun again," Loki protested as a raindrop plopped onto his nose.

A roaring wind accompanied the rain. All of them ducked into the open hatches of the shuttle and the lander. The feeble light from the drowning fire and the portable illuminators revealed a ghostly silhouette descending from the heavens. All of the locals crossed their wrists and flapped their hands.

Loki felt an unreasonable urge to mimic the ancient ward against the bloodthirsty demon Simurgh. Kim crossed himself, murmuring silent prayers.

"You mangy traitor! I'll feed you to an Anubian blood worm." Another string of curses, in a language

Loki did not recognize, as Kat's husky voice split the air.

Uneremoniously, the dragon thudded to the ground. Kat's spine must have jarred, for she bit off the last diatribe. Then the dragon rippled his back and extended his wing. Kat slid from her perch and landed in the soft dirt directly above the buried king stone.

"Oh!" She rubbed her abused bottom. With her legs splayed and her hair drenched she did not look happy. Or comfortable. "You promised to take me back to my own people," Kat spat at the dragon.

(*What are your people other than blood kin?*)

"I don't claim them. I don't like them or their way of life. I belong with His Majesty's Imperial Military Police."

The dragon looked down his long nose at her. For a moment the spiral horn on his forehead looked as if it would lift Kat off her feet and toss her into the air.

Loki smothered a smile.

Kim had a sudden coughing fit and had to turn his back. He snaked out an arm to keep Hestiia from running out to assist Kat to her feet.

(*Irythros,*) the dragon announced his name.

"Welcome, Irythros. Loki here."

"You didn't welcome me!" Kat protested.

"You, baby sister, are a pain in the ass. What happened, Kat? Did the dragon foil your escape plans?"

She did not deign to answer.

"May I come in? I'm cold and wet, sunburned, and I have a headache," she spat through gritted teeth.

"Survival often depends upon the hospitality of others. By custom we honor your request for shelter. May you return the favor to others so benighted." Loki bowed to her in the same manner he had witnessed Raaskan greet newcomers to the village.

She muttered something that sounded like, "Extremely unlikely." To put it politely.

"Your word of honor as an officer in His Imperial Majesty's Military that you will honor the custom of hospitality." Loki braced his feet and stood firmly in the hatchway. He kept reminding himself that they all had to learn to live together on this planet.

"Lieutenant Talbot!" Cyndi pushed past Loki and ran to help Kat to her feet. "At last, a civilized person. Tell these people to return me to the ship immediately. I shall perish in the cold and the damp. Who knows what bacteria lurk in this filthy air!" she gushed.

Kat shook off the helping hand and stiffly got her feet under her. She shot the dragon a malevolent look. "I suggest you keep your thoughts and words to yourself, Ms. Baines. Return to the ship is dangerous at the moment and unlikely to help the situation."

Cyndi stared at her, mouth agape.

Loki racked his brain trying to remember why he ever thought Cyndi attractive let alone the most beautiful and desirable woman in the galaxy. Thoughts of Paola Sanchez jumped to his mind's eye. Determined, energetic, independent, her stark beauty held much more appeal at the moment.

Cyndi dominated by manipulating people, like Mum. Paola led.

The dragon took off in a huff, leaving behind a flurry of windblown debris that cascaded over Kat and Cyndi. Dragons were big enough and powerful enough they did not have to hide their emotions or cater to the whims of others.

Loki wished he were a dragon at that moment. Or had the respect proffered to them.

"Your word of honor, Kat," he reminded them all of the reason for the delay.

Kat returned his glare for a long moment before firming her shoulders and thrusting out her chin. "My word of honor. I will honor the custom of hospitality and deny it to no one who asks properly for shelter in my abode."

"Full of loopholes but good enough for now. You'll learn the value of honor and hospitality and a bunch of other qualities alien to civils of the GTE." Loki turned his back on the women and retreated deeper into the shuttle.

"Qualities totally alien to the O'Hara brothers who have broken nearly every law honored by civilized humans since time began," Kat retorted.

Loki froze. The weight of his crimes came crashing down upon his shoulders. He wanted to justify his actions, blame them on others who had cheated him. The truth was, he enjoyed the danger and excitement of defying the law, always one jump ahead of arrest.

Suddenly he needed to punch someone and did not like himself very much for the thought. How could he lead this ragtag group of refugees when he could not properly exhibit the qualities he professed?

* * *

Konner drifted slowly to the surface of his meditation. A bird chirped a tentative inquiry.

A soft glow of predawn light shimmered around the edges of Konner's awareness. A gentle shaft of warmth struck his back. Then all of the birds came alive with songs of greeting to the sunrise.

Konner heaved a deep sigh of release and opened his eyes. He looked around before moving. Nothing but the birds and a slight breeze filtered through to this grassy creekside. He might be the only person alive on the entire planet.

Except that his heart ached for the one missing.

Best let her continue resting until she awoke naturally. The healing magic of a cat's purr needed time. Even the more intense ultrasound treatments of modern medicine needed hours to show an effect.

The muted roar of Iianthe's throat rumbles ceased abruptly.

"Wake up, Konner," Dalleena whispered. Her hand touched his shoulder.

He scrambled to his feet and encircled her with his arms, needing to protect her from whatever had roused her. "What's wrong," he asked quietly.

"They come."

There was only one "they" that would make her eyes go wide with alarm. IMPs.

"How far away?"

"Not far."

"Can you travel? Is that still sore?" Konner asked, exploring the bump on the back of her head with his fingers. She winced but stayed within the circle of his embrace. He peered at the spot, not daring to touch it. He wished Kim were here. His brother could hasten the healing started by Iianthe.

(*I cannot fly today,*) the dragon announced. His mental voice sounded as hushed as Konner's and Dalleena's whispers, as if he feared alerting the approaching soldiers.

"We must hide," Konner decided. IMP officers used hostages as bargaining tools. Their captain must be desperate to regain the king stone by now. If they had to, would Loki and Kim trade it for Konner's safety?

He did not intend to give them the opportunity.

"We have to get to the clearing. I have to leave today to get to my son in time." He wanted to shout and pound things with his fists. No time.

Muted voices came from a spot due west, a few hundred meters away.

"Can you climb?" He shoved Dalleena toward the tallest tree he could see.

She stretched one arm above her head. Grimaced. Nodded hesitantly, then shook her head. She looked as if she might cry.

(*To me,*) Iianthe called.

Shafts of sunlight seemed to concentrate upon the mossy rock where the flywacket crouched. Surely the IMPs must see the blinding explosion of light. Konner whirled Dalleena around so that both of their backs were to the transforming dragon. She clutched her middle from the abrupt motion. When the glare dissolved, Konner peered over his shoulder.

(*Your enemies see only the sunrise.*)

Konner hoped that was so. True civils like Pettigrew had probably never observed a sunrise. Looking east they might mistake Iianthe's shedding of light as nothing more dangerous.

(*To me,*) Iianthe repeated. He lifted his good wing a little.

"I hope this works." He and Dalleena slipped beneath the wing. They lay flat upon the cushion of moss.

(*Do not move,*) Iianthe admonished them. (*Color and movement betray the hunted.*)

"What about your purple-tips?" Konner asked as quietly as he could.

(*Inconsequential.*)

The voices came closer.

"Heat sensors indicate the quarry has . . . I can't find them anywhere, Lieutenant Commander M'Berra," a female voice said. "Must be something wrong with the handheld. All I see is one block of heat half a klick square."

Konner wished he could see through Iianthe's wing. He needed to read body language as well as vocal tones to judge the degree of danger.

"People cannot just disappear into thin air," replied the deep bass voice of *Jupiter's* second-in-command.

Iianthe's skin rippled in sympathetic vibration. His own voice had much the same timbre.

"Begging the Commander's pardon, but the O'Haras have been known to do that on any number of occasions," the woman with the sensor corrected her superior officer.

"Tricks," M'Berra insisted. "Smoke and mirrors. Now where are they? This is the place they hid just a few femtos ago."

"Sensors can't find . . ."

"To hell with the sensors. Use the eyes and the nose God gave you. Use your hands to feel every micrometer within a square klick. Now spread out, all of you, and find the two escaped prisoners."

CHAPTER 40

KAT LAY MOTIONLESS in the hammock slung across a corner in the body of the lander. Somehow, she had to get out of here. She could salvage this mission and save many lives with a little luck and more skill.

Half a dozen bushies snored in other hammocks around her. She was boxed in. Big warriors slept to each side of her, more between her and the hatch. The slightest movement would set the portable beds to swinging and awake the occupant. No easy escape.

She'd graduated top of her class in "Escape from Hostile Territory." But she'd never had to actually do it before. She had no doubt that the bushies who guarded her would kill her if they caught her. They were not bound by the conventions of civilization.

Holding her breath, she rolled out of the hammock, keeping one hand on the mesh to prevent the bars at head and foot from knocking into something and making a noise. Her knees bent, absorbing her weight. Did the others hear her soft landing?

She counted to one hundred. The man next to her snored a little louder, mumbled something, and heaved himself over. His hammock careened back and forth. Kat dropped to her knees to avoid being hit in the back and thus awakening the man.

Eventually the hammock swings slowed. Kat crawled around and beneath the other hammocks toward the cockpit. Once clear of the sleeping men, she eased to her feet. The cold cerama/metal decks reminded her that the season changed toward autumn and winter. Loki had taken away her boots and socks. The soft synthleather wasn't much protection in the bush, but better than bare feet. She shivered in the cold morning air.

Someone moved behind her. She froze in place. Barely daring to breathe, she peeked over her shoulder. The guard nearest the hatch scratched, then settled back into sleep. Predawn light filtered through the portholes. Everyone would wake soon. Except perhaps Lucinda Baines. The diplomatic attaché had a different circadian rhythm than anyone else. Kat had found the woman prowling *Jupiter* at odd hours, no matter which shift had just ended.

Kat crossed the last open space on tiptoe as rapidly as she dared. Silently, she moved aside the curtain that separated the cabin from the cockpit. Loki lay sprawled against the control panels, his hand firmly on the interface that locked all pilot controls.

Through the windscreen she saw a burly warrior prowling around the lander and the shuttle. He carried a spear and an iron sword as long as her arm.

A new plan glimmered in her mind. She'd bet a month's pay that Kim did not guard the cockpit of the shuttle as well as Loki guarded this one. He'd not separate from his wife so readily.

One micrometer at a time, she eased away from the cockpit. Down on her knees again, she crawled back the way she had come to the small hatch giving access to the engines and the all-important fuel cells.

The hatch opened on noiseless hinges. Kat dropped into the belly of the lander just as two of the guards dropped out of their hammocks, scratching and yawning. She eased the portal shut, letting it latch only as the men began speaking.

If they questioned the extra noise, she did not hear. The emergency lights did not come on. She bit back curses as she stubbed her toes on protruding equipment. Where was the switch? SBs handled this sort of thing, not officers. Still she should have memorized the layout of every micrometer of the vessel. It was her job to know about light switches and such.

Blindly, she reached to her left. The bulkhead was blank. She moved her hand around. Still nothing. But then she was left-handed. Most people, including designers used their right hand. Her fingers met the recessed plate on the first try to the right. Soft red light flooded the cramped compartment.

A quick scan showed the fuel cells right where they should be, along the two exterior bulkheads. Six to a side. A cubed meter each in size. Paired. The ship would operate under reduced power if some of the cells were damaged or empty, but only if the operating cells were paired with an equally fueled one on the opposite side.

Kat knew precisely how to disable the lander. Quickly, she yanked connecting cables from all the cells. She opened others at random, letting the energy held under pressure dissipate.

Sometimes in combat a cell took too many hits and absorbed the energy directly into the storage coils. Crews needed to get rid of it before it exploded. She opened the jettison port.

Then she unbolted two of them on the same side and heaved them out beneath the lander. She heard the casings crack as the two cells hit the ground.

As a final desecration she crawled backward through one of the jettison tubes, pulling a cell behind her. This one she cradled in her arms as she dropped to the ground. Bulky and awkward, it nearly toppled her. She braced her feet and gritted her teeth. A pebble pressed against the soft skin on her sole. She felt a bruise forming and needed to hop and curse and get rid of the offending rock that felt as big as a boulder.

Somehow she managed to carry the fuel cell across the clearing to the shuttle. She expected the watchman to shout an alarm at any moment.

Now for the tricky part. She hid herself and her purloined treasure behind one of the wheel struts. Not a great hiding place for long. Clouds obscured the sunrise. Tall trees and adjacent hills ringing the clearing would keep it dark here until the sun was well above them. She prayed that she had enough time.

One by one the locals trooped out of the two vessels, including the gloomy Lucinda Baines. That surprised Kat. Dared she leave the diplomatic attaché to the not so tender mercies of the brothers O'Hara? No matter. Kat would be back soon with reinforcements. Besides, Ms. Baines seemed to have a prior acquaintance with Loki. If she had survived his friendship before, she would again.

The moment the last occupant of the shuttle stumbled toward the remnants of last night's cooking fire, Kat sneaked aboard with the fuel cell. She coaxed the hatch closed and dashed for the cockpit.

"Controls keyed to O'Hara DNA," Kim had said yesterday. She laid her hand flat upon the lock.

"Retina scan," a voice from her past demanded. She almost choked with tears at the sound of her mother's voice. Then Kat remembered how the woman had abandoned her. Their moment of communion in the desert had sickened Kat from first contact with Mum's obsessed mind.

"Override. Emergency," she barked in as deep a voice as she could muster.

"Emergency password," Mum's voice replied in an equally gruff tone.

"St. Bridget and all the angels," Kat cursed.

"Password accepted." The engines roared to life.

Kat almost laughed. Mum's archaic religion was not popular in the GTE. No civil would think to invoke a saint for a password. She scanned the screens quickly. She didn't have time for more. Already her brothers and their lethally armed guards dashed toward the shuttle. She set the VTOL jets and lifted off.

*   *   *

"Well," Cyndi huffed. "She could have at least taken me with her."

"Oh, shut up," Loki retorted.

"Do you know who you are talking to?" she fumed. Hands on hips, hair disheveled from sleep, she almost looked like a woman worthy of this planet.

Then Loki noticed how her makeup had smeared, darkening her eyes and blurring her mouth. She'd be a lot prettier without the enhancement.

"I know precisely who you are," Loki said with a calmness he did not expect. "You are my prisoner. A hostage. Rank means nothing here. You have to earn respect—not be born to it."

Cyndi narrowed her eyes in deep concentration. Loki had always feared that expression. He never knew if the result of her intense thinking bout would produce brilliance or trouble. Trouble for him. Trouble for her father. Trouble for the universe.

He no longer cared. Fear of losing her love had always made him succumb to her moods. Now he knew deep in his gut that she had never truly loved him. She loved the adventure of an affair with an

outlaw. She loved outwitting her father and his security. She loved manipulating people. Just like Mum.

"Kim, are the fuel cells repairable?" he called to his
brother rather than waste any more time with Cyndi.

S'murghit, he should have put the force bracelets
back on Kat. Restrained both her hands and her feet
with the blasted things. But he'd spent a few sleep-
less nights in jail cells wearing the electronic shackles
until Mum either organized a rescue or bailed him
out. He hated the thought of doing that to another
human being. Especially his sister.

"I think Kat made more of a mess than actual damage," Kim said. He stood up from his close examination of the cracked casings. "A little cerama/metal
caulk ought to repair the exterior." He headed for
the hatch.

"What about the energy that's leaking out?" Loki
racked his brain for a solution. "Where is Konner
when we need him most?"

"He should have been back here before us," Kim
said. He reached under the pilot's seat for the emergency repair kit.

"I'm getting worried," Loki admitted.

"Well, we have plenty to worry about. The caulk
is nearly used up in this kit. Not enough to fix more
than one or two cells." Kim emerged from the hatchway shaking his head. "Maybe some of the local
moss will fill the cracks."

"Raaskan," Loki called to the people gathered near
the fire. "We need to explore and forage. We're going
to be stuck here for a while."

Raaskan nodded, then began a conversation with
the other warriors accompanied by many pointing
gestures.

"I'm not going anywhere until I get a shower,"
Cyndi announced.

Hestiia looked at her with contempt. "Bathe in
the creek."

"You mean with . . . with water! Fish crap in that water." She stared aghast at Hestiia. When that evoked no response, she tried logic. "Water is inefficient, barbaric, and probably contaminated. I need a sonic cleansing. You all do." Cyndi wrinkled her nose. "I've never smelled anyone so . . . offensive."

Hestiia looked as if she would slap the GTE diplomatic attaché. Cyndi deserved it, but violence would not settle the issue.

Rain dropped on the top of Loki's head. Cyndi screeched and ran for the interior of the lander. Hestiia shrugged and returned to reheating last night's leftovers. Kim muttered and cursed as he scrounged around the cockpit for tools and caulk. The warriors spread out and disappeared in pairs behind the tree line.

"Now what?" Kim asked.

"When Konner gets back, tell him to start building a still. I think we're going to need it." Loki pulled a toolbox from the lander and dumped the contents on the ground. "Bathing the coils in alcohol might enhance the effects of sunlight in recharging the cells."

"What are you going to do?" Kim eyed the discarded tools as if they might hold the answers to all of their problems.

"I'm going to collect some of the fruit of the Tambootie and make some dragon wine."

CHAPTER 41

"WHERE ARE YOU, Martin Konner O'Hara?" Martin Fortesque slammed his fist against his Lazy-former®. The cushions absorbed the impact and eased none of his frustration. The vid screen remained quiet, unable to answer his question.

"Marty, I found it!" Bruce Geralds popped onto the screen almost as if summoned. He sounded breathless and a little frightened.

"Found what?" Martin sat straighter. He peered into the screen as if he could penetrate the pixels to delve across space and time directly into Bruce's terminal.

"The will."

"My grandparents' will?"

"Yes," Bruce breathed. He looked over his shoulder as if afraid of being observed. "I'll shoot it to you directly . . . and file a copy with the local courts." His eyes refused to look directly at the screen.

"What is it, Bruce?" Even as he spoke a document appeared in the lower right corner of his screen.

"Read it. Then destroy your file. I've secured the official copy where your mother can't find it."

Bruce disappeared.

"Scaramouch, enhance document." The screen enlarged the document enough so that Martin could read the fine print from his chair.

"Where as . . . wherefore . . ." he skimmed the legalese looking for the core of the document.

" 'Everything to daughter Melinda Georgina Fortesque.' No surprise there."

The next paragraph jumped out at Martin. He began to chill. His mother's police record followed. Embezzlement, blackmail, conspiracy to falsely accuse another for a fatal accident involving loading equipment at spacedock. "Sale of a controlled substance on the black market. Smuggling of same said controlled substance. Any other person would have spent a number of years in prison undergoing psychiological rehab, possibly even a mind-wipe.

Obviously Melinda's parents had bought her suspended sentences and paroles.

Since taking over Fortesque Industries, Melinda had been a model of propriety. No whisper of scandal ever attached to her for long. Record of her crimes had been scrubbed from local courts—and probably from GTE jurisdiction as well.

"Principal and seat on board of directors to be held in trust until her thirtieth birthday or her marriage," Martin read the last sentence.

His mother had married Konner O'Hara within two months of her parents' death.

· Martin scrubbed the will from his files as well as any record of having received a document from Bruce.

Slowly, almost reluctantly he called up the minority report of the accident that had killed Melinda's parents.

"Evidence suggests the explosion was caused by external weapons fired from a small independent merchant vessel."

He began to shake uncontrollably.

"You murdered your parents. You hired a Sam Eyeam to do it for you. All you ever wanted was control of the corporation. Nothing else. Not even me."

*   *   *

Konner tried frantically to think of a way to distract the IMPs long enough for Dalleena and him to run away. But where would they run to? How could they run with her ribs still paining her?

She seemed to have fallen asleep. He hated to awaken her for any reason until she healed.

He was about to give himself up and hope the enemy would settle for him, without looking further for her. Then the skies opened up. Huge drops of water pelted the IMPs.

M'Berra cursed in a dialect full of fluid syllables Konner did not recognize. His tech screeched something about drowning. The scattered footsteps of the rest of the squad returned.

"We're screwed, Lieutenant Commander." Was that Ross Duggan's voice? "The changing air pressure and temperature is fouling up all our readings, sir. The rain and cold are dulling our own senses. We need better gear to do more than exist in this climate."

"We are Marines deployed with the Imperial Military Police, Sergeant. A little rain should not deter us."

"The crew are not acclimatized, sir," Corporal Paola Sanchez interjected. "In our haste to recover Lieutenant Lotski's patient, we left most of our foul weather gear behind."

Konner almost laughed out loud at how his new allies sabotaged their own people.

"With your permission, sir, I'd like to take the men back to our landers and equip them with rain and cold weather gear," Duggan said. "The quarry cannot go far in this weather. The female is severely injured. Lieutenant Lotski was surprised she could even walk beyond the hut."

"We'll find them faster with rain gear and shields for the tech equipment," Sanchez finished.

"Very well. Sergeant, recall the crew and return to the lander in close formation. No strays. I'll take the point."

More rustling and stamping and uncomfortable mutters. Then a few moments of silence.

"Wherever you are, get out now. I figure you've got one half a metric hour at the most to disappear into thin air," Duggan whispered. Then his footfalls retreated.

Konner waited. He counted one hundred heartbeats. He was about to speak to Iianthe when the dragon lifted his wing. Konner crawled out from beneath its shelter. Immediately, the rain drenched him. He shivered and clutched his arms close against his body.

"We need a better hiding place," he said.

(*Help comes.*)

"My brothers?" Hope remained dormant. The IMPs would hear the shuttle and open fire with the heavy guns aboard their lander.

(*Irythros!*) a second dragon voice chimed in. This one was brighter, higher in pitch, and more enthusiastic.

"Konner here." He looked up into the pelting rain against the gray sky. He saw no shimmering form outlined in red. He saw nothing but more gray clouds dumping more cold rain on his face, clinging to his eyelashes and dripping in chilly runnels down his back.

The sound of a large splash blended in with the rain dropping into the creek. Konner peered in that direction. Only a few meters away and he still could not see much detail.

The splashing continued. Eventually, Konner detected a pattern in how the water cascaded around a bulky form.

"Are you here to take Dalleena and me to safety, Irythros?" he asked, still peering through the rain.

(*Yes. I love flying against the weather.*) He almost chortled.

Konner was reminded of a puppy he'd had as a kid. All feet and ears, the dog had much more enthusiasm than sense.

(*Awaken your lady, Konner,*) Iianthe said politely. His deep bronze bell of a voice sounded much more mature. Perhaps his pain added weight to his years.

All of their problems seemed trivial compared to getting Dalleena to safety where she could mend in peace and quiet.

And what of his appointment with his son, Martin. He needed to leave today if he was going to make it to Aurora on time. He prayed the shuttle had enough fuel to get him back to *Sirius* and the crystals had finished growing. Would his brothers ever forgive him for deserting them at this terrible time?

In short order he managed to hoist a reluctant Dalleena aboard Irythros' back. She seemed more alert this morning and moved with more ease. But she still walked stiffly and cautiously.

"What about you, Iianthe? How will you fare, grounded and alone?"

(*I am not without defenses, Stargod Konner. Go. Keep your lady safe. I respect her courage and your dedication to those you love.*) A curl of steam snaked out of the dragon's nostrils.

"Farewell, friend. Take care. I hope our next meeting is less fraught with danger."

(*Danger will always follow you, Stargod Konner. Take care that you defeat your enemies with honor.*)

Now what did that mean?

Konner did not have time to reflect on it. Irythros pranced down the creek, splashing through the rain until he had enough momentum and lift for takeoff.

He flapped his wings vigorously until they were secreted among the thick clouds. The air was a little drier up here. But not much. Thoroughly soaked and chilled, Konner clung to Dalleena and the dragon for warmth. He clenched his teeth so they did not chatter.

Soon Dalleena began to shudder violently in the cold. Konner wrapped his arms tighter around her, letting her draw what little warmth she could from his body. He clamped his knees tighter against the dragon's back, hoping for a smooth flight and gentle landing.

(*Understood,*) Irythros said. He sounded more sober and mature than Konner remembered. Had he curbed his youthful energy out of concern?

Konner sensed more than felt the land rising beneath them. He presumed they headed south, toward the clearing. The clouds and the cold deadened all of his other senses.

And then they lost altitude abruptly. Dalleena swallowed a yelp of surprise. Or was it dismay.

Konner's stomach flipped and his balance distorted. He dropped one arm from around Dalleena to clutch the dragon's spinal horn. The clouds stayed with them until they were barely fifty meters above ground. Irythros circled lazily. Dalleena spotted a fire and pointed it out to Konner. The stolen IMP lander came into view. He made out Loki's and Kim's red hair among a scattering of people.

As promised, Irythros landed slowly, gently, working his wings to cushion them.

"Where's the shuttle?" Konner shouted to Loki before Irythros had fully settled.

Loki's face looked grim. Kim's looked just as bad. They told him in blunt terms of Kat's escape, her sabotage, and her theft of the shuttle. They had few rations and were far from help. The IMPs would come and find them as soon as Kat revealed their hiding place.

Even if Konner could get the lander up and running he wasn't sure he could get past his own booby traps aboard *Sirius* with any vessel other than *Rover*.

"Forgive me, Martin. I think I'm going to miss your court date and our one chance to be together."

CHAPTER 42

KAT PARKED the shuttle out of sight and weapons range of the camp. No sense in being shot down by her own people in a notorious smuggler's vessel before she could explain herself.

"Where is Captain Leonard?" she asked the first guard she encountered on the perimeter of the village.

Her feet ached from wearing the too thin and too large boots she'd found thrown into a locker aboard the shuttle.

The guard shrugged and gestured with his head toward the cluster of cabins and huts. Kat proceeded. She asked everyone she met where to find their captain. No one knew.

"Captain is still aboard *Jupiter*. She's vowing to remain aboard until we find the crystals or until the ship's orbit decays beyond repair," Josh Kohler, the navigator, said. "M'Berra's out chasing an injured native kidnapped by one of the outlaws. Guess that puts me in charge as senior officer."

"What about Pettigrew?" Kat did not like to think about the self-righteous Marine in charge of the mission. They needed level heads and careful plans to capture her brothers and reclaim the king stone.

"Lotski has him doped up and pumped full of antibiotics. She's ordered bed rest until she's certain his wounds do not infect."

"Wounds from what?"

"He claims that a dragon dropped him onto ancient razor wire soon after first landing." Kohler worked his cheek muscles to keep from laughing out loud.

Kat did not see the humor in the situation. She knew from personal experience just how big and dangerous a dragon could be.

"The man is delusional." Kohler sobered. "But then we all knew that before this mission. Can't have him charging into the fray and possibly damaging one or more of the crystals in his enthusiasm."

"He'd likely do that."

"Yeah. Pettigrew wants revenge. Been raving about it for hours. Word from the latest batch of refugees is that the enemy sneaked back aboard *Jupiter* with a bunch of bushies. All armed to the teeth. They killed a bunch of people who opposed them and stole the rest of the crystal array."

Kat's knees grew weak. She did not want to believe the three men she had met capable of the atrocity of murder. Bad enough that they deprived animals of life to feed themselves. But to kill another *human!*

Somehow, the legendary exploits of her brothers did not match the image she now had of them.

"I know where the O'Haras are hiding," Kat blurted out before she had time to rethink her plans. "But we have to move fast if we are to capture them and recover the crystal array."

"I think we need a superior officer, Kat," Josh refused to look her in the eye.

In that moment she knew he'd never move much higher than navigator. He was good at that job, but he did not have the self-confidence and initiative of an officer of the line.

Kat had no intentions of letting this man hold her back just because he outranked her by one degree and had two years' seniority on her.

"Fine. I'll fetch M'Berra. Where did he go?"

"That way," Kohler pointed vaguely to the south and west. "He took a squad out before dawn, as soon as Lotski discovered her patient missing."

"Dalleena, Konner's lady. The middle brother hadn't returned to the hiding place as of two hours ago. I bet he stayed behind to grab her. He's the only one who could correct the sabotage I left behind. We'll leave Konner to M'Berra. Our first officer will keep the man busy and away from the clearing. Best to strike the others while they are divided. They have Ms. Baines." She hoped the last statement would spur Kohler to action. He'd been watching the diplomatic attaché with lustful eyes for weeks.

"My orders are to secure this compound at all costs. Unless M'Berra counters his own orders, or Captain Leonard tells me otherwise, I and the people under my command will stay here and prevent the locals or the O'Haras from stealing the stores or burning the place down." Kohler bit his lip and refused to look Kat in the eye.

"Very well. I'll get Captain Leonard's orders to move out. Where's communications?"

"Uh . . . James is missing. His escape vessel must have landed in a different sector. Our communications are rudimentary, just what Brewster could cannibalize from a lander that's out of action. Some local bacteria is eating away at the cerama/metal."

Kat did not like what she was hearing. Not one little bit. Disorganization, lack of leadership. Fear. Why had they all evacuated? The ship should still be manageable, even without the king stone.

"We'll need a mechanical genius to get that lander in the air again."

"Just don't let Konner O'Hara near it," she muttered. "Any other vessel that comes within hailing distance will have to be dunked in the saltwater bay to kill the bio-gunk in the upper atmosphere. Otherwise, we'll lose them all." She captured Kohler's gaze with her own until he nodded. "Permission to contact Captain Leonard aboard *Jupiter*, sir." She saluted smartly. At least she'd make it look like she proceeded through proper channels.

"Permission granted, Lieutenant Talbot." Kohler returned her salute. He stepped back and began scanning the horizon with a FarSight® sensory visor. The infrared detectors would reveal more than his eyes peering through the gloomy clouds. At least the rain had let up a little down here in the valley.

Kat sloshed through mud churned by too many boots toward the largest hut in the center of the village. A mess sergeant had managed to boil up some grains for a cereal breakfast.

He shook his head and grumbled. "First salvage trip back to *Jupiter*, I want the hydroponics tanks and all of the food stores. First priority. No questions." He pinned Kat with his gaze. "Growing food in the dirt is most inefficient. If these grains had been tanked, I could feed twice as many people on half the amount. This planet needs civilizing. Fast."

"I'll do what I can," Kat replied. She grabbed the next bowl of mush and chowed down. No telling when she'd eat again and she'd had nothing since last night's meal of roasted vegetables—she had refused the rabbit so proudly caught by one of Loki's warriors.

From the chow line, she made her way to the largest hut. She figured she'd find communications there.

A harried Sergeant Brewster sat at a collapsible table with six handheld communicators and pieces of the lander's more elaborate system configured to beam data among them. Eight other noncoms crowded around her with demands to contact this person, that officer, a love interest.

"Silence!" Kat cut through the jumble of people with the authority of her rank, her training, and her superior height.

"Communication with *Jupiter* has to take priority," she announced.

The noncoms met this demand with loud protests and indignation.

"We can sort out units after we recover the crystals. I know you are missing friends, people you care deeply about. We can only hope they have landed in friendly territory. But we have no hope of reuniting any of you until we get those crystals back. Now disperse and see to your gear." She leveled a stern gaze at each of them.

They snapped to attention, saluted smartly, turned, and departed on a quick march.

The sergeant heaved a sigh of relief. "Thank you, Lieutenant," he said realigning some of the handhelds. "Maintenance has been slack on the landers. We've been too peaceful for too long. There are parts missing. Weird atmospheric fluctuations and a lack of satellites are interfering with communications. I think that green layer in the upper atmosphere is creating havoc."

"Are the missing parts a lack of maintenance or sabotage?"

"Your guess is as good as mine. First landing party had all their comms and weapons stolen by the locals the first night, then returned—inoperative. I vote for sabotage."

"Can you reach *Jupiter*?"

"Sometimes. But even if I can get through, there is no guarantee the captain will answer." He began fiddling with and adjusting his units.

"Why wouldn't a comm officer answer a hail from the surface?"

"Captain's the only one left aboard. Who knows what she's doing to maintain orbit. Might be too busy to answer."

"Keep trying to reach her. If she answers, tell her I'm on my way up with the captured smuggler's shuttle *Rover*." Kat took off at a run for her brother's vessel. She could not allow mud and drizzle and discomfort to slow her down.

"Take a squad with you," Josh Kohler called as she hastened away. "Start salvaging what you can."

Kat grunted a noncommittal reply as she ran.

The shuttle was fast. Faster than any lander designed by a GTE engineer. Almost as fast as a two-man scout, or even one of the new cyber-fighters where the controls were linked to the pilot's brain synapses. Commands happened as fast as thought. Still, the trip took hours. Far too long.

With the dragons at his beck and call, Konner could easily have eluded M'Berra's squad and returned to the clearing. A few more hours would see the crystals connected and buried. The confusion field would snap into place soon after.

When *Jupiter* finally came into view, Kat shook her head in dismay. The cruiser was a mess. It listed at an odd angle, half pointed toward the planet below. It no longer spun to generate gravity. The troops had fled the ship with too much haste to secure bay doors. Only a few lights showed in those open bays. It looked dead.

She had less time to save the ship than she thought.

Kat prayed that Captain Leonard had kept enough power generating to provide atmosphere.

She docked without challenge. In the back of the shuttle she found an EVA suit that fit remarkably well. Her uniform EVA had to be custom tailored to her tall frame.

Atmosphere did not register on the suit until she found the bridge. The first air lock did not want to close behind her. She slammed the panel with her fist. Sparks flew. Her faceplate instantly polarized and her helmet light dimmed. After a few moments her vision cleared and she found the door closed.

Another fist to another control brought air into the lock. When it reached point zero five atmospheres, Kat dared release her faceplate. And wished she hadn't. The air smelled stale, as if the scrubbers were overtaxed or only working at half capacity.

Another few moments brought the pressure up and the inner door creaked open slowly.

Lieutenant Commander Amanda Leonard swung her chair to face the door, a needle pistol in her hand. A huge bruise covered the right side of her face and swelled that eye closed. Her upper lip curled in a sneer.

"So you've come to finish the job your brothers started," she snarled and tightened her finger on the pistol.

CHAPTER 43

"**M**ASTER MARTIN." His Super Snooper, enhanced with the latest features thanks to his friend Gerald, appeared on the screen in front of the graph Martin was building showing shipping lanes of the Galactic Free Market.

"What?" Martin replied querulously. He almost had enough data to put this portion of the program into the hologram star map he and Bruce and Jane were composing.

"I have detected activation of the rescue beacon assigned to Melinda Fortesque's agent-at-large, Sam Eyeam."

"Where?" Martin sat forward eagerly. He sent his graphs into the background. The Sam Eyeam could be anywhere in the known galaxy. But Martin was willing to bet that Melinda had sent him in search of Konner O'Hara, to keep him from returning to Aurora in time for the custody hearing.

"Unknown. The signal is faint and irregular."

"Guess."

"Star charts do not extend to the location suggested."

What to do? "My dad needs help. I know it."

"May I suggest, Master Martin, extrapolation from the merchant charts."

"Yes!" He'd designed the project to show anomalies in the ever-changing borders among the GTE, the Free Merchants, and the Kree Empire.

A three-dimensional swirl of colored lights appeared in the far corner of the room. The hologram had swelled since the last time he'd set it into motion. GTE solar systems appeared in blue, the Free Merchant stars in green, and the enemy empire in red. Known jump points flashed yellow. The chart nearly filled the room. Even then, the vast distances between stars were hardly representative.

As he examined the troubled borders, several stars changed color, from red to green, green to red, and blue gobbled up three from each. Aurora changed from blue to green and back again in less than one digital minute. Melinda frequently used the threat to withdraw from the GTE as leverage in negotiating trade concessions or waivers in the judicial system. Martin had no idea what today's switch involved.

He hoped his mother's threats did not have anything to do with the custody hearing coming up in just a few days. Or worse, the arrest and conviction of Konner O'Hara.

"Scaramouch, show me the beacon."

"Insufficient data."

"Extrapolate."

"Insufficient power."

"What?" Martin pulled up a diagnostic. Sure enough, the huge mapping program and holographic display had eaten up almost all of his spare memory and speed.

Dared he ask Melinda for a few upgrades?

No. "Melinda can't be involved in this in any way," he muttered to himself.

He called Bruce and Jane. Neither one had a solution.

Martin paced the room. He wandered through the

hologram, watching the changes in colors, looking at how the jump points connected star systems in seemingly random patterns.

Crystal drives made jumps possible, bridging the light-years. Crystals made near instantaneous communications between the planets possible. Crystals . . .

"Scaramouch, locate souvenir crystal from camp." The icon of two fencers moved back and forth across the screen.

Two years ago Konner had given him a tiny crystal, a miniature of a king stone. "My dad said it would be a tangible reminder of our friendship."

Perhaps it was something more.

Experiments on integrating crystals into computer components had drifted through the scientific journals several times over the last decade. Always the government had classified such experiments as top secret and made the growth of miniature crystals illegal.

Martin did not question how Konner O'Hara had come by such a thing.

"Your crystal is secreted inside your personal terminal." The computer's voice sounded almost animated.

Of course. Martin had been hiding childhood treasures in there for years. He'd cleaned it all out last year on his birthday, feeling too old for such things. But he'd left the crystal there. It was more than just a memento from a favorite camp counselor.

He yanked open the wall panel revealing the guts of the machine. He remembered now that he had hidden the crystal, about the length of his palm, here, because this was one place Melinda would not search, one place his tutors and companions had no need to access. Konner and his unique gift were parts of his life he had always needed to keep separate and secret from his mother and her flunkies.

He reached deep into the recess, fumbling around for the cool, glassy feel of the faceted crystal. He brushed his knuckles against . . . could it be? . . . a Klip. Cautiously he drew out the thumbnail-sized clamp. It remained attached to one wire. The primary wire.

Melinda was tapping into his programs. At the same time, she drained memory and power from his system to severely limit his capabilities.

Anywhere else in the GTE this little device would be illegal. So was murder.

Melinda had gotten away with both here on Aurora where she owned everything.

Not anymore.

With cold determination, Martin slipped the clamp off the primary wire. Nothing changed overtly. No alarms beeped and no surge of power changed the holographic display. He dropped the Klip back into its hidey-hole.

Then he retrieved the crystal. He dredged up from memory the last report he'd read on crystal experimentation. If he placed it between the processor and the Q drive, connected to both by fiber optics . . .

Where would he get nitrogen to bathe the crystal?

No, this was not a crystal star drive. The mini crystal would not be a monopole seeking an opposite pole in an array of crystals. This was a single king stone that wanted to be connected to a mother stone.

He connected it to the communications port where it could tap into whatever theoretical energy bigger king stones used to connect to the rest of the universe.

Instantly the hologram of a star map began filling in details. New stars and jump points appeared. Star systems Martin had not charted became blue, green, or red.

The entire thing shifted and rotated to a new alignment.

"North!" Martin chortled. "My crystal is now galactic north."

And then the jump points changed. Some remained stable and yellow. New ones wandered, taking on paler colors. Some became so intense they changed to orange.

Martin noticed very pale lines of white connecting the jump points to their destinations.

And at the core of it all remained a huge blank spot with no jump points entering or leaving. It stood strategically bordered by all three political entities.

"Scaramouch, what is this hole?" Martin asked his computer.

"Define hole?" the computer replied.

"This area without any stars." He circled the dimensions of the hole. It was big enough to contain fifteen or twenty star systems, but none showed.

"Unknown. No charts exist for that area."

"Scaramouch, correlate the distress beacon with this area." Martin tapped his foot anxiously while he waited for the computer to make calculations. It seemed to take an inordinate amount of time.

Finally a tiny violet light blinked at him from an area of the hole farthest away from Earth. But only a few jumps from Aurora.

"Scaramouch, highlight jump points into this area."

"All known jump points shown." The area remained free of entry.

"Scaramouch, calculate probability of a black hole in this area."

"Insufficient data," the computer replied.

"Martin?" Melinda Fortesque appeared on the vid screen. "I need you in my office immediately." She did not sound happy.

"What is it, Melinda?" he asked, careful not to call her "Mother."

"Stop questioning my orders and come here," she

snapped. Her image disappeared so quickly he almost heard the pixels pop.

"Uh-oh, she sounds mad. Really, really mad. She must have discovered the Klip is now disconnected." Martin hastened from the residential wing to Melinda's office. He paused at her door long enough to straighten his rumpled shirt and trousers and run his fingers through his hair.

His mind spun with lies. He plastered a blank expression of supposed innocence upon his face.

Melinda, of course, was impeccably groomed, wearing one of her expensive suits. This one had a longish skirt rather than her usual trousers. Who did she intend to impress? Certainly not Martin.

"What is this?" Melinda thrust a handheld screen at Martin without preamble.

The harbormaster's calendar lay before him, the date of Martin's last birthday highlighted. And a week later the date of Konner O'Hara's banishment from Aurora stood out in bold red letters.

"Looks like a calendar." Martin shrugged and returned the screen to his mother's desk. He bit his cheeks rather than ask her about the Klip.

Maybe she hadn't discovered it yet.

"Do not feign ignorance with me, Martin. Your computer's telltales are all over that entry." She tapped the entry regarding Konner.

Martin opted for silence. He tried to keep his face bland and his eyes level. He'd learned the art of a masterful stare from the best. His mother.

"You moved the entry," she accused.

He maintained his silence.

"I have to respect your perseverance, if not your actions. Do you know who this man is?"

"Yes, Mother, I do."

She returned his silence. He knew he could not out-stubborn her in this mood.

"Martin Konner O'Hara is my father. You cannot

keep me away from him after my fourteenth
birthday."

"Yes, I can. He will not arrive in time for your
birthday. He will never arrive in Aurora. My latest
intelligence says that he is dead. Killed in a battle
with the Imperial Military Police five months ago. I
have just received a copy of his official death certificate on file with the GTE. Any man appearing with
his name is an obvious imposter and will be arrested
and extradited immediately."

Martin swallowed the sob that threatened to escape his throat. He had to blink back hot tears.

Rather than show emotion in his mother's presence, he turned and marched back to his own quarters. He slumped into his Lazy-former®. Black
despair threatened to drag him deeper and deeper
into himself until he disappeared completely.

"If your father is dead, Master Martin, why would
Sam Eyeam activate the beacon?" the Super Snooper
asked.

"Scaramouch, trace agent Sam Eeyam's movements over the past three months and display in purple on the hologram."

*   *   *

"How did you know the O'Haras are my brothers,
Captain?" Kat asked. She kept her attention on Leonard's eyes, knowing they would signal any change
in her intent to fire before her finger reacted. In minimal g, could she avoid a spray of needles aimed at
her face?

"I had the displeasure of meeting one of your
brothers. The family resemblance is remarkable, Lieutenant Talbot. No wonder you are obsessed with
finding them. The one who stole the king stone did
this to me." Amanda Leonard gestured with her free

hand to the bruise that marred her face. The fingers of that hand were swollen and hung limp, as if she had broken them. "He stunned me in the face, then kicked me." Her words began to slur.

"I think you have a concussion, Captain. You've been breathing bad air, too. May I relieve you of the weight of that weapon?" Kat asked blandly. She crept forward, wincing at the clank of the boots of her EVA suit.

"No, you may not." Leonard steadied her grip on the pistol.

"We can still recover the king stone, sir. If we act fast."

"I will not desert my ship, Lieutenant."

"I am not asking you to, sir. But the others will not act without your orders. It's chaos down there. We need you to take command and restore order."

"Chaos. Rats deserting a sinking ship. It's all Judge Balinakas' fault. He ordered the evacuation while I was unconscious. He took the crystal techs away from their terminals at gunpoint. He caused the panic. Ever since the day I came aboard as captain he has challenged my authority. Just because he has served aboard *Jupiter* since her commissioning does not give him authority over *my* crew. Only over judiciary . . ." Her words trailed off.

Good. Her animosity diverted her attention from Kat and her brothers. "Would you like to prove your superior ability to the judge, Captain?"

Amanda Leonard's eyes brightened a bit and she looked at Kat with a glimmer of hope.

"Sign an order, sir. I know where the smugglers are hiding. I watched where they buried the king stone. We can retrieve it along with the rest of the crystal array. But I need your authority to command the Marines." Kat bent over Leonard, fixing her with her gaze. When she had the captain's complete attention, she folded her hand around the pistol and pulled it free. She breathed easier.

So did the captain. "Your eyes are different from your brother's. His are blue. Midnight blue. I almost lost my soul looking too deeply into his eyes."

"The orders, Captain. I need you to sign the orders."

"Very well. Take every Marine, lander, and piece of equipment you can scrounge." She whipped out a handheld and scribbled with a new electronic pencil from her earring.

"Sir, this puts Lieutenant Pettigrew in charge of the mission." Kat gulped back her dismay. "I'm the only one who knows . . ."

"You are too close to the situation, Lieutenant. If you give the orders, you might jeopardize the mission in a misguided attempt to spare your brothers."

"I assure you, Captain. I have no love for any man or woman with the name O'Hara. They abandoned me when I was a child. They left me without a backward glance." That was not exactly true. A flash of heat flushed her face as she remembered the moments of laughter and reminiscence with her brothers during yesterday's adventures.

Then she remembered the incredible experience of reaching out through the universe and touching her mother's thoughts; of feeling bound to everything and everyone. Especially her family.

But she did not want to be bound to the woman whose obsession to recover her daughter had become an excuse for gaining wealth that would never be used.

"Pettigrew is in charge. He outranks you."

"What about M'Berra. He's your second-in-command. He should lead."

"M'Berra needs to remain at that rustic headquarters and coordinate everything. Pettigrew leads the mission to retrieve the crystals. You will obey him, Kat. I'm depending upon you to behave yourself and obey."

"Yes, sir." Kat snapped a salute.

"Take a hydroponics tank back with you and as much food as the droids can carry. You're all going to be very hungry if you fail."

"I won't fail, sir."

"I have my doubts, Kat. Do this for me."

"Captain . . . ?"

"I intend to sail my ship back home with the O'Haras as my prisoners and Judge Balinakas in chains, or go down with it in flames."

"Not if you keep breathing bad air with a concussion. Sorry, sir." Kat slammed her fist into Amanda Leonard's jaw. As the captain slumped into unconsciousness, Kat slung her over her shoulder and tromped back to the shuttle *Rover*.

"We need you dirtside more than you need to remain aboard a sinking ship, Captain."

CHAPTER 44

"THEY COME," Dalleena called to Konner and the others. She stood at the edge of the clearing, facing north, her right arm extended palm out. In her left hand she clutched the small ultrasound device Kim had given her. She did not need the healing machine much now.

"Where? How many?" Konner poked his head out of one of the many holes in the ground.

"How long?" Loki asked. He and Irythros, the red-tipped dragon, dug yet more holes opposite Dalleena's post.

So many holes for so many crystals. Everything counted in twelves, the crystals, the holes, the distances that separated them. She did not pretend to understand the why and where of Konner's operation. She knew only that he considered it important and the others followed his directions.

"Landers lifting now. Thirty, no fifty people."

"Your talents are getting more precise," Konner said as he vaulted out of a hole. He still carried the intriguing weapon that shot fine ropes over long distances.

She could think of many times such a tool would have aided her in rescuing lost ones. Especially sheep and small children who tended to get into awkward places where adults could not fit.

Konner came up beside her. He rested a hand comfortably upon her shoulder, as if it belonged there. As if each of them was incomplete without the other.

"This place . . ." She shrugged at her lack of understanding. Perhaps the crystals made her tracking sense keener. She knew without thinking that fifty hearts beat against her palm.

Konner's hand tightened. Fifty minds brushed against hers. The fifty minds separated, became individuals. She shared fifty different emotions. One stood out from the others, determined, focused, single-minded.

"They are angry and afraid," she said. The pressure of that anger made it hard to breathe. Perhaps this refinement of her talent was not for the better.

"Fifty troops, that's two landers." Loki joined them at the perimeter of the clearing.

"Four," Dalleena corrected him. "They plan to leave with the crystals.

"The confusion field anywhere near ready?" Loki asked.

"No. I need another full day, even if you and Irythros finish the digging and placement of the directionals," Konner replied.

"The Others will be here in two, perhaps three hours. The leader pushes them hard. He . . . she seeks vengeance." The force of the personality swamped Dalleena's senses.

She swallowed hard, trying desperately to reclaim her sense of self.

"Your sister."

"Kat," Konner said at the same moment.

Sadness swept from brother to brother, then through Dalleena. With her talent engaged and heightened she became a part of their anguish.

"We will have to fight our own sister. Mum will kill us." Konner choked.

"Do not think about it, Konner." Dalleena dropped

her seeking hand to wrap it around Konner's where he clutched her shoulder with desperate fingers. She felt her skin bruising beneath his grip.

"We cannot engage them here." A note of panic crept into Konner's voice.

Dalleena's chest felt as if an iron band squeezed it. She needed to sever her physical contact with him in order to keep breathing. Yet she could not. He needed her. She knew with absolute certainty that he would break something in his mind if she removed his hand from her shoulder, her hand from his, his mind and emotions from contact with hers.

"We have strategic advantage here. They will have to come at us uphill, over rough terrain," Loki countered.

"If we fight them here, I will have to kill one of them." Konner's words came out, barely above a whisper.

Dalleena could not breathe. She saw the man he meant, Lieutenant Pettigrew. For three very long heartbeats she relived with Konner the vision of the man turning into a skeleton, of a bright tunnel swirling, drawing them in, like the dragongate, but without a destination.

Was that what it was like to die? She shuddered.

Loki stared into Konner's eyes for a long moment. Then he nodded as they came to a silent agreement.

"They can't land four vessels here and Kat knows it. Two were a tight fit." Loki began to pace.

Kim joined them, Hestiia close on his heels, as if one could not act without the other. "Perhaps one of us should go up with Irythros and scout."

"I don't think that will be necessary. Dalleena is following them," Konner said.

"If I were Kat, I'd land at the foot of this hill and hike up," Loki said. He picked up a stick and began drawing a rough map of the area in the loose dirt.

The brothers called Raaskan and Niveean over to consult.

Dalleena tuned out their conversation and listened to the emotions of the Others. The similarity of Kat's thought patterns and emotions to Konner's frightened her. She tried to block out the leader, Kat. She raised her hand again, seeking the practical information of speed and direction.

"Six small vessels, two men each, approach very fast. They are surrounded with energy. Dangerous energy," she called to them. "Fighters with weapons charged." The alien words invaded her mind and heightened her fear.

Konner went rigid. The image of the bright tunnel swirling, faster and faster, pulled her closer and closer toward death. A death she/he/they would inflict? Or a death they would suffer?

She had to break free of this man. Now. Forever. She could not live with this terrible knowledge.

* * *

"Heads up," Loki whispered into his comm. He spotted movement through the tall ferns and scrub. The intruders came. Right on schedule.

He watched from the vantage point of a tall tree. The only reasonable path from the flats to the clearing lay within his view. He hoped that Kat would not take the unreasonable route over cliffs and dead-end ravines. If she had skilled rock climbers among her Marines, she might be able to reach the clearing unobserved.

Loki had gladly left Cyndi gagged with duct tape and bound to a tree half a klick before the clearing. The IMPs would have to rescue her. Her protests and demands ought to slow the IMPs further and alert anyone left in the clearing.

Loki's few warriors had a chance to pick off the intruders one by one as they negotiated obstacles, natural ones and those created within the last two hours.

"See them," Raaskan confirmed. "Pettigrew leads." A long pause. "Taneeo guides him." The last came out on a hiss.

"Expected that," Loki muttered. One more piece of evidence that Hanassa's spirit had taken over Taneeo's body. Hanassa had gone to great lengths to remove the Stargods from the land of the Coros. He hadn't given up, even in death.

Where was Kat, if not up front? He sought a different vantage point. A rock outcropping offered him clear line of sight of Raaskan's position. Unfortunately, it also gave Pettigrew the slanting line of sight to Loki. He stayed prone, shielding his eyes against the westering sun filtering through the cloud cover, searching for the tall female and whatever company she might lead.

Thank St. Bridget, Pettigrew kept his eyes focused straight ahead. He prodded Taneeo with a sharp finger every few meters and barked questions. He should have kept scouts ranging ahead and placed himself in the middle of the column for his own protection, but the cocky lieutenant had to lead. He probably saw this as his one chance at promotion.

But Pettigrew had to get past Loki and his warriors first.

The Marines all wore helmets and battle armor that hid hair color, complexion, and gender. At this distance he could distinguish few features other than relative height.

Where was Kat?

Raaskan popped up behind the last private in line. A knotted vine twisted about the throat left the hapless Marine choking. A quick snap of Raaskan's powerful arms and his victim's head lolled limply on his neck.

Unbearable pressure built within Loki's chest, robbing him of breath. The cords along his nape burned and ached. He had to close his eyes and concentrate upon Pettigrew. If he watched the grisly work of his warriors, he'd share the deaths. His orders to render the IMPs unconscious whenever possible had not registered with the locals.

Tribal warfare had been their way of life for generations.

Fifty meters farther along the path Hestiia took out a straggler with a well-placed arrow—again to the vulnerable throat.

Loki was prepared for this death. With his feet braced and his hands locked behind his neck, he kept his focus on Pettigrew and Taneeo. The slight priest seemed to know the path better than Loki's own warriors.

About every one hundred heartbeats Loki scanned the area for signs of his sister and a squad of specialized bush troops. Nothing.

Surely he should be able to find her. If not with his eyes, then he must seek her with his mind and his heart.

Three deep breaths. His mind cleared of the confusion of dying men. Consciously, he blocked out his awareness of each of his own troops. He filtered through the company of determined soldiers. Seeking, always seeking, something familiar.

A whisper of thought brushed against him. He honed in on the pattern of logic that could only be Kat. Behind him. Close. Getting closer.

"Freeze, Loki, or I blast you from here to kingdom come." Kat stood at his feet, braced against a tree with ten men behind her. All of them held stunner rifles, fully charged and aimed at his heart.

*   *   *

Large rocks crashed down hills and through brush.
Their fall echoed around the clearing. A cloud of dust
drifted through the trees.

(*Trouble,*) Irythros called.

Konner peered through the brush toward the path.
Niveean and the two blacksmith's apprentices
jumped up and down in triumph. The rockfall continued beneath their feet. They had fulfilled their part
of the ambush and levered a boulder into the path
of the approaching IMPs.

Konner bowed his head a moment, praying that
no person stood in the path of that rock and the
others it released as it plummeted downward.

He caught a flash of bright light on the periphery
of his senses. Quickly he rolled to his right.

Fighters whizzed past the clearing. An energy bolt
singed the saber fern to his left. The next blast fired
across the top of the clearing as if engaging more
fighters rather than enemies on the ground.

Then Konner caught a flash of a dragon wing and
a wild chuckle from Irythros.

(*They waste their ammunition on what they cannot see
and will never catch.*)

Konner shook his head. The dragon did not take
this battle seriously.

He should.

The clearing was a mess. Piles of loose dirt littered
the place along with uprooted ferns, shrubs, and
grasses. Konner had to expand the open area by
nearly five acres to accommodate his measurements.
One crystal lay within feet of the edge of the pool.
The hot spring there fed extra energy to the crystal.
The stone, in turn added heat to the water. All of the
crystals drew power from the iron and nitrogen in

the soil, shooting energy back and forth among themselves and the king stone.

At last the stones had stopped singing their unharmonious wail in the back of his mind. They waited now in tense silence for the connections that would make them a family again.

At their urging he'd finished the hard work of placement and connection twelve hours ahead of schedule.

Now he just had to establish the programming of the confusion field and bury a small handheld computer within a force field beside the king stone. This would be easier if he had access to the database aboard the shuttle. But Kat had stolen that.

(*You must leave the clearing. The fighters leave. They have no more ammunition or fuel. But the Others come. Quickly,*) Irythros said. His tone sounded very insistent.

"Not yet," Konner replied. "Dalleena, can you see anything?"

"Just dust." She stood on the opposite side of the clearing, keeping acres of land between them.

He did not understand her coolness. Or her silence. He did not have time to wonder.

"Just a few more moments and I can engage the field." He ran back to the center and the king stone. He dropped into the deep hole.

"Konner!" Dalleena called. "Konner, help me!"

He could not ignore the plea.

(*Stay hidden.*)

"St. Bridget help me, I can't." Before Irythros could counter the argument, Konner nearly flew up the crude ladder from the depths of the hole.

Taneeo held Dalleena from behind, a knife at her throat. Fifteen armed IMPs ranged behind them, Pettigrew at the fore.

Konner still had the unconnected handheld in his

pocket. No time to finish the last few commands. No time to keep the IMPs out of their hiding place.

No time to save anyone.

Konner's gaze was drawn to the strange object suspended upon a thong and hanging around the priest's neck.

The second distress beacon. How had he gotten it from the freelance merchant with the good teeth?

A feral grin spread over the traitor's face. "Any move from you or the dragon and I kill her where she stands," he snarled.

"I see you have returned from the dead to terrorize innocents again, Hanassa."

CHAPTER 45

"**P**SST!" KIM signaled Loki. From his vantage point on a ledge below his brother, he could not see if Loki heard him or not. Or if Kat heard and would send her shock troops after him.

He counted one hundred heartbeats. He heard only the muffled sounds of strident conversation above him.

"I can do this," he told himself.

Slowly, he breathed in and out three times, clearing his mind. When he felt disembodied, he pictured in his mind exactly where Loki should drop off the top of the rock outcropping. Dangle here, drop there. Avoid this rotten foothold. Take this less obvious one. Then he sent the images to his brother.

Behind him, he heard the confused thrashing of the IMPs freeing themselves from the rockfall. He had to leave the mop-up to his people. Hestiia and Raaskan would dispose of as many as they could.

Best if Kim did not know how many or where. He forced himself to think in terms of obstacles removed rather than people.

He was just about to give up on Loki and concentrate on diverting Kat, when his brother rolled down the rock face. He slipped dangerous meters, then grabbed a tree growing horizontally out from the cliff. He swung there for many long moments until he balanced and added his other hand to firm his grasp.

Shots buzzed in Loki's wake. Kat's red head appeared above them. "I'm not finished with you yet!" she shouted and fired her stunner blindly.

Kim ducked back into the shrubbery to avoid the shot.

Loki laughed. The landscape picked up his mocking and reverberated it up and down, back and forth until it lost meaning and direction.

More shots followed. Kat let loose a string of curses and epithets that would have earned her one of Mum's frowns of disappointment.

At last, Kat and her squad retreated from the edge of the rocks.

Now, Kim urged Loki with his mind. *Before she finds a way around.* He sent mental images of a likely route of descent rather than exact words.

You sure about this?

Kim felt Loki's uncertainty.

As certain as I am that your sister will be upon us before you get down here if you do not hurry.

Loki let go of his branch and dropped one and a half meters to a narrow ledge. He teetered on the edge.

Kim braced himself to break his brother's fall.

Loki found his balance and dropped to all fours. Clinging to the ledge by his fingertips, he proceeded downward.

Kim kept urging speed. Loki took his time, testing each hand and foothold before committing his full weight to any of them.

Kim heard the clatter of ten armed and armored people winding downward by a circuitous path.

Then he saw Kat drop over the top and grab the same tree Loki had.

Kim inhaled sharply, willing Kat to use both hands to climb down and leave her weapon holstered.

She did. But she moved faster than her older brother, showing more recklessness than Loki ever had.

At last Loki dropped the last few meters. Kim braced his feet against a tree trunk and grabbed Loki to keep him from tripping and rolling on the rough ground.

"Where?" Loki asked, panting. He glanced over his shoulder at the uniformed figure still working her way down the cliff face.

Kim pointed out their path. "Shuttle," he mouthed. The hair on his nape tingled. Kat was very near.

Loki's eyes brightened and he grinned without mirth. "Comeuppance," he mouthed.

At least Kim thought that was his word. A few obscenities would fit the same syllables.

A shot burned above their heads. It severed a tree limb and dropped it in their path. Wild shouts and more fluent curses from Kat followed the bolt of energy.

Kim pelted through ferns and bracken, slid on mud and tripped across a roaring creek. Loki followed close on his heels.

Scratched, bruised, and filthy, they emerged from the tree line onto the flatter surface of a fertile plateau. Before them waited their own shuttle *Rover*, its cerama/metal hull dulled by a layer of green. Beyond it rested three landers.

More shots.

No time to disable the landers.

They ran faster, diving into *Rover*'s open hatch. Kim slapped it closed while Loki scrambled for the cockpit. "Break out the weapons, Kim," he called over the roar of the engines.

Before Kim could belt in and take command of his screens, they rolled toward the sea.

The cliff edge came too soon. Not enough lift beneath the wings. Below them treacherous rocks played peek a boo with the crashing waves. Gravity pulled them down into the teeth of the broken shore.

At the last minute, Loki fired the VTOL jets and lifted. A cannon pulse blast rocked them. They dipped lower, losing the little bit of altitude they had gained.

"She's got a lander up already," Loki cursed under his breath.

"And she's shooting to kill." Kim locked his own tiny blaster onto the looming target of the military vessel. It gained on them by the millisecond. The next shot would be at point-blank range.

He fired.

The energy burst in front of the cockpit windscreen. The pilot did not falter. The lander kept coming.

"I've got nothing to match that thing."

"I'm not sure I can outrun it," Loki admitted. "She's one hell of a pilot, matching me move for move in a bigger and clumsier craft."

They skimmed the surface of the waves and bounced up again. The lander could not match the maneuvers. It did not need to. Kat bullied forward.

(*You need a bath,*) Irythros reminded them.

"So we do." Loki slowed abruptly and plunged *Rover* into the waves.

*   *   *

Hanassa! Dalleena swallowed. Felt the knife scrape her throat. The priest's muscles shifted. The tip of the knife pricked her skin. She winced and started. Warm liquid trickled down her neck.

"I will not be a sacrifice to your perversion," she whispered. Anger fueled by fear sent jolts of energy through her veins.

Silently, she contracted her abdomen and shoulders, testing the level of pain lingering from her injuries.

"Irythros warned me against you, Hanassa."

"Irythros!" the man spat. "A child among dragons. A meddler who breaks the law and reveals secrets!" He pressed the knife a little closer against Dalleena's neck. She winced and prepared herself for pain.

"What will you gain by taking a life?" Konner asked the IMP casually. His attention seemed to focus upon the man beside the priest rather than the man with the knife.

"I do not take a life," the IMP replied, equally casual.

"You employ the assassin. By your own laws, that makes you an accessory before the fact. Punishable by five years imprisoned rehabilitation after a mind-wipe."

"What about the twenty men you and your brothers killed?" Heat rose in the man's voice. "You are as guilty as the men who unleashed an avalanche of boulders."

Out of the corner of her eye, Dalleena saw the man lift a black box of a weapon. A stunner, Konner had called it. At the same time, he moved forward.

The priest did not like that. He shoved Dalleena forward, elbowing the IMP aside. He stumbled and fought for balance. A blast of red light shot from the stunner into the shrubbery. Well away from Konner.

Konner lunged.

Dalleena rammed her elbow into the priest's gut. Then she stomped upon his bare foot. As he doubled over, she whirled and slammed the heel of her hand against his jaw and her knee into his groin.

Her ribs protested. She clenched her jaw against the pain.

Hanassa thudded upon the ground, rolled to his knees, and bounced upward.

"It will take more than your puny efforts to fell me," Hanassa snarled. Gone were all traces of the priest's mild tenor voice, replaced by a deeper, harsher baritone. His body was bulkier than the man she had found suffering from a severe beating. Had he done that to himself?

She did not wait for an answer. Her foot swept across the back of his knees, and she turned and ran for the creek.

Heavy footsteps pounded after her. Booted feet that crashed through the underbrush.

"Stop or we shoot!" the IMP called.

"Shoot her and you die!" Konner replied. Sounds of a struggle.

The pool came into view. Dalleena angled southward and uphill. A tangle of calubra ferns slowed her down. She pushed them aside, vaulting over them. Pain lashed her ribs with each harsh breath. She tripped and rolled upon landing. The ferns loosed their pungent perfume. A sedating aphrodisiac.

Holding her breath, she jumped up and climbed the hill. A new, sharper pain began in her side. Breathing came hard. Her legs grew heavy.

Then miraculously, Konner was beside her. He braced her with an arm about her waist. Running became easier. His strength guided her back toward the sound of the cascade of water. After a long, dry summer, boulders formed a damp ford across the upper creek.

Konner leaped to the top of the first boulder. She grabbed his wrist with both hands. She clambered up beside him.

"We have to get outside the field," he said when she faltered. "I'll activate it with them in and us out. They shouldn't be able to follow." He bounded across a gap to the next boulder.

She followed more cautiously, afraid to imitate his

leap and jar her abused bones upon landing. She slipped at the edge. He held her hand tightly, keeping her from falling over the cascade and landing upon a pile of broken rocks below.

"Stop," the IMP leader yelled. He managed to shinny up the first boulder on his own.

Someone behind him fired one of the stunners.

Moss sizzled at their feet.

Konner halted and raised his hands. Dalleena did the same. They turned slowly to face their pursuers.

"I have no quarrel with you, Lieutenant Pettigrew," Konner said.

"But I have a very large one with you," the IMP replied. He rose from his crouch upon the first boulder. "You have broken the law many times and resisted lawful arrest. You have sabotaged an Imperial vessel. And now you flee again. Judge Balinakas will dish out many long sentences to you and your brothers."

"We do not have to live with this animosity. We can share this planet in peace," Dalleena offered.

"I have no intention of allowing you to strand me in this godforsaken wilderness, O'Hara. Where is the king stone?"

"Practically under your nose."

Pettigrew looked down. So did the IMPs behind him.

A cold wind blasted Dalleena in the face. A thunderous beating of wings. She brought her right palm up and jerked her head right and left.

Irythros burst from the cloud cover. He screeched. The IMPs grasped their ears in pain.

Dalleena wanted to hunker down and cover her head. Konner remained standing. So she did, too.

A stream of flame ejected from the dragon's mouth. It brushed the top of Pettigrew's head, singeing his hair.

The lieutenant screeched to match the dragon. He

bent so far over he fell into the creek, deep here near the cascade. How deep?

The IMPs let loose a volley of shots.

Konner jumped into the water. He flailed about, dove. Surfaced. Gasped. Dove again.

Dalleena peered into the churning water, scanning with her palm as well as her eyes. She couldn't sense anything.

The IMPs stood, rooted in place, exchanging worried glances. Hanassa danced around them in glee.

"Help him!" Dalleena screamed.

Konner surfaced again, flung water out of his eyes. Then once more he kicked up and back and plunged back into the water.

Favoring her ribs with one arm clutched across her midriff, Dalleena slipped into the water. Only a little deeper than Konner was tall. She felt about with toes and hands and senses.

Nothing but more water, sand, and a few slippery green things.

The current gently wove around her.

She dropped below the surface, caught a glimpse of a white foot to her right. She grabbed. It kicked. She came up with a firm grasp of Konner's ankle.

"They can't swim in armor with field kits on their backs." he choked out. "No time to undress." The agony on his face mimicked what she had seen when she shared his vision.

Two IMPs struggled out of their heavy packs while their comrades unfastened shin guards and breastplates. They still had arm, back, and thigh armor to remove. They'd never get into the water in time to help their lieutenant.

"You are not responsible if he dies, Konner," she called to him as he dove once more.

"Yes, he is!" exclaimed Hanassa. He jumped up and down on the bank, brandishing his knife toward anyone who tried to enter the water. "Konner O'Hara alone determines if the petti-man lives or dies."

Dalleena went under once more. When she could hold her breath no longer, she gave up. Clinging to one of the rocks while gulping long draughts of air, her right palm began to tingle. Then she spotted him.

"Konner!" She did not wait for him but swam a few strokes to her left, toward the opposite bank. She tugged on a limp white hand drifting above a tree snag.

Konner splashed right behind her. He plunged deeper.

Dalleena tried to clear branches and roots. The man beyond the visible arm remained stuck.

"Help us," she called to the IMPs. "We can still save him."

Hanassa drove his knife into the throat of the first man who tried climbing onto the ford of boulders.

The remaining IMPs felled him with a concentrated blast of stunners.

Not enough. Hanassa twitched and moaned, then rolled to his knees and crawled into the underbrush, still alive, still able to menace them all.

CHAPTER 46

KAT BIT HER LIP. Did she dare plunge the lander into the bay in pursuit of her brothers? She'd watched Loki and Konner closely when they executed this maneuver. She knew she could duplicate it. Was it worth the risk? Perhaps she should hover and monitor, waiting for them to emerge.

On the other hand, the lander needed a bath to clean off the growing green gunk.

"Go after them!" her Marine sergeant urged. "We can shoot them underwater."

"Efficiency?" Kat snapped at him.

He ran numbers through the weapons array. "Saline content of the water will dissipate the focus by twenty-three point six percent."

"Intensity?"

"I'm not a data tech," the sergeant protested.

Kat glanced at the data. "Fifteen point zero two percent drop." Close enough.

She aimed the craft into the water. She had to slow to a near stall to allow the transition of pressure to hit the hull gradually. Sensors distorted the moment she hit the water.

The ten men with her were combat troops, not pilots or techs. They understood weapons. She had to fly (drive) the lander and interpret the data.

"Look for this symbol in the data stream." She pointed to the glyph that represented the cerama/metal alloy common to any hull that could be exposed to the high radiation of space or intense heat of reentry. The same specs protected them from water seepage from increasing pressure.

The sergeant gulped and nodded. "Starboard. Seven point three degrees."

"How far ahead?"

"Sixty meters to firing range. Sixty-five. Seventy."

"Damn."

"Port. Twenty-five degrees."

"Can't. There's an outcropping between us." Kat steered around it. By the time she cleared the pile of jagged rock, she'd lost contact with her quarry. Frantically, she searched the water ahead and her sensors for the tiniest glimpse of a man-made object.

"Something big on the ocean floor," the sergeant said excitedly.

"Show me?"

He pointed to the sensor screen. Sure enough a long and dense object glowed with the distinctive glyphs of cerama/metal.

"That's one of the landers the O'Haras stole." Disappointed and frustrated, she steered for it. "Suit up, Sergeant. You and two others are going to fly that thing back to base."

"I'm no pilot."

"You are now. You know how to fire the engines, rock it a bit to get it off the bottom and aim for camp."

"How about if I take this one back to base and you maneuver that one off the bottom?"

"Fine." Alone, Kat would not have to report to anyone. Alone with a lander, she could take her revenge without the restrictions of GTE military protocol.

"The controls are yours, Sergeant. I'll retrieve the lost one."

* * *

Konner fought the white vortex. His mind swirled ever deeper into the whiteness. He clung to Dalleena's last words to him. "You are not responsible."

His heart wanted to protest. Of course he was responsible. Pettigrew had chased Konner and become a victim of the chase.

His logical engineer's brain scoffed.

A violent, mechanical roar tugged him back toward reality.

He blinked rapidly. Outlines appeared before his eyes. Then color began to fill in the blank spaces.

"Dalleena?" he called.

A muffled grunt.

"Dalleena, where are you?"

"Here," she croaked, less than a meter from him.

"How do you fare?" He swam the single stroke from his side of the snag. Her face looked pale. Tight lines drew her mouth down and furrowed her brow. He stroked the lines with a delicate finger. They did not fade.

"I tracked him and lost him," she muttered.

"You are not responsible."

"Neither are you," she said. Then she shivered.

"You're chilling. We have to get out of the water."

"We have to retrieve the body."

"Leave it for the IMPs."

"Tracker's code. I *have* to bring him back to his people for proper burial."

"Later." He tried dragging her away from the snag. She resisted. The glare she shot him should have sizzled his hair. "Very well."

Without the press of time to save a living man

making his movements clumsy and ineffectual, Konner freed Pettigrew's trapped foot with only two more dives beneath the surface.

The mechanical roar became a pulsing weapon. Konner looked shoreward. The IMPs crouched low, weapons drawn and aimed at *Rover* hovering above them.

A red electronic charge skimmed the edge of *Rover*'s nose.

"Damn it, Loki, not now!" Konner grabbed two handfuls of moss and tore them free of one of the rocks. The moss that chinked gaps in cabin walls, lined baby diapers, and served as a fire starter. "Stuff this into your ears. Tight. Follow me. And hurry."

He pulled himself up onto the ford, pausing only to grab Dalleena's wrist and haul her up. She choked off a scream.

Still holding her hand, he ran as fast as he could for the opposite shore.

* * *

"St. Bridget and all the angels, save me!" Kat stared at the sunken lander through the faceplate of her EVA suit. The long vehicle tilted on the edge of a trench. If it had touched down three meters farther, it would have plunged thousands of fathoms deeper, well beyond her reach, possibly beyond hull tolerances.

"You say something, Lieutenant?" the sergeant asked over the comm unit.

"Nothing worth repeating. Stay close, Sarge."

"Will do. Easier keeping this hunk of bolts in one place than swimming to the surface."

"Until the currents get you," Kat subvocalized. No need scaring the man into doing something stupid.

Kat half swam/half walked the twenty meters to

the rear air lock of the lander. Her heavy magnetic boots dragged her down to the sandy bottom. The water felt as thick as soy pudding. Her suit kept beeping alarms, not liking the pressure she endured at this depth.

She punched in the codes to work the air lock. The keypad responded sluggishly. She checked her air supply. At this rate she'd be breathing water by the time the chamber pressurized to equal that of the ocean bottom.

"We're sinking!"

"Give her a little juice, Sergeant Brewster," Kat ordered. She fought to keep her voice calm.

A blast of water swirled around her. She braced herself against the air lock, desperate to keep her feet. A hasty glance over her shoulder showed the other lander swaying back and forth, creating its own current.

Her lander rocked in response.

A flood of curses spilled out of Kat's mouth.

Then the air lock opened. The change in pressure rocked the lander again.

Kat held her breath, praying it did not tip over into the trench.

A few rocks back and forth, then it settled into the sand. Was it a fraction farther forward?

"Don't go anywhere just yet, Brewster. Gotta make sure I can get this baby off the bottom." She stepped into the air lock and closed it behind her.

Agonizing moments passed before the automatic system flushed out the water, replacing it with air. Her wrist monitor looked stuck in the hazard position. Finally, the numbers crept upward showing breathable atmosphere.

"You still there, Brewster?"

"Barely. I'm really uncomfortable at these controls, Lieutenant."

"Can you fly an air car? Take your girl out on a date back home?"

"Yeah." He sounded hesitant.

"Real hot shot, I bet. Show off for the ladies."

"Yeah." His voice brightened.

"Same thing. This is just a bigger vessel, a little clumsier, a lot more powerful."

"You make it sound easy, Lieutenant."

" 'Cause it is. Now stick around until I give you leave. I want this thing off the bottom before I see your tail in the viewscreen."

Kat opened her faceplate. The air tasted stale and salty. She hadn't much time.

Edging forward on the slightly tilted deck, she stayed near the outer bulkhead as much as possible, keeping the lander balanced. "So far so good," she breathed as she neared the cockpit.

Her third step toward the middle of the craft sent shivers through the hull. She grabbed the nearest handhold, riding out the rocking of the hull. When the lander finally settled, the deck tilted forward at least five additional degrees.

She gulped and waited.

"You okay, Kat? That thing looks mighty unstable."

"Yeah, Kent. Give me a few more moments. I think I can get to the copilot's seat without any more disturbance. Firing up the engines could shift the balance." Before she lost her courage, Kat slid into the nearest chair. She unlocked the legs and scooted along the rail that ran along the deck at the base of the circle of terminals.

Halfway to the viewscreen she found systems control. A quick check showed the essentials working, navigation, weapons, environmentals, hull integrity, and fuel. When Konner had ditched the vehicle, he'd set it to go through automatic shutdown at some point after launch. The family mechanic couldn't kill a machine any more than he could kill a king stone.

Kat fully intended to take advantage of her brother's weakness.

She breathed a little easier as she ran through ignition. A comforting rumble answered her commands. Ever conscious of her precarious position, she edged her chair further along the rail. She came to command position and looked out the viewscreen. The trench yawned before her.

A behemouth swam across her bow. It flipped its tail twice and shot upward. The crush of water pressed downward against the nose of her vessel. She tilted farther forward and slid . . .

*   *   *

"Sonics, now," Loki ordered Kim.

His little brother reached for the red interface on his screen in the upper right-hand corner. Out of the way of any casual brush of his fingers.

"No. Wait!" Loki stayed the command with a tight grip on Kim's shoulder. "That's Konner and Dalleena down there."

"IMPs taking aim at them." Kim hesitated, his index finger one micro above the screen. "I've got to down the IMPs."

"If Konner and Dalleena fall off the ford, they'll either drown or break their necks going over the cascade.

"If the IMPs shoot them, they face the same choice."

"Two more femtos and they'll be on firm ground."

"Damn, there's Taneeo and his knife. He's going to kill one of the IMPs." Kim dropped his finger onto the blinking red interface.

Muffled echoes of the piercing blast of sound penetrated the hull. Annoying. Almost painful.

The figures below doubled over in pain, hands holding ears, grimaces of agony on their faces.

Loki could not find Konner among them, or on the opposite bank.

CHAPTER 47

KONNER DOVE behind the upended roots of a huge fallen tree. The tangled roots, rocks, and mud, with infant ferns growing in the middle stood between him and *Rover*. Dalleena crawled behind him, burrowing deep into the leaf litter that collected between the root ball and the tree trunk.

He mounded more of the plant debris around their heads as he lay on top of her, shielding her head with his body.

Less than a heartbeat later his ears rang with the harsh pulses of a highly illegal sonic weapon. Every hair on his body felt as if it stood on end. His teeth ached. Tears streamed down his face.

"I love you, Dalleena," he whispered, fighting to stay conscious.

"Loving you can be very dangerous, Stargod Konner O'Hara."

*   *   *

Kim counted each IMP as he fell victim to the sonic blast. Taneeo fell last, his wickedly curved knife still clutched in his hand.

When the traitor's body stopped twitching, Kim breathed a sigh of relief. But he left his hand upon the sonics trigger.

The moment Taneeo succumbed, Loki signaled Kim to cease firing.

The silence after the sonic blast seemed to echo around Kim's head. Unnatural. Surreal. How much hearing had he lost? How much had the IMPs lost after the full exposure?

"Where's Konner?" Loki's eyes were wide, nearly bulging out of their sockets.

Kim searched with his eyes and every other sense he could muster. He saw fifteen IMPs and Taneeo all lying unconscious at the edge of the pool. Konner remained elusive.

"I have to land this thing, quick. We have to find them." Loki sounded as frantic as Kim felt.

Loki moved *Rover* into the center of the clearing and dropped to the ground. Not the smoothest of landings. Kim hardly noticed. They ignored Cyndi, still gagged and bound, slumping against the tree where they'd left her hours ago. The sonics had silenced her, too.

Together, Kim and Loki pelted down the narrow path toward the creek.

"Konner!" Kim yelled across the water.

Taneeo moaned and twitched. Loki pulled a set of force bracelets out of his pocket and slapped them on the little priest. "What's this?" he held up the missing second beacon. Ungently, he yanked it away from Taneeo, snapping the leather thong that suspended it.

The strained leather did not leave so much as a mark on the traitor. Loki felt along the man's neck.

"*St. Bridget*! Hide toughening, exoskeleton forming. He's turning into a dragon. Just like Hanassa."

Kim examined the man's neck and torso. His fingers met hard cartilage becoming as dense as bone.

"We'll have to make another trip back to the volcano and destroy that beacon, too," Kim muttered.

He pulled a length of vine away from the shrub it

nearly choked. Viciously, he twisted it into convenient lengths, ignoring how it looped back upon his hands and arms, trying to snare him. Bloody welts appeared beneath its thorns. Devil's vine the locals called it, with good reason.

He used it to bind the wrists and ankles of all of the IMPs. The thorny weed gouged any skin it contacted, wrapping easily where Kim guided it. If one believed the locals, the plant was almost sentient. Kim had a hard time keeping it from tangling his own hands. The IMPs would not break free easily.

"Konner!" Loki called again.

"Here," came a strangled voice.

"Can you handle these guys?" Loki asked.

Kim nodded grimly. "We can dump them a few kilometers from their camp after dark. Make them walk back." He twisted a length of vine securely on the last of the IMPs. Then he yanked off their boots. All fifteen of them began to stir and moan.

*   *   *

Loki leaped from slippery rock to jagged boulder across the ford without care for his own bare feet.

He landed on the opposite muddy creek bank clumsily, sliding to his knees. Irythros had been digging here and left a mess. Desperate to find his brother, he regained his footing with only two backward slides toward the water. Behind him he heard the groans of recovering IMPs. Ahead of him, only silence.

"Konner!" he yelled again.

Was that a soft whimper ahead and to his right?

"Konner, get your sorry ass out of whatever hole you crawled into."

"Do we have to?" The voice was weak. No, soft. Like an intimate whisper.

"Where are you?" Loki began peering under bushes and around the massive root ball of a fallen forest giant.

"Ow." Konner's protest was followed by a soft, feminine giggle. "Get off my foot, Loki."

Loki looked closer at the mound of leaf litter and plant debris filling the triangle between the root ball and the place where the tree trunk met the ground. He found a foot. Big and callused. Konner. Then a second foot, smaller and booted. Dalleena.

"Do I need to leave you two alone? If so, then make it quick. We've got a clearing full of IMPs and our sister on the way in a lander."

* * *

"Coming," Konner said. He sighed heavily. "Dalleena and I have the rest of our lives to be together."

"Well, I'm glad that's settled." Loki's sigh sounded relieved, as if he'd been waiting a long time for Konner to find a life mate.

"How did you manage?" Loki asked. He spoke louder than normal and mouthed his words carefully.

Konner pulled the wads of moss out of his ears. Dalleena did the same. "I'll have to analyze this more thoroughly. It does more than fill chinks in the cabins and insulate against the cold."

"It lines baby diapers, too. Quite absorbent," Dalleena added with a glint of mischief in her eyes.

Konner kissed her again, needing to linger. Other matters pressed upon his conscience.

"I have to activate the confusion field before Kat arrives." Konner crawled out from his hidey-hole, followed closely by Dalleena. He kissed her palm the moment she stood upright, then captured her hand in both of his. He did not want to break the contact, as if their skin had bonded as well as their hearts and minds.

"We need to get across the creek first." Loki moved toward the water, keeping his back to his brother, giving the couple a moment more of privacy. "I want to be well inside the field when you close it. Who knows what happens to someone caught in the boundary when it snaps into place."

Konner lingered only a moment longer. He grabbed another quick kiss from Dalleena and followed his brother quickly.

The moment they dropped from the last boulder of the ford onto the ground, Konner pulled a handheld from his pocket. He peered closely at the screen a moment and logged in a few more codes.

"Are we ready for this?"

Loki and Kim nodded.

Konner tapped the screen three times.

"I don't see anything different," Loki said. He turned in a full circle, examining everything.

"My sense of anything beyond the circle is dulled." Dalleena scanned the entire area with her hand extended in tracking mode.

"That's the beauty of this cloaking," Konner chortled. "No one sees the field. But if anyone without O'Hara DNA tries to penetrate from either direction, they get pushed back, misdirected, deluded into believing they move forward instead of in a circle around our private enclave."

"How do we open it?" Kim asked. He monitored the pulse of one of the IMPs who remained still long after his fellows twitched and squirmed for release.

"Harmonics." Konner grinned. "All we have to do is hum Mum's favorite lullaby and we will match the resonance of the crystals."

A lander moved up the hillside. It looked perfectly clear to Konner, but the roar of its engines seemed slightly removed, more distant than it should. He doubted it was a lingering aftereffect from the sonics.

"Loki, Konner, and Kim O'Hara, where are you," Kat called to them from the lander's exterior speakers. She circled the area, never quite steering directly above them.

Konner walked back to the shuttle and opened a frequency to his sister. "Lose something, Kat?"

Loki and Kim stayed close upon his heels. Dalleena squeezed in as well. Konner pulled her into his lap at his customary terminal.

"Yes, I lost you three. Open the field and let me land."

"Sorry, little sister. We can't trust you," Konner said.

"I'll find you eventually. You know that. The dragon showed me how to use my latent psi powers. I'll penetrate the field one way or another."

"Probably too late to save *Jupiter*, Kat," Konner said.

"We'll see about that. You have to come out of the clearing soon to go rescue your son, Konner. I'll be waiting."

"It's too late for that, Kat. I can't reach Aurora in time to gain legal custody."

"Since when has legality stopped you?"

A slow smile spread across Konner's face. "I think I have a plan."

EPILOGUE

"YOU SEE, MARTIN? Konner O'Hara did not arrive at the custody hearing. He is dead. You are well rid of him," Melinda Fortesque said brightly. She paused long enough to pat Martin on the shoulder. "Now that there is no question of where you belong, I have authorized an increase in your allowance as well as a lump sum as a birthday present. You may purchase that jet pedcycle you have lusted after for so long." Then she marched down the palace corridor. Clearly the custody hearing had taken too much time away from her busy schedule.

"Even if Dad lives, he can't get me now," Martin muttered. He hung his head and scuffed his feet, reluctant to retreat into the privacy of his own suite. He did not care if the servants, toadies, petitioners, and corporate employees saw him cry. He did not care that his mother knew of his intense disappointment.

A question niggled at his brain. "If my dad is dead, then why bother with the formality of a custody hearing?" He scooted into his room and activated Super Snooper.

"Status on the distress beacon?" he demanded before the icon figure fully formed.

"The signal has ceased," Super Snooper replied.

"What about agent Sam Eyeam?"

"He has not responded to your mother's hails."

"What about tracing his movements? Scaramouch, display star map hologram with Sam Eyeam's last known movements."

The map came up. A scattered series of purple lights flashed. The last one faded and disappeared at the edge of the vacant anomaly.

Martin's heart skipped a beat.

"Show area suspected to contain the beacon."

The entire anomaly lit up in a violet haze.

"I think I'll have to find the jump point into the hole in space by myself." Martin made a brief detour into his bank account. Sure enough, Melinda had deposited a huge amount of money; more than enough to buy two jet pedcycles, with all the accessories.

"Super Snooper, find out which ships in port are available for charter, and a pilot who can be bribed into silence. Make a conference call to Bruce and Jane Q, they'll want to be a part of this. Then open a new account in the commodities market. We have to make a bit more money for this project."

Irene Radford

"A mesmerizing storyteller." —*Romantic Times*

THE DRAGON NIMBUS

THE GLASS DRAGON
0-88677-634-1

THE PERFECT PRINCESS
0-88677-678-3

THE LONELIEST MAGICIAN
0-88677-709-7

THE WIZARD'S TREASURE
0-88677-913-8

THE DRAGON NIMBUS HISTORY

THE DRAGON'S TOUCHSTONE
0-88677-744-5

THE LAST BATTLEMAGE
0-88677-774-7

THE RENEGADE DRAGON
0-88677-855-7

THE STAR GODS

THE HIDDEN DRAGON
0-7564-0051-1

To Order Call: 1-800-788-6262